# No Enemies Within

# No Enemies Within

## A Creative Process For Discovering
## What's Right About What's Wrong

*Dawna Markova, Ph.D.*

Conari Press
Berkeley, CA

*To those who,
even at the gates of midnight,
still dream of the dawn.*

*For workshops and further information, please contact the author at
Conari Press, 1144 65th St., Suite B, Emeryville, CA 94608*

*Copyright © 1994 by Dawna Markova*
All Rights Reserved. No part of this book may be used or reproduced in any manner whatsoever
without written permission, except in the case of brief quotations in critical articles or reviews. For
information, contact Conari Press, 1144 65th Street, Suite B, Emeryville, CA 94608.

Distributed by Publishers Group West

Excerpt used as opening quote from *The Bean Trees* by Barbara Kingsolver.
Copyright © 1988 by Barbara Kingsolver. Reprinted by permission of HarperCollins Publishers, Inc.

Cover design and illustration: Christine Leonard Raquepaw
Cover photo: Hollie Noble
Charts: Linda Ottavi

ISBN: 0-943233-63-1


Library of Congress Cataloging-in-Publication Data

Markova, Dawna, 1942-
    No enemies within : a creative process for discovering what's right about what's wrong / by
Dawna Markova.
        p.  cm.
    Includes bibliographical references and index.
    ISBN 0-943233-64-X (pbk.) : $12.95
    1. Self-help techniques.  2. Mental healing.  3. Self-actualization (Psychology)
BF632.M33   1994
615.8'51—dc20
                                                                                    93-40614

*"Wisteria vines thrive in poor soil. Their secret is something called rhizobia. They are microscopic bugs that live underground in little knots on the roots. They suck nitrogen gas right out of the soil and turn it into fertilizer for the plant. They're not part of the plant, they're separate creatures, but they always live with it, a kind of 'underground railroad' moving secretly up and down the roots. There's a whole invisible system for helping out the plant that you'd never guess was there. It's just the same as with people. The wisteria vines on their own would barely get by, but put them together with rhizobia and they make miracles."*

—*Barbara Kingsolver*

# Appreciations

*To the earth that roots me alive,*
Andy Bryner
*the sky that pulls me toward my dreams,*
Mary Jane Ryan
*the soil that fertilizes those dreams,*
Milton Erickson, M.D., Thich Nhat Hanh,
Richard Kuboyama

*To those who are the rhizobia of this work, indeed, of my life:*
David Peck, Joan and Lewis Sapiro, Tommy Sapiro, Jimmy Sapiro
Karen Bouris, Will Glennon, Emily Miles
Shauna Frazier, Peris Gumz, June LaPointe, Dale LaPointe, Anne Powell
Rita Cleary, Fred Kofman, Peter Senge
Beth Renniger, Peggy Tileston, Jody Whelden,
Jodi Cohen, Riki Moss, Hollie Noble, Robert Ostermeyer, Marjean Bailey
Maria Chiriboga, Lisa Caine, John Moody, Lonnie Weiss
The East Coast Study Group, "Hearts and Hands," The Brownells, The Bryner Family
The inhabitants of Madison, Wisconsin

*To the unseen beings who shine on it all:*
Terry Dobson
William Mechanic, Edith Mechanic
My grandmother
Bambi, Muppet, Domino

# No Enemies Within

# Meeting the Demons:
## Healing As Liberation

*I write this as a baby sucks its toes,*
*fusing inside to out.*
*I write this to re-create my moments,*
*to squeeze them into tiny mirrored fragments,*
*to salve my wounds and mend my broken dreams.*
*I write this so that your eyes can feel,*
*so that your heart can ease,*
*so that your soul can crawl from its hiding place*
*and gaze upon a mystery*
*which can be neither solved nor explained.*
*I write this to breathe our spirits live.*

*Once upon a time, a long time ago, and very far from here, a great Tibetan poet named Milarepa studied and meditated for decades. He traveled the countryside, teaching the practice of compassion and mercy to the villagers he met. He faced many hardships, difficulties, and sorrows, and transformed them into the path of his awakening.*

*Finally, it was time to return to the small hut he called home. He had carried its memory in his heart through all the years of his journey. Much to his surprise, upon entering he found it filled with enemies of every kind. Terrifying, horrifying, monstrous demons that would make most people run. But Milarepa was not most people.*

*Inhaling and exhaling slowly three times, he turned towards the demons, fully present and aware. He looked deeply into the eyes of each, bowing in respect, and said, "You are here in my home now. I honor you, and open myself to what you have to teach me."*

*As soon as he uttered these words, all of the enemies save five disappeared. The ones that remained were grisly, raw, huge monsters. Milarepa bowed once more and began to sing a song to them, a sweet melody resonant with caring for the ways these beasts had suffered, and curiosity about what they needed and how he could help them. As the last notes left his lips, four of the demons disappeared into thin air.*

*Now only one nasty creature was left, fangs dripping evil, nostrils flaming, opened jaws revealing a dark, foul black throat. Milarepa stepped closer to this huge demon, breathed deeply into his own belly, and said with quiet compassion, "I must understand your pain and what it is you need in order to be healed." Then he put his head in the mouth of this enemy.*

*In that instant, the demon disappeared and Milarepa was home at last.*

Beginning is difficult. It feels as if I've never been here before and, at the same time, it feels as if I'm coming home. I'm afraid in the ways people are always afraid when they face the unknown, when they struggle with themselves to begin a journey through the dark geography of their own minds. I am sorely tempted to turn away, run away, go away. To rewind the video tapes or vacuum the refrigerator coils or alphabetize the travel receipts for next years' income taxes. To cook a cheese souffle and then eat it. To mix a vodka collins and then drink it. To find someone else who needs something, anything—a wound, a bruise, a neurosis into which I can pour my attention.

I turn on the radio. At 4 a.m. there is only static. The voice inside my left ear whispers, "Turning away from what you're afraid of isn't the same as turning toward what you want. What do you want?"

I hate that question. "What do you want? How can I help you?" I've been asking it throughout my thirty years of working with people who are struggling to learn how to get through hard times, to recover from the loss of love, spirit or meaning in their lives. Suddenly, I see their faces flashing across the screen of my mind—men, women and children, confused, agonized, suffering, wanting an answer or a solution, wanting advice or direction, wanting to get rid of some problem, wanting it to be fixed.

I see their hands stretched out, groping, reaching, fumbling for something to hold onto, for some connection—with themselves, with the ones they love or are trying to love, with the world around them; raw fingers searching for a source of comfort and wisdom that is more than the pain they find in their daily lives.

I see their lips moving, hear their voices, thousands of voices, telling me stories about the demons they grapple with, stories that shape the landscape of their minds. Stories that are all different, yet somehow all the same. Stories about cervical cancer or divorce from a twenty-year

*"To heal is to touch with love that which we previously touched with fear."*

–Stephen Levine

*"In dealing with fear, the only way out is in."*

–Sheldon Kopp

*"In a dark time the eye begins to see."*

–Theodore Roethke

4

marriage; stories about addiction to cocaine, or work, or food; stories about a seventy-year-old grandfather violating a seven-year-old child, and stories of that same man being violated by his father.

The entire night spills over with so many faces etched in so much pain. I can hardly bear it. I float in thirty years of sorrow. I have no rage left, no outrage. All I can feel is compassion. An entire ocean of it fills me, opens me up where before there was only bone, blood and belly.

*"Nothing human is alien to me."*
*–Terence, 161 BC*

Now they're asking questions behind my right ear, questions that are all different and yet all the same: How can I be at peace with the war in my mind? How do I free myself from the anguish and abuse I experienced as a child? How can I love my life? How do I heal? Thirty years of questions I have only begun to answer.

Thirty years of accompanying people on journeys to find their way home. All those faces and hands; all those questions and stories. Beneath the meaningless labels of psychotherapist and client, or teacher and student, we are all tied together at the root. We are all wounded healers. We are all wounded warriors. We have all been struggling across a dark and mountainous landscape to find a way to heal our lives.

*"If there is no enemy within the enemy outside can do us no harm."*
*–African Proverb*

Now my own face of fifteen years ago appears on the blank screen of my mind—the etched face of a woman battling the enemies of a terminal illness, addiction, and a history of abuse; a woman at an intersection she was totally unprepared for; a woman ravaged by questions she could not answer: What is a source of comfort deeper than all this pain? What do I want to be in my heart at the moment I die? At that moment, will I know I have loved well? Will I have been true to my own path? How do I find my way through all of this?

*"We cannot heal the mess we have made of the world without undergoing some kind of spiritual healing."*
*–M. Scott Peck*

Many of us who have never been to a battlefront have nonetheless survived our own private wars. The landscape of our lives is a combat zone of ongoing skirmishes, with internal enemies we've never defeated. No matter what we've tried, be it frontal assault or hasty retreat, we've survived. But we all have been damaged in some way; we all have been victims. We all are veterans who struggle to tell our story so it will no longer fester inside of us, so we can bear the pain, so we can learn from it, so we can teach from it, so we can once again belong to the world.

*"When I had to stop my exploration because the path faded beneath my steps, I found a bottomless abyss at my feet, and out of it comes . . . arising I know not from where–the current which I dare call my life."*

*–Teilhard de Chardin*

I am writing this book because fifteen years ago I needed to read it. Desperately. I was searching for a raft to carry me through the turbulence. I was very fortunate to find a few people who could teach me that a wound could be a doorway to healing.

Carl Jung said that we experience trauma in order to know the soul, to give our lives meaning. The Dalai Lama teaches that the transformation of difficulties is a path to spiritual awakening. And we need to awaken as a society as well as personally. The human community can evolve from the lessons learned through individual suffering. But how can people live their lives so they learn to heal and, conversely, how can people heal in order to learn how to live their lives? How do calloused fists soften into open palms that divulge the secret stories of how they saved their lives?

I know what I want to do with all I've witnessed these past thirty years. In my heart I hold some things I want to tell you about these people, their questions and journeys. Until I write these things, I have failed as a witness. It's all inside me like a heavy stone, all these untold stories that push and demand, needing to be born into a world that will learn from them so all the pain can have meaning.

Their stories are gleaned from my memory, as well as recordings and notes of workshop sessions my husband Andy and I have facilitated. They are all true and happened as described. To protect the confidentiality of the people involved, I've changed names and identifying characteristics, such as gender, occupation, and geography.

I ask that you listen as deeply and as openly as you can. My hope is that, in the process, you will learn new ways to relate compassionately to the things, inside and out, that you've been opposing, and to use the unique resources of your mind to save your own life.

Milarepa was a great sage who met his enemies with an open heart and an enlightened mind. Most of us have not yet achieved his wisdom, and still need to learn new ways to relate to the demons we face on our path. We can learn that illness is not a failure, disease is not a sin, and confusion is not a weakness. Rather, they are all indications of the direction healing needs to go in. Every path to Hell is a possible road to Heaven.

In the chapters that follow, I offer a simple yet profound transformative process for perceiving your problems as solutions, creating safety within yourself, acknowledging and expressing your pain, remembering your disowned resources, and reclaiming your choice to decide how any given event determines your life. I call it reconnective learning. It is a fusion of learning through awareness, imagination, and compassion so that, like Milarepa, we can face our problems and demons in a way that creates harmony instead of opposition, wholeness instead of fragmentation. Face them with awareness so we can dig in with the fear, pain, and rage. Face them so that we not only survive them, but are transformed by the experience.

What is shared here is what I have realized through my own experience, and used effectively with others who have moved through turning points in their lives. It is their emergence that informs me. The amalgam of stories, ideas and experiences I offer are an indigenous truth extracted from the exploration of a dark landscape; the fruit of the many turnings and journeys I've followed in the last three decades as a psychotherapist, teacher, and educational consultant. This is earned wisdom.

The process is meant for anyone who has been brought

*"Many people are praying for mountains to be moved when all they need to do is climb them."*

*–Anon.*

to a moment of torment by a personal problem that will not be solved, and is ready now to stop running and turn toward it. It offers a handrail for your mind to cling to as you travel through the upheaval and loneliness your wounds may cause, the muck life sometimes offers.

We are all on a journey, through and beyond our personal struggle, in search of spiritual maturity. It is a solitary adventure, but one that ultimately reconnects us to the world in a deeper and truer way than ever before. When you travel with your enemies as your companions, when you offer them hands well-worn with compassion, when you shelter them in your wonder, then who you are and who you might become converge. You experience a sense of responsibility for the world around you–not because you are trying to be good, but because you are able to love.

This is not an instant how-to book. Healing is not a weekend project. Rather, it requires an unfolding, as one does with a mystery. There are no instant answers or magical powers. What is shared here is simple but not easy. For too long in my own struggle with addiction, I kept trying to find the easy way out. I switched from one brand of cigarettes to another, smoked a joint once a week instead of every day. When I finally allowed my pain to touch me, when I held my struggle at arm's length and acknowledged it, listened to it, saw it, and experienced it, then, and only then, did I begin to have a change of heart and become willing to risk living the unanesthetized life. That's when healing truly began.

I believe each of us is the ultimate healer of his or her own condition, no matter what the cause. However, we can learn to use tools that can be immensely important for helping us to uncover the map to our own path. I offer you signposts and, if you are willing to receive it, a hand, open and extended on the other side of the door as a companion for the journey across this dark landscape.

*"It may be that when we no longer know what to do we have come to our real work and that when we no longer know which way to go we have begun our real journey."*

*–Wendell Berry*

*"The technique is not the healing; it is the vehicle for the healing."*

*–Rachel Naomi Remen*

Many of the ideas you'll encounter in the weaving of these pages are not new. They are spun with precious fleece from many disciplines: Charlotte Selver, Thich Nhat Hanh, and other Buddhist teachers wind the warp of awareness and mindfulness; Clarissa Pinkola Estes, Deena Metzger, Natalie Goldberg, Gabrielle Rico, and other teachers of creativity use the loom of the power of imagination to foster self-realization; Jack Kornfield, Ram Dass, Victor Frankl, Joan Borysenko, Stephen Levine, and Joanna Macy interlace the weft of compassion. Jeanne Achterberg and Milton Erickson, M.D., Stephen Gilligan and Yvonne Dolan use the shuttle of the unconscious mind for healing; the martial arts, aikido in particular, offer resilient strands of teaching about creating harmony with an opposing force by blending and using its power to diffuse and redirect the attack; and Stanley Siegel, Sheldon Kopp, and other revolutionary psychotherapists tie in the raw silk threads with their perceptions of the adaptive ingenuity of the human mind.

There are also fibers of my own that give a unique texture to this particular material: the emphasis on uncovering your individual pathway to accessing, receiving, and recognizing the messages of intuition; the use of the revelatory power of imagination; the specific instructions for how to use the combined core qualities of awareness, compassion, and imagination to deal with the difficulties you face. The structure of this book, the experiences, the integration and the conclusions are drawn from my own life.

One of the most transformative experiences I had was when I died on an operating table for four-and-one-half minutes. I know four-and-one-half minutes does not make me an expert. But it did help to straighten my path in some places where it had gone crooked; and it took me a long way from where I had come. In my family of origin, we never mentioned the "D word." I never went to a funeral

*"One day I would like to teach just a few people many and beautiful things that would help them when they will one day teach a few people . . . ."*

*–Anon.*

9

until I was twenty-five. People didn't die; they just stopped showing up places. Death was the ultimate failure.

My own small four-and-one-half minute experience was so different from that. It is still difficult to put into words–I have not found the form to hold the intensity of the kind of rapture I experienced. I've tried to describe the patterns of light shifting, surrounding me, but my tongue ends up stumbling on clouds. It was as if my soul were grabbed up and spread out into the universe, or rather the universe and my soul were so enmeshed that it was impossible to tell where one began and the other left off. I became a cyclone of intense alertness. In the biggest classroom you can imagine, I learned a geometry of living in which all things added up. An infinite number of separate, unrelated strands spun into one strong thread.

I looked down from a thousand miles and saw my poor body draped in green on that metal operating table, the doctor administering adrenaline, the nurse scurrying frantically around the linoleum floor. At the same time, a voice all around and within me welled up and asked, "Have you had enough joy?" I realized in that instant that out of all the billions of moments I had lived, I had actually experienced only a very few. I missed most of them while frantically racing into the future or running from the past. I came to that realization like a small bird flying into a wide glass door—stunned.

A second question came, "What's unfinished for you to give?" Then there was a kind of crackling, a soft rushing around me, a pulling, tugging, floating downward that brought me back to the operating room, back into my body.

Such a small, private and ultimately timeless moment, but nothing has been the same since. I was emotionally and spiritually relocated to a way of thinking where "getting"—getting rich, getting loved, getting ahead, getting approval—was no longer so important for me. I missed too

"A spiritual crisis is an attempt to find oneself, to acquire new faith."

–Audrey Tarkovsky

many moments "getting."

Those four-and-one-half minutes shaped me the way a river does a canyon wall. Giving has replaced getting as a compass point—a giving where I don't give myself away. Learning to experience as much joy as possible has become my magnetic North, insisting that I create a life so alive and full of joy that I wouldn't want to leave it.

This book is not an end in itself. It is a means of having a conversation, a collaborative communication. Without you at the other side of the page, it could not exist. You are the arrow, and it is the bow. Without you, there would be no point.

There are frequent places in the pages that follow where you are invited to stop and use the tools offered so that this journey will become a lived experience. There are also many stories, all true; but they aren't meant as formulas for action. The most ancient form of education, stories, teach without telling. They remind us that we don't stand alone. They bind us together at the heart.

*"We are the ones we've been waiting for."*

*–June Jordan*

*Let's begin here. Everyone has a geography that can be used for change, some place that you can renew yourself, a territory that relaxes and rejuvenates. For some people it needs to be abrupt and rugged like the mountains. For others, wide and expansive like the seashore.*

*If you were on a journey, what would the geography be like? Are you in a desert or a forest? Are the forces that challenge you like storms or river rapids? What are the questions or quests that are at the root of your life now?*

## Healing As Liberation

At the beginning of most airline trips these days, there is a destination check: "This plane is going to Pittsburgh. If that is not your destination, please depart immediately." It seems like a good idea, therefore, to make sure we are headed in the same direction on *this* journey. In order to do that, I'd like to distinguish healing from curing.

Curing uses the same kind of thinking processes that problem solving does. It is focused on an end result; a diagnosis and treatment are necessary. When you talk about cure, you mean that the goal is for the disease or disturbance to leave. You stub your toe, and put some antiseptic and a band-aid on it. Cured is a finite state, not a process; it involves separation of the disease or disturbance from the person. Curing is necessary. I am deeply grateful for the treatments that were essential to the cure which allowed me to live so that I could learn to heal my life.

Healing is not an "alternative" to curing. It is ancillary to it, a companion process. To treat only our illnesses and problems is not to reach the root condition: The symptoms may recede, *but no learning has taken place.* In our sore toe example, healing would involve receiving the sensations of your wound, and being curious about what the conditions were that provoked the injury so you could learn what you needed next time.

Therefore, when you talk about healing, you are including the way you live your life, whatever time you have left. Sometimes it involves alleviating symptoms, but it always includes changing the conditions under which you are living. You don't heal *from* something you are afraid of, you heal *toward* something you deeply desire.

Healing insists that you re-examine everything—all of your habits, ideas, beliefs, values, passions, inhibitions, assumptions—until you find those things that are truest at the core, discarding everything else. It demands that you nurture your questions until you discover how to create the kind of environment where you have integrity with yourself and the world on a daily basis.

Curing implies a specific treatment for a specific dis-

*"What is to give light must first endure burning."*

–Victor Frankl

ease. Healing, on the other hand, involves a very personal medicine that only you can divine. Because it is not a linear process, questions are not answered directly, but rather responded to—images emerge unpredictably, insights pop into your mind erratically. There is no known formula except one: You must gradually liberate yourself from everything that does not help you create the life you took birth for with a sensitive ferocity.

*Your turn to set your own course on this journey, to find your own definition. You're invited to let your mind wander for awhile. You may have a favorite way of doing that—walking or swimming or hitting golf balls or driving on a back road. Just let it go wherever it wants, while you notice your breath going in and out. Then ask yourself the following questions, one at a time:*
*"What does healing mean to my body right now?"*
*"What does healing mean to my heart right now?"*
*"What does healing mean to my soul right now?"*
*Rather than expecting answers after each question, just notice what images and thoughts rise and fall in your mind with your breath, as if you were noticing clouds or stars while lying in a summer field.*

When we are children, we fear what can harm us. As adults we often fear that which has the greatest capacity to heal us. I believe that real safety lies in your willingness not to run away from yourself.

Will you travel with me? Our destination involves both learning and liberation. It focuses on a process, not a goal to be produced; it is a matter of finding new meaning, not new mechanics. The enemies you face will break you open, so that what needs to come through has a passage-way. Your wounds will become an evolutionary threshold for the expression of who you are in your most natural, divinely human, extraordinarily ordinary, authentic self.

*"Healing is embracing what is most feared; healing is opening what has been closed, softening what has hardened into obstruction, healing is learning to trust life."*

*–Jeanne Achterberg*

13

# 1 The Bounded Self:
Recognizing the Enemy Within

*"The heroes and leaders toward peace in our time will be those men and women who have the courage to plunge into the darkness at the bottom of the personal and the corporate psyche and face the enemy within."*

–Sam Keen

I used to love to watch my grandmother make bread for the Sabbath. Elbow-deep in flour, she taught me kitchen psychology while braiding the dough. One morning, when I was five or six, she said, without lifting her eyes from the table, "People have energy which makes their lives yeast. Their souls get sick if they don't let it out. It gets confused. It doesn't have a way of rising so it twists and strangles instead of becoming a new pattern." Her fingers tangled in the dough as she spoke and her beautiful bread became a mass of chaos. She struggled to free her hands. In the process, the shape of the bread was destroyed.

"Then we have to go back to the beginning and start again with the kneading and the rising," she said as she began to punch the dough flat again.

☆    ☆    ☆

*"Nothing can be sole or whole that has not been rent."*

*−W.B. Yeats*

We carry on wars within ourselves, our families and communities, among races and genders, nationalities and nations. I see them as a reflection of that inner twisting of conflict and pounding of fear my grandmother taught me about so profoundly.

As we stop the war within, we find the thing from which we have been running. What has to be healed will surface and resurface in some form, like a corked bottle filled with air and dropped into the ocean of our minds. It is that innate rising, the yeasting, inner creative force that we search for. To uncover it is to reclaim our lost selves.

I am thinking now of a television documentary I saw of Mother Teresa unwrapping the bandages of the lepers in Calcutta, washing their wounds, and stroking their foreheads. Even though the image was captured behind glass, even though it happened thousands of miles away, even though they spoke a language I couldn't understand, I wanted to turn away and not watch. At the same time, I could not pull my eyes from the screen. How could she

*"Whatever you bury, you bury alive."*

*−Anon.*

17

touch them? How could she see what she saw and still smile? For an instant, I was there beside her, holding the bowl of water. Then I shook my head and was back on my green couch. I knew I was watching connection, relationship, and healing in the truest sense of the word.

A few weeks later, I sat on that same green couch watching buildings in Iraq erupt in smoke, tanks rolling over a desert landscape, Scud missile launchers. I saw generals in camouflage and berets explaining what was happening in a press conference, how many buildings had been destroyed, how many babies. . . . No, there was no mention of babies. No people were mentioned. Just "the enemy." Casualties meant planes, how many planes were lost, shot down, missing.

Even though the image was captured behind glass, even though it happened thousands of miles away, even though they spoke a language I could not understand, I wanted to turn away and not watch. At the same time, I could not pull my eyes from the screen. How could they blow up other human beings? How could they pretend they didn't hear the screaming and see the wounds? How could they still smile? For an instant, I was there, speaking into the microphone about victory. Then I shook my head and was back on the green couch. I knew I was watching disconnection, out-of-relation-to, war in the truest sense of the word.

I don't believe anything happens "out there" that does not also exist, in some form, within me. There is a warrior inside my psyche who disconnects daily to do battle, who explains away the shrouds and scars, while bragging about victory. There is also a healer, who kneels and relates to the leprous wounds I carry in my heart and bathes them clean, salves them with compassion, smiles into the eyes of my fear.

Healing, whether from a debilitating disease, a broken heart, or a horrifying past, entails establishing a relationship

*"The greatest warrior is one who never has to use his sword."*

*–Anon.*

*"Every war is against the world and every war against the world is lost."*

*–Alice Walker*

between that warrior and that healer, thereby creating a possible future for yourself, for all of us. It requires that you create a context where both of them can exist, where you can teach the warrior to protect you without destroying others; where you can allow the healer to expose your wounds without destroying yourself. To do that is to ultimately transform the way we are thinking about our problems or enemies; it is to punch down the old shape and let it rise before re-braiding it into something new and whole.

*"Since wars begin in the minds of men, it is in the minds of men that we have to erect the ramparts of peace."*

*—UNESCO Charter*

## Re-Thinking the Nature Of the Enemy

For me, growing up always seemed like a camp color war with the world divided up into opposing teams, the good guys against the bad, the white hats against the black, the right side against the wrong. Home meant hot wars with my father erupting in rage, or cold wars with my mother silently sabotaging him. My dad taught me that the other guy was always the enemy. My mom taught me the enemy was always myself. Home was the place I learned to do combat with blame and vengeance, resentment and retaliation.

My mother was the captain of the victim team. The rules were not to see, speak, or know how my father hurt us. Her eyes and mouth and mind, in the name of mothering, orphaned me. My father was the captain of the enemy team. His rules were to always have a reason for beating me. If you were right, you got to do the beating. If you were wrong, you got beaten. His hands, in the name of fathering, orphaned me. As I grew, I played internal color wars, making myself wrong, beating myself up, orphaning myself with eyes and mouth, hands and mind.

When I was in graduate school, trying very hard to be

*"The judging specter gives fears a familiar face and personifies them—as the parent, the teacher, the political tyrant. It is easy for us to externalize him, to turn him into the Enemy, to look for him outside ourselves in all the persons or factors that may be putting us down, getting in our way.*

*—Stephen Nachmanovitch*

professional, I was taught to become obsessed with pathology. I learned to identify what was wrong with everyone I worked with, to find their deficits, to label them. The assumption in all of my training was that there were "enemies" inside of people, "bad" things that had to be removed as soon as possible, things that needed to be treated or improved. Of course the vocabulary was quite sophisticated, but that was what they meant in plain talk. I was taught that my unconscious mind, in the core of my being, was a seething cave for dark, libidinal forces which "caused" certain things to be "wrong" with me. When I mentioned to my Freudian analyst the abuse I experienced as a child, he explained to me that it was really a fantasy generated by my unconscious mind.

When I was trying to heal from terminal cancer, I thought of the enemy as alien cells which had to be demolished. When I was struggling to recover from addiction, I thought of an enemy inside of me who wanted a bad substance. Recovery meant getting rid of that monster, and praying that a good guy named Will would somehow triumph. Likewise, "getting over" being raped was another war between the enemy inside of me who had somehow created the reality by doing something shameful that deserved punishment, and a good girl who pretended it never happened.

"Curing" each of these problems—cutting out the malignancy, not using the toxic substance, analyzing the reasons for the abuse and then forgetting it—has the same effect as sewing wings on a caterpillar: It still isn't a butterfly. My body was cured, but my soul needed a metamorphosis if it was to take flight again.

Cancer was the first challenge of my life where intellectual knowledge was worthless. The best heads in America had no idea how to fix my body; in fact they told me I would not survive. In a frenetic attempt to find some cure, solution, or expert who could help me when the medical

*"Nonviolence means avoiding not only external physical violence but also internal violence of spirit. You not only refuse to shoot a man, but you refuse to hate him."*

*–Martin Luther King, Jr.*

profession gave up, I worked my way through a variety of healers. Several psychotherapists suggested I pound on pillows to release my hostility. I tried a famous German bodyworker who had callouses on her knuckles like cigar butts and dug into my "muscular armoring." A psychic "channel" charged me several hundred dollars for the message that my soul had created the disease to correct a spiritual inadequacy. A social worker volunteered to help me "make arrangements" for the guardianship of my son. My best friend, trained in Rogerian empathetic communication, could not listen to the agonized moans that escaped through my tightly locked jaws. Other friends came with crystals and wheatgrass, all trying valiantly to help me get rid of this enemy disease and solve my problems.

Most of the people that were supposed to be helping me were basically terrified of illness, pain, and death. They too considered them "bad" things, mistakes to be fixed, failures to be eliminated as soon as possible. New Age healers were more benevolent toward my disease, but they shone the light of responsibility in my eyes by explaining how I had caused the illness. I needed a lifeline and they threw me a noose.

> "At the root of all war is fear."
>
> –Thomas Merton

It was only when I stopped thinking of these challenges as problems to be solved or enemies to be vanquished, and started exploring a new way of relating to them, that transformation began.

*Try it for yourself for a minute. What if, instead of thinking of your problem or enemy as something wrong, you thought of it as a story in need of a change of direction? What if you thought of it as a path to someplace important, gone crooked? What if you thought of it as a messenger? What if you thought of your problem as a solution, of your enemy as an ally in disguise?*

> "There is a time, when passing through light, that you walk in your own shadow."
>
> –Keri Hulme

Enemies are really a case of mistaken identity. Someone back then taught you that you are what you do, or even what was done to you. I was wounded. I am a victim. I am sick. I am helpless, abandoned, depressed. Your effectiveness is increased, however, when you follow in the tracks of Gregory Bateson who said, "I consider myself to be a verb." Or Dr. Milton Erickson, psychiatrist and medical hypnotherapist, who was most interested and curious about the patterns people brought to him, patterns of communicating, experiencing, behaving, interacting. In other words, a problem isn't something wrong with you, it's something wrong with what you're doing. And there might even be something right about it.

There are no enemies within me. Not really. Or you. Not when we make room in our hearts for what we have been struggling against. But in order to truly know that, it is necessary to face what is most repugnant and most terrifying in ourselves. If we run from it, we will inevitably want to destroy it when we meet it "out there." As we unwrap the bandages, we find the wounds and needs of our history waiting to be tended.

I once saw an ad in the *New York Times* magazine section for a new kind of safe. It was pale green plastic and shaped exactly like a moldy cabbage, made to look and feel so much like the real thing that any burglar who found it in your refrigerator wouldn't bother to inspect it any closer. Only you would know that if touched in just the right place on the middle seam, the whole thing would open to reveal your most valuable jewels.

This clever cabbage is a wonderful model for the work of transformation, because it springs from the places within where we feel the most inferior, despicable, uncontrollable—the moldy cabbage that only a truly curious and unconditional soul would be willing to touch with compassionate fingers—and when that happens, what is revealed is of the greatest value.

In the Buddhist tradition, this is the work of the spiritual warriors, those who are willing to face their darkest selves

"Our best hope for survival is to change the way we think about enemies and warfare. Instead of being hypnotized by the enemy we need to begin looking at the eyes with which we see the enemy."

–Sam Keen

"Healing, as the Tao-te Ching clearly indicates, does not come from increasing the amount of light in our lives but from reaching into the shadow and drawing up unreconciled elements of ourselves into the light where they can be healed."

–Greg Johanson & Ron Kurtz

and recognize them for what they truly are. This turning is no small thing. Those darkest selves are far more than character flaws. They are shadows at the very core of our being, looming larger than life, refusing to be shrugged away, controlled, ignored or eliminated. And we are very resourceful in keeping ourselves from knowing about them.

A story to bind this together: Sylvia had been living in a religious cult for years. She sold little booklets on the streets of a major city to raise money for the man who was the head of the organization, and whom they all called "Father." At first, Sylvia came seeking help because she could not spell, which she identified as her stupidity—the thing about herself she most hated. She also could not form an intimate relationship with anyone, and described herself as feeling disconnected from her own life. Within a short time, it became obvious to me that she was blocked from the resource of her long-term visual memory because of some great trauma in her history. This woman was a walking wound with a person attached. My intuition said not to interfere with this "problem" by trying to improve her spelling. I suggested instead she use a computer with a spell-checker.

Sylvia maintained contact with me, and three months later I received an emergency phone call from her. She was sobbing hysterically. When we finally met the next day, she told me that her father, whom she hadn't seen since she was eleven, had just died. She went to the funeral home and when she stood in front of his casket and actually saw his dead body, a flood of visual memories rushed through her. The door to the prison cell had opened.

She remembered being sexually abused by him from the age of five. He had sold her on the streets as a child prostitute until she was eleven when her grandmother took her to live at her house. That memory had stayed hidden in Sylvia's core until her unconscious mind knew he

*"My most formidable opponent is a man named Mohandas K. Gandhi. With him I seem to have very little influence."*

*–M.K. Gandhi*

*"You may my glories and my states depose, But not my griefs. Still, I am king of those."*

*–William Shakespeare*

23

was dead. Without her being aware of what was happening, it had drawn her to a similar situation (the cult family where she was selling something little to make money for her "father") in an attempt to heal that early wound.

Sylvia's problem, "the stupid" lack of visual memory, was a noble accomplishment on the part of her unconscious mind—it saved her sanity until such time as it was safe to open up and heal. Chances are that your enemies, the things you'd most like to get rid of or change about yourself, may also be valiant attempts at adaptation to traumas you've experienced in your past. They may not necessarily be as extreme as Sylvia's, but woundings nonetheless.

## The Enemy Hiding In the Shadows

*"To confront a person with their own shadow is to show them their own light."*

*–Carl Jung*

More than forty years ago, Carl Jung expressed his concern that humans had come to a turning point. In the aftermath of World War II, he realized that at no other time in history had the extermination of so many rested in the hands of so few. He was concerned about the bomb, overpopulation, and the mistreatment of the environment. Jung believed it was within the individual psyche to turn the course of this malignant tide. He said we could survive if a sufficient number of people could "maintain the tension of the opposites." He was referring to those parts of ourselves which we hold in the light of our awareness, and their opposites—those that lurk in what he called the "shadow" of our psyche.

We learn to disconnect from this shadow in two predominant ways—by projecting it up and out where it becomes an external enemy or by pushing it down and into our muscles, bones, and hearts, where it becomes a symptom or affliction.

Think about a seesaw. On one end are those aspects of yourself that you've been taught to consider acceptable. On the other—in the shadows—are those feelings and forces that you've been taught are not who you're expected to be. If, for example, you spend a lot of time in righteous dieting, it's likely that on the other end there will lurk an out-of-control binger. Often, people who seem to be controlled and unemotional on the surface may have a hotbed of feelings concealed in the shadows beneath their calm exterior, waiting for a few drinks to explode in a fit of temper or tears.

Think for a moment of a mask. It has one side—convex, which shows to the world at large, and another—concave, which is closest to your skin. It is this second one that is the shadow or enemy. If you didn't take off the mask once in a while, you would not even be aware that the hidden side was there.

My father was a lion of a man who insisted he was never afraid of anything. He was repulsed by people who "had no guts." They were exposing what he was hiding from— fear. Since each of us is always trying to create wholeness, it is a spiritual necessity to reclaim that unlived side of the mask. When my father had a heart attack at age 75, he was overwhelmed by fear—fear of everything. He had finally met his gutless enemy in a hospital bed.

## Up and Out

We tend to unconsciously surround ourselves with people who play out the hidden aspects of ourselves, and who behave in ways we don't dare. An emotionally warm, engaging woman, for example, may be attracted to someone who is distant, aloof. A parent who has always worked hard, always done the right thing, has a child who loves to

*"The more we ignore the animals we are, the more likely it is that the fearful beast will be released."*

*–Sheldon Kopp*

*"No matter what area of your life seems to you to be blocked or thwarted, stop and reconsider: you will recognize the outer 'enemy' as but a reflection of what you have not, before now, been willing or able to recognize as coming from within."*

*–Ralph Blum*

25

take risks, break rules, walk the edge, be lazy, just enjoy life. A man described by everyone as a complete "sweetheart," good-natured but a worrier, marries a woman who is described as explosive, manipulative, "a complete bitch who doesn't care about anybody or anything."

An external enemy, be it Hitler, Sadam Hussein, or the person at work you just can't stand, is constructed from the disconnected aspects of yourself, the hidden side of your mask. Like most people, I took some inner enemy from the underbelly of my mind, and cast it out of my awareness by projecting it on the people in my life. When I first met my husband Andy, his outstanding quality was a sensual, healthy awareness of his body and the physical world around him. At first, I found that very attractive. It seemed completely foreign and desirable to me. However, in time, I started accusing him of being lazy, of just hanging around all day enjoying the moment, never caring about the disasters going on in the world or the future. It took a great deal of time and effort to turn toward myself instead of against him. What I found there was my own fear of feeling—anything. Feeling to me meant I had to feel my own pain at the moment. As long as I could worry about the future, I could ignore my own suffering. For years, I justified my numbness by explaining how much good work I was doing in the world. Symptoms were as close to feelings as I could allow myself to get. I was more loyal to his body than I was to my own, and that was a spiritual emergency. Andy was the waking part of me and I was the sleeping part of him. If I didn't learn to awaken my own feeling-sensual-body self, I would die.

*In order to make this concept relevant to you, it would be helpful to consider the people with whom you have the most problems. Think, now, if you will, of five people, past or present, who frustrate or annoy you. The overall person may drive you crazy or just some particular behavior of theirs (i.e., "I just can't*

*"What is the beloved? She is that which I am not."*

*–D.H. Lawrence*

*"If we could read the secret history of our enemies, we should find in each person's life sorrow and suffering enough to disarm all hostility."*

*–Longfellow*

stand Millicent; I don't know why." or "Saddam Hussein's arrogance infuriates me.") Consider particularly "types" of people or behaviors that keep popping up over and over in your life. (i.e., "I don't know why, but I seem to fall for one abusive man after another.")

Next step, write down three qualities, actions or behaviors that especially bother you (i.e., neediness, righteousness, etc.).

Now read over what you have written, and ask yourself:

Is there a part of me that acts like this also?

Is there a part of me that admires this behavior in some way?

Is there anything about this behavior that could be "right?"

Is there a part of me that would secretly like to behave that way, but has never dared?

## Down and In

Many of us are exiles from our childhood. We are struggling with issues of recovery from a disease, an addiction, a failed relationship. As we turn to face each of these enemies, what we often discover are wounded histories of abuse and molestation. We approach them, protesting all the while, saying "It didn't really hurt so bad. I survived. I'm all right now. It's just that I'm feeling a little despair. It's just that I feel as if I'm invisible. It's just that I have to be on anti-depressants. It's just that I have an eating disorder, am disconnected from my body, am working myself to death, can't form an intimate relationship. . . ."

Every time we disconnect and make someone or something into an enemy, it really is a disguise for a disowned aspect of our own suffering. Frequently, there is a psychological wound hidden in the shadows, causing old fears to invade our current experience. We are responding to the past rather than to the present. Like a series of nesting dolls that hide one inside the other, the enemy hides the wounded history, thereby hiding our unmet needs and our internal resources to meet those needs.

*"Every part of our personality that we do not love will become hostile to us."*

*–Robert Bly*

27

*"The truth about our childhood is stored up in our body and although we can repress it, we can never alter it. Our intellect can be deceived, our feelings manipulated, our perceptions confused, and our body tricked with medication. But someday the body will present its bill, for it is as incorruptible as a child who, still whole in spirit, will accept no compromises or excuses, and it will not stop tormenting us until we stop evading the truth."*

—Alice Miller

*"Who is it we spend our entire life loving?"*

—Kabir

Before children have a bounded sense of themselves, they tend to internalize the bad things that happen around them in an attempt to fix them. When parents fight, the child swallows it, believing it is his or her fault that they are fighting. A pet dies and the child believes it is because he or she didn't love it enough.

Our culture encourages us to put the problem inside: "It's your fault, Sally. If you had been a good girl, Daddy wouldn't have had to hit you." It also encourages us to put solutions outside of us: "Buy this new toy/drug/car/therapy and you'll live happily ever after," which keeps us consuming. Unfortunately, we are being consumed by our consumption.

Internalizing the problem and externalizing the solution in this way creates the belief that we have no internal resources and thus that something outside of ourselves will make everything all right. A beautiful lover, more money, or job success may work temporarily. But ultimately they won't meet the needs of our wounded histories, because our centers of gravity will always be in that lover, that money, or that job. We begin to worry about "what if": What if the woman leaves me, or the stock market crashes, or I get sick and cannot work? Even if the woman loves you, you may spend your time worrying about when she'll leave and so you miss her presence when she *is* with you.

In the moment we are wounded, we realize the world is not safe. Our lives distort and warp. Our souls begin to leak. We stop seeing the width and depth of things, stop feeling the texture and only speak what is mutually agreeable. The edge between where we end and danger begins blurs; the membrane that defines our personal, private space shreds. We learn to live in the cold vise of either having other people inside of us totally, or withdrawing so far behind stony barriers that no one and nothing can affect us.

Cynthia had been traumatized by her mother as a child.

As a forty year old, she developed an "unreasonable" terror of the next-door neighbor, who frequently yelled at her children with a piercing voice. Whenever Cynthia walked out of the house and heard her, she felt as if she were a terrified five-year-old. She begged her husband to sell the house so she could get away from "that ghastly voice." She even knew that the neighbor reminded her of her mother. She knew the woman was *not* her mother, yet she could not stop her reaction to her.

Children who are traumatized often feel like aliens in disguise, strangers in a strange land, as if there is no place they belong. Since they cannot make boundaries in the outer world, they build walls in their inner world between "me" and that part which they have disowned. That wounded self becomes isolated from the child's own resources and other life experiences. The child grows into an adult who continues to relate as if he or she *is* the problem, the memory, the trauma. It is as if a computer froze the material on screen and could not access any of its memory. The person's awareness becomes narrowed. All attention is focused on the problem. The perceptions become tunneled into that continuous loop—a "can't-do-anything-about-this" loop. It is as if a spell is cast and he or she is imprisoned in a dark forest.

Because it is trapped in the deepest part of our unconscious mind, the wounding event seems to be like a virtual reality drive-in movie, perpetually playing even when we lose conscious awareness of it. After the violation has ceased, we continue to be wounded by the stories we tell ourselves about it, the real-life images we see on the screen of our minds and the feelings that seem to arise out of nowhere. We lose connection with our resources, our bodies, our support system. The self becomes a "me" without an "I"—a kind of non-being who is neither safe inside nor out. It is as if we are captured inside of a timeless memory, outcasts from our present selves. In that place,

*"The ultimate dragon is within you."*

–Joseph Campbell

29

we are still being terrorized, beaten, abused, or abandoned. I call this phenomenon "trauma trance." The bridge between the person, the present moment, and the rest of his or her learnings is washed away.

At the time of a deep wounding, basic survival needs go unmet, such as the need to be protected, nurtured, touched, looked at, listened to, the need for freedom and belonging. These are universal, ongoing needs that do not disappear as we grow, but follow us from womb to tomb. Our survival instinct urges us to fulfill them, to complete what was unfinished, to evolve. That's why in the depth of our wounds, at the core of our enemies, lie the needs that have been waiting to be fulfilled: the needs of incest survivors, for example, to learn how to make boundaries that will keep themselves safe, and give choices about what goes into them and what doesn't. A woman who grew up under the constant dominance and direction of her mother needs to have her individual identity acknowledged. A workaholic man driven by an abusing father needs to be guided, to be supported when at rest, to become conscious of and nurture his own feelings, and to express his own pain.

We need to break the silence: to receive our own pain and have it received by our community; to show our wounds; to be held and touched with clean hands; to grieve and teach; to be heard and to reach. The deaf say it all in a language deeper than words. The sign for "home" is fingertips to lips, palm cradling ear—a place to eat and sleep, but more I think. Each of us needs, and has always needed, a place to be harbored and nurtured, where we may sleep in safety and trust. Each of us needs to find a way to speak of our wounds and to know that other hearts are listening.

Our wholeness is based on reclaiming those aspects of ourselves that, due to our personal circumstances, we've had to leave along the way. Most likely, you've thought

*"I owe much to my friend but . . . even more to my enemies. The real person springs to life under a sting even better than under a caress."*

*–André Gide*

about your problem as an enemy to get rid of for a long time. Beginning now, I'm going to ask you to think about it and relate to it in an entirely new way—with compassion, which is the way the heart perceives the true identity of all things. In the martial art of aikido, there really are no attackers. The opponent is called "uke," which means "the one who falls," or "partner." As with all partnerships, the goal is to find a common ground.

*Let's begin. Take me along as a companion in your journey to find a safe space, a haven, the best place you can think of, real or imagined, a place to turn and face what you've been running from. Take me to that place in you where your truth is rooted. Walk with me for awhile in a park, a quiet street, a cornfield you love. You have given me such fine attention. Allow me to do that for you. Walk with me under a night sky or on a plain, clear morning with the smell of Spring clinging to your skin.*

*When we get there, tell me about an enemy you've found inside yourself with which you've been struggling. Perhaps one came to mind when you first saw or heard the title of this book and wondered what it meant. Perhaps as you have been reading, your mind has gone on an internal search, matching the words to your own experiences. Tell me as much or as little as you would like. What you say at this point isn't nearly as important as creating a safe space for yourself to acknowledge the struggle you've been experiencing.*

Who are we divorcing? Who are we drugging and bombing and abusing? I know that it is possible to come out of opposition with oneself, to reconcile one's internal warfare. I know it is possible to discover that you are more than your suffering, more than your trauma, more than your violations. You *can* learn to turn and face your enemy, to make room enough for it so that you can find out what it needs. You *can* learn to access and depend on your internal resources to meet those needs. You *can* form a healing alliance within yourself, not to change or fix the

> *"You cannot overcome the enemy until you've healed in yourself that which you find despicable in them."*
>
> *—The I Ching*

> *"Dip into the unconscious well of your own disowned darkness with a wide brush and stain the strangers with the sinister hue of the shadow. Trace onto the face of the enemy the greed, hatred, carelessness you dare not claim as your own."*
>
> *—Sam Keen*

31

past but rather to create environments in the present where your needs can be satisfied.

Underneath the symptoms of physical illness, addiction, despair and helplessness, beneath the enemies that you are facing at this point of your life, is the demand to change your life and the way you relate to the world. Ultimately, we cannot go around, under or over all of this. The only way out is through. We do have internal resources. We do have guidance, which comes in the form of images from a source within us. Those images are channels for the energy that is expanding. They are stained glass windows bringing illumination into the denseness of matter. Enemies challenge us to dance light into the dark mass of disease and trauma, to drum it, paint it, carve it, story it; to use our creative energy to reconnect who we have been with the radiance of who we can become.

*"Why shouldn't there be a chance for an entire civilization if as many of its members as possible can dare to look their own truth in the eyes without fear?"*

*–Christa Wold*

## Putting It All In Your Hands

*Somewhere around your house or office there must be a rubber band—the bigger the better. Slip your two hands between it, facing palm to palm. At first, allow only one hand to move. Let it represent the warrior within you. Let it describe itself to you kinesthetically, through movement.*

*Then allow your other hand to describe the healer within you.*

*If possible, let them both move simultaneously, within the rubber band. Allow your eyes to be soft, curious and removed, as if you were watching a puppet show of how they now relate to each other within you. You can extend this by changing the movement, so that they describe how you would like them to be relating.*

*What words would you use to articulate the changes you would have to make to be living that relationship?*

# 2 Losing Life, Heart, and Mind:
## Disconnecting From Your Resources

*"Mr. Duffy lived a short distance away
from his body."*

–James Joyce

Milton Erickson believed that people who are traumatized get stuck in one frame of reference, in one way of thinking about the world, themselves, and their difficulties. It is that "stuckness" that imprisons us, because it knocks us out of connection with our bodies and senses. We feel as if we have lost the spirit from our lives.

By the time we reach adulthood in this culture, most of us have learned appetite, but our appetite to learn has all but vanished. We are not only estranged from the resources of our minds, we're also disconnected from an awareness of our bodies' messages, so that illness becomes the only way we can give ourselves permission to change. We are also detached from an awareness of the present moment. Life becomes what happens while we wait to go on vacation. (Vacate shun = the one week when we shun vacating!) We have been taught to divorce ourselves from the inner world of intuition and imagination as a source of guidance. And we are fragmented away from our compassion—thinking of ourselves as a collection of parts to be gotten rid of or sold to the highest bidder.

As a consequence, when we come face to face with an internal or external challenge, we tend to get stuck in our one-way-to-think-about-it prison. We attempt to relate to it the "right" way. Whether we are facing the "enemies" of cancer, an estranged partner, loneliness, depression, or addiction, we do the best we can to make ourselves safe in a tiny cell of control, which means to exercise dominance over. Keep that disease under control. Control that anger. Control your feelings of helplessness. Control your partner, your children, your body, your neighbor. When a challenge won't be controlled, we rattle the bars shouting, "It's not fair!"

However, safety doesn't lie in the absence of danger or in our capacity to control the world at large, but rather in our ability to shape whatever happens to us. We are well trained in pleasing others. But where do we learn how to

*"When the power of love overcomes the love of power, then there will be true peace."*

*–Sri Chin Moi Gosh*

35

navigate through the challenges we encounter in our lives? Who teaches us to relate creatively to difficulties?

Acknowledging the way we've gotten into this prison of disconnection, and turning around to notice how we've been ruptured from our awareness, imagination, and compassion is the first step to finding our way back to wholeness.

## The Routine Way We Lose Our Lives: Disconnection From Awareness

*"Forfeit your sense of awe, let your conceit diminish your reverence and the universe becomes a market place."*

*–Rabbi Heschel*

When we are children, we are fully attuned to the present moment. That's why we ask such "inappropriate" questions: "Mommy, why does that man have such a funny smelling mouth?" Noticing sensations in our bodies is almost always considered inappropriate and something to be controlled. How else could we "learn" to sit in hard, little chairs for hours on end, paying attention to chicken-scratching on a chalk board? We're taught how to think *about* our bodies rather than how to think *with* and *in* them. We're taught how our bodies are supposed to look, rather than how to look at things through a "sense-able" perspective.

Listen to this poignant description of physical discon-nection by Betsy, a young woman who was recovering from a history of abuse: "I'm beginning to see how inhabiting my body is a choice I make, and how being fully human does, in the end, require me to inhabit my body. A question I have had since I began my healing, and one I still have, is: Who is in my body when I'm not? Who has been controlling, making decisions about, for instance, my pelvis, all these years that I haven't been there? The fear, as I re-enter, is like returning to one's village after a bombing— not knowing what atrocities one will discover, what violence, what destruction. Yet it is one's home, my home, so return I must or stay a refugee."

In Japanese, the word for sickness means "absence of mind." Conversely, the word for health means "presence of mind," or "awareness." I was brought up to believe that an absent mind was a safe one. In my family, we frequently said, "I don't mind" and shrugged. When I asked my mother if she were upset when my father went on one of his rampages, she shrugged and said, "Oh, that's just the way he is. I don't mind." In the same way, I learned to deny or ignore whatever was challenging me: "Just don't pay any attention to it, Dawna, and it'll go away."

Disease was the only alarm I couldn't ignore. When I was challenged with cancer, it became obvious that my mind had become very estranged, very absent, very un-aware of anything below my chin. I was forgetful of my entire body, except as a fleshly taxicab for the really "important" part of me, my brain. I was a disinterested passenger involved with important ideas and things that needed to get done. Re-entering my body was a slow, frustrating process, similar to bringing styrofoam to life. My intellect, that well honed, over-educated instrument which so neatly defined how I was distinct and separate, was totally useless. It was the sword of my nobility, my crown, but it had also impaled me and was my cross. It was designed to control, and I had controlled every drop of awareness out of my body until I could no longer experi-ence any joy in, or through, it. I had been living in my work, in other people's minds, in fantasy and television sets. I had little private time, little time for friends, for leisure, contem-plation, puttering or, the worst sin of all: Doing nothing!

Ultimately, healing for me has come to mean forming an intimate relationship with my body, coming to under-stand it in a way no one else could. I had to learn to see in the dark, hear the unspoken, feel what else existed in the spaces between pain. I had to learn to travel in a mysteri-

*"Illness is the most heeded of doctors. To goodness and wisdom we make only promises; pain we obey."*

*–Marcel Proust*

ous landscape where I was totally ignorant of the terrain.

Through the inspiration of a friend, Ilana Rubenfeld, I became intrigued with the work of Moshe Feldenkrais, an Israeli physicist and black-belt judo practitioner who developed a system called "Awareness Through Movement." One of the first things I heard him say was, "Where there is awareness, there is circulation. Where there is circulation, there is health. Where there is numbness, there is more likely to be decreased circulation, and increased chance of injury, and disease."

Feldenkrais developed thousands of small movement sequences which were designed to increase one's awareness of physical sensations, while also creating new neural pathways in the brain. Here's a simple one you may want to try:

*Fold your hands, fingers interlaced, in the habitual way you have folded them since you were a child trying to appear good. Look at your hands and notice whether your right fingers are on top of your left, or vice versa.*

*Now uncross them and refold them in the opposite way. If your right fingers were on top before, the left ones will be now.*

*Keep folding back and forth between the habitual way and the new way as you ponder these questions: Which is more comfortable? Which is more familiar? Which feels strange? Which feels more secure? Which one increases your awareness of all your fingers and the spaces between them? Which makes your hands feel more alive? Which makes you more aware of the fact that you have two separate and distinct hands?*

When I first experienced this practice, I kept crossing and uncrossing my hands and mumbling, "familiar = secure, known; strange = weird, unknown." I couldn't believe it! The *strange* way increased my aliveness! I had been living for over three decades trying to do whatever was necessary to make myself secure, and what I had really been doing was to make myself numb! If I wanted to

---

*"The body should be studied not only by those who wish to become doctors but by those who wish to attain a more intimate knowledge of God."*

*–Al-Ghaz Ali*

*"If we believe it's wrong to love ourselves, as most of us do, then we can't really love anyone, not our enemies and not our friends. Instead we reach for security: a promise that someone else will love us, an insurance policy from Allstate, an antimissile missile defense."*

*–Sy Safransky*

become more alive, if I wanted to understand the strange language of sensation that my body was speaking, I was going to have to do things in ways that were awkward and unfamiliar. I had to turn toward that which I'd been running from and receive it with awareness.

## The Logical Way We Lose Our Minds: Disconnection From Imagination

Our culture does everything it can to discourage us from becoming aware of our inner life. It's considered a waste of time, a distraction from the really important things. There are no rewards for contemplation. You don't get degrees, promotions or bonuses. In fact, we are taught to be as externally-oriented as possible; every sense we have is flooded with beckonings from the outside world.

We are meticulously taught that wisdom is always outside of us. Even the people I teach who are spiritually sophisticated spend five hours traveling to weekend workshops so they can to listen to an "entity" being channeled by someone they wouldn't normally ask for advice on how to bake a potato. They return, exclaiming how wise and deep the entity was, and explain that they've just been too busy to meditate or write in their journal. An addictive system of any kind references externally; it evaluates and motivates based on outside opinion. A man I worked with who struggled with a cocaine habit was always worried about what other people were thinking. He had done so since he was seven years old, trying to get smiling faces drawn on his papers by Mrs. Chalkdust and waiting for Mr. Stencil to tell him when he should be finished working on his multiplication tables. He had absolutely no internal reference point experiences for evaluating whether something he did was worthy or not, or for estimating how much

*"We've built a way of life that depends on people doing what they're told because they don't know how to tell themselves what to do."*

*—John Gatto*

39

was enough. Remember how the shadow balances on the other end of the seesaw? The harder the externally-oriented self would try to please everyone else, the deeper his internally-oriented, sabotaging self would entrench in its no-one-can-make-me-do-anything-I-don't-want-to-do behavior. While the conscious aspect of his mind was busy worrying what everyone else thought, the unconscious aspect of his mind that cared only about what *he* thought was sabotaging any external goals by secretly indulging in pleasures that led directly to pain.

That's why no matter what challenge we face, be it of body, heart, or soul, the first stage to healing is withdrawal into ourselves. We have to learn to switch our allegiance, from being loyal to outside people, situations and toxic substances, to becoming loyally committed to finding the things that nurture the sacredness in us, silencing the tired, old voices in our heads that moan about how selfish and inappropriate we are being.

A woman I worked with who was struggling with a failing marriage, sorely in need of her attention, explained to me that she couldn't put time into her relationship because she had to work sixty hours a week in order to save up enough money to retire in ten years. I questioned her logic: "You are telling me that you have to give up the time you have now to make enough money so you will have time ten years from now?" She looked at me blankly and nodded her head, bemused under the spell of disconnection from her senses, which is cast upon all of us when we are taught to be "reasonable."

We are, in fact, all longing for our own company and don't even know it. The faster we run, talk and act, the more numb we get. Our liberation begins when we choose to stop running around and around and rest. Back up, back down, back off. Rest physically, of course, but more importantly, rest mentally, psychologically, spiritually. The heart grows when the mind is at rest. Magically or logically

*"It's as if we're driving down a road at night, speeding faster and faster, and at the same time, we're turning our headlights down dimmer and dimmer."*

–Peter Senge

(depending on your perspective), when *we* retreat, cancer can retreat, rage can retreat, alienation and fear can retreat. They are all messengers who demand with increasing insistence that we stop, feel, see, and listen to how we are using ourselves. They insist that we bend back our lives enough so that our souls can catch up with the rest of us.

In a crisis of body, heart or soul, the habitual ways of problem solving grow less and less effective and learning to think creatively is what is needed. In order to do this, we must first sit curiously in the place of *not* knowing. Nothing in our schooling prepares us to do that; saying "I don't know" is an admission of weakness and failure. As soon as we hit the border territory of the unknown, where we are confused and lose our certainty, we are taught to contract fearfully and do whatever we can to avoid experiencing it.

*Try it for a few moments now. You're invited to put the book down and think about some way you get stuck in your present life, something you don't know how to do, or can't figure out. Notice what happens to your energy, your breathing, your muscles as you do that for a few minutes. Do you contract? Get tight? Does your breathing get shallow?*

> "The suicide rate of American high school kids is up 500% since 1970. The major cause of injury to women in this country is beating by the men they live with. People don't know how to get along with house-mates, soulmates, roommates, love-mates or themselves, because they haven't been given the skills to do so."
>
> –Colman McCarthy

We have mastered using our brains to solve problems quite efficiently. But problem solving and learning to heal require very different thinking processes. Our culture equates learning with taking in and putting out information. In fact, a more effective definition of learning would be one offered by Peter Senge, systems thinker and author of *The Fifth Discipline*: "enhancing our capacity to produce results that really matter to us."

Considered this way, it becomes obvious that very little true learning happens in school. Completing graduate school in psychology and education brought me no closer to producing a loving relationship with my son or with my

41

body, which was what really mattered to me. I had been taught how to solve problems for twenty-one years. That meant I knew how to make things go away. But I didn't want to make my son or my body go away. And the smartest of the smart could offer me no solutions on how to make the cancer or my grief go away.

In Chinese, the two symbols which express the word learning are "studying" and "practicing constantly." You can never say that you learned something, only that you are practicing. When solving problems, we are taught to contract when we become confused. In practice, however, confusion can expand into curiosity and ultimately into wonder: "I wonder how I can do this simply, more elegantly?"

There are many situations where problem solving is an effective way of thinking. It can help us cure disease as well as do our taxes. The point is that problem solving is not the *only* way of using our minds and, as the chart below indicates, it is not the kind of thinking that healing requires.

| PROBLEM SOLVING | LEARNING |
| --- | --- |
| eliminating | revealing |
| discriminating | adding possibilities |
| avoiding the unknown | entering the unknown |
| disconnecting from | connecting to |
| finite | infinite |
| answer-oriented | process-oriented |
| oppositional | relational |
| acquiring information | developing ability |
| short-term | long-term |
| contracted, focused | expansive, wondering |
| linear | creative |
| reactive | proactive |

As the chart reveals, we are taught how to fit in, but not how to create or relate. We are taught to separate "from," to do "to" and do "for." We need to learn how to do "with," how to connect. True learning is a much more connective and imaginative process of uncovering new patterns of action and thought. In being disconnected from our imagination, we are in fact disconnected from our ability to learn.

The human imagination holds tremendous untapped power. Every one of us is born naturally creative. As children, we have imaginary companions, talk to trees, highways and ants, and invent new ways to approach just about anything. But all too quickly we are taught that this is, at best, a useless way of thinking. Our imagination as children was spliced, sliced and shredded. All too often when I ask someone I'm working with to draw, or dance, or sing what an illness or stuck place is like for them, he or she will look at me as if I had just asked a gorilla to tango. "But I'm not creative, Dawna! I couldn't do that."

Creating stories was the first way I could reach out into the world all by myself. I made up stories as my ladder to everything that was beyond reach—too far, too high, or too big to understand. Stories took the strange and made it familiar. While my best friend Joycie would crouch down in a plain brown dress and draw things in wild colored chalk on the sidewalk, I'd hug my knees next to her and make up stories about a land where the crayons took over and elected Purple the king, and gave Scarlet a robe of ermine. We'd find sheets, cotton and soap flakes and make the living room into a magical land where nothing was plain, nothing was brown and everything was possible.

Our kindergarten teacher, Mrs. Corsette, took away all of Joyce's crayons except for green and brown. She told her the right way to draw a tree was with a green circle and two brown lines for the trunk. I was given Dick and Jane and Spot. In my family, the phrase "telling a story" was

"Psychopaths and sociopaths can't imagine the other. An education that in any way neglects imagination is an education into psychopathy. It is an education that results in a sociopathic society of manipulations. We learn how to deal with others, and we becomes a society of dealers."

–James Hillman

"When I was a little boy, they called me a liar, but now that I am a grown-up, they call me a writer."

–Isaac Bashevis Singer

43

synonymous with lying, and said in a sneering tone of voice, head turned away: "Oh, you're just telling a story." I was humiliated into believing that I was untrustworthy, because everything that happened to me was spun by the kaleidoscope of my mind into a story which was, in essence, true, but in "fact," a flight of fancy. I tried my best to stifle these stories but they were as irrepressible as my dreams. My mind didn't invent things; it re-perceived them as if it were a prism.

I did the best I could to learn which were the right kinds of stories to tell and which were not. My mother tried to control my wild and unruly red hair in tight neat braids and I tried to control my obstreperous mind in tight neat facts. As a result, something in me curled up tight, got pushed under and down, and the world became alien and strange.

Both Joyce and I lost our innate capacity to explore our intuition and express our creativity. I got smart and memorized all the right answers. Joyce got good and learned to stay within the green and brown lines. At home, I was told I was too smart for my own good. At school, I got the message that smart was the only way to be. It was like being allergic to myself. No wonder that, as I got older, my immune system couldn't tell what was me and what wasn't. When Joyce reached adulthood, she had what was called a "nervous breakdown." We both became bad and stupid by getting addicted to substances. We both used drugs to escape into the closest thing we could find that resembled creativity. Joyce ultimately found her own way to fly out of darkness by spreading her colors over canvas; I reclaimed my stories.

When I first heard Milton Erickson lecture about hypnosis, my unruly mind had been ordered into a neat series of little concrete categories. I listened carefully as the staff psychiatrists asked the renowned hypnotherapist very linear questions: "Tell us, Dr. Erickson, why did you find it necessary to disorient the patient from her traumatic

*"None of us got here by control. We got here because our parents loved each other enough to lose control; that is part of the universe's ecstasy."*

*–Matthew Fox*

*"When soul is neglected, it doesn't just go away, it appears symptomatically in obsessions, addictions, violence and loss of meaning."*

*–Thomas Moore*

inhibitions and libidinal responses?" I was amazed to discover him responding by doing what I had been taught to be so ashamed of. He began to weave and bob his head in that peculiar way he had, looking directly past them into space, and told those starch coats *stories*! "Well, I'm glad you asked me that, because it reminds me of the time when . . ."

Erickson was a brilliant psychiatrist, but what was most important for me at the time was the discovery that the talent I had been ashamed of for so long could be a tool for teaching and healing. The day I heard him tell a "teaching tale," a smile that had been trapped inside my mouth for ten years unfurled.

My grandmother told me that every soul is born with something to give, something to experience, and something to learn. There is a creative force at the very center of each of our beings—a flow of energy, pushing, stretching, demanding to be transformed into the world. Because of how we are treated and taught, we lock that truth in, blocking it from breaking free. I believe my body manifested it as cells that were growing in crooked and crazy directions. That growth needed to be turned inside-out. That truth needed to be given voice and image and movement.

Writing, storytelling, and creating have ultimately been the medicine my soul has needed to mend itself. Life without it would be senseless. It gives me a home, a path, a purpose. The writing owns me, yet I refused it for so long. I believe I paid a dear price for betraying such a deep part of myself. As I write these words to you now, in this moment, I am healing.

*"The artist is not a special kind of person, rather each person is a special kind of artist."*

*–Ananda Coomaraswamy*

*"Story . . . the most precious container of the spirit."*

*–Laurens van der Post*

## The Fragmented Way We Lose Our Hearts: Disconnection From Compassion

"Trapped in our tradition of rugged individualism, we are an extraordinarily lonely people. So lonely, in fact, that many cannot even acknowledge their loneliness to themselves, much less to others."

–M. Scott Peck

Quantum physics teaches us that there is an intrinsic wholeness to things. Healing is the revelation of, and movement toward that wholeness, tending and nurturing that process. But what we've been taught to do when we come to the chaos of a crisis is to disconnect from it by fragmenting or fracturing: "A part of me hates him, but another part is afraid and wants to . . ." To disconnect from wholeness is to lose our compassion, our ability to integrate all of who we are. For, as with Milarepa, the practice of compassion involves a willingness to partner with something or someone and relate to it in such a way that you can understand deeply what it is at its core.

Not everyone is willing to do this. The oncologist who treated me for several years was in his late seventies. When it became obvious I wasn't going to die immediately, as he had predicted, I waited for him to ask me what I was doing to heal myself. He never did. My check-ups got further and further apart. Finally, I was only going into New York once every six months. We greeted each other the same way each time: I'd ask, "Are you still alive?" and he'd say, "Sure am. Are you still alive?" I had been trained in avoidance and denial at an early age, but this man was a pro.

Finally, I could resist no longer. I had to ask. "Tell me, Dr. Stethococus, since you said that no one who was challenged with this kind of cancer has ever survived, why haven't you asked me what I am doing to make it?"

He swiveled in his maroon leather chair and looked out the window. The lines in his cheeks were deep grooves. His silvery eyebrows hung down over his eyes. The sill was covered with gold framed pictures of his children and grandchildren. He turned back, stood up, and began to pace, his hands stuffed into the pockets of his white coat

"And the trouble is, if you don't risk anything, you risk even more."

–Erica Jong

46

like discarded tissues. His steps were hesitant, uncon-scious. His words finally came when he was walking away from me. "All of my patients die, you see. I'm an old man now. I'll retire soon."

He ran out of space, turned to the left as if on a parade ground, and walked silently to a small mahogany table in the corner. His pipes were neatly displayed in a rack. He picked up the closest one, intricately carved and mel-lowed. I'm not even sure he was aware he was holding it, as his words continued: "I went into medicine to save lives, you see?" He faced me directly, his eyes swimming, his words stretching across the room. "If I knew what you've done, it would mean there may have been something more I could have done to help my other patients. I'm an old man. I'm going to retire soon. I don't think I could live with that. Can you understand?"

I didn't want to. I felt the struggle twisting and churning in my mind, where a voice was screaming, *"But how could you not want to know?"*

In the next instant, I heard myself sigh. A long, slow, easing sigh that released my chest. I felt my hands unclench. I hadn't even noticed that the nails were digging little red half moons into my palms. One hand lifted, opening upward, outward, toward him. I did understand. On a level deeper than the screaming in my mind, deep as bones and blood, I understood.

*"You shall love your crooked neighbor with your crooked heart."*

–W.H. Auden

Like the good doctor, I, too, had not wanted to know. I had denied my truth and cut it off from my self. I had stuffed the ways I had been wounded deep down in the darkest closet of my body. This was at the root of my disease. I felt powerless to keep any threat out of my system, be it my father, the man who raped me or illness. That's why it seemed "natural" to have a menace inside of me. I had no real sense of boundaries to separate what was me and what was not me. The immune system helps us to discriminate between what is beneficial and what is toxic;

47

it sorts and rejects what is foreign. Without boundaries, I was like a palm opened face up, waiting for its fortune to be told. The only way I could be safe was to create barriers to hide behind, but they kept the wounds isolated and me cut off from my own resources. I had become a no-body, a no-thing, a non-self.

These barriers, however, also prevented me from taking responsibility for my own healing. I was trained to believe that responsibility meant that I was responsible for causing my disease, but it was inconceivable to me that I could use my abilities to respond compassionately to the needs that were hiding under that disease.

Our healing is made, not given. Ultimately, we are the way we are because of *how* we think. Until we change the way we think and interact, nothing else will change. The traumas we have experienced can be regarded as incomplete learnings. A crisis invites us to awaken from the habitual ways we have been doing and thinking about things and create an open space where we can learn. The disconnections must be uncovered, enacted and re-woven into our lives as a daily practice of integrity.

*Let's ground this in your own experience. Where are the opposing forces in your life? When do you hear yourself saying: "A part of me wants . . . but a part thinks that . . . ?" Make an ongoing list of these contradictory desires—i.e. there's the part that always wants to take care of everyone else's needs and the other part that just wants to play and not care about anyone else.*

*If I could wave a magic wand over your head enabling you to "get rid" of any part(s) of yourself, what would it/they be? Write each one down on a slip of paper.*

*Arrange them in the order of the one you most want to eliminate on top. Hold them in your hands one at a time, while thinking about each as vividly as possible. Then rip the slip up and notice how that affects you. What is lost after you have let go of it/them?*

"We used to wonder where war lived, what it was that made it so vile. And now we realize that we know where it lives, that it is inside ourselves."

–Albert Camus

# 3 The Turning Point:
## Choosing To Reconnect With Your Lost Self

*Let my wounds be my teachers,*
*Let my pain be my guide,*
*Let my monsters be companions*
*to the loneliness inside.*

*I stopped making choices,*
*turned my back to the truth,*
*let it all happen to me,*
*lost the best of my youth.*

*I learned to be loyal*
*to things which would betray*
*my heart, my mind, my spirit*
*my right to a clean, clear way.*

*Let my bruises be my advisors,*
*Let my scars be my guides,*
*Let my pain teach me truly,*
*how to be on my own side.*

Any personal crisis is a turning point. You come to this intersection as a way of being is about to die—a relationship, a role or occupation, an addiction, a long-held secret. The word crisis is from the Greek, meaning "a moment to decide." A turning point is, in essence, a spiritual crisis. It occurs when we have become disconnected from our souls, and thus are challenged to awaken from numbness and stagnation. It is, then, when our hearts break, that we have a choice: to disconnect further or to allow them to break open and learn a whole new way of relating.

It's like being at a glass revolving door in an airport. I have known some people to come right up to the door, stop on the outside, stand still and observe it turn for the rest of their lives, refusing to acknowledge that a change is within their reach. Others propel themselves into the door, but then go round and round, aware of their problem but unable to move through it.

If we are stuck in a pattern of disconnection from our awareness, imagination, and compassion, we find ourselves going through turning points as if they are the same damn thing over and over. Believing the solutions will be found externally, we follow the same pattern of behaviors—withdrawing behind barriers, escaping through back doors—until we are among the walking dead. But because our systems do whatever possible to complete the learning and reconnect with our own unmet needs, we'll find ourselves back at the same turning point again and again.

For those brave enough to go through the door, there is an unfamiliar emptiness on the other side. Anyone who has made that passage knows about the void, the abyss, the nothingness, the yearning that is the dark face of wholeness. It can be so terrifying that we fill every emptiness we find in our lives—with food, talk, work, television, drugs—anything and everything to stuff up the space. For in that emptiness, there is no sense of power or control or orderliness. You are left on your own in the unexpected,

> "The recurrent moments of crisis and decision when understood, are growth junctures, points of initiation which mark a release from one state of being and a growth into the next."
>
> –Jill Purce

> "Therapy helps you go from life being the same damn thing over and over to life being one damn thing after another."
>
> –John Weakland

facing the brutal truth of yourself and your pain, screaming into the darkness, "I don't know how to do this!"

It is from moments such as these that we learn that faith is not something you have or can lose. It is something you practice because your life depends on it.

A turning point challenges us to decide to reclaim our shadows and resources, to re-perceive the world and our relationship to it, to re-integrate our fragmented selves, and to re-direct our lives so we can channel more energy into the world. Thus, more than anything else, it is an opportunity for emptiness to open into a space for learning. For when we no longer know which way to go, we have begun the real journey home.

These fulcrum moments, the experiences that we don't choose, which we might give anything to avoid, provide us with the precious opportunity to reconnect with our souls, to forge an ongoing relationship between our hearts, minds, and bodies. It is here we have the chance to learn the lesson that no one studies willingly—that it is possible to grow from suffering. It is in these moments that we can experience the inner shift that occurs when our difficulties really touch us enough to cause the most powerful change of all—a change of heart.

I don't know how to bring you to the point of choosing to enter the door. I don't know how to help you cure your cancer, renounce an addiction, or decide if you were sexually abused as a child. There is no one right formula. After all these years, I still have no idea of what really causes someone to choose to move through that door, what "makes" them change. Everyone I've witnessed and supported has found a unique path, an individual way.

When I was challenged with cancer, the best oncologists, internists, and endocrinologists could explain in multisyllabic detail the history of my pathology (how I got so sick). They were quite sure that I had very little chance of living more than three months, but were totally speechless and empty-handed when asked how I could get well.

However, while I was preparing to die, without knowing it, I was also preparing to heal. Until that point I had always been able to run, divorcing myself from anything with which I didn't know how to deal. I'd find a back door, a side door or a trap door. But I couldn't escape from cancer. "Vanity runs and love digs in." Someone gave me a framed sampler with those words cross stitched on it in pink and yellow embroidery thread. I had to dig in. Ninety days. Nowhere to go. I had arrived. Finally. The only way out was through. Cancer became the path. Dying became the path. Fear became the path.

When you prepare to die, you reduce everything to the simple and essential things—family, beauty, prayer. You turn away from objects and toward heart. You have no time to be distracted. No more "Someday, I'll get around to it." Guilt or blame means wasting what little time is left. No more time for doubts or petty criticisms when you could be feeling your son's soft cheek. No more time for rage and ranting when you could be smelling the air turn willow yellow as it does in April.

This was the turning point in my trip through the revolving door. How could I die as my own enemy? Was there time enough left to learn? Everyone seemed concerned with how long I was going to live. But to me, living longer meant perpetuating the misery of a life that was hollow, numb and grasping. If I were going to live, I wanted to live wider, deeper. I wanted to live for the experience of being alive. I wanted transformation, not just preservation.

I have always believed that change is possible if a person can learn new ways. Could I learn to live as fully as possible while I was still alive? Could I learn to embrace what sustained me? Could I learn new ways to come into a relationship with my life and with the things I had labeled as other, as enemy?

*(About a girl who was blind)*

*"Today, near eventide, I did lead the girl who had no seeing a little way into the forest where it was darkness and shadows were. I led her toward a shadow that was coming our way. It did touch her cheek with its velvety fingers and she too does have likings for shadows. Her fear that was is gone."*

*–Opal Whitely, four years old*

*"The only hope Mother Earth has for survival is our re-covering creativity–which is of course, our divine power. Creativity is so satis-fying, so important, not because it produces something but because the process is cosmologi-cal. There's joy and delight in giving birth."*

–Matthew Fox

Although it usually portends a death of some kind, a turning point is experienced by many like the transition stage of labor during childbirth: it happens when you have been pushed open by a rapid change; you may feel hot, cold, disoriented, sick to your stomach. You can't get comfortable, and are frightened; then everything seems to decelerate. You may feel crazy, curse, pray loudly, be angry with those you love—sure that it's all their fault—want to go home and forget about the whole thing; you may be held in place when what you want is to stand on your own two feet or hunker down; you may feel irritable, need quiet, not want to be disturbed, need to go inside.

*I'd like to invite you to pause and consider this particular time as if it were a rite of passage for you. What is it too late for? Too soon for? Just the right time for? What has or is dying? What ways of relating don't work for you anymore? What is trying to be born? How are you being challenged to awaken? What do you need to reconcile within yourself to be at peace?*

## Choosing To Reconnect

Many years ago, when visiting Japan, I saw a group of monks carry a cage of white birds to the top of a hill. It was an unusual sight, so I followed them. I was as discreet as I could be with my heavy Nikon camera hanging around my neck from a thick, red embroidered strap. It was a long and hard climb. I began to tell myself I was nuts and should turn back. My chest heaved. My calves screamed. It was foggy, damp, cold.

And then we arrived. Encircling the cage, the monks chanted in low and resonant tones, their palms pressed together, their shaven heads bowed, their orange robes dancing as the mist rolled around their ankles. One of them

54

leaned over and opened the cage door. A score of white doves erupted into the sky—rising, circling, flapping their way to freedom.

I was clicking the shutter wildly when one of the monks tapped me on the shoulder. In very halting English, he asked me about my camera. I put it in his hands. As he was looking at the lens, I asked him why they had released the birds. He smiled softly, responding, "One of our brothers has passed. These birds will be companions for the liberation of his soul."

In considering my healing process, it is clear to me now that what I have done that has been the most significant is slowly to liberate myself. Cancer was the cage. Addiction was the cage. Abuse was the cage. Living my life as if it were a perpetual audition was the cage.

I am also the monks opening each cage, one by one. I am the white doves winging free. I am the monk who died. I am the woman taking photographs.

What my healing demanded was that I learn to live my life from the inside out, instead of from the outside in. I kept myself captured by feverishly pursuing external objectives. Round and round I went on the little wheel, accomplishing one thing after another. Being inside of it enabled me to forget that *I* had an inside. It kept me from being wild. And it kept me from being free.

Someone once told me that illness is the Western form of meditation, meaning the only circumstances we sanction for inner exploration. Even if I had known I had an inner life, I wouldn't have known how to access it before I got sick. My life needed to have depth as well as outcome, pleasures as well as accomplishments, a sense of purpose as well as a goal.

I don't mention my "terminal illness" much these days. It's not that I've forgotten. I can never afford to forget that life is not a given, but a chosen gift. Once in awhile, people ask me what I've done to cure my cancer. I'm always at a

*"The spiritual path is one of falling on your face, getting up, brushing yourself off, turning and looking sheepishly at God and then taking the next step."*

*–Sri Auribindo*

55

loss. I begin by explaining that I no longer "have" cancer. Lumps have come and gone. None of them have been malignant. Though the cancer is apparently "cured," I am still healing. I will continue to heal in the same way that I will continue to recover from the disease of addiction, and a history of abuse—every day, reconnecting one by one with awareness, imagination, and compassion.

Reconnection is another way to relate to challenges besides going rigid, or giving up, not caring or becoming a caretaker. It's what is between fight or flight. It is the series of small changes, tiny gestures, seemingly ordinary actions that are the essence of healing.

The root word of heal means "to make whole." Thus, by definition, healing meant I could no longer try to get rid of any part of myself. I could no longer live with one aspect of myself at war with another—my whole system would have to be respected.

I'm not sure whether I am free of illness, addiction, or abuse, but I know down to the level of marrow and breath that I am liberating myself from the cages. Writing this book is a matter of giving and gratitude, an act of faith, and a wonderful way of releasing the lessons I've learned, allowing them to rise in the mist, circling and flapping their way to freedom.

*"Healing is the very ground of being. Everything is moving toward wholeness. And that's all healing is, that movement."*

*–Rachel Naomi Remen*

## What's Your Favorite Scar

*"We must seek God in error and forgetfulness and foolishness."*

*–Meister Eckhart*

Milton Erickson once said that healing involves reconnecting and reorganizing one's experiences in such a way that memories and events that had once been perceived as limitations become resources for growth. When asked, for example, how he developed such phenomenal observational skills, he replied, "Oh, I was luckier than most. I was paralyzed as a young man, so I got to lie around and study people for quite some time."

Instead of being victimized by those situations and events which you may consider "enemies," I'll be asking you to re-perceive them in such a way that, like Milton, the darkness opens to discovery.

Let me give you a small example of what I mean. What is your favorite scar? What's the story of how you got it?

I usually tell people about the one on my calf that I got when I was six years old and riding on the handlebars of Stuie Stillman's bike down Rugby Road. We were going so fast, faster than I had ever gone before, and I didn't notice the loose spoke of his front wheel cutting into my right leg until he deposited me at my front door and I saw a wash of blood pouring onto our porch.

Each time I tell the story, I find myself touching the scar with affection although it was a place of terror when Dr. Goldfarb stitched it up. For two or three years afterwards, I expected the thin red skin to burst open at any strain, and I was sure the ugly mark would keep me from my true destiny as a prima ballerina.

Scars are the strongest, most flexible tissue in the body. Most people I know tell their scar stories with the same delight and nostalgia that I do, although the original wound was often the site of agony and fear. I am very fond of scars. They teach me that healing is, in its essence, the task of re-creating yourself. They affirm that as a human you are, after all, capable of a most tender invincibility.

## Getting Out Of A Trap By Getting Into It

So here we are—you've decided to go through the revolving door, and you're standing on the other side, at the place between what was and what is yet to be. It is in this open moment that you have the power to choose.

*"The word hero needs to be reserved for the man or woman who is willing to take the solitary journey to the depths of the self, to re-own the shadow, to exorcise the ancient warrior psyche, to discover the power and authority of wholeness. "*

*–Sam Keen*

Instead of doing the same thing over and over, hoping for different results, a turning point always gives you the opportunity to learn another way, to exercise what Victor Frankl calls "personal freedom."

There are people who, though we never meet them, inspire us to change the course of our journey—through a book, a song, a piece of art, the way they live their life. Victor Frankl was such a "random act of kindness" in my life. I read about his life for a psychology final exam. He is a Jewish psychiatrist who was imprisoned in the death camps of Nazi Germany. His entire family, except for his sister, perished. He suffered excruciating torture. He never knew whether he would be inside of the ovens or outside removing bodies and ashes. As the months and years wore on, Frankl slowly became aware that there was one thing, "the last of the human freedoms," that his Nazi captors could not take away: he could decide within himself how all of this was going to affect him. Between what happened to him and how he responded to it lay his power to choose. I was so fascinated by what I was reading that I forgot to take notes, underline or highlight. All I wrote on my index cards that dawn was, "Between an impulse and an act, we have a choice. It is within our sphere of influence to choose how to respond to the things that happen to us that we do not choose."

I don't remember what questions were on that exam. My hand and heart wrote an entire blue book about Victor Frankl without any interference from my conscious mind. When I was finished, I closed the cover and put an A+ on it.

In essence, the entire process of reconnective learning is meant to help you choose how you respond to what is challenging you at this time of your life. If you've read this far, you know that fighting or fleeing only leads to more fighting or fleeing. In aikido, they teach that the less resistance you create, the more efficient and effective your action can be. What I know in my bones is that you are free the moment you stop fighting.

I'd like to invite you to try a practice that I learned from Terry Dobson, a wonderful aikido sensei and neighbor.

*Think about those straw puzzles where you stick one finger in each end and pull. Like the tar baby in Uncle Remus, the more you struggle, the more you are stuck. Try sticking the index finger of one hand inside the fist of the other and pull. The more intensely you try to pull your finger away, the more your fist will clamp down.*

*Experiment with an alternative: push in briefly and then quickly slide your finger out.*

Once you know how, do you find yourself wanting to do it again? Perhaps you can even allow yourself to enjoy the secure feeling of being held inside the fist for a moment. As you continue to play with this paradox, you may discover that when you respond to the fist by moving into it, by making room for it to be there instead of trying to get away from it, you are free, as illogical as that may seem.

This is the same principle student pilots used to learn when they went into a tailspin: If you try and pull back on the joystick, the nose of the plane won't come up. If you move it down in the direction of the spin, like a miracle the plane stops turning and you are in control again to pull the nose up out of the dive.

> "I have been waiting twenty years for someone to say to me, 'You have to fight fire with fire' so that I could reply, 'That's funny—I always use water.'"
>
> –Howard Gossage

## Hardships As Messengers

Most of us are learning disabled in the skills that will enable us to connect and respond to our enemy. Instead of running away or struggling against it, we need to learn about the verb *to relate*. How do I relate to . . . my loneliness, the wounds of my past, my terror, sadness, the pain I feel, the fear, my body?

Milton Erickson demonstrated that everything the human mind does can somehow be used. He called this *utilization*. The approach offered to you here uses the symptom as part of the template for change. The mechanism of the problem is the mechanism of the solution. It gives you the possibility of metabolizing wounds from your personal history into messages which you can then go out and teach in your community.

Learn, heal, serve. Thus, the more we have suffered in the past, the stronger a healer we can become. We can learn to transform our suffering into the kind of insight that forms circles of protection and purpose binding people together.

Throughout history and across cultures, undertaking this kind of transformation has been called a spiritual journey, or pilgrimage. The traveler is considered a seeker of the truth.

A spiral is the ancient symbol for a labyrinth, the twisted pathway for a journey to the core of being, complete with secret passages and mystical ways through, as well as dead-ends. Many years ago, I had the opportunity to travel through the labyrinth at Chartres cathedral in France. It is an allegory for a spiritual journey. Soon after entering, the pilgrim is brought directly to a place close to the center—near enough to see it, yet separated from it. The first glimpse of the light is very powerful. It pulls on you, but as you try and reach it, you must travel the entire maze out to its edges, spiraling back and forth. It is at this point that you realize you are, in fact, going further and further away from the light.

Now your initial vision and passion must sustain your long journey through the dark passageways. You may even forget it, and what keeps you going is your faith. When even that falters, all you can do is put one foot in front of

*"Trouble? Life is trouble! Only death is nice. To live is to roll up your sleeves and embrace trouble."*

–*Zorba the Greek*

*"We need a path not to go from here to there, but to go from here to here."*

–*Jakusho Kwong*

the other. Your footsteps begin to join the rhythm of your breath and, very shortly thereafter, you turn the last corner and are clear on a path to the center, the Source, the light.

My grandmother called a person's spiritual path in this life "traveling on the wisdom trail." She said it is a spiral, bringing us closer to the truth at our core each pass round. What this means is that we keep coming to the same places, intersections, and struggles over and over again, only each time we've expanded out, collecting more wisdom. Wherever you go on a spiral, there is no escaping from yourself.

I'll be using the metaphor of a rite of passage or a journey of initiation as a unifying theme for the rest of this book. In some cultures, it is described as having three distinct stages. The first is separation, and involves withdrawing from the rest of the world, moving away from the familiar habits of daily life.

The second stage was described by my grandmother as "straightening by fire," because it involves turning inward, to the chaotic world where you meet the demons. You become receptive to them, receive "medicine" from them, and find renewal through the powers stored in your mind. It is an initiation which, if successfully completed, yields the gift of, and for, healing.

The last stage, called "the open moment," requires you to turn back to the outer world, bringing the lessons you have gathered into your daily life where you can share them with your community.

> "The end of one turn of the spiral becomes the beginning of another . . . we are designed for possibility."
>
> –Gabrielle Rico

> "If properly understood and treated as difficult stages in a natural developmental process, these experiences, 'spiritual emergencies' or transpersonal crises, can result in emotional and psychosomatic healing, creative problem solving and personality transformation."
>
> –Stanley Grof

# The Wisdom Trail

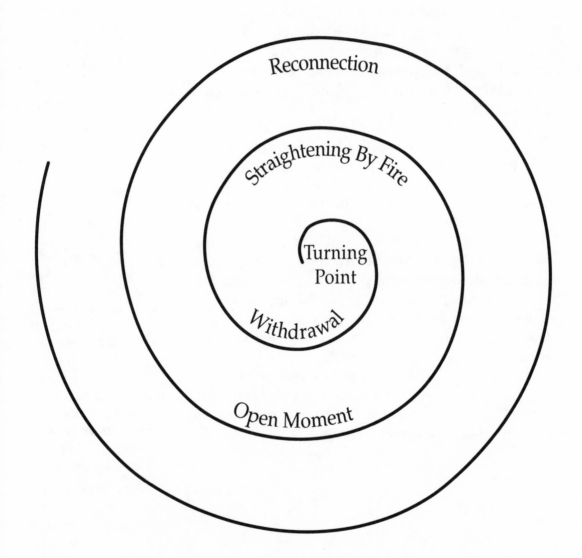

I'm proposing that you enter this dimension of healing with me. We'll find our way together. Our aim will be to learn how to use awareness, imagination, and compassion to turn toward your enemy, bow and sing to it, and recognize the needs that have been hidden in the shadows of its belly, so you can respond to it in ways which support your healing. Maybe we'll even be able to touch each other's heart in the process.

First, we'll begin by withdrawing in order to learn to increase awareness through centering and receptivity, so you can calm your mind and open your heart.

Then we'll begin the straightening by fire, crossing the threshold into the world of imagination so you learn:

> to access your intuition and consult the deeper source of guidance that rests there;
>
> to use creative expression and imagery as a means for facing your problem and establishing a healing dialogue with it.

In the last stage, you'll need to foster all the compassion you can find to:

> recognize the unmet need in your enemy;
>
> find the inner resources to fill that need;
>
> create a relationship between that need and your personal resources;
>
> transform the experience into a message of personal truth;
>
> and express that message—teach it, share it with the rest of the world.

This is not a one-night stand. Each of these stages is a signpost in the maze of turning points. What is shared here is an ongoing process—the way you live with yourself—the way you learn to hold your pain in one warm palm, your love in the other, and bring the two together.

*"We must learn–not teach or preach–our way from here."*

*–Don Michael*

*"The difference that exists is that the White doctor's medicines tend to be very mechanical. The person is repaired but he is not better than he was before. It is possible in the Indian way to be a better person after going through a sickness followed by the proper medicine."*

*–Ernie Benedict, Mohawk elder*

I have used this process to great effect with countless people in private sessions and seminars around the country. However, the one thing it will not give you is hope. I believe that those of us who have been wounded have lost some very basic enchantments. We know the world is not a wonderful place. But this process can help you reclaim your faith. You can come to feel as if you belong, that you have a place. You can use what you learn here to generate a rich and possible future from the debris of a life, to walk within the dignity of your own boundaries with a full and unbounded heart.

*Some questions to carry in your pocket and run through curious fingers as we travel together: What do you want to be in your heart the moment you die? What will you answer to the questions, "Have you loved well?" "Were you true to your own heart?" "What story did you live out in the years you had?"*

As you may already have guessed, I am a passionate advocate of the possibility for change. I believe your turning point, dear reader, is a moment that invites you to remember, reclaim, speak, create, heal, share, and teach your own truth. I would like to accompany you on your search for the ally that hides within the enemy. I would like to help you replace that cage with a nest of your own design, to home the feathered mysteries that live waiting inside your darkest corners, yearning for release.

# Bowing To the Demons:

## Calming Your Mind, Opening Your Heart

*"Anybody who counts days is more grateful for the present than worried about the past or future. My view is that you grow by adversity. It's the dread of being removed from the scene that makes you appreciate being on the scene. If you presume endless days, then no day has particular value. I think of all the fathers who have young children and play golf all day Saturday and Sunday. They've never had cancer. I think of the husbands who never voice their affection for their wives. They've never had cancer."*

–Paul Tsongas

$B$uddha was visiting a village in the countryside. The strange thing was, all the townspeople were hiding in their huts. He questioned them and discovered that there was a local terrorist who frequently came down from the mountains and killed anyone he found on the streets. Buddha considered this very carefully. The next morning, as he was preparing to go out for his walking meditation, the innkeeper tried to stop him. "Please do not go, you will surely be killed. The terrorist is coming today." But Buddha just smiled kindly and then silently went on his way.

Sure enough, within a half hour, the terrorist came storming through the streets. As he approached Buddha, he drew his sword and screamed piercingly, "Stop, or I'll kill you!"

Buddha continued to walk and breathe, smiling kindly at the terrorist. When he was a few feet away, the dirty ruffian shouted again, "Stop, or I'll kill you!"

Buddha didn't break his pace: One step, one breath. When he was within arm's reach, the terrorist raised his sword and screamed, "Are you deaf, old man? Didn't you hear what I said? Stop, or I will run my sword right through you!"

Buddha took another step. And another breath. Then he said in a voice as calm as a summer breeze, "But, my good man, I have stopped. It is you who have not."

The terrorist's arm hung suspended in mid-air, his mouth was agape. "What do you mean? It is you who have not."

Buddha took another step, another breath. By now he was so close to the man he could smell his stale sweat. He replied with fierce tenderness, "I have stopped terrorizing myself. You have not. Thus, you must stop, for it is your own self you are truly killing."

—adapted from a story told by Thich Nhat Hanh

A turning point leaves you trying to find your way in a funnel of questions that seem to have no answers. As the questions get bigger, if you are to make it through, you learn to take solace in the small things closest to you: The smell of a wet June morning, an eruption of irises, the light glinting off of the golden hairs on a baby's arm.

If you allow yourself a graceful withdrawal into this awareness, you'll notice a yearning, a hunger, which is at first indefinable, then identified as a need to touch beauty in any form. It is beauty which can feed you, filling you so that you can deal with the emptiness that suffering brings. It is the small things that anchor you through the vast storm of unanswerable questions major challenges can bring.

Awareness means coming fully into the present moment, what Thich Nhat Hanh calls *mindfulness*. It is a movement toward connection, with all of oneself in the same place at the same time, unified. It is the realm of the undivided self. But what makes it so hard to stop and notice the present moment?

When I was in private practice, people would often return from vacations reporting that for the first few days they'd run fiercely around trying to play until they dropped. Then they'd wind down and stop. Great! No. Awful, because most of them said that when they slowed down from fifty-five mph to thirty mph, they felt grief, fear, rage or pain. They'd have external fights with their partner or internal fights with themselves. It wasn't the stopping which caused the pain or the fights. Stopping just helped them see what had been there all along, but held below the level of awareness.

Two essential facets of awareness that make this first stage of healing possible are a calm mind and an open heart. Together, they give you a lens to search through the geography of your mind without being swept away by what you think or controlled by what you feel. In other words, awareness doesn't help you look for calm in your

*"Healing is to give a person the skills to see the miracle of their own existence and that of a flower's. And, even further, how the two are connected."*

*–Shawn May*

mind, but helps you look at your mind calmly.

You can't change anything you don't accept. This first part of your journey, then, is dedicated to finding and learning how to re-create calmness in your mind and receptivity in your heart. Having done that, you can stop running and face your demon with equanimity, respect it as an agent in your own evolution, and honor its energy without allowing it to sweep you away.

Awareness is a light of attention that you shine in one place or another. When you fall in love with someone, you shine that light on all of the adorable and delightful things you notice—the way an eyebrow lifts, a dimpled knee, a crooked nose. When you fall out of love, the light shines on pores that are too big, a voice tone that rubs your ears raw, the way the person won't stop jiggling.

*Try it for a moment. What happens when you become aware of the space between the toes of your left foot? Those spaces have been there all along—I guarantee it. Your awareness, however, until a moment ago was somewhere else. That foot is now in the present moment in a way it wasn't before. Can you keep it there with you while you continue reading?*

I believe our souls are constantly trying to correct us when we get crooked on our paths—by broadcasting a continual message, a homing beacon of guidance through the symbolic language of our dreams and intuition. The purpose of the first stage of this journey is to reconnect you with your own stillness; to relearn how to wrap a soft blanket of calm and quiet around your fear so that you can be receptive enough to find this truth in yourself.

*"On beyond ideas of right doing and wrong doing there is a field. I will meet you there. When the soul lies down in that grass, the world is too full to talk about."*

–Rumi

*"We cannot finally understand, but we must try."*

–Teresa of Avila

# 4 The Center of the Storm:
## Bringing Your Mind Back Home

*"Heaven is right where you are standing
and that is the place to practice."*

–Morehei Ueshiba

Ythe ou can't really go anywhere until you know where
you are to begin with. Facing a turning point means living
in external chaos. When you are challenged in such a way,
the first thing you need to do is to come home to yourself.
Where are you in the current of the moment? Are you
noticing your breath? What's going on inside of you?
Where is your stability? In order to answer those questions,
you literally have to "in-corporate"—to experience being in
this body, in this moment, in this place. Those are your
hands. Those are your feet. You have all possibilities there,
in your belly, which is your center of gravity. Having an
unchanging awareness of a steady center of balance within
creates the possibility for change.

Sound simple? It is. Sound easy? It's not. What do you
do when you're in a crisis? What if you are the one person
in a million who has no center? What if you can't find it, or
you lose it?

An agitated mind is like a shaking bowl filled with
churned up water—you don't have to smooth the water,
you just need to find a way to hold the bowl still and the
water will settle by itself. In this chapter, we'll be learning
a variety of ways to do just that.

> "Winning means winning over the mind of discord in yourself. This is to accomplish your bestowed mission."
>
> –Morehei Ueshiba

## Coming Home To Yourself

I used to think that having a calm mind meant having
a totally still mind. Calm meant blank, passive—or so I
thought. (The only time I actually experienced my mind
being like that was when I had to speak to a group of two
thousand people without a previously prepared speech!)

Sensei Richard Kuboyama, who teaches ki-aikido in
Hawaii, explains that a centered mind is *calmly energized*.
He describes a way of achieving this: Imagine all the
energy of the universe condensing into one dynamic point
in the center of your pelvis. Andy says it feels as if he

> "Quietness of the mind is master of the deed."
>
> –Gandhi

belongs in the world and is entitled to take up space.

Imagine your whole body yeasting—poised yet stable, like a sea gull on a wave, pulsing with possibilities. Standing firm in yourself in this way roots you to a source of energy that is more than your own—a universal source, a higher power—in the same way that a jellyfish is powered by the might of the entire ocean.

Centering also involves becoming proactive: moving from within yourself outward, instead of the other way around, or moving forward from your own values. In this culture, many of us, by the time we have become adults, have lost our center of balance: We don't know what our individual values are; we don't know what is really important to us. We have opinions, but opinions are not values. A value is a spindle that aligns everything, as if it were a spine running through one's life: "This is so important to me that my whole life is about making it happen." Centering brings us back to that spindle again and again.

Centering is a natural process. It involves allowing your body to return to its home position, making it possible to condense all your scattered energy. My friend Will does it just by touching a golf club. Bonnie does it whenever she gets in front of a loom to weave. Karen goes to the ocean and lets her mind run out to the horizon. Rachel gets menstrual cramps and remembers she has a pelvis. Don plays with his dog, Sampson, and presto—he's embodied in the present moment.

You already know how to center. You used to do it naturally as a young child. This is not another new thing you have to learn; it's a process you need to remember. If you know how to swim and you jump in a cool green lake on a hot summer's day, your body will recall what to do, even if you haven't been swimming for thirty years. Maybe you'll hold your breath at first. Maybe you'll tense your muscles and "try" to recall the act for a few minutes; but soon, you'll release your breath and surrender. Voila! Your body will float you.

*"It's not a matter of moderation. It takes one kind of courage to wait patiently, another to get on with it."*

–Sheldon Kopp

*"He flung himself upon his horse and rode off in all directions."*

–Anon.

The practices that follow will help you find a way to reconnect with your center. They may be more useful and fun if you can get someone to "challenge" you by pressing backwards gently and firmly on the front of your shoulder. If you are doing this with a partner, you may want to take turns centering and challenging. What you will probably notice when you are challenging a partner who is centered is that they feel like closed-cell foam rubber—flexible, yet condensed—yielding, yet solid. If they think about a stressful situation, they'll feel rigid. If they think "I don't mind" pathetically, they'll feel like fish flab. But if they're centered, you can't move them off their spot, even though they aren't actively resisting you. It's time to slip into the water.

*"Occupy the space you occupy."*
*–Adrienne Rich*

## Centering In Your Own Way:

*Think of a time or a situation in which you felt self-confident, self-contained, calmly energized. Think about it quite vividly, as if it were happening now.*

*Notice what happens to the way you're seeing the world, to your sense of hearing, to your breath, to your awareness of your body. Notice what "home" can feel like.*

*Now lose it on purpose. Think about what you have to do tomorrow. Think about that as vividly as possible. Notice, as you did before, how this affects your sensory experience. What are the things that make it easiest to lose your center? Does talking to yourself in a certain tone of voice inevitably cause you to lose it? How about loss of peripheral vision? Or holding your breath? Everyone has his or her habitually "favorite" way to lose center. And if you learn how you lose it, you can reverse the process to find it—by widening your vision or by hearing, breathing, changing your tone of voice, etc.*

## Centering Through Movement:

*Stand on the balls of your feet with your heels just an inch or so off the ground. Shake your arms vigorously from your elbows for a few minutes, as if you had wet hands. Let your shaking move your whole body up and down. Allow your body to release.*

*Notice your pelvis, and feel how gravity pulls on the underside of everything—your buttocks, your fingertips, your earlobes.*

*Increase the awareness of your breath going in and out and the spaces between each breath. As you lower your feet, your heels barely caressing the floor, imagine the whole universe condensing down to one point in your belly. If you can't "feel it," that's fine. Find the center of the place where you can't feel.*

### Centering Through Your Values:

*Think about something that is really important to you—a value to which every cell in your body is committed. Notice how this affects your sensory experience.*

*Now lose it on purpose. Think about a situation where you are habitually stressed out or apathetic. Notice how that is different.*

*Shift back and forth between thinking about what is important and "not caring," until you can clearly identify when you lose your center, and trust in your ability to find it again.*

"Be tough in the way a blade of grass is: rooted, willing to lean, and at peace with what is around it."

–Natalie Goldberg

# Finders Are Not Keepers; Losers, Don't Be Weepers

The good news is that centering is a natural process that you've learned quite simply. The bad news is that centering doesn't last. Like a gyroscope spinning on its axis, you'll align briefly, and then lose it. You find it again. And lose it. Your center is not a fixed static place; it's an expanding, contracting axis of energy. It is like coming home. If you had to stay there all the time, home would become a prison. The two things you need to know are *how to recognize when you have left and how to find your way back*, which isn't always easy. As infants, we center, lose it and re-center all the time. It's as natural to us as the instinct a cat uses to land on its feet. At a certain point in

"Renewal requires a return to the basic source from which all personal and cultural myths are ultimately forged–the human psyche."

–David Feinstein

our development, however, most of us learn to get outside of our bodies and not come back.

Our minds often disconnect us from our centers of gravity in order to prevent us from feeling pain. When I was being raped, I left my body. I was without an exit, as a knife was at my throat. So, I immediately left through the trap door in my mind. I watched it all from some dark place in the wall. Afterwards, I told myself that because "I" had been in that wall, my soul was still a virgin. It had never been violated.

The solution for me back then became a problem later in life, because I couldn't feel alive inside my own skin. A psychoanalyst labeled me frigid and that was that. So, when I first learned centering with Kuboyama Sensei, I was terrified at a cellular level. It wasn't logical. My body vibrated. My adrenaline pumped. Centering was literally bringing me back to the scene of the crime—my body. The memory was in my tissues. The cells remembered what had happened. The only way I could become aware of my pelvis was to find the centermost place where I could *not* feel a thing. I had to learn new ways to come home, to make myself safe in my own body.

Many of us are taught to put our centers of balance outside our own bodies: to go blind, deaf and numb to what our senses tell us. Thus, we are taught to always be slightly on edge, "off-center," uptight in preparation for the impending doom that might happen at any minute if we're not "lucky." Avoidance (a void dance) becomes a substitute for awareness. If we get scared, we turn to Valium, vodka, or marijuana to numb out.

Losing one's center is, in my experience, a spiritual crisis. Your basic instinct to survive knows that a calm, alert mind, centered in your body, is how you're meant to function. If you habitually put your center in something or someone external, your unconscious mind will do what it can to sabotage that unhealthy state and bring you back to

"My own feeling is that there's a body wisdom that our skin, our muscles, our nerve fibers possess, and we need to activate that wisdom to gain courage and transform our lives."

–Miryam Glazer

"People cannot be alone with themselves. They need the TV, the phone, the stereo—something . . . because to be alone is to see all the stuff we spend so much of our time trying not to face."

–bell hooks

yourself. I learned to put my center in suffering people. I worked sixteen hours a day with any walking wound that came my way. My system finally created a larger wound inside my body and I was forced to come home to myself, whether I liked it/me or not.

Brian is another example of that phenomenon. He grew up with a mother who burst into abusive verbal rages at his father and older sisters. Each of them fought back, and were then attacked physically. He was so scared that he just "left his body." Knowing he was no match for his mom, he "put his mind inside of her," so he could understand what she was feeling. As an adult, Brian repeatedly became involved with abusive women. In the business world he was a dynamo, but at home he vacated, putting his center in the raging woman of the moment and understanding her in ways that no one else ever could. Eventually, he'd find himself hating the woman. Then he'd break up with her and find another. People told him he should stand up for himself, and he agreed; but each time he stayed inside his own skin around an angry woman, he became terrified all over again.

If you have your center outside of yourself, you will respond to a challenge in one of three ways: you'll get *rigid*—"Go ahead, make my day!"; or you'll go *limp*—"Hey, I'm mellow. I'm easy. I go with the flow."; or you'll go *rigid and then limp*—"You gonna make me? Hey, I was only kidding!"

Conversely, if you center inside your body, your awareness is increased: The lights are on and there's somebody home! You are safer, because your reaction time is heightened. Your body is loose, flexible, able to maneuver easily. Your mind can function readily, drawing on all your resources instead of freezing up. Between any stimulus and response, you have a moment to choose. It is in this state that choice and, consequently, change, is possible.

*"The body is the outward manifestation of the mind."*

*–Candace Pert*

## Noticing Me Noticing You Noticing Me

Because of the different ways our minds work, we may have different things that help or hinder centering. Some people need to close their eyes momentarily; some need to hum to themselves; some move; some bring an image to mind, such as pretending to have roots in their feet. Enjoy experimenting with what makes centering difficult and easy for you. Notice the situations that may make it more challenging to center—a room full of noise, looking into someone's eyes, or just being in a certain position. I had great trouble learning to center lying down, because that was the position I was in when I was abused. It was the most difficult to reclaim, and also the most important.

When you come into the present in this centered, embodied way, you are connecting with what is challenging you. You are receiving it, instead of trying to keep it out. This enables you to utilize the energy of that challenge. For instance, if a lot of noise or words is difficult for you, you can use that to help you center by telling yourself, "The more I hear those words, the more I'll feel my own pelvis." Though this may sound illogical to your conscious mind, your unconscious mind has no trouble making these kinds of connections. It is, after all, no more logical to tell yourself, "When I stand in front of a group of a thousand people to give a speech, I'll feel terrified." Either way, it's just an association.

Some delightful associational "triggers" that people I've worked with have used successfully to center are: "The crazier it gets on the outside, the more I'll feel the calmness in my center." "The more he tries to push me around, the more I'll feel the stability of my own center." "As she whines and begs for attention, I'll attend to the stillness in my center." "While she is nagging me on the outside, I'll be curious about what I need on the inside."

*"To see virtue takes a very calm mind."*

*–Suzuki Roshi*

*"People are like tea bags. You find out how strong they are when you put them in hot water."*

*–Anon.*

*Here's an opportunity to experience a natural tranquilizer, yet another way of holding the bowl so your mind can calm: Describe what you are hearing and seeing outside of yourself and what you are feeling in your own body. Describe just the information your senses give you—not thoughts, comparisons or opinions. For instance: "Right now, I'm seeing my fingers move across the gray plastic keys. I'm seeing the white letters and shadows under my fingers. I'm hearing the hum of the ceiling fan and the sound of the dishwasher downstairs. I'm feeling my butt resting against the chair and I'm feeling the sweaty place behind my right knee. I'm feeling the itch of a mosquito bite on my arm. I'm hearing a cricket . . ." Continue this way for five minutes.*

Narrating your sensory experience in this manner slows the whole thing down. It puts your mind in neutral, calming it, while bringing you to your center, back into your body and into the present moment. It does not make for fascinating conversation, so I suggest you do it when you are alone or with someone who knows what you are doing. At first, it's important to say what you're noticing out loud, because otherwise your thoughts bleed into each other too quickly. If you cannot bring yourself to say it out loud, or are in a library or board meeting (or bored meeting for that matter), write your sensory experience down in the same way.

The practice is simple. The results are remarkable. I've used it with people who have high blood pressure, as well as with people who blow their stacks and get abusive. They learn to scream just what their sensory experience is: "I'm feeling my fists clench and a fire building in my belly. I'm feeling my head pounding and seeing your brown eyes, and I'm hearing you gnash your teeth." Rather than increasing the pressure, yelling their awareness causes it to settle, while increasing their mental, spiritual, and physical circulation.

*"Not gifted with genius, but honestly holding his experience deep in his heart he kept his simplicity and humanity."*

*–Sakaki*

*"In the beginner's mind there are many possibilities; in the expert's, there are few."*

*–Shunryu Suzuki Roshi*

## Centering With Your Enemy

Aikido master Terry Dobson once said, "If you meditate on your upset, you'll lose your center. So meditate on your center, and you'll lose your upset." Remember, center isn't a noun or an adjective ("I'm a centered/uncentered person"). It's a verb—something you do, a way of coming back to yourself again and again.

Chances are very high that you uncenter when you think about your enemy. But you don't have to take my word for it—practice.

*Find someone who will push gently on the back and front of your shoulder after you have centered in your favorite way. Then, think about your enemy: a substance you've abused; a person who has abused you; your abuse of another . . . you get the idea. Pick an enemy. Think about it and have the "someone" challenge you again. (You don't need to tell them what you are thinking about.)*

*Keep practicing until you can center while thinking about your enemy. A hint: Sensei Kuboyama suggested that we can think in our abdomens about anything we want and it will help us center. Andy's version is to say to himself, "The more I think about X, the more I'll feel my own center." Totally illogical; but it works.*

The outcome of doing this is that you take your power back. It (the enemy, or anything on the outside for that matter) no longer *makes* you feel miserable. The enemy is just as awful, obnoxious or pathetic as ever, but *you* are balanced inside of yourself again.

"If I'm going to die, the best way to prepare is to quiet my mind and open my heart. If I'm going to live, the best way to prepare for it is to quiet my mind and open my heart."

–Ram Dass

"I say to my breath once again, little breath come from in front of me, go away behind me, row me quietly now, as far as you can, for I am an abyss that I am trying to cross."

–W.S. Merwin

# 5 The Opening Heart:
Developing Receptivity and Release

"Silence–not of the hostile variety, but rather of the kind that simply expresses beingness–was apparently, and I believe unconsciously, seen as threatening. It was as though something potentially dangerous would emerge if the talking were to stop for anything longer than thirty seconds. What is being avoided are the questions of who we are and what are we actually doing with each other. These questions live in our bodies and silence forces them to the surface."

–Morris Berman

Traveling through a turning point on the wisdom trail is an inquiry in action and, as such, leaves no room for attempts to control. The desire to control things, to make them what they were in the past—instead of allowing them to be what they are so they can challenge us into the creation of a new future—is an indication of the soul sickness that brought us to the intersection in the first place.

We have been trained to see through the filters of our fear, to listen through the baffle of our projections, and to feel through the callus of our prejudice. Our perceptions have become distorted and limited.

So what are we supposed to do? How do you *un*learn to not feel or hear or see? How do you find the time to slow down enough to notice what's going on around you when you've got a crisis on your hands? And what about the fear and grief? Are you supposed to receive those too?

This chapter addresses the issues of re-inhabiting your awareness, receiving yourself in the present moment—including your most difficult feelings—and receiving your enemy, so you can bow to it with respect and dignity.

The challenges we face on this journey will not be controlled for long. They require that we relate to them as one would clay on a turning potter's wheel: with hands that are firm and sensitive enough that the clay can be contained, yet rise up naturally to emerge into a new form.

> "Real fearlessness is the product of our tenderness. It comes from letting the world tickle your raw and beautiful heart."
>
> –Chogyam Trungpa Rinpoche

> "In a sword match with live blades, the person who cannot sense what is coming next will lose. It doesn't matter how hard the opponents can cut. What matters is how sensitive they are."
>
> –Lloyd Miyashiro

## Receiving What Is Now

It is morning in northern California. Andy and I are on a retreat with Thich Nhat Hanh, fondly known as "Thây" (Vietnamese for "teacher"). The rain and I were both mizzling. I was watching the peculiar little wisps of shapes that float inside my eyelids. I had slept poorly the night

85

before, in a tent on a redwood root, and I was lulled by Thây's soft voice. His words followed me and then resonated in my awareness as if a bell were being rung.

Thây explained that it is only when we take the time to notice what peace we have, that it can be absorbed by our systems and straighten out what has grown crooked: "You all say you want more peace, more peace. But have you noticed the peace you *do* have, in this moment?" I shook my head a little, as if something loose had rolled into place. What he was saying was so simple, so obvious.

He told us how important it is to notice what he called "the un-toothache"—those moments when we are not in pain or danger—and to drink them in deeply, down to the parched places in our histories.

As he spoke, I thought of how closely related my short temper was to my being short on time, short on resources, and short on help when my son David was growing up.

"If you are going to work with suffering, it is essential that you balance it out with joy. If you have listened to suffering for three hours, go walk in the woods and hug a tree until you come back in balance again. You owe it to yourself, to the people you work with, and to your family. People can't help relieve suffering if they don't have a broad base of joy."

As he spoke, I remembered how I was taught to use a reasonable facsimile of joy as a denial of suffering: One drink and I was peaceful; two and I was happy. No more suffering in the world. But that was an escape, a temporary cessation of fighting, not peace.

Thây went on: "Peace is present right here and now, in ourselves and in everything we do and see. The question is whether or not we are in touch with it. We don't have to travel far away to enjoy the blue sky. We don't have to leave our city or even our neighborhood to enjoy the eyes of a beautiful child. Even breathing can be a source of joy."

Joy and peace collected in small doses—by noticing the

*"Drinking a cup of tea, I stop the war."*

*–Paul Reps*

*"The notes I handle no better than many pianists. But the pauses between the notes–ah, that is where the art reside."*

*–Arthur Schnabel*

delight of a long hot shower, the softness of a pillowcase under your cheek, the absence of pain in your body—are not escapes. They form a resiliency in your mind, a nest, an open hand in which suffering can rest, a soft embrace in which pain can find a home. The more moments of simple peace you weave into that nest, the more you will be able to help do something about your suffering. Your system will know you have a core strong enough that you won't be consumed by it. The more moments that are collected in that nest, the more space there will be for the suffering you experience to be transformed into something fine and straight that can be passed on to those around you.

Opening your heart entails receiving the world, as Thich Nhat Hanh describes, and also being received by it. Here's a practice which only takes a few moments, but will give you a reference point experience of the receptivity you knew as a child:

*For a moment, imagine you are lying on the shoreline, a foot or so away from the lapping of warm, gentle waves. Your eyes are closed and your mind is reaching out receptively, keenly aware, yet uncertain of how or when you'll be touched by the water. You draw it to you as the moon does the tide. The waves creep closer and closer to your sun licked skin. You become aware that your body is inside of a wider "you," which is feeling those waves before they actually touch you, and which follows them each time they recede.*

> "As a lover of life I cannot keep out of any field of life . . . just as one naturally responds to the lack of clean water in the villages [of India], one responds to a lack of understanding and peace in the hearts of those in the West. As a lover of life, how can I separate any part from the whole?"
>
> –Vimala Thakar

## Is Yesterday Over Yet?

Here's a tale of one woman's struggle to find her way back to the present moment: I was undulating across a hideous brown-and-yellow-splotched carpet in the former convent where we were teaching. Twenty full-grown adults were galloping, cavorting and rolling around the room with

> "Your ears are wiser than you are."
>
> –Senegalese proverb

87

me. It was the sixth day of a week-long training seminar. We were examining the group process metaphorically, by choosing the first animal that came into our minds and becoming it. The whole time I had been pretending to be a dolphin, a voice in my mind kept whispering that this was not one of my more brilliant ideas.

At the end of a very long half hour, we reformed into a circle and I asked what people had learned. One woman, who had chosen to be a whale, said, "I couldn't find the space I needed."

"Is that true in your life? Do you have trouble finding the space you need to wail?"

She smiled, looking shyly at her hands, and released a long breath. "I never even realized that's what I was saying or that's why I chose to be a whale. But of course—I need space in my life to wail! And I'm always telling myself I take up too much space."

I was delighted to have her share such a perfect example of how the mind can use the same word to express two different meanings. I also could not avoid realizing that the dolphin my conscious mind had chosen was, in essence, a message from my unconscious mind to "delve in." After a week of paying attention to everyone else, that was exactly what I most needed to do for myself.

Then it was Marga's turn. She was a short, chubby woman in her mid-sixties, with severe asthma. She had been studying with us for several years, and this week had been a strain on her body. She had to walk hunched over, her breathing labored. Each day, when we talked to each other, her words flew around my head in circles, looping backwards into some story from her childhood, about how much her parents had neglected her or how hard it had been to be born a girl. I became frustrated at not being able to find a way through her windshield of words.

Marga called out her animal—a sea otter—and said she didn't really think it was relevant to her life in any way. Andy moved in front of her, his face soft, his open hand reaching out, as if offering something: "Could 'see others' be true for you, Marga?"

She turned her head sideways, staring blankly at the wall behind Andy. Her hands fluttered around like moths trapped in a jar. "Well, how does that fit? My whole life I've been noticing others, and no one ever notices me. No one cares if I live or die. I remember when I was six and my dog died, there was no one to comfort me and that dog was the only one in the whole world who. . . ."

Andy persisted: "I care, Marga. Each night I hear you moving down the dark hallway toward the bathroom. As you struggle to breathe, the air moving in and out of your lungs sounds as if it's moaning '. . . see . . . I . . . see . . . eye see . . .' and I remember the times when I've called out in the dark passageways of my life and no one was there. I'm here with you now, but I'm not feeling received. Will you notice that you're surrounded by support and caring in this moment, Marga?"

She glanced down at her feet and then turned her head toward the opposite wall. "I was always told not to make noise. When I was a girl, my mother used to yell at me whenever I cried at night, so I tried to be as still as a mouse. . . ."

I was sitting on a bed of coals with sparks crackling in the dark of my mind. I centered, feeling my feet on the floor, released my breath and with it, the words: "Is yesterday over yet, Marga?"

Every person in the room was startled. The crucifix on the wall tilted.

Amazingly, Marga's breathing steadied. "I don't know what you mean, Dawna. I was only saying that I don't want to bother people with my breathing, but it's hard being my age and all alone in the world. I have to do everything for myself you know. Years ago, my mother would . . ."

This time, I came close to bellowing. "Is yesterday over

*"We look back and we forget to look around."*

*–James Hillman*

*"The best way to cope with death is to focus on your life. Don't be on your deathbed saying, I should have had more fun. Say I really couldn't have used my time any better."*

*–Anon.*

yet?! Marga, look at Andy, just look at him. There is a man sitting right in front of you who cares deeply about you and you're not even seeing him."

She turned her head toward him. His chin trembled as he said, "I don't want to be lumped in with all those people who ignored you. I care that you're in pain, Marga. It makes a difference to me if you live or die."

Her hands began to flutter again, her breathing labored, and she looked at me. "I know he cares, of course he does, but it's just that no one really ever did see that I was hurting and . . ."

"Marga, look at Andy and see him. Let your eyes inhale him. Yesterday is over. See the caring that's here for you in the present moment. Receive it now, Marga."

Her head turned slowly toward Andy, as if the rusty vertebrae of her neck had just been oiled. I went over and sat behind her, back-to-back. Her breathing slowed. I inhaled as loudly as I could. She began to cry. "I see you, Andy. I do. I see you. I see you caring. I'm afraid. When I was little, the caring I needed wasn't there. So . . . but I am doing it now, I am seeing you here with me, caring." She reached her shaking fingers towards his face, tracing the tears that etched pathways over his jaw.

Andy spoke again, "Some day *I'll* be struggling down long dark hallways in the night, Marga. I hope I'll see the caring that's there for me, instead of the hollow yesterdays when I was alone."

People in the room reached out to each other, one hand finding another. It was as if there were a binding in tears of the alienated self in each of us. As Marga and Andy finally embraced, I heard myself ask once again, "Is yesterday over yet?"

## Finding the Now

In order to deal with what seems to be the random chaos of our experience, our minds weave stories to act as scar tissue between the facts of wounds and the pain of them. In Marga's case, the facts of her early life were that her parents often ignored her needs. Her inner experience was of pain and isolation. The story she told herself over and over was that if she had been born a boy, they would have cared about her, but since she was a girl, they despised and neglected her and she had to be alone. Night after night, year after year, this story ran through her mind as a way of adapting to the world from her wounded place. It was as if she built a castle with tiny slits for windows to protect herself from the arrows of her childhood, and all she could see forever after were narrow slices of the landscape.

The arrows were real—the facts of deprivation and her inner experience of pain. But the castle was her own creation, and needed to crumble if she were to come into the wider horizon of choices in the present moment. Until she changed the story, she couldn't change the way she was living her life.

The practice that follows will help you dissolve the mortar of old stories that lead to blank walls and dead ends:

*"There is no such thing as talent, only awareness."*

*–Chogyam Trungpa Rinpoche*

*What are the facts of your current struggle to find your lost self or deal with your enemy? Just the facts. If you were perceiving it all on a large movie screen, what actual occurrences would you see and hear?*

*What is your inner experience, i.e., tightness in your throat or knots in your belly?*

*What is the story you tell yourself about those facts and inner experiences? For example: "What happened was that Jackie said she never wanted to talk to me again. When I heard that, I felt a pain in my chest and then a walling-off there. The story I told myself was that she thought I was the worst person in existence, and that there would never be an opportunity for resolution."*

"Because human consciousness must involve both pleasure and pain, to strive for pleasure to the exclusion of pain is, in effect, to strive for the loss of consciousness."

–Alan Watts

Be gentle with yourself as you do this, and stay curious. Sometimes, it can be like unthreading a sticky cobweb, with pliers that are too large for the job and fingers that are too awkward. Chances are, you've been taught not to discriminate between your stories and the facts of your experience. But you can separate out the facts from the sensations and stories you create about them.

## Receiving Yourself

When we give external attention to others, but ignore our internal needs, it is likely that we will sabotage what we give. This may take the form of resentment, withdrawal, alienation, or abuse. If I find that I'm not receiving Andy, David, or a friend who calls up to ask for support, I know it's time to turn inward. When my eyes glaze over and I look without seeing, hear without listening, do without feeling, I know I need to receive myself. I need to be curious about what's going on without trying to change me, fix me, treat me, lecture or improve me. I have to turn in first, so that I can turn out clearly.

You carry the truth of yourself inside in a sheltered place, the way a fruit carries its possible future inside the hard stone at its center. You can find it, help it crack open, and emerge only when you turn inward receptively to cut away the rotting flesh of everything that is no longer you. Here's a story that traces such a turning.

"When you are in the heart of a summer's day as inside a fruit."

–Anais Nin

I was fighting like a samurai to stay alive, while also being in a great deal of pain. I was considering suicide from every perspective. Oncoming traffic enticed me. I fantasized about walking into a field of snow and freezing to death. There was a month when I carried an empty hypodermic needle in my purse in case the pain got too intense. I'm not sure I would have known what to do with it, but the mere sight of it, the promise of an exit, was reassuring. The best I could do was to begin every day staring into the mirror and vowing that I would not kill myself for the next twenty-four hours, no matter what.

Andy came to give me a massage one day. We were just good friends back then. He was the only bodyworker who didn't try to fix me or dig deep into my resistant fascia "for my own good." It seemed he was working *with* me instead of *on* me.

As I lay down on the brown leather massage table, I told him about all the places that were in pain or out of balance. It took fifteen minutes. I expected a response similar to the one I got from the acupuncturist, the shiatsu lady, the physical therapist, the oncologist, the endocrinologist and the psychotherapist. I expected him to go to the place of pain and try to fix it. He didn't. He listened intently to my tales of agony, but didn't do anything about them. Instead he asked, "Where *don't* you hurt?"

I had no idea what to answer. He went on to explain, "Well, I'm interested in where you are hurting right now, but I'm much more curious about where in your body there would be room for you to experience some peace, if not pleasure." He rubbed almond oil into his palms. "Your feet, for example. You didn't mention your feet; do they hurt?"

I thought he was either nuts or coming on to me. The first seemed much more likely than the second, given the circumstances. I decided to placate him. "No, my feet don't hurt. What are you gonna do about it?" (Is this the kind of woman anyone would want to come on to?) He picked up one of my feet and just held it. That's all he did. He held it. And he breathed a few times.

"What are you doing, Andy? Do you have a foot fetish

> "In a way, intelligence is measured by the intensity with which we can enjoy our senses."
>
> –James E. Lovelock

93

or something?" He smiled, but didn't laugh. His deep set eyes swam as he said, "No, dear friend, I do not have a foot fetish; but I am enjoying holding your foot. You seem so convinced you're going to die soon, I may not be able to feel it much longer, so I thought I'd just enjoy holding it."

I had no idea what he was talking about. But his hands were quite hot and the warmth was moving through my ankle, so I put my head down on the table and forgot to think for a minute or two. Having someone just enjoy holding my foot—without trying to relax it or improve it in any way at all—was a very unique experience. Everyone else had been giving me attention for being in pain. I could not compute what was happening. There was nothing I could do to deserve this warmth.

I tried to tell Andy a funny story while he was holding my foot. Humor had always been an automatic way to hold any feeling or any person at arm's length. But he told me to be quiet; then he held my other foot. I tried to think of other things, but that damned heat from his big hands had a very strange effect on me: I began to cry. Not great big sobs or anything, but not meager, cold tears either. My tears were warm, and they had no reasons for being. Remarkable. I didn't know there *could* be tears without reasons. I began to feel a strange sensation in the center of my chest—that same warmth. When I commented on what I was experiencing, he just said, "Good. I'm glad there's room in your body for peace too. It seems only fair, doesn't it?" My face was stuck in the hole of the massage table, but I nodded anyway.

Andy went on to hold my hands, my neck, my forehead and face, my calves and knees, "with enjoyment," as he said. No rubbing or aligning or fixing or treating. When I turned over to lie on my back, I sneaked a peek through my closed lids, and he did seem to be enjoying just holding different parts of my body. And the heat in his hands was remarkable. Soon the heat moving through my body was

*"When we make music, we don't do it in order to reach a certain point, such as the end of the compo-sition. If that were the purpose of music, then obviously the fastest players would be the best."*

*–Alan Watts*

remarkable. Not a sexual flush—more like the feeling you have when you've been sleeping on an arm and then roll over and the blood begins to flow back through it. Pins and needles at first and then . . . "vitality" is the best word I can come up with. Warm tears kept on spilling, my chest kept on filling. I felt an immense void filling up, spilling over. A waterfall of light.

As he was folding up his massage table, Andy said, "Well, old friend, at least now if you die tomorrow, I've enjoyed you, and that enjoyment is mine. No death can take it away."

For once, I had no words with which to reply. How could I? I don't think anyone had ever enjoyed me like that—for no reason, wanting nothing back, having no motive, with nothing I had to do to earn it. I had spent years railing against being used as a sexual object for some man's mindless pleasure, and here I had been used as a spiritual object for some man's mindful pleasure, and I loved it!

What's more, I'd felt myself! I could actually feel places that were *not* in pain. When Andy had arrived, my body consisted of 55 percent pain and 45 percent styrofoam. When he left, 50 percent was in pain and 50 percent was alive, a palpable kind of alive. A knowing, not a knowledge. A reality, not an idea.

I mumbled something incoherent and stumbled into the bathroom. I looked into the mirror. My face was luminescent, as if I held the moon in my mouth. I asked myself if I were in love. The answer was yes, but not with Andy. I was in love with the experience of being alive, with feeling my . . . everything. The hollow in the center of my chest—the place that had been a void for as long as I could remember—was now filled with a warm pulse that I didn't have to touch in order to know. It murmured, "I'm here. Live now. I'm here. Live now."

I touched the face in the mirror with one hand and traced a tear trail with the other. "I promise to experience

> "But still existence for us is a miracle; in a hundred places it is still the source. A play of absolute forces that no one can touch who has not knelt down in wonder."
>
> –Rainer Maria Rilke

95

as much life as I can in the next twenty-four hours, no matter what." I knew I could learn to be with myself the way Andy had been with my foot. I knew there was enough time for that.

Each day after that began (and still begins, fourteen years later), with the same commitment in the mirror: I promise to experience as much life as I can in the next twenty-four hours, no matter what.

## Personal Exploration:
## A Date With Your Self

"Life is not lost by dying; life is lost minute by minute, day by dragging day, in all the thousand small uncaring ways."

–Stephen Vincent Benet

Now it's your turn. This practice asks you to care directly for your own well being as though you were your only child. I suggest you retire to some place where you won't be disturbed—a bathroom, an oak tree, or library. This is a simple date. No fuss or fanfare. You may feel awkward at first, but not awful. Remember, unfamiliar *is* awkward.

You may also find this boring. That's fine. We give our attention to lots of external things we find boring. Water filling up a glass can also be perceived as boring. Yet, if you remember as you are drinking it that the only water that is known in the entire universe is here, on this earth, then suddenly you are swallowing a sacred gift that took twenty billion years to create and make flow.

Please feel free to choose your own sequence of doing this practice.

*You'll be receiving yourself in three different ways, for three minutes each: kinesthetically, through your sense of touch and motion; auditorily, through listening; and visually, through see- ing. If you choose to start kinesthetically, touch your body somewhere—your neck, for instance. Just touch it to feel it, as if it were something strange and wonderful, not to fix it or improve* it. Just receive it as your hand is receiving what it feels with each breath, as if every pore is a little mouth, breathing in the feeling of that neck. At the end of three minutes, stop and notice how that has affected you.

Switch to another way. If you choose visual next, imagine the pupils of your eyes can inhale each time you take a breath. Look at one of your hands and receive it through your eyes. Rather than looking at how wrinkled it is, or how you need to trim your nails, just see it as it is. After those three minutes, stop and notice the effect.

Switch to the last way of receiving yourself. In this case, that would be auditorily. My suggestion is that you begin with the phrase "no enemies within" and then let yourself say anything that comes to your mind. You don't have to be logical or give a speech, and your thoughts don't have to be connected. Let whatever comes just roll on out. If you run out of things to say, repeat "no enemies within." At the same time, allow your ears to become as receptive as were your eyes. Imagine they can simply inhale what you're saying, rather than trying to judge or figure it out. Just let the words float through as if they were clouds: "No enemies within. It makes me think of a thousand tiny soldiers kneeling on the shores of a blood vessel, putting their helmets turned upside down to float downstream. No enemies within. I'm seeing the words on a movie marquee. No enemies within. I'm thinking of a Mylanta commercial. I'm thinking of my sister coming to visit me in a yurt in the woods of Vermont . . ."

You don't have to understand what you say, or have explanations for the words. They have no meaning. Just receive your words as they are. (This is best done out loud; but if that is too much, say them in your mind as slowly as you can.) At the conclusion of these three minutes, notice the effect.

The nine minutes you've just spent with yourself may make it possible for you to begin to allow yourself to be received by others on a much deeper level, as well as to bring the truth within you that much closer to home.

> "To be awake is to walk the border between control and abandon."
>
> –Carlos Castenada

## Receiving Your Feelings

My friend Dale has a painting of the Madonna and Child hanging over the small gas stove in her kitchen, next to the telephone. I went in there to call home for my messages one day, and while my machine in Vermont reeled off voice after voice, my eyes in Boston were transfixed on this painting. I kept pushing "rewind" to play the messages over because every time I was about to write down what someone said, my eyes were captured by Her again. As one person after another poured out their story of suffering, all I could see was the Madonna holding this beautiful infant close to her heart, while gazing out at the wide horizon.

*"If you are totally vulnerable, you cannot be hurt."*

*–Ruth Gendler*

I wished she could teach each of the people who were calling me how to do that with their pain, fear, rage or grief. I remembered Thich Nhat Hanh saying that mindfulness can be a companion for our anger. We were in California, home of the emotional discharge, and he declared that all pounding on pillows does is make you tired! He suggested that anger, fear, and sadness shouldn't be repressed like toxic waste, but, rather, held like an infant.

There, in Dale's small kitchen, his words were woven together in my mind forever with that painting. I have been angry since, in despair, grieving and terrified, but each time, within minutes, that image rises up in my mind, and I find myself wondering what it would be like to cradle that fear, that rage, close to a spacious heart while gazing at the horizon of all of my life experiences, at all the resources that are available to me at any given moment. To walk with my suffering as I did with David when he was an infant, to croon to my shame, all the while noticing the enormous width of the horizon of possibilities. The Madonna has taught me that when I find myself afraid to love, what I need to be doing is loving my fear.

Most people are afraid to feel what they're feeling, because they have no idea what to do with all of it. They have histories of negative experiences with *reactions to feelings*. They are afraid of their fear, angry at their anger, and despairing about their despair. Indeed, a great deal of what we call pain is really resistance to pain. Can you imagine allowing your heart to be open enough to make room for your pain, your anger, your terror?

I worked with John, who was struggling with AIDS. He said what was hardest for him was getting others to listen to him talk about the problems people with the disease were facing. I suggested that they were afraid of really letting themselves know about the suffering, because they wouldn't know how to respond to it. I asked how his parents responded to his fear when he was a child.

His experience was the same as it is for most of us—they told him that there was nothing to be afraid of and to stop feeling it. I asked him to consider for a moment what it would have been like to be a frightened child whose parents held him and breathed with him, listening to him talk about his fear. John just snorted. I explained that although he had grown up, his fear hadn't, nor had his need for it to be received.

Like a sweater worn thin at the elbows, John's defensiveness tore open. All the nightmares trapped inside broke through. Instead of responding to them as his parents had, I asked him if he was listening to what his fear was saying, listening deeply enough to hear what it needed. The voice he responded in was completely different than the one he had started with—all traces of tension and cynicism were gone. What he said was quite simple: "Dawna, my fear is not a failure." In that moment, I knew he was reconciling with himself, and would be able to build compassionate bridges to those who were willing to meet him halfway.

There are two other lessons I learned from Thây that

> "Spiritual warriors are courageous enough to taste suffering and relate to their fear . . . suffering is not seen as a failure or a punishment. It's a purification."
>
> –Sogyal Rinpoche

> "The trick is not to rid your stomach of butterflies but to make them fly in formation."
>
> –Outward Bound

99

have taught me more about responding to emotions with grace and compassion than all my years of training in psychotherapy. The first one suggests that when strong feelings come up, moving down from your head to your body is always helpful. He uses the metaphor of a tree in an intense storm to suggest that if you climb into the upper branches, trying to be bigger than the things you are afraid of, you'll get whipped around. Climb down the tree, hugging tight to the big stable trunk, and then go crawl in a cave at the base of the tree. There, nestled in the root of it all, you have a much better chance to notice what you do need until the storm passes. It will widen your perspective and deepen your understanding, and allow you to consider what resources you have available to you to meet those needs.

The second gift is about impermanence. We all suffer because we know we will die. We know everything that is precious to us will be lost. But in this dark reality, there is also the gift of change, the abundance of new forms that are continually being born. Have you ever noticed how quickly a wonderful feeling passes? In truth, *all* thoughts and feelings are like clouds that pass on a wide open sky. The sky embraces everything; it is without territory or boundaries. I've never known anyone, no matter how persistent or stubborn, to experience an emotion that lasted for more than thirty breaths when it was examined with awareness. Anger turns out to be a moment of fear dissolving into a moment of rage, changing into a moment of self-pity, transforming into a moment of helplessness. Knowing that prepares you to notice and enjoy the passing moments of joy and healing that also will inevitably cross that sky in the ever-changing weather of your mind.

In this culture, we use the word "emotions" to mean both body sensations and thoughts. So I invite you now to take a few moments to notice all you are feeling. I suggest you follow the tides of your breath back into your body,

*"In us, there is a river of feelings, in which every drop of water is a different feeling, and each feeling relies on all the others for its existence. To observe it, we just sit on the bank of the river and identify each feelings as it surfaces, flows by, and disappears."*

*–Thich Nhat Hanh*

following the sensations there for awhile.

*Allow your thoughts to silhouette against the screen of your awareness. When you are ready, you can notice the feelings that arise into your awareness, perhaps naming each one. You can notice the images, stories and memories that float from those feelings. You may want to use the image of the tree or the Madonna to receive them, or perhaps you'll choose to notice them through the lens of impermanence.*

*You can allow the awareness of your breath to be a dry ground for whatever arises. Is it long or short? Does it change? Is it warm or cool? Is the rising longer than the falling or the other way around? What are the spaces like in between? What would it be like to wrap your breath around what you are feeling like soft swaddling?*

*"Denying anger is as destructive as expressing it excessively."*

*–Harold Bloomfield*

There's another practice I've found very helpful in relating to a feeling rather than reacting to it. I learned it from Ira Progoff, depth-psychologist and author of *At a Journal Workshop*:

*If there is an emotion that seems to be controlling you, or one you know you keep denying and avoiding, develop a correspondence with it. Some people like to do this by writing a whole letter to their anger, for instance, and then on another sheet writing a whole letter from their anger. An alternative way is to write it as dialogue. For example:*

*Me: I don't understand why you just come over me in a flash. I hate how destructive you are.*

*Anger: Talk about destructive! You destroy every desire I have.*

*Continue this way of relating as long as you are interested, perhaps stretching it out over weeks or months.*

## Receiving Your Enemy

Each enemy we find in ourselves is, on some level, an energetic contraction built out of fear. We respond to it with patterns of holding—holding our breath, holding ourselves in, back, and down. These patterns are like knots of energy tied around our memories and images. If you hold something tightly in the palm of your hand long enough, numbness will set in and you'll forget that you're holding anything. Acknowledging each demon loosens its grip on us and expands our capacity to be free in its midst.

In aikido, there is a maxim that says the faster you tighten up, the quicker the punch reaches you; whereas, the more you relax and open, the more time you have to choose the best response. The following practice will give you an experience of releasing your heart, untying the knots. Perhaps, like Milarepa, you will find yourself bowing to your demons.

*"The only real meaning of life is the experience of it."*

—*Mark Salzman*

## "My Friend, the Enemy"

*After centering and noticing the sensations in your body as you did above, turn the light of your awareness on any physical discomforts or tensions you've been fighting or ignoring. Rather than analyzing or trying to change them, just notice them with kind interest. In each area of struggle you find, allow your energy to release and soften around it.*

*When you are ready, move your attention to your emotions, noticing feelings and thoughts with which you have been struggling. With each discovery, you have the opportunity to open to what you are experiencing—without fighting it, but softening around it, expanding your energy as you release.*

*When you are ready, bring your awareness to the battles that exist in your life with this demon, this enemy, this lost self. Once again, just notice them kindly, with attentive curiosity and a heart*

*"Peace is neither the absence of war nor the presence of a disarmament agreement. Peace is a change of heart."*

–*Richard Lamm, former governor of Colorado*

*that releases around it all softly.*

*You can allow your mind to wander lazily over the following questions: When does your awareness of this enemy arise? Is there an image that triggers it? How long does it last? What ends it? What follows it? What is asking for acceptance?*

*Bring yourself back to the present moment—as fully aware, alert and refreshed as you would like to be. You may want to walk around as you notice how this practice has affected you.*

Between resignation and rebellion, tedium and terror, lies the present moment, waiting to be received. It is the only place where loving and learning is possible. To lose it is human. To find it is divine.

*"Tomorrow is a long way away."*

*–Tahitian saying*

# Singing To the Demons:
## Thinking For A Change

*"Learning is a companion on a journey to a strange country. Learning is strength inexhaustible."*

–from *Hitopadeso*,
a collection of Hindu writings

People watched the stars move around the heavens for ages, knowing they turned. But it wasn't until they were able to transfer this understanding into an imaginative symbol—the wheel—that civilization could be profoundly changed by that awareness.

Most of us go through our lives as if we were climbing one rung after another on a ladder. We graduate from one school so we can go on to the next. Then we graduate from that one, so we can get a job. We work so we can get a promotion, so we can move to a better neighborhood.

It's known that we use only fifteen percent of our brain's capacity for "ladder thinking," the kind of problem solving that our society requires of us. I believe that the rarely-used 85 percent is the largely unexplored territory of the imagination. When someone does something, such as compose a symphony or invent Velcro, we say they are remarkably talented. When someone heals from terminal cancer or triumphs over a history of abuse, we say they are lucky or their doctors were talented. But what if they are, in fact, tapping into the resident capacities of that remaining portion of their brains? What if their minds are "wheel thinking?" What if, instead of thinking that some have it and others don't, we explored the possibility that we all could expand the scope of our capacities far beyond anything we now consider "normal?"

The imagination is an integral part of our minds' make-up, a vital force without which we can exist, but not truly live. Yet we have been taught that it is the part we can most easily sacrifice, since it is extraneous, trivial, or the sole property of a few "talented" ones. As a culture, we over-educate and over-emphasize the linear to the exclusion of the rest of our abilities. This leads to fragmentation: Figure things out by breaking them down into pieces. It's either this way or that. You're right or you're wrong. You work on Monday and have fun on Sunday.

One of the consequences of this linear emphasis is that

*". . . to climb the ladder of success only to discover it is propped against the wrong building."*

*–Joseph Campbell*

*"Where the spirit does not work with the hand there is no art."*

*–Leonardo DaVinci*

*"The most beautiful understanding in the world is that of the mysterious."*

*–Albert Einstein*

we seem to be bereft of creative ways to deal with conflict or struggle. We have starved our capacity for wonder and severely neglected the unique inner abilities of our own imagination.

Something fundamental in our soul gets twisted when we lose access to our creativity. Recently, there's been an increasing awareness of how imagery can affect healing, but we have been so ingrained to believe in external sources of wisdom and internal sources of problems, that we've turn to someone else's standardized formula for affirmations, visualizations, and rituals. I believe that no formula will work for everyone, that each person must find his own creative pathway to healing, her own unique route to what works best. But that doesn't mean you have to flounder in the unknown. You just need to know how to begin. This section is about coming to recognize and access your unique way of knowing.

I once worked with a man who was attacked by a shark while surfing. One of his arms was bitten off, the other severely mauled. He lost a great deal of blood, but nonetheless did what everyone later said was impossible—he swam through half a mile of rough surf, crawled across a deserted beach and up a rocky hillside, and dragged himself an additional half mile until he came to a road where he found help. When I questioned him as to how he had done it, he said he just didn't pay attention to his wounds. Instead he found himself pretending there was another self—a future self—who knew he would make it; "he" cheered on and guided the traumatized man. When I asked him if he had ever done any imagery work in his past, he rolled his eyes and explained to me that he wasn't the creative type! In spite of this negative belief, during the shark crisis a door had opened to that other portion of his mind, and out walked an imaginary friend to help him.

Throughout time, imagination has always been an integral part of the healing process. Yet, these days we're more willing to consider its destructive capacities than its healing ones. Most of the people I work with understand that the way they "think" contributes to their illness or problem: "It's because I worry so much. I know it drives up my blood pressure, but I keep imagining my boss's beady eyes as he screams at me for all the mistakes I'm going to make tomorrow. . . ." Few, however, believe that they can use that very same imagination to contribute to their own healing.

We *can* make ourselves ill through the imagination, and we have all had a great deal of teaching about the process. But Nature creates few one-way doors so the reverse must also be true—we can learn to make ourselves well. But, in order to do that, we need to open ourselves up to explore the geography of our imagination. We need to not only discover our deepest truths, but create new models, stories, and images from which to craft the kinds of experiences for which we've been longing. Following the path of Victor Frankl, we can search the terrain of our minds until we find the meanings that guide us toward illumination and healing.

What follows is a guide for moving through this second stage of our pilgrimage—the straightening by fire. Its purpose is to explore new ways of using your mind to support healing. We'll be doing what I call "insearching," inner research to help you discover how to shift into the wheel states of mind, so you can resource all the possibilities that exist to find a way of relating to your struggle that serves you well. You'll learn how to recognize and access the different states of consciousness your mind uses for creative thought, and come to identify the sequence of imagery that is most effective for you. You'll learn how to experiment with several different ways to dialogue with your unconscious mind, in order to gather the information you need to find your way to wholeness.

By thinking "wider," more globally, you can create an

> "I pray and I sing and sometimes my prayer is my singing."
>
> –Bobby McFerrrin

> "It is in changing that things find meaning."
>
> –Heraclitus

*"Before a month had passed, writing became my safe place, a way to get in touch with me. . . . Without my knowing when, there was a shift in my identity. I wrote, therefore I was."*

*–Barbara Gordon*

inner spaciousness where your enemy can exist within the whole landscape of experiences, skills and wisdom you've collected in your life, without being able to control you. When you change to thinking in this way," I am the problem" becomes "I have the problem" becomes "I do the problem." Ultimately it becomes just one of the many patterns of thinking and behaving that the kaleidoscope of your unconscious mind can use to sing to the demons.

# 6 The Changing Mind:

Exploring the Nature Of Imagination

*"The idea that there is one culture, one reality–that things can be put neatly into one little box which works for everyone–simply is not true. That way of thinking is crippling, and it's almost a criminal thing to do to the human spirit."*

–Elena Featherstone

Crossing the threshold into this stage of our journey means entering a confusing dark world that is both strange and unfamiliar. There are no signposts here, or right angles. Thinking in the old way just doesn't work. The challenge is for you to learn to trust yourself in this world. And that requires understanding the vehicle you'll be using to move through it, and knowing how to shift into the new ways of thinking that are most effective here.

But how do you do that? How do you think in a different way from the one you've used for your whole adult life? What if you believe you can't be imaginative? What if you feel handicapped in the world of symbolic thinking? What if you open your mouth to sing to the demons and all that comes out is "My Country 'Tis Of Thee?," in the wrong key?

Telling someone to think in a new way is like telling her to shift into third gear when she's only driven cars with automatic transmissions and has no idea where to find the clutch! Even among those who espouse the importance of imagery in body-mind healing, there is one widely-held misunderstanding—*that all minds create images in the same way.* I hear people all the time say things like, "I tried to use my creativity, but I just can't visualize," or "I've been saying these affirmations for two years, but nothing seems to happen." It is as if we are taught to believe that a bicycle is the only kind of vehicle, and those of us who drive a sports car, and get nowhere by trying to make the pedals go round and round, are not trying hard enough.

It seems so difficult for our culture to conceive of diversity, yet the truth is that there are as many languages of the imagination as there are of rational thought. This morning at the local Mobil station, I overheard a woman sitting behind the wheel of a red van, yelling at her husband who was filling the tank. "How could you even think that way?!" she screeched. It was inconceivable to her that his brain worked in a different way than hers worked. So, she

*"This very world is seen by the five senses as matter, by the very wicked as hell, by the good as heaven and by the perfect as God."*

*–Vivekananda*

*"I refuse to be intimidated by reality anymore. What's reality? Nothing but a collective hunch!"*

*–Lily Tomlin*

113

*"The most interesting thing about wood for me is that it has a grain, as people do. That is, each piece of wood has a personality and, as we know from our relationships with people–trying to work with them, live with them–personality could almost be defined by the way resistance (to what I want) is expressed in it."*

*–Carla Needleman*

*"Looking for God is like seeking a path in a field of snow; if there is no path and you are looking for one, walk across it and there is your path."*

*–Thomas Merton*

decided it was wrong. Maybe crazy. Certainly not orderly or organized like her brain.

She's not alone. The assumption that all of us use our brains in the same way to think has led to mis-appraisal of our core competencies, as well as ruptured relationships. When some of us learn easily and others don't, we've been told that the reason is some people are smart and others not, some are creative and others not. Too many of us have been exiled from our native truth because we have not been taught to listen or speak in its tongue. When we fail to imagine our own lives, we become the victims of someone else's imagination.

What we will uncover in this chapter is that we *all* learn in several different ways. Each of us is imaginative once we understand and honor the unique ways our minds function. To know how to access the unique pattern of imagery that your mind uses is to know how to navigate with the map of healing that waits in your widest, wisest consciousness.

And it does wait. Your imagination, creativity, intuition, whatever you wish to call it, is remarkably loyal. It sits like a spring-fed lake waiting for you to dip into it, waiting for you to notice it. In thirty years of working with human beings, I have never found one whose imagination has abandoned them, though I have met thousands who have rejected their imaginations! You just have to know how to find it. In order to understand how your mind moves from linear thinking to imaginative thinking, I'm going to invite you to explore with me the three modes of thinking.

## Exploring the States Of Consciousness

As those of you who are familiar with psychology are aware, there are three states of consciousness: conscious, subconscious, and unconscious. What we are less aware of is that every thought goes through each state. As a single thought moves through your conscious mind into your subconscious, then unconscious, your mind expands outward as you get more and more receptive to imagine. When you become more alert to focus into action and expression, it contracts back to a single point. Expanding, contracting, expanding, contracting, like a bellows or lungs; widening as your mind turns in towards your unconscious, contracting as your conscious mind concentrates to express.

The diagram here is a map you may choose to follow as we track this expanding circumference of our minds. It's illustrated as a spiral because that is the ancient symbol of personal power and purpose, death and rebirth.

> *"The totality of the psyche can never be grasped by the intellect alone."*
>
> *–Carl Jung*

# The Spiral of Thinking

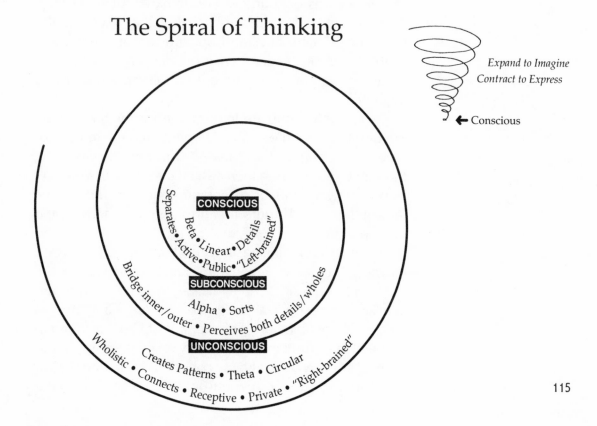

*Expand to Imagine*
*Contract to Express*

← Conscious

**CONSCIOUS**
Separates • Beta • Linear • Details • Active • Public • "Left-brained"

**SUBCONSCIOUS**
Bridge inner/outer • Alpha • Sorts • Perceives both details/wholes

**UNCONSCIOUS**
Wholistic • Creates Patterns • Theta • Circular • Connects • Receptive • Private • "Right-brained"

115

## Organizing Thoughts In the Conscious Mind

We are taught in school that there is one way to think: "Pay attention!" That's the conscious mind.

*In this moment, I'd like to invite you to do your best to "pay attention." What do you do to think that way? How do you shift into that way of thinking? Notice what that state of consciousness is like for you.*

Did you sit up straighter, narrow your focus, make your body more still, listen for details? This is called linear thinking or, as some people refer to it, left brained thinking, logical, conscious, "reasonable" thinking. I call it the "one way mind," because when we think in this way, we are certain there is only one way to think about something. This way gets right to the point. When the brain uses this mode of thought, facts and opinions are gathered, and problem solving occurs. Here is our detail mind where we organize everything, separate it into compartments and fragments.

Here we accumulate information for the short term, but don't necessarily "learn" it. I once studied fiercely for a geology exam and got an "A." The next day, walking through Central Park, a friend asked me whether a particular boulder was igneous or metamorphic and I didn't have the slightest idea. The information had gone in one eye and out the other.

This mode of thinking, in which the brain is producing the most Beta waves, is your most familiar and alert mental state, and your least receptive. It likes the tried and true, the familiar and recognizable. Possibilities are eliminated as quickly as possible here. For example, if I hear a sound in the night that is unfamiliar, not the way I think things should sound, I get very alert, and my conscious mind does its job of separating out that sound from every other one in the

"*What people call thought is mostly a hunt for the right opinion.*"

*–Carla Needleman*

house until I can identify it: "Ah yes, that's the new refrigerator making ice cubes." If you couldn't think in this mode, your world would become a chaotic whirlpool. But because this state of mind thrives on repetition of the known, it plays a large part in addiction, which is progressive and repeated familiar behavior.

It's from the conscious mind that we can express ourselves quickly and precisely, and from here that we can compete quite easily. My father was my primary teacher of this state, pushing me to struggle to "climb the ladder of success. It's a dog-eat-dog world. You've got to fight to get ahead." This state (and my father) does not deal well with change. The conscious mind loves stability and will do whatever is necessary on the surface to achieve it. In a relationship, a person making change from this place would go for the kiss-and-make-up technique, while an organization would go for the quick fix.

*"Addiction is linear, a progressive degenerative disease. But creativity is regenerative and cyclical, a process of death and rebirth."*

*–Linda Leonard*

We have been taught that if we aren't in this state, we aren't thinking or learning. In fact, this is only the very first stage. It is like the mouth of the mind that takes information in and chews it up.

## Sorting Thoughts In the Subconscious Mind

*Now, let's shift states of mind and go a little wider. To do this, you'll have to get confused and space out a little. Let your thinking get a little fuzzy, as if you can't make up your mind about something. Notice what you have to do to achieve this. Stop trying to pay attention to the outer world and let your mind wander. What do you do to think that way? How do you shift into that way of thinking? Notice what that state of consciousness is like for you.*

Some people find they must stare or rock or talk to themselves to get to think in this way. Yes, this too *is* thinking, no matter what Mrs. Chalkdust told you in fifth grade. In fact, if you allow yourself to be comfortably perplexed, you may discover your "confusion" has changed altogether and instead become "curiosity."

This state of consciousness may be called alpha or the subconscious mind. It is a trance-itional way of thinking, for here the brain is going into trance to metabolize information and explore options by sorting. It is thinking in dualities, a two-way mode: "Either I do this or that; either his side of the story is wrong or hers is wrong; either I see it this way or that." It is like the stomach of the mind, churning things around, deciding what will be digested and how. In the case of the new refrigerator, I might listen to it for awhile and figure out whether I want to go on listening to that noise or get up and close my bedroom door. Because it links the conscious and unconscious mind, this way of thinking can perceive the details of something and the whole of it.

My mother was my primary teacher of the subconscious mind. She was always weighing both sides of any decision, terrified to act lest she make a mistake: "Well, you could wear the red dress, but it's a little flashy. On the other hand, you could wear the blue one, but it's too casual." Since most of us are taught in school that this way of thinking means we don't know what we're supposed to, we develop the habit, as my mother did, of contracting ourselves here, getting "up-tight" and uncomfortable when we hang out in this mode for any length of time. When people feel pressured, they are usually stuck here, thinking they need to get back to the certainty of the conscious mind.

In fact, this way of thinking is vital for decision-making and image making, for it is the bridge between our inner and outer worlds. Without it, we'd swallow everything whole, never thinking about whether something is right for us or not. Knowing this makes it easier to expand when

*"Until you are willing to be confused about what you already know, what you know will never grow bigger, better or more useful."*

–Milton Erickson

we're "confused," giving our brains the time they need to cross that bridge comfortably.

Change from this state is effected by centering, taking time to step back and reflect, by not deciding until the information is sorted and completely digested, by taking a "wait-and-see" attitude. Giving ourselves time to be here, to wait and not know, is crucial to healing, and often uncomfortable until we get used to it.

## Creating in the Unconscious Mind

*Now it's time to shift wider, to get even more receptive. Have you ever driven on a highway at night when you were at exit 15, when suddenly you notice you are at exit 19? What happened to exits 16, 17 and 18? Who was that masked person driving your car?*

*Allow yourself to space out as completely as you can for a few minutes—get lost in your thoughts. Put the book down after reading this paragraph and just allow your mind to wander wherever it wants to go for a few moments, as it does when you're listening to a boring lecture or waiting alone in a movie theater for the show to begin. . . .*

*What do you do to think that way? How do you shift into that mode of thought? Notice what that state of consciousness is like for you.*

> "A dream is a being that travels from wild mind into the dot/monkey mind/ conscious self to wake us up."
>
> –Natalie Goldberg

This way of thinking is often referred to as unconscious, right brained, entranced. Here, the brain is producing mostly theta and delta waves. Here you think about the way things could be. It is like the intestines of the mind, constantly changing the form of what has been digested and connecting the nutrients to every part of the system. You probably learned to apologize for thinking this way in school, for "daydreaming" and not paying attention to the teacher. In fact, in this state, your brain was processing what you were learning, searching internally for how the new information fit with what you already had experienced, making new patterns from it, storing information for long term, and dreaming new possibilities for the future.

Here, the brain thinks in many ways at once, circularly, creating and carrying messages indirectly through dreams, symbols, and imagery. Because it can think in so many directions simultaneously, this mode enables us to be alive in the contradictions that challenges offer. It searches for the pattern that will reveal the whole of something, the forest rather than the trees. In the now-famous case of the refrigerator, the unconscious mind might incorporate the sound into the whole of my night by giving me a dream about being in a hailstorm.

This mode of thinking is devoted to understanding how things are interrelated and connected. It functions very much like a kaleidoscope, recombining bits and pieces to make new images and symbols. Thus, to your unconscious mind, change is *of* the system, not just *to* it. When change comes from this place, you become a non-smoker rather than switching brands. You go into therapy to study the process of how you are or are not relating to your spouse. Your business decides to do an overview of how information is moving throughout the company rather than firing the computer operator. The state does an in-depth overhaul of its financial system rather than starting a new lottery.

I think of this most receptive thinking state as the "tomb, the loom, and the womb," since all of our life experiences are stored here, constantly being woven into ever-changing patterns with our new experiences, and seeding our creativity with unlimited dreams of possibilities.

Because it is the mode of thought most capable of understanding the whole of something, the big picture, the

*"In the course of living, from infancy on, you acquired knowledge, but you could not keep all that knowledge in the foreground of your mind. In the development of the human being learning in the unconscious became available in any time of need. When you need comfort, you can feel comfort."*

–Milton Erickson

*"Metaphor is right at the bottom of being alive."*

–Gregory Bateson

widest landscape, this is also the place of deepest spiritual connection and healing, of that elusive inner voice or insight or gut feeling. This is where innovation originates, where we find the unity of melody beyond separate tones. This is where we need to learn to go in order to find out what our enemy needs.

My grandmother, who delivered hundreds of babies into the world and sat with an equal number of people as they died and left the world, was my teacher of this mind. She taught me indirectly, through stories, symbolic rituals and ceremonies, how things were interrelated.

This expansive state of mind, where curiosity becomes wonder, awe or surprise, is often the most difficult for us to access and, for many people, where they feel the most shy, awkward, or vulnerable. That's because we have been taught that to think this way is to waste time. In our culture, we are supposed to be in action or reaction as much as possible. No one gets good grades or promotions for thinking in this way. If someone is busy "doing" something, we are taught not to interrupt. But in the east, where reflection is honored, no one would interrupt someone who was sitting quietly in contemplation!

Remember, nature devoted approximately 85 percent of your brain to this wider thinking. For learning to be complete, information must move all the way through this state of mind. For healing to happen, we must be able to think in wholes, and that is best done "spaced out,"— musing, contemplating, pondering, meditating, and ruminating. In order to incorporate change, we need to expand the circumference of our minds and explore the possibilities at the edges.

Therefore, shifting to this non-linear state of mind helps you to:

Move through the unknown;
Go from confused to curious;
Generate imagery;

"A human being is part of the whole, called by us universe; a part limited by time and space. He experiences himself, his thoughts and feelings as something separated from the rest, a kind of optical delusion of consciousness. This delusion is a kind of prison for us, restricting us to our personal desires and to affection for a few persons nearest us. Our task must be to free ourselves from this prison."

–Albert Einstein

Connect with internal resources;
Fuse inner reality and outer reality;
"Relate to" a problem rather than solving it;
Understand the whole story, the "big picture,"
    the landscape;
Find linkages within self and community;
Trigger your immune system;
Become more comfortable with pain;
Think globally;
Transform raw emotional "garbage";
Comprehend.

## Expanding Your Mind

*"Wisdom is the intelligence of the system as a whole."*

*–Gregory Bateson*

Some people talk about going deeper, deeper, deeper into the unconscious mind. I like to view the process as expanding your mind. This means you become more and more aware of your periphery. You literally allow yourself to see more of what is on either side of you, instead of just focusing on a detail in front of you. You hear the sounds all around you, and feel all of your body, where and how it makes contact with the floor, etc.

In ki-aikido, I learned to imagine I was inhaling what I saw through the pupils of my eyes all the way down to my belly. This is called "soft eyes." It's possible to do the same thing with your auditory channel by imagining you're inhaling sound through your ears with each breath, and with your kinesthetic by imagining you're breathing what you feel through the pores of your skin. What you exhale in each case is curiosity.

*Let's experiment. Start by thinking very intensely about one thing—tension in your back, for example, or your wretched Uncle Charlie, or that mortgage bill you have to pay. Become as focused as possible.*

*Now shift. Widen your senses so that you are aware of your periphery. Soften your eyes so you can see all around you. Expand your feeling so you are noticing your whole body and listen to both the sound of your breath and any noises in your environment. For five breaths, imagine you are inhaling what your senses perceive and exhaling curiosity.*

*Notice how that effects your thinking, your energy, your blood pressure.*

Most people say they relax, feel "spacier" and that the quality of their thinking changes. The problem, or Uncle Charlie, doesn't go away; but how you respond to the thought does change. Perceiving this way puts what you're focused on in a larger context, which means more options and possibilities have room to emerge. In fact, that's exactly what you are doing—stretching your mind wide enough so that it has room to perceive the possible connections. You literally give your brain room to maneuver, to ponder, to create and generate. You may remember the exercises a chiropractor gave you to do for your back; you may think of Uncle Charlie as a five-year-old boy; or realize the problem is just out there, not taking over your whole life.

> *"The significant problems we face cannot be solved at the same level of thinking we were at when we created them."*
>
> *–Albert Einstein*

*Let's go in the opposite direction. Space out, expand your periphery and float there for a few minutes. Now, narrow your senses down, contract your mind and energy until you are listening to, looking at and feeling just one thing. Notice how that affects your thinking, your breathing, and your blood pressure.*

No state of consciousness is good or bad, particularly if you know how to shift from one to the other and when to use each. In situations of immediate danger, a single focused "fight or flight" response can be very useful. If a lion is about to pounce on you, most likely you will go wide for a moment—"Oh my God what am I going to do?"—and then snap alert, into that adrenalinized, detailed state of consciousness that helps you act immediately.

But there are limitations to thinking in this way. The word "re-act" means to act over and over in the same way, which is exactly what this state of mind most likes to do. The conscious mind loves repetition. It also thinks in pieces, details or fragments. It loves compartments, because they are neat and separate.

In the case of that lion, if you stay in your conscious mind, you might freeze and forget you have a knife strapped to your calf. You might even forget you have a calf or a leg, for each of those awarenesses is neatly tucked in another compartment of your mind. The lion is in one compartment with your pounding heart. Your legs, calves, and ability to run are tucked into another.

However, if you do what you always did, you get what you always got. Not every problem we face is a drooling, snarling, fanged lion. As a matter of fact, fewer and fewer problems are as fiercesome these days. More are situations that require our deep reflection until we can perceive the whole situation, the relationships within it, how one thing will affect another, the entire system of actions and reactions. From this place, we can create new patterns of response.

I worked with a woman several years ago who kept getting stuck in a fight-or-flight response to her daughter. On the surface, Sandy seemed to be very easygoing about almost everything. The "almost" represented her grown daughter, who "drives me up a wall." Sandy told me that she believed her daughter really hated her and whenever they were together, all she wanted to do was run away or scream at her. She described their relationship as oppositional: "Whatever is important to me, you can bet she'll do exactly the opposite."

I asked several deep and revealing questions, but Sandy ignored all of them. When I made a suggestion, she

*"A people who would build a nation in which strong, democratic institutions are firmly established as a guarantee against state induced power must first learn to liberate their own minds from apathy and fear."*

*–Aung San Suu Kyi*

slipped into "yeah, but. . . ." So, I just listened for awhile, and then asked her to give me an example of when this had happened recently. She put her right hand over her eyes and said, "Just yesterday we were having lunch together. We always have lunch together on Tuesdays. We always go to this Greek restaurant because I'm a vegetarian and can get a great salad there." Sandy's voice began to get tight, intense. Her words came faster. Her hand dropped but her eyes were staring directly ahead, seeing something I couldn't see.

"She ordered a hamburger, rare. She was sitting right in front of me and, when it arrived, she slowly picked it up and bit into it. The blood dripped down her hand and wrist. I swear I felt as if it were *me* she was eating. I just couldn't stand it, which I told her and then ran out of the restaurant! Even now as I think about it, my heart is pounding and my mouth is dry."

Obviously, there was a lot of learning that needed to be done, but people tend not to be very open to learning when they are in a fight-or-flight response. What Sandy wanted was to be comfortable with her daughter and to understand why she got so triggered. I told her I could help her get comfortable, and then she could explore the origins of her feelings more easily.

After teaching Sandy how to widen her periphery, I made the following suggestion: On their next Tuesday outing, she was to take her daughter to a completely new restaurant, one where neither of them had ever eaten, one that had a visually intriguing environment. She was to sit next to her daughter, not across from her, and when they began to eat, Sandy was to widen her periphery by noticing what she could see and hear all around her, as well as the feelings in her entire body.

I was very curious to find out what happened when she came to see me the next week. She bounced into my office, ran her hands through her silver hair once and then

*There will always be conflict in human affairs because of the simple fact that I'm hungry when you're thirsty, I want to sleep when you want to get up, I want to go left when you want to go right. The issue isn't conflict itself, but how we deal with it."*

*–Riane Eisler*

said, "It was amazing! I did everything you told me to, although I was sure it wouldn't work; but I paid for that suggestion, so I decided to give it a go. This time, my darling daughter ordered rare roast beef, but I took those five breaths through my eyes and ears and feet and all I noticed then were the paintings on the wall behind her. There was one of a sailboat, and I remembered when she and I used to go to the beach in Nantucket. She couldn't have been more than four, and kept taking off her bathing suit because she wanted the waves to tickle her skin. I reminded her of that time and we spent the whole lunch laughing and reminiscing. We haven't had such a good time together in I don't know how long."

I asked Sandy if her daughter finished the roast beef sandwich, but she looked puzzled and told me she hadn't noticed. But now that she knew how to get comfortable, she felt she was ready to get down to figuring out what was underneath all those feelings she had been having before I made my suggestion.

*"Any time that is not spent on love is wasted."*

*–Tasso*

## Getting Unstuck By Widening Your Mind

*The next time you get stuck with a particular person, or think about an issue that habitually slams you right into a wall, or try unsuccessfully to make a decision, or find yourself in the middle of a "hamster wheel" argument with someone:*

*Expand your periphery. Get wide. Use your breath to inhale through your ears, eyes and skin, and exhale curiosity five times. Notice the effect.*

## The Languages We Think With

When I was training in psychotherapy and observed people in a hypnotic trance, I noticed that as they shifted from one state of consciousness to another, the language they used to describe their imagery also shifted. Hank, for instance began one session quite alert as he described the words of a fight he had with his wife: "And then she said I was cold and indifferent. And then I said she was an inarticulate fool. And then she said . . ."

As he became more comfortable, shifting to a more internal, wider state of mind to ponder what he really wanted, his words slowed down, and he began to speak of visions he had: "I . . . uh . . . don't see clearly how I could make this happen; but I need a new perspective . . . so I can show her I care . . . and . . ."

After awhile, I told him some stories, suggesting he could float into a free period of learning, unencumbered by limitations of any kind. He then shifted to an expanded state—his eyes closed, his breathing deep and steady, floating in the ocean of his unconscious mind. When I asked him what resources he had that would be of assistance, his words were very slow, dream-like and referencing his feelings and kinesthetic imagery: "I'm beginning to feel waves of steady warmth . . . in . . . my belly . . . as if I could feel . . . all the memories of loving moments we ever shared . . . like a spring . . . filling my heart . . ."

Years of exploration led me to realize that as thought moves through the conscious, subconscious and unconscious mind, it also changes form. I think of how a melting ice cube starts solid, becomes liquid, and then evaporates into a gas. Like an ice cube, as an experience is being processed by the mind, it goes from one of three basic symbolic forms to another. In Hank's case, from Auditory (words and sounds), to Visual (pictures and colors) to

*"It appears that even the different parts of the same person do not converse among themselves, do not succeed in learning from each other what are their desires and intentions."*

–Rebecca West

127

Kinesthetic (feelings, actions and experiences.): A-V-K.

Experimenting with this, I realized I could influence Hank's state of consciousness by presenting information in one form or another. If I drew with him, for example, he would quiet down and be in two-way thinking, being present both with me and with himself. However, when I suggested kinesthetic activities, working with clay or playing a drum, Hank became speechless and enraptured, almost losing contact with the outer world altogether. There was only the clay or the drum and his inner world. The ice cube had transformed into a puddle and then vaporized. When we went back to a discussion, Hank would become very animated again, logical and alert, highly aware of the effect his words were having on me and my responses to them, signaling the return of the solid ice cube.

At first, I assumed everyone would "vaporize" if I did something kinesthetic with them, and that they would remain solidly logical if we talked. But Mindy, whose session happened to follow Hanks', became very alert and conscious when we sculpted (K). When I engaged her in conversation about her problem (A), magically her mind turned to liquid. She slowed down, became more receptive, began to tell stories, use metaphors, and talk on both sides of her issue—all indications she was entering her subconscious mind. And when I asked her to draw (V), she went over the edge into the trance state so indicative of unconscious thinking: her pupils dilated and her facial muscles flattened; she was sitting next to me but was, in fact, a thousand miles away in the world she was drawing. A totally different pattern of response (K-A-V) from the one triggered for Hank.

Thirty years and thousands of people later, I have come to understand that for each of us, each of the three states of consciousness is linked with one of three perceptual channels: Visual, Auditory, or Kinesthetic. Conscious thought is triggered by one kind of input, subconscious by

*"To generate thought is to create life, liveliness, community. What's important is how the generative power of our thought makes our life vivid and burns out the dead brush, dead habits, dead institutions."*

–James Hillman

another, and unconscious by the third. For example, when some people look at the visual symbols in a book, they "space out" into their unconscious mind, while others become quite alert with the printed word. Some people are confused into their subconscious mind by hearing many spoken words while others are triggered into being consciously energized.

It seems that at some point in our neurological development, the brain selects one of six different patterns to sequence the channels, so that it can integrate experience efficiently. I call these habitual sequences each of us use personal thinking patterns.

*"Thought and analysis are powerless to pierce the great mystery that hovers over the world and over our existence, but knowledge of the great truths only appears in action and labour."*

*–Albert Schweitzer*

| CONSCIOUS | SUBCONSCIOUS | UNCONSCIOUS |
|-----------|--------------|-------------|
| V | A | K |
| V | K | A |
| A | V | K |
| A | K | V |
| K | A | V |
| K | V | A |

Many of the differences between us that we believe to be personality traits are actually a result of the different operational characteristics of these patterns.

## The Six Personal Thinking Patterns

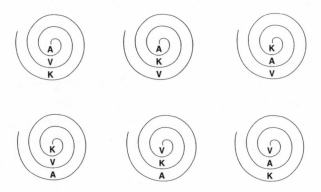

## Implications For Healing

*"Conflicts of a marriage are the crucible of the spirit."*

*–Sam Keen*

I have found the implications of this very simple discovery for healing to be very profound. For example, Hank had been in verbal analysis (A) for seven years, and could understand all of his issues very logically. He found his sessions stimulating and interesting; however, they did not help him change his life, or understand what he was feeling (K). He still flew into temper tantrums that would not be controlled by his logical, auditory mind. Since his analyst had only observed Hank in his conscious mode, he assumed Hank's wife's reports of raging battles were all due to her over-active imagination.

After completing analysis, Hank heard someone lecture about the power of affirmations, and he spent a year mumbling in the mirror as he shaved, "I am a loving and kind man. I can control my temper with ease." Even so, over and over again, he would fall into a verbal argument with his wife (A), begin to see movies flash by in his subconscious mind (V), and then go blind to his unconscious kinesthetic rage (K) as he threw things and became physically abusive. Hours later, he apologized profusely by explaining that "something just came over me," and then went off to recite more affirmations. The obvious problem was that it was not Hank's conscious auditory mind that needed support, but his feelings—which he couldn't get to with spoken words. He needed a visual bridge between his words and his feelings. So I had him draw how he felt.

In our sessions, Hank's drawings of the "something that came over him" were powerful and revealing. His hand, with a mind of its own, drew a balled up fist. When he looked at it, he began to see images of his father beating up his mother, and he remembered the terror he felt in his body as a child, and now as a man. He could then speak of these memories and what they triggered in him. Soon he took a large pad of paper and markers home, and when verbal arguments began to trigger his newly conscious feelings and needs, he turned to the pad and began to draw and write what was going on inside him. He was neither controlling nor being controlled by what was going on; rather, he was witnessing and responding to what he was feeling instead of blindly reacting to it. But what Hank needed to do to relate to his rage would not work for people with other patterns—and that's why formulaic therapies work for some people and not for others. If it happens to fit your pattern, it might work. If not, it won't.

Since we all assume that everyone else's mind works in the same way ours does, all forms of therapy and healing are based on the model of the world of the person who originated that form. For example, Fritz Perls, the founder of Gestalt psychotherapy, used auditory information consciously (A), kinesthetic information subconsciously (K), and visual information unconsciously (V). Thus, his primary method (A-K-V) was to ask someone to sit in a chair and talk about their feelings to an imaginary person in another chair. Sometimes he would ask the person to pound on pillows or scream, so their words and feelings were congruent. There was no visual "reality," just invisible imagined people sitting in chairs or laying on pillows. If a person could not scream his or her feelings or discharge them with a tennis racket on a pillow, Perls assumed he or she was repressed or resistant.

A famous dance therapist I worked with would not engage in words until the second half of the session. She had each person walk into her studio, and describe with his or her body what was going on for them (K). Then they discussed what had been experienced (A), and ended their sessions by looking in the mirror and stating learnings or drawing them on large pieces of paper (V). Her preferred method was, therefore, to follow the K-A-V pattern. Anyone who wanted to be shown what to do or talk before

*"The crisis is in our consciousness, not in the world."*

*–J. Krishnamurti*

131

*"And this is the simple truth–that to live is to feel oneself lost. He who accepts it has already begin to find himself to be on firm ground."*

–Jose Ortega y Gasset

moving–such as me with a V-A-K pattern–was considered to be avoiding the real issue.

I usually went from these sessions to my doctor's office. He'd smile, quietly look me over, write down whatever I told him (V), and then do a physical examination (K). When we were finished, he'd tell me what he found, but his statements were quite circular, more like musings or questions (A). His V-K-A pattern caused him to get scrambled and frustrated when I wanted verbal explanations *before* the physical examination.

Because most healers do not understand mind patterns, they rarely consider that although a method may work perfectly for them, it might be completely incorrect for a person with a different pattern. Mindy, for example, was struggling to heal from breast cancer. She came to me because her oncologist had suggested she visualize the cancer cells being overwhelmed by her chemotherapy treatment. The problem she was having was that she "could not" visualize. She was convinced she wasn't "an imaginative sort of person," but she wanted desperately to get well and believed visualization could help her. Can you guess why she was having so much difficulty visualizing?

Mindy's pattern was K-A-V. Her conscious mind's attempt to be aware of the unconscious part was a bit like a hand trying to scratch an itch on the back of itself, or looking this way and that for your own head. When she attempted to make pictures in her mind, she instantly blanked out, triggered into an unconscious trance state. "The same thing happens when I try to read a book, you know," she explained to me, blinking rapidly and looking down. As with most people whose minds worked as her's did, prolonged eye contact was extremely difficult, leaving her feeling disoriented and vulnerable. "I get as far as the first paragraph and then it reminds me of something that happened to me. The next thing I know, I'm sound asleep or gone off into the ozone."

Mindy was in a lethal double bind: she was told her imagination could save her life, and yet she believed she was not imaginative. As we talked, I asked her what would happen if her cancer recurred. She told me a long and desperate story about the effect that it would have on her husband and family. When she was finished, I pointed out to her that she was quite creative, after all, for she had imagined that entire story. Mindy laughed and acknowledged that she did tell herself gruesome stories about the various feelings she experienced. "I never thought of that as my imagination. I mean, aren't you supposed to *see* images?"

I explained that "images" could in fact be "feelings" or stories, songs or rhythms, ideas of what to do or smells, an inner voice or pictures, or some combination thereof. In her case, it seemed that her visual channel generated her images, but she didn't start to become aware of them until they were in her subconscious mind in the form of stories she could hear.

Since Mindy, like most of us, was used to paying most of her attention to the outer world, we experimented with beginning in the channel that was most conscious and comfortable for her—kinesthetic—and working backward from there. She had no trouble using clay to model a detailed replica of her breast receiving, and benefitting from, treatment. She then felt what she had sculpted in her body and sang, "Be at rest, be at rest" to accompany those feelings, while dancing slowly around the room. As her voice became softer and softer, her movements stilled and she slipped into a comfortable meditative state for fifteen minutes. When she awakened she reported, "I don't remember visual images, but I feel very confident that my imagery will be effective. I can't explain how or why; I just know it in my cells."

Because of the way Mindy's mind works, it was most effective for her to use healing imagery by following the

*"I am accustomed to going at everything, even thinking, with the energy of my physical body. . . . My thoughts go out fueled by 'muscle' power. Watching, on the other hand, requires a different sort of alertness, a tonus more relaxed than muscle tone."*

*–Carla Needleman*

sequence of Kinesthetic (sculpture and movement), Auditory (song), and then, unconsciously Visual. This is a completely different sequence than that used by her oncologist. His brain dealt in exactly the opposite pattern (V-A-K), so his method was to visualize first, then talk or sing, and lastly, perhaps, do something or move.

Likewise, what worked for Fritz Perls (talk—feel—see: A-K-V) would not have worked for Sigmund Freud (whose brain, like Hanks', most likely followed the talk–see–feel pattern: A-V-K) even if they both lived in California in 1973!

Some people need to write or draw as their entry point and then walk or do something with their hands or body. Only then can they talk about it or create music in some form (see, feel, sound: V-K-A).

Lastly, we have people whose minds use the opposite sequence of Hank and Freud. They want it concrete, in hand or in body somehow as an entry place (K), and shift next to visual (V) by writing, drawing or sitting with their eyes open and visualizing. From here, their unconscious mind will shift into auditory (A) by making music or poetry, sounds or even words (K-V-A).

Each one of these patterns has different needs and multiple pathways to access intuition, imagery, and spiritual guidance. Without understanding this basic truth, we keep running into the same old assumption—that there is one right way and if it doesn't work for you, try harder. If it still doesn't work, you are resistant or lacking in sincerity, ability, or sensitivity.

I repeat, the right way is only right for the person who developed the method, and for anyone else whose mind uses that same pattern. Consider a prominent teacher of meditation who has a mind that follows the K-V-A pattern; his meditation method follows that pattern. He teaches people to sit or walk, noticing their breath (kinesthetic), and, with their eyes closed or unfocused, to visualize four images he gives them (visual), saying simple words with

*"God made everything out of nothing, but the nothingness shows through."*

*–Paul Valery*

each (auditory).

Another famous meditation teacher has a mind which visualizes first, then shifts to words and finally to feelings and actions (V-A-K). His approach has people sit for long periods of time, "watching" their thoughts arise, then has them name the thoughts or listen for inner stories, and finally feel the physical energy under the thoughts.

Anyone can learn a great deal about meditation from both of these fine teachers. But it may be more effective for some people to walk when they meditate, and it does not mean they are spiritually remedial if they cannot sit still for an hour. Others, understanding how their mind works, can release tension and find stillness with more ease if they name their thoughts verbally, because holding visual images might actually stimulate their conscious mind and make it quite difficult for it to settle. Still others are better off sitting rather than walking.

As these examples indicate, any vehicle can transport you to Topeka, but if you're trying to do it by pedaling on your roller skates, you're going to do the roller skates and your journey a great disservice! So if you're attempting to work with a spiritual or healing approach and find you are having difficulty, rather than assume you are resistant or spiritually deficient, consider your unique way of knowing as valid. Find a way to make the method fit you, instead of the other way around.

> "You spent the first half of your life becoming somebody. Now you can work on becoming nobody, which is really somebody. For when you become nobody there is no tension, no pretense, no one trying to be anyone or anything. The natural state of the mind shines through unobstructed–and the natural state of the mind is pure love."
>
> –Ram Dass

# The Treasure Hunt: Identifying Your Pattern By Following the Clues

So, how do you discover *your* mind's pattern? You'll find clues to your pattern in your everyday life, in what you love or hate to do, in what's important or frustrating, in what's been a life-long struggle. Did you hate gym class as a child? Do you need to see the big picture? Do you find it hard to stay awake while listening to a lecture? Can you walk and talk at the same time? What confuses you, what spaces you out or enlivens you, what makes it hard for you to concentrate are all signposts of how your mind processes data.

I love this information, because it's empowering. You'll begin to realize how easy it can be to take charge of the times you space out and those when you don't; the process is as simple as standing up and moving around, or closing your eyes and rocking back and forth. Old ghosts of self-doubt and discouragement can be replaced by new awareness and self-appreciation.

Here's an illustration: Patricia came to me during a break in one of our workshops. Her eyes darted around the room and then she blushed when she was about to speak. "I'm embarrassed to ask this, Dawna, but maybe you'll be able to explain something that happens when I meditate. It's kind of important, because I have high blood pressure and I need to learn to calm myself down." Her words were halting and I nodded encouragement.

*"I will take with me the emptiness of my hands. What you do not have you find everywhere."*

*–W.S. Merwin*

"I close my eyes and then, before I know it, my hands kind of float, and move in really weird ways. My meditation teacher suggested I fold them in this specific way called a . . . uh, I forget the word he used. But it doesn't matter; it doesn't help. As soon as I begin to relax and calm my mind, my hands take off like . . . uh, like birds with a mind of their own. Do you think I'm crazy?"

I reassured Patricia that she was not crazy, and asked her to sit and meditate so Andy and I could notice what happened. Sure enough, within three or four minutes, her hands began to float. A man nearby who was a yoga teacher leaned over and began to whisper a technical explanation. I hushed him up, all the while also hushing my own rational mind, which was whispering intellectual explanations drawn from my previous studies of hypnotherapy.

Instead, I just read her hands. Andy sat across from Patricia. When she opened her eyes to come back to a conscious state, I asked her to watch him as if she were looking through a window at a very wise person—a guru—who had answers to the questions which were most pressing for her. She began to rock back and forth as Andy's hands made the same movements as hers did.

Tears began to slide silently down her cheeks, and when she was finished, she wrapped her arms around herself and nodded. I asked her to share what she had learned. Without hesitation she replied, "I needed to remember about grace and harmony. I don't want to explain what that means, but I know. Oh how I know. I'm amazed that all this time my hands, which I thought were signs of my craziness, were really trying to give me the sacred message that I was searching for."

Recognizing that Patricia's mind used the see-do-say sequence (V-K-A), helped me to support her in finding her own wisdom. Not understanding the way her mind worked had led her and others to assume the movements were an indication of something wrong or "just" a phenomena to be ignored. But people with this mind pattern often have kinesthetic images which may come in movement or "gut" feelings. By watching those movements mirrored back, her intuitive message could become consciously available to her.

It is worth noting that everyone's unconscious mind is highly receptive, which means that we have the least protective filtering there. Thus, we often feel naturally vulnerable, and are most easily violated in this channel.

I worked for a time in a prison. Many of the inmates had minds which used the visual channel unconsciously. (I suspect that these patterns suffer the most from our visually detailed and demanding educational system.) They were "eye shy," naturally needing to avoid prolonged eye

*"As long as you are trying to be something other than what you actually are, your mind wears itself out."*

*–Krishnamurti*

contact—not because they were "shifty," but rather because their unconscious minds could take in with one glance what others received by staring for long periods of time.

I noticed that a lot of hostilities began for these particular prisoners when people were "in their face," violating their need for visual space, and causing their brain to—as one man put it—"fritz, go haywire, short circuit."

In a similar way, people whose unconscious minds use the auditory channel are highly sensitive to tone of voice, and remember sarcasm and nasty words for years. When they are with someone or in a situation where they are flooded with words, their brains seem to go on overload. People whose unconscious minds use the kinesthetic channel may "get the creeps" when they are touched casually. They may remember rough or probing physical contact for years, and often sense what everyone around them is feeling without being aware of it.

One of the most significant and important aspects of understanding how your mind processes information comes with the realization that the state of consciousness which is most difficult to access, *your unconscious mind, is the source of your personal creativity.* What you may experience as the most "private" channel, the most frustrating, the least "brilliant" and competitive is, in fact, the storehouse for all you have ever experienced. It is the generating station for your wisdom and guidance, and the ultimate navigator of your life's path.

Thus, people whose unconscious minds use the auditory channel may be anxious about speaking to groups of people or remembering the name of someone they met in the parking lot, but they can delight in their ability to listen deeply and hear multiple harmonies, perhaps speaking the unspoken essential truth in a large meeting. People like Hank, whose unconscious minds use the kinesthetic channel may be frustrated by all of the accidents they get into

*"We need to recall the angel aspect of the word, recognizing words as independent carriers of soul between people. . . . Words, like angels are powers which have invisible power over us."*

–James Hillman

or sports equipment they break, or by how shy they are about being touched casually. On the other hand, their feelings run deep and true; their touch can be exquisitely sensitive, and what they experience can be sacred to them. Those like Mindy, whose unconscious minds use the visual channel, may be disheartened by how long it takes them to read a book or write a letter; but their global vision, that ability to see the very big picture, can inspire, induce and intrigue the rest of us as surely as the first photos of the earth did taken from a spacecraft.

*"It's hard to face that open space."*

*–Neil Young*

## Investigating Your Mind's Path

I've been sharing a lot with you about other people and how their minds work. Now, let's explore this natural choreography of your different states of consciousness from the inside out. We're not searching for your pattern, just being curious to notice whatever you can about what helps you refine, define and organize your thinking, sort out possibilities, and generate images.

*To discover what triggers different states of consciousness for you, begin by noticing connections. For instance, if you amble on a walk to no place in particular, or give yourself a foot rub, how is your mind affected? Does it expand or contract? How does kinesthetic input affect your state of consciousness?*

*Now, I'd like to invite you to play some unfamiliar music— whatever you'd consider your favorite type, but new to you. Notice how listening affects your state of mind? What happens when you listen to the radio or to a lecture? How does this auditory input affect you?*

*Lastly, visual input. When you read, or watch a movie, or wander around in a museum or a store where you aren't looking for anything in particular—just glancing around—what happens to the circumference of your mind? Does it expand or contract?*

As an example, my pattern is V-A-K, so visual input such as reading or window shopping brings me alert and focused in a pleasant way. It narrows my mind down to one thing, which can be a relief. My husband Andy (K-A-V), however, is asleep at the title page. When the book falls on his face and he awakens, he's usually got an idea about how to do something or an insight about a problem he was struggling with—which has nothing to do with the book, but everything to do with floating in his unconscious mind for awhile, where ideas are generated.

In Andy's and my common middle channel, auditory soothes and relaxes. Listening to music helps me drift back to an awareness of what I'm feeling or how I'd like to move and what I'd like to do. Andy finds listening to music helps him stop "doing" and start being, drifting in and out of visions and drive-in movies that dissolve like dreams.

Kinesthetic input has exactly the opposite effect on me than it does on Andy. If he's getting a massage, which he loves, he becomes pleasantly alert and quite detailed and logical about which muscle is releasing where. A walk or ten-mile bike ride (which is an amble for Andy) refreshes him and helps him to organize his thoughts. I, on the other hand, travel throughout the galaxy when I'm receiving a massage. And my mind starts generating one idea after another, in no particular order, when I amble (which would probably be up and down the driveway). Those ideas come in the form of auditory words or quick visual flashes, but it is the walking or the massage or dancing which gets them going. And speaking of dancing . . . When I do it, particularly if I am alone, it becomes a sacred experience. Fragments of feelings, unremembered aspects of myself, disconnections of any sort in my heart or soul begin to bond, fuse, connect. My brain automatically shifts into poetry, whereas prose comes much more readily after I've walked.

The chart that follows summarizes the differing charac-

*"I never knew how to worship until I knew how to love."*

*–Harriet Ward Beecher*

teristics of people whose states of consciousness are triggered by various perceptual input.

Now is the time to say that charts help some people learn; but they just confuse others, because they see themselves in everything they read. If they confuse you, that may indicate that your subconscious mind is being triggered. Or maybe you only like charts that have very few words in them, preferring visual symbols. This may indicate that your unconscious mind is triggered by visual input. If you love the chart that follows, if it clarifies everything for you, then perhaps like me, your conscious mind is triggered by visual input. If you're still not sure how your mind works, there is an inventory in the Appendix which may be of use in identifying your pattern. You can also find more detailed information on personal thinking patterns in my two previous books, *The Art Of the Possible: A Compassionate Approach to Understanding How People Think, Learn, and Communicate*, and *How Your Child Is Smart: A Life-Changing Approach to Learning.*

"The reasonable man adapts himself to the world; the unreasonable one persists in trying to adapt the world to himself. Therefore all progress depends on the unreasonable man."

–George Bernard Shaw

# Triggers to States of Consciousness

| If Kinesthetic Activity Triggers: | If Auditory Activity Triggers: | If Visual Activity Triggers: |
| --- | --- | --- |
| **CONSCIOUS MIND** *Alert* <br><br> • learns most easily by doing <br> • immediate access of physical sensations <br> • does things logically <br> • movement is strong, direct <br> • jiggles, constantly in motion <br> • touch energizes, brings alert <br> • touch is casual, natural <br> • organizes in piles | **CONSCIOUS MIND** *Alert* <br><br> • learns most easily by discussing <br> • immediate access of names, what was said <br> • says things logically, no hesitation <br> • describes abstract ideas with complex language <br> • constant and intense talking <br> • speaking energizes, brings alert <br> • verbal contact is casual, natural <br> • organizes by talking about what needs to be done | **CONSCIOUS MIND** *Alert* <br><br> • learns most easily by reading, watching <br> • immediate access of the way things look <br> • writes things logically <br> • shows and illustrates ideas <br> • constant and intense eye contact <br> • writing energizes, brings alert <br> • eye contact is casual, natural <br> • organizes in lists |
| **SUBCONSCIOUS MIND** *Confused* <br><br> • movement helps to sort thoughts <br> • feels pent-up energy frequently <br> • feelings right beneath the surface <br> • often pulled in two directions <br> • hand gestures accompany words <br> • feels what they see or hear <br> • touch/movement is bridge between inner and outer worlds | **SUBCONSCIOUS MIND** *Confused* <br><br> • talking helps to sort thoughts <br> • hears both sides of a story <br> • metaphors right beneath the surface <br> • can hear inner voice while listening to words on the outside <br> • may hesitate slightly to find words <br> • can hear the whole and details in a conversation <br> • words are the bridge between inner and outer worlds | **SUBCONSCIOUS MIND** *Confused* <br><br> • writing/drawing helps to sort thoughts <br> • sees things from two directions <br> • visions right beneath the surface <br> • can see visions with eyes open or closed <br> • has to look to side to find words <br> • can see whole and details <br> • vision is bridge between inner and outer worlds |
| **UNCONSCIOUS MIND** *Entranced* <br><br> • feels the whole of something <br> • doesn't like to do things in same way repeatedly <br> • needs verbal or visual instructions to learn to do new things <br> • needs to close eyes to access body sensations <br> • feelings can be overwhelming <br> • very sensitive and shy to touch <br> • touch entrances <br> • movement generates images <br> • does things non-linearly, creatively | **UNCONSCIOUS MIND** *Entranced* <br><br> • hears the whole of something <br> • doesn't like to speak in detailed way to groups of people <br> • may forget names, initials, words may take a long time to access <br> • hates to have words filled in by others <br> • words may be overwhelming <br> • can hear harmonies internally <br> • sensitive to tone of voice <br> • auditory input entrances <br> • sounds generate ideas <br> • hears things creatively | **UNCONSCIOUS MIND** *Entranced* <br><br> • sees the whole of something <br> • doesn't like to write detailed things in same way repeatedly <br> • shy and sensitive to prolonged eye contact <br> • visual stimulation can be overwhelming <br> • visual input entrances <br> • visions generate ideas <br> • sees things creatively |

As you continue through this book, and through your everyday experiences, I'd like to invite you to continue your investigations. What helps you generate images? What helps you sort out possibilities? What helps you express and refine your thinking? You may begin to notice that when anyone talks to you for more than just a few minutes, you shift into your unconscious mind. Now that no longer means you're just rude and inattentive, but rather that your unconscious mind gets triggered by auditory input! Similarly, if you discover that every time you are touched casually by an acquaintance you want to crawl out of your skin, remember that no longer indicates that you're uptight and insensitive. Rather you can suspect that your unconscious mind is being triggered by kinesthetic input. And if you find your eyes darting all over the place when reading, well, you can forget the idea that you've got a short attention span. Rather you can guess that your unconscious mind uses the visual channel to daydream and create visions wide enough to get lost in!

You may discover that you don't need to change your mind after all. Just notice how it changes already, particularly as you turn inward to find your own wisdom.

*"A journalist cannot accept 'No Trespassing' signs on his curiosity. We're beachcombers on the shores of other people's experience and knowledge. We roam the world picking up interesting pieces of driftwood, debris and sometimes treasure."*

*–Bill Moyers*

# 7 Living Between the Answers:

Turning Inward To Learn

*"There is no reality except the one contained within us; that is why so many people live such an unreal life. They take the images outside them for reality and never allow the world within to assert itself."*

–Herman Hesse

Your intuition is a pipeline to your heart and inner resources—the feelings, memories, abilities, and wisdom that flow through your deepest self. It can shepherd you, lead you, as if you were a mountain goat moving through a dark forest. It can guide you through the difficult emotions you will encounter on your journey to reclaim yourself. It can inspire you, validate you, and help you trade addiction and abuse for a pen, a paintbrush and a keyboard. It can take you to the place in you that is deeper than fear. Most important of all, I think, it can help you trust yourself wholly.

*"The seat of the soul is there, where the outer and the inner worlds meet."*

*–Novalis*

Accessing your intuition means becoming more comfortable in the realm of your imagination. Like Wonderland, this terrain is enlivening, energizing, surprising, full of possibilities, spontaneous, and anything but dull. It is Behind the Beyond—a wild territory where nothing grows in straight lines. It is an integration field, where there is room enough for things that seem to be in direct opposition to each other to co-exist in harmony. It is the place between answers. It is the place where you can live your questions.

But traveling here is a bit like being in a foreign country. Everything is strange, unknown and unpredictable. Nothing is habitual or controllable. In the last chapter, you found a map that guides you to this state of mind. You now know about the different continents of consciousness, and the unique languages that are spoken in each. But now that you've fallen through the rabbit hole, what do you do once you're there? How do you access your intuition for healing? How do you shift into symbolic thinking?

*"Jesus was all virtue and acted from impulse not rules."*

*–William Blake*

Although you cannot control things here, you can be in charge of how you travel through. And that's what this chapter is all about. In the pages that follow, you will find pathways that will guide you inward toward your own intuition. You will be exploring how to inquire of it, receive guidance from it, and advocate for its support in creating wholeness with your enemy.

This chapter will be interactive. There are no chauffeured rides across this part of the journey. No sitting back and letting it all happen to you. Not now. Healing suggests participation and we need you to sift your way through your own experiences.

*"Sometimes I go about in pity for myself and all the while a great wind is carrying me across the sky."*

*–Ojibway*

## Wandering In Wonderland: Turning Inward

Milton Erickson said that a powerful mind is one that can take its learnings from one situation and transfer them to another. This opens a free flow of interchange between your experiences, so that lessons learned on the tennis court or in the delivery room are readily available and transferable to the board room or kitchen. This kind of power enables you to transfer the easy feeling of tumbling on the floor with your child, to tumbling through challenges at work.

Thus, before you take in any more information from the outside about accessing intuition and learning through imagery, I'd like to invite you to notice what you already know—and to *use the power of your mind to transfer it to your own healing.*

The word "intuition" comes from the same root as the word "contemplate." It means sensing without the use of rational processes. In one way or another, you've been following your intuition since you were born. You may have become disconnected from it; you may have ignored it, betrayed it or invalidated it, but there is a footpath in your mind that has led you there again and again. Let's meander back on that route for a start and clear away the brush:

*"First I stand still and try to get my mind to quiet down. To do that I usually start by listening intently to the sounds around me. That prevents me from thinking about a past memory or what I'm doing this afternoon. "*

*–Stephen Nachmanovitch*

*Please think of a time when you turned inward in some way and paid attention to your intuition. Make it as real as you can.*

*What do you become aware of as you think about that time? How did you turn in? What actions did you take? What did you say or see that helped you to take the actions?*

*How did you recognize your intuition? Was it kinesthetic, visual or auditory? Or was it a combination? What was the quality of the images you received? Were they songs, sounds in your body, moving pictures, black and white still shots, sensations of motion, feelings in one part of your body, etc? Notice in as much detail as you can what it was about that way of thinking that identified it to you as "intuition."*

*Now bring to mind another time when you know that you definitely ignored your intuition or were thinking in a way you would describe as the opposite of intuitive. As before, notice the quality of how you were thinking in that situation. You may want to shift back and forth from counter-intuitive to intuitive a few times until you can clearly identify the characteristics of your own intuitive thinking, and what you need to do to "tune in" to it.*

You might want to jot down, tape, talk to someone about or just go for a walk with what you've just learned, as a way of transferring what has worked for you in the past in accessing your intuition to this current healing work you are doing.

I once worked with a man who was highly successful as an expert consultant helping states get rid of toxic waste. When I asked him how he knew what to advise these people, he said blithely, "Well, I just seem to know intuitively. I've got a lot of experience, and somehow the right thing to tell them just comes to me when I need it. I've learned to trust my gut."

His expertise ended at the doorway to his own home, however. He told me how he had gone from one failed

> "Anyone who has insight into his own actions and has thus found access to the unconscious, involuntarily exercises an influence on his environment."
>
> –Carl Jung

149

relationship to another, always picking partners "who dump all over me and contaminate my whole life with their shit." My jaw dropped open as I listened, waiting for him to make the connection between his use of intuitive skills at work and his needs at home; but they were in different compartments, isolated from each other as if separated by a lead shield.

I finally asked him if he realized that he could apply what he was teaching others about getting rid of the toxic waste to getting rid of the "stuff" that was poisoning his state of mind and heart. He looked at me for a very wide moment, and then started to laugh. "I never thought of that. I never heard the parallel before. How amazing! How stupid! How deaf!"

After reassuring him that he was neither stupid nor deaf—just caught like any other human in the abyss between resources and needs—I asked him a lot of questions such as the ones you just answered. I asked him about the different ways of thinking he used at work and in his relationships.

His path to intuition involved restating out loud the words he heard his clients ask (A)—then staring into space, seeing full color moving images fill his head (V)—finally stepping into the images and describing them from that vantage point to his clients, doing what he suggested (K). With lovers, however, his path to "counter-intuition" involved being silent, while trying to make black and white still pictures behind his eyes of what they were saying (V). That action caused him to hold his breath a lot and feel as if he were shrinking and being controlled (K).

It didn't take much for him to dissolve those compartments. He imagined what it would be like with a partner— to listen to her words *and then restate them out loud*, staring into space until there was a full color moving image to step into, and speaking from *that* place. It was hard for him to believe at first that he had this option to change how

"How many times have you connected with yourself at all in your whole life?"

—Chogyam Trungpa Rimpoche

he was thinking, but as he practiced it several times, his amazement at the difference in how he felt grew beyond any doubt. Subsequent check-ins in the months that ensued revealed that he was using the new way of thinking with ease and comfort, and that he was delighted at the unleashed power of his mind.

A woman whose mind used the A-K-V pattern was shown (V) articles about the form of cancer she was manifesting, then told (A) by her doctor that the only thing she could do was to have a very invasive treatment of chemotherapy. She couldn't decide what to do. When she explored other times that she had consulted her intuition successfully, she discovered she had talked it over with someone (A) until she knew what she felt about it (K) and then a "movie" would pop in her mind (V) of her following that feeling.

On the other hand, the times she had been filled with resentment or regret after a decision was when someone had painted a picture for her in words, or given her a vision of the perspective (V) she should have, then talked (A) to her about what action she should take (K).

Armed with this awareness, she went to her support group and talked for a half hour about her feelings regarding the treatment. When she was done, people were silent at first. Then they gave her feedback about the tone in her voice and how they sensed her energy. She told them that when she thought about a treatment of surgery and radiation, her chest opened and she could see many possibilities for follow through. What became obvious to her was that she needed to be completely supportive of whatever treatment she chose and that surgery/radiation was the only one she could support wholeheartedly.

*"Only one feat is possible, not to have run away."*

*–Dag Hammarskjold*

## A New Intuitive Path: 5-4-3-2-1

Since you now have your own experience as a compass, I'd like to share some more possibilities with you. The practice that follows is an almost instant way to get in touch with your intuitive mind. It's delightfully simple and produces mindfulness as well as an expanded state of consciousness for any pattern. I'm told Betty Erickson, Milton's wife, originated it.

*You begin by choosing the perceptual channel that you are most aware of in that moment and naming five things you perceive in it, i.e., "I'm seeing the white letters move across the screen. I'm seeing the stars through my window."; or "I'm hearing the door squeak as it's opened. I'm hearing the cat purr on my foot."; or "I'm feeling my feet on the carpet. I'm feeling a gurgling in my stomach." Just as simple as you can get. No comparisons, no judgments, no interpretations.*

*Shift to another channel and name five things. Then to the last channel and name five things. You don't have to choose these in your perceptual pattern, if you don't know it. This will be effective no matter what progression you use.*

*Next, do the same thing, except with four awarenesses in each channel. Then three in each; then two in each; and finally, one in each. You'll be into your intuitive cocoon in a lovely way.*

"The only way out is through."

–Goethe

## Guidelines For Intuitive Inquiry

The charts that follow are the result of countless "mindtrackings" I've done with people who used imagery for healing. As they turned inward to inquire intuitively of themselves, I asked them questions that were designed to increase their awareness of the natural choreography of their thoughts.

It is not necessary to know your perceptual pattern to

use these charts. You may just be aware of your uncon-scious mind's channel for now. Fine. Go to that page and play with what you find there. Then use the other pages to experiment with—noticing how your state of mind is af-fected by the different channels.

Although these charts start with the conscious mind, expanding outward from there, altering your state of consciousness depends on where you are when *you* start. As an example, let's say your mind uses the visual channel consciously, auditory subconsciously and kinesthetic un-consciously (V-A-K). Let's assume you've been spending the afternoon on the telephone, talking. It might be most effective for you to shift directly to the kinesthetic channel, by going for a slow, meandering walk first to find and ask your question. Then take a long bath and, finally, sit still so you can notice the whole of what you're feeling, giving your intuition a chance to respond to you. Remember, movement through your mind is cyclical. Your conscious-ness spirals. So where you begin depends on where you are and where you need to go.

Please, do not use these as you would directions to a paint-by-the-numbers kit. Not everyone with the same pattern is interested in the same things. Because of mis-education and woundings, most of us have short-circuits and short-cuts, by-passes and favorite by-ways that we take as we shift into symbolic thinking. Remember the spirit of Thomas Alva Edison who, when asked how many failures he had in inventing the light bulb said, "None. I discovered 99 ways not to make a light bulb, and one way to make one." Play around until you catch the drift, see the pattern, understand the logic. Above all, replace criticism with curiosity. Avoid paralysis by analysis, disabling by labeling. Just have fun wandering and wondering.

*"Learning is the very essence of humility, learning from every-thing and from every-body. There is no hierarchy in learning."*

*–Krishnamurti*

# Turning In

| | Auditory | Visual | Kinesthetic |
|---|---|---|---|
| **Conscious Mind**<br><br>*General Guidelines:*<br>Evoke curiosity, slow thoughts, direct attention | Tell someone or talk into tape recorder about the question that is important to you, so you can hear yourself say it. Avoid trying to answer it.<br><br>Stop talking. Listen to sounds around you or music you love until your thoughts slow.<br><br>Ask yourself the question internally in a tone of voice that is intriguing and curious. | Doodle or write the question that is important to you.<br><br>Stare into space, at a blank page or fixate your gaze on something external that is interesting to you to slow your thoughts.<br><br>Close your eyes and notice any visual images that are attached to your question. | While doing something that requires no thought, pace or move in a way that helps you get a grasp of your question.<br><br>Give yourself a lot of space away from people and notice your rhythm.<br><br>Still yourself as you notice what you're feeling in your body and your breath to slow your mind. |
| **Subconscious Mind**<br><br>*General Guidelines:*<br>Intensify attention inward | Listen around you while asking the question internally in a curious tone of voice.<br><br>Give yourself permission to take as much time as it takes.<br><br>Listen to spaces *between* thoughts.<br><br>Remember a time you trusted yourself. | Allow your eyes go to wherever they want.<br><br>Let their movement slow until you are staring at one thing. Close them and go blank.<br><br>See your question in your mind's eye.<br><br>Remember a time you trusted yourself.<br><br>Notice your breath as you move, pace, walk. | Notice your body sensations and energy without attaching meaning to them.<br><br>Come into stillness and get a felt sense of your question.<br><br>Remember a time you trusted yourself. |
| **Unconscious Mind**<br><br>*General Guidelines:*<br>Become the question, explore connections | Listen deeply with wonder, in silence.<br><br>Sing/chant the question repeatedly or ask it while standing in front of a mirror or in nature, using wondering tone.<br><br>Listen to your breath and everything in your mind, including the silences. | Let eyes go to a favorite view or picture or object.<br><br>With eyes closed, see as if you were inside of the question.<br><br>Allow your inner vision to be as wide as it can, to see the big picture. | Stop all doing and move slowly, rhythmically, or give yourself a foot rub, etc.<br><br>Notice the cycle of your breath many times, feeling the whole of your body.<br><br>Step into the question and feel its energy. |

## Getting Unstuck: A Few Basic Principles For In-searching

A most useful guideline in this process is to understand that the *human mind is rarely stuck in all three perceptual channels*. Thus, when one is blank, numb or calcified, go to another. If that one is stuck, shift to the third. For example, if you find yourself at a loss for words, make a picture in your mind of some place that represents what you want to say—or write it down first. If you need a new perspective, sense into your body and feel what it is you want there. If you're stuck trying to see the direction you want to go, take yourself for a walk to stimulate your kinesthetic channel, which may ignite your vision.

It's important to remember also that *it's not possible to be in the front and back channel at the same time*. Like dominoes, there has to be a direct connection. Thus, for someone whose mind has to hear it (A), see it (V) and feel it (K) to know what she is feeling and be able to talk about it, there needs to be some kind of visual channel bridge making that connection—perhaps writing it or taking photographs, sketching, etc. A person using the see/hear/feel pattern (V-A-K), on the other hand, must shut out visual input by closing their eyes, and have some auditory input to know what they are feeling. Questions help, or listening and moving to music, or verbalizing the sensations being experienced in different places in their bodies. Likewise, if someone whose brain uses the feel/hear/see (K-A-V) pattern wants to live out their deepest dreams and visions in the world, they need to talk about them to someone or translate them into song or sound.

When you say "Oh my God!" (or the equivalent in your vocabulary), *remember to wait for an answer*! That's often a point where people contract, making it impossible to get intuitive guidance. So use that favorite phrase as a re-

*"Go by the way of ignorance. That's the calling card of the unconscious. Let go of predicting and say, 'I don't know and I'm interested in finding out.'"*

–Milton Erickson

155

minder instead to breathe and expand, giving the guidance time and space to rise to the surface.

Another opportunity to expand comes when you forget something. This is especially for people whose unconscious mind uses the auditory channel, or for those of us whose minds are increasing the spaces between things as we age. *Each time you forget something, expand.* Not only can this help you remember, but what happens is you get a delightful moment of peace when your mind blanks out, shuts up, is still. I have noticed that even when I meditate regularly, my mind is never as empty as it is when I forget what I was going to say! The problem occurs when we respond to the emptiness by contracting, which makes it very uncomfortable. The choice is yours. If you're human, you will forget something, sometimes. Why not have each time be a little moment of peace?

Competing or performing from your unconscious channel is a crown and a cross. That state of consciousness is highly creative and collaborative, as well as private. Often, people push themselves to be first in line, at the top of the heap, the best, all of which are foreign concepts to this state of mind. Athletes, for example, whose unconscious mind uses the kinesthetic channel, are highly creative and can feel ecstatic in their sport; but if they try to compete aggressively, they may break equipment or parts of their body. One young man I know who played football because his father wanted him to do so was in the hospital with injuries fourteen times in one season! And a woman I worked with, whose unconscious mind used the auditory channel, developed nodes on her vocal chords when she forced herself to join a debating society.

Often, we give everything away and keep nothing for our own pleasure. I have worked with too many artists, musicians, dancers and artisans who are sharing from their unconscious mind and keep nothing for themselves. A pianist, whose unconscious mind used the kinesthetic

*"Being an artist means not numbering or counting, but ripening like a tree which doesn't force its sap and stands confidently in the storms of spring not afraid that summer may not come. It does come. It always comes."*

*–Rainer Maria Rilke*

channel, stopped playing for his own pleasure when he began giving concerts. Within two years, his music was for the public-at-large. Within three years, he had crippling arthritis and had to stop all concerts.

Similarly, an artist, whose unconscious mind used the visual channel, became quite successful, with shows in major galleries. His art had gone from creation to performance and he was painting what he knew would sell. Within a very short time, he developed eye inflammations, infections and, eventually, cataracts, unusual for someone so young.

The guideline here is that if you choose to share yourself or compete with the rest of the world from your unconscious channel, save some time and effort for your own pure personal pleasure and revelation. Ski for the goose bumps as well as the glory. Give one hour every day to singing for your audience of one. Write poetry that no one else will ever see.

Your unconscious mind has a logic all its own. Two contradictory realities which seem to your conscious and subconscious mind to be in opposition to each other and tearing you apart, can exist in harmony and comfort when you are in this state of consciousness. This is illustrated in experiments done by Ernest Hilgard in the 1950s, with people who were experiencing severe chronic pain. When they were in trance, functioning from their unconscious mind, they reported the pain was there, in one part or level of themselves; but they didn't notice it in the comfortable other part they were in when in trance. Thus, comfort and pain were no longer in opposition to each other in this state of mind.

This relational logic of the unconscious mind becomes relevant to us here because *if you are caught in an either/ or contradiction*, most likely you are being torn apart in a battle between the supreme allied commander and the dark enemy within. *Expand!* Go in. Go wide, to where there

*"The people I met experienced religion as a Great Perhaps and not as a doctrinal certainty, and it was their faith in the midst of the ambiguity that sustained them—and taught me."*

*—Bill Moyers*

*"It is the paradoxical secret of transformation itself, since it is in fact in and through the shadow that lead is transformed into gold."*

*–Carl Jung*

is room enough to recognize the relationship between them, and a middle third place where there is space enough for peace to occur. Turning toward your imagination is a way of making room in your mind to explore possibilities. By knowing how to go inward and move from confusion to wonder, we have entered the place of revelation—where we can discover what is bound up, what it needs, and how to extract the lessons from the bindings that hold us in and back.

Now, we can move one step closer to using our struggles as a pathway to wholeness—understanding imagery, the language of intuition.

# 8 Guidance From the Source:
## Establishing a Healing Dialogue With Your Intuition

*"The image is a midwife that allows inner experience to be birthed into conscious expression."*

–Matthew Fox

Chaos is creativity seeking a form. An image is that form. It is the "stuff" of intuition—the language spoken in the vast land of Wonder we've been exploring. The right symbol, image, or metaphor becomes a secret password with which you can bridge the ravines between body, mind and spirit. It can open the gates between hurt and healing, and unlock the doors between head and heart.

*"Wherever I go, I find a poet has been there before me."*

*–Sigmund Freud*

There are as many ways of using imagery as there are ways of being used *by* it. This chapter offers some introspective tools for working with imagery in all its forms. They will help you understand and recognize the responses that come from your intuition, as well as make suggestions for healing to your intuition.

As you may realize from the previous chapters, imagery is not just inner pictures, any more than English is the only language. A feeling of longing in your chest is an image. A poem that unfolds meaning in the chaos of your life is an image.

I'm using the terms "image," "symbol" and "metaphor" interchangeably. That would not be precise if we were being linear. But this is the territory where everything has multiple meanings.

As an example, what does the image of a wave say to you? When I ask this question to a hundred people, I get many different responses. Some people talk about cresting a wave; some talk about moving their hand in space to greet someone; others talk about permanent curl in one's hair. But if I told you that a wave of sadness came over me, you'd know in your deepest place what I had experienced, and you'd probably flash to a time when a wave of sadness came over you. This is the power of an image, symbol, or metaphor to have multiple meanings, and at the same time to connect and to create a relationship.

In Greek, metaphor means to transform energy. As we will see later in this chapter, imagery can be used as a tool for transforming the meaning of any given situation so it no

*"Consciousness is forever interfering, helping, correcting and negating and never leaving the simple growth of the psychic processes in peace. It would be a simple enough thing to do if only simplicity were not the most difficult of all things."*

*–Carl Jung*

longer has the power to block change.

Your images are influencing you every moment. In fact, you change your very body with the stories you tell yourself. To your unconscious mind, an image can have as potent an effect as a "real" event. Let's say you're going for a walk in Arizona on a hot summer's afternoon. You wander through a stretch of arid, barren desert. You're thinking about your plans for next Thursday, when suddenly you hear a sound—a hiss. Instantly, you interpret this random outer event by telling yourself a story about a rattlesnake that is directly ahead of you on the rocky trail. What happens to your biology? Your respiration increases immediately. Your heart rate and blood pressure go up. Simultaneously, your saliva production decreases markedly. You take one more step and a prairie dog rustles past the sagebrush in front of your boot. You breathe a sigh of relief and go on, relatively unaware of the powerful influence your imagery has just had on your biology.

The following exercise, which I learned from Ilana Rubenfeld, a pioneer in the field of psychophysical education, demonstrates the powerful effect imagery can have on your body:

*Standing, move your head as far to the right as it will go comfortably, noticing where you are staring when the movement stops.*

*Then come back to the center, and stretch your right arm overhead, hand bent back at the wrist and palm facing upward. Stretch so that you can feel it all the way down your right side. Lower your arm. Stretch your right leg, extending the toes as you bend at the ankle.*

*Come back to center and, without straining again, rotate your head to the right, measuring how far it goes comfortably this time. The chances are, because of the muscular stretching, it goes farther.*

*Now, rotate your head to the left and observe what you can see when you go as far as you comfortably can. Come back to center.*

*This time, without moving, vividly imagine (so you can feel them) doing the stretching movements with your left arm and leg. Without straining, measure how much you can actually now rotate your head to the left comfortably.*

Most people report that their heads also moved farther after this mental imagery, even though there was no "actual" stretching.

Imagery similar to this has been used by a wide variety of people—from professional athletes to public speakers to people recovering from surgery. I taught it to a man who had knee surgery on his right knee, after injuring it with a chain saw. His doctor said he would not walk again for a year. He did actual rehabilitation movements with his left leg and then, daily, vividly imagined those same movements on the right side. He was on crutches in six weeks, walking with a cane in three months and unassisted within five.

As far as I've been able to determine, not one medical school text mentions the power of an individual's imagery to raise and lower blood pressure, alter saliva production, or effect the body in any way! It is the intent of this chapter to increase your awareness of the options you do have to both guide and be guided by this inner source mind. From that, you'll find a whole new way to relate to your struggle.

> "[The image] is an important instrument for preventing the disorders that are known to be directly or indirectly induced or made worse by stress. To date virtually every disease under scrutiny has been associated with stress in some measure, including cardiovascular disease, arthritis, cancer, diabetes, the auto-immune disorders, cancer ad infinitum."
>
> –Jeanne Achterberg

## Imagine That! Exploring Your Images For All They're Worth

Everyone has images, even you. Since most people have been exiled from this territory, imagination has been barricaded behind lead-lined walls, with "Irrelevant" scrawled all over them. Those compartments are reinforced by cynicism and lack of trust. I don't believe we can

*"To end fragmenta-
tion, we don't need
to gain some special
knowledge, we need
less knowing about
how life should be
and more openness
to its mystery."*

*–Jack Kornfield*

*"First, it is impossible
that you have no
creative gift. Second,
the only way to make
it live and increase is
to use it. Third, you
cannot be sure that it
is not a great gift."*

*–Brenda Ueland*

ever get rid of them, but if we soften the walls with curiosity and trust, there can be leakage between the compartments. Wisdom is a permeable membrane between those compartments that enables us to cease dividing our life into isolated fragments. It enables us to create relationships between disparate elements that can inform each other—between work and play, between sacred and secular, between our bodies and our minds, between our problems and our resources, between our values and living those values with the people we love. Healing is a continual movement away from fragmentation, toward wholeness and connection.

Current knowledge and ancient wisdom supports the observation that attention directs action. What this means is that the more attention you pay to your imagery and intuition, be it in dreams or daydreams, the more readily available it will become to you. It is as if your brain is saying, "I thought you weren't particularly interested in this capacity since you were a child, but since you seem to be, let's reconnect the circuits." Once again, awareness heals!

When I was in graduate school, I worked at night monitoring meters in a laboratory that studied patterns of dreaming. Our main subjects were medical students. I'd watch these little needles swing back and forth each night indicating the occurrence of one dream after another. I'd listen each morning as the students insisted they hadn't dreamt all night. One of the young men who protested the most emphatically was a psychiatric resident. He swore on Sigmund Freud's whiskers that he did not dream. Midway through the year, he was required to enter Jungian analysis where the subject of every session was to be his dreams. Lo and behold, within two weeks, the medical student was remembering four to five dreams a night.

I'd like to give you a few handholds as you increase the awareness of your imagination from the inside out. We'll begin by identifying an image and then examining the perceptual quality of it.

*Play with me. I'm going to give you a really stupendous present. Right now. I'm about to step out of the pages of this book and join you for just a moment, so I can deliver it to you wherever you are. Move over a little.*

*Now, this is an outrageous gift. There's no way you could possibly deserve it. Or not deserve it. This is the kind of gift that someone who knows you really well just gives to you for no reason. All I'm going to tell you about it is that it's something that will be really helpful to you right about now. So after you read the next paragraph, please put down the book, get receptive, and put out your hands. OK?*

*Here it is.*

*You can hold it and heft it around for awhile, if you want. Do you like how it's wrapped? Do you hear the sound when you shake it? Do you want to guess what's in it? Open it whenever you'd like. Rip it open or unfold it very carefully. It's yours to do with as you please.*

*Fine. Now . . . What do you think about it? Do you like it? Will you ever use it? Tell me how.*

*Walk around with it and describe it to yourself while you hold it. Maybe you'd like to sit down and write out a description of this gift, or orally describe it into a tape recorder. If you have a really good friend, you could show them the gift and tell them about it. If they do not see it at first, don't worry. You just describe it as vividly as you know how.*

> "The Bible teaches that creation is going on all the time. Every time a flower blooms or a child is born or a movement is organized or a friendship is struck up, there is God creating, co-creating with us and with the rest of creation."
>
> –Matthew Fox

At the very least, this gift reveals to you that you do have an imagination, dusty and rusty though it may be. If, however, you couldn't find the gift I left for you, it does not mean you've had an imaginectomy. Merely that the compartment walls are thick enough to require a little more trust and patience on your part. You'll have many more opportunities.

Let's move on to explore the qualities of your imagery. You'll need to use the chart that follows, and the image of your gift, as a reference point. (If you still can't find where

I left it, then use the image that arose in your mind when you read about Milarepa and the demons at the beginning of this book.)

*Begin with the channel which is most apparent. Notice as many things about the quality of that particular aspect of the image as possible. For instance, my gift is an immense apple green plastic recycling box. I'm most aware of the visual aspects of it first. So I'll turn to that page first and scan the qualities, then go back to my box. It definitely is in color and translucent, without texture. It's like a photo, with letters on the box. I see it inside my forehead, as the little black letters are spilling on the screen, etc.*

*If you have no idea about a particular quality—the location of your auditory image, for example—that's fine. Just skip over it and go on. There's no way you can be wrong.*

*When you've explored one channel, overlap to another. If I go to auditory, for instance, and scan the chart to reference my image, there is only silence at first; but then I notice a voice in my head describing the box to me. It's my own voice, originating on the left side of my head, inside and over my ear, etc. Finally shift to the third chart and channel. Then notice the quality of combinations of channels.*

This psychic survey should only take a few minutes of clock time. The more curious you are, the richer the results will be. Just stay as open and avid as if you were exploring the mind of a new lover.

## Expanding Your Abilities

Each mind seems to have a range of qualities of imagery. For instance, my mind will not make a three dimensional visual image, no matter how long I practice. I don't consider this a limitation. As a matter of fact, it has become extraordinarily useful. Knowing the range of my own imagery helps me to identify when I am "picking up"

# Increasing Awareness of the Quality of Imagery

*(With appreciations to Peggy Tileston)*

| | **Visual** | **Auditory** | **Kinesthetic** |
|---|---|---|---|
| **Traits** | Are they in color, black and white, toned, bright, pastels, opaque, translucent, clear, fuzzy, cartooned, textured? Can you "see" words, letters? | What is the tone of voice? Pitch? Is it male or female? Does it sound like you or someone you know? Are they of different ages? | Do they have texture? Weight? Pressure? Temperature? Intensity (vagueness or obvious)? Moisture? Can you feel movement when you are actually still? |
| **Location** | Where is the image? Is it movable? Is it close or far? Foreground or background of your mind? | Where does it originate? How near or far? Does it stay in one place or move around? | Are they overall sensations? Are they specific to physical organs? Are there any places you never have "feelages"? Usually have them? |
| **Size** | How big is it? Is it wrap around? | Is it soft or loud or varying? | What size is it? What's the biggest it will go? The smallest? |
| **Speed** | Is the image moving or still? What is the range of speed? Can you increase or decrease it? | What is the tempo? What is the range of fast and slow? What is the rhythm? | Fast, slow or varying? |
| **Boundaries** | Is it bounded or bordered? If so what is it like? Can you find edges to it? | Are there silences? What are they like? Are there words, sounds, tones of voice or all? | Does it have a shape and external boundaries? Fixed or flexible? Thick or thin? Permeable or solid? |
| **Dimensions** | Is it two-dimensional, three-dimensional, like a hologram? | Is there music? Melodies? Lyrics? Harmonies? Are there more than one voice? Do they dialogue back and forth? | Is it three dimensional or one dimensional? Holographic? Are there more than one at once? |
| **Connection** | Are you in the image (associated) or observing another you in the image (disassociated)? If dissociated, from what perspective? Does it happen to you? Can you make it happen? | What pronouns does the voice(s) use, i.e. "You should. . ." (disconnected) or "I should. . ." (connected)? Does the voice narrate what is happening or speak as if it is in the image? Or both? Does it happen to you? Can you make it happen? | Is it inside of you? Outside? Does it happen to you? Can you make it happen? |
| **Flexibility** | How much choice do you have to change and vary these images? | How much choice do you have to change and vary these images? | How much choice do you have to change and vary these images? |

*"Whoever said we have only two beings wrestling within us underestimated the number by a consider-able amount."*

*–Goethe*

images from someone else. If I am working with someone and notice, as I expand my mind, that I am seeing three-dimensional images, which are beyond my normal range, I assume the images are coming from the other person. I check out the assumption with questions to determine if he or she makes three dimensional visual images. If the answer is yes, then I feel quite comfortable offering them up for further examination.

I don't consider this "extra-sensory abilities." I've trained hundreds of people to do it, and prefer to think of it as "expanded abilities," which is the Russian term. As so often happens, the more you know yourself and the workings of your own mind, the more confident you will be in the boundaries that separate you from others and, paradoxi-cally, the safer you will be to know others deeply.

Let's switch to a new image as a base line, and notice what you can do to expand its range:

*If you reach out an imaginary arm, you'll notice there is an entire bookshelf in front of you, with volumes of every size, shape and design. But one will indicate that it's "the one," exactly the book which I wrote just for you and you alone. Let it just fall into your hand.*

*Do you like the cover? That took me the longest to do. Flip through it at your own rhythm. Make sure you check out the last paragraph on page 28. It will tell you something you really need to know right now.*

*This is a book full of wisdom, but the very last line is particularly significant advice for dealing with your enemy. Don't worry about ruining the rest of the book by knowing how it'll all come out. You can read this last line and not ruin anything!*

*When you're ready, you can close the book and put it in your pocket or back on the shelf. If you'd like to write down or tell someone or audiotape what you discovered, please go ahead.*

I hope you like your present. I've found that even people who normally don't like to read, or children who can't read, can always enjoy the books on this shelf with total ease. Some kids have talked me into helping them make the books they find on "real" paper, so that they can dictate the words to me and read them over and over. I do it because I find most children's reading books much less interesting than these; but I think keeping them on this bookshelf is much neater and takes up less room.

Now that you have a new image, let's notice what expands it. After playing with each suggestion, notice the effect it has had on the image of your book:

**Breath:** *Take a few shallow breaths, then a few deep ones. How does each affect it?*
**Touch:** *Find a place on your body that would like to be touched and do that while noticing how that effects your image.*
**Rhythm:** *Explore a variety of rhythms as you drum on the floor or your chest and notice the effect.*
**Movement:** *Try a variety of different movements, swaying, walking, dancing, noticing the effect each time.*
**Taste and smell:** *How do each effect your image?*
**Humming:** *Try it out loud at first, then in your head. What effect?*
**Singing:** *Try it with words.*
**Talking:** *Speak to yourself, then out loud. Narrate what you are experiencing, including a description of your image. Notice the effect.*
**Listening:** *Open to the sounds around you, to music on a stereo.*
**Staring:** *With your eyes open, focus on something a short distance away. Notice the effect on your original book image.*

*"Last night I dreamed I was a butterfly. Today I wonder if I'm not a butterfly dreaming I am a man."*

*–Chuang Tzu*

# Receiving and Recognizing
# Intuitive Responses

*"As an improvising musician, I am not in the music business. I am not in the creativity business. I am in the surrender business."*

*–Stephen Nachmanovitch*

A few words of advice from your friendly advocate for battered intuitions. Remember that when you ask a question of your unconscious mind, it does not necessarily respond in words. It's rare that you ask, "What is this about?" and a voice responds "Let me explain it to you." (Unless your intuition has been psychoanalytically trained. Even then, be doubtful. You may be channeling the ghost of Sigmund Freud and he's had more than enough air time!) What's more likely is that you'll find yourself staring out the window, then snap back. What you find yourself thinking about is a movie with Robert DeNiro. You rummage around and remember it was called, "Raging Bull." Then, instead of discarding that, become curious about it. Perhaps your unmet need was to be able to scream and yell, "Bull Sh . . !"

You may just go blank. Then, minutes later, a song will pop into your mind. Or you may just notice that you have an impulse to do something different, or to try something new, such as walking or swimming or playing the banjo. You may have an urge to join a little theater group, or to write a screenplay for a movie. Depending on the pattern your mind uses to process information, your intuition may give you visual images, ideas of what to do, songs or feelings. Or you may just find yourself doing something in a different way than you ever have before.

These "random ideas coming out of nowhere"—these hunches—are, in fact, bubblings rising from your unconscious mind. It's not that most of us don't have intuitive, creative minds. It's just that we've been educated to ignore the messages that come from them as "meaningless" or arising from "absentmindedness." Remember, your conscious mind thinks in straight, ruler-like, ideas; your subconscious zig-zags and your unconscious wanders all over the place, thriving on chaos.

Betsy, a young woman I worked with whose mind uses the K-V-A pattern, describes the change that occurs for her when she uses writing to turn inward: "Normally, when I write, I just feel my fingers on the keys and look at them moving. Once in awhile, I glance at the words on the screen of my computer. They seem to come out in separate, tightly bound packages. But to get intuitive guidance, I've learned to use a slightly different approach. I notice my breath and I center. I don't look at my fingers on the keys; instead, I lose myself in the images I see in my mind with my eyes open, and I begin to hear the sounds of an inner voice. Later, when I look at the screen, there's a whole stream there, a seamless story. It's a completely different process. The first one is for communicating with everyone else. The second is for communicating with me."

Sheldon, whose mind uses the K-A-V pattern, came to a workshop because his wife made him. He was skeptical that his intuition ever gave him any guidance: "Once in a great while, an idea pops in my head, but it's about as trustworthy as a newspaper advice column!" I asked him to notice the sensations in his body for awhile, and then rhythmically ask himself a question that he really wanted guidance with—not an answer necessarily, but guidance.

He readjusted his shoulders, crossed his legs at the ankles, glanced sheepishly around the room and then closed his eyes. I suggested that he feel inside of what he was feeling, as deeply as he could, while he asked the question several times. "Then just surf on your breath for awhile and notice if any songs or stories come to mind." Within minutes, his bright blue eyes flew open. "How'd you do that?" he demanded of me.

"How'd I do what?" I had no idea what he was talking about.

"How'd you make that song just pop into my mind?" He was almost laughing, but his fingers were gripping the

> "Good ideas must come welling up into you. Wait for them. They come from the dreamy idleness of children."
>
> –Brenda Ueland

*"Once in a while it really hits people– they don't have to experience the world in the way they have been told to."*

*–Alan Kingsley*

edge of a blue cushion.

I laughed also, and in all honesty told him I had nothing to do with anything that popped in his mind. "Listen Sheldon. It's only been in the last ten years or so that I've been willing to admit I have anything to do with what pops in *my* head. What was the song, by the way?"

He cleared his throat and took a sip of water before answering. "It's a song we used to sing at Sunday school when I was a kid. The first line is, 'It's in everyone of us to be wise.' I can't remember the rest."

Mike and Sally, from the opposite corner of the room, began to sing spontaneously. "It's in everyone of us to be wise. Find your heart. Open up both your eyes. We can all know everything without ever knowing why."

We all exploded into applause and laughter. When it subsided, Sheldon shook his head and said, "That's amazing. I haven't thought of that song in twenty years. The question I asked was, 'How will I know what I need?' The truth is, songs come into my mind all the time. I just usually don't pay any attention to them. Do you?"

Instead of answering, the whole group sang another chorus of "It's in every one of us to be wise."

*"What we nurture in ourselves will grow; that is nature's eternal law."*

*–Anon.*

You can use what you have discovered about your unique imagery system to expand the scope of what you have previously called "hunches" or intuition. Hopefully, it will help you to stay open to *any* of the above kinds of images, rather than dismiss them as irrelevant. Hopefully, it will help you to respect the multi-dimensionality of your mind.

What follows is the gleaned collective wisdom of people from all of the patterns about how they recognize intuitive responses when they arise. Images are generated in the unconscious mind but, as with dreams, most people lose awareness of them almost immediately. That doesn't mean the image is "gone." It can be much more easily retrieved in the subconscious mind, and then brought forward to the conscious mind where it can be "understood."

## Receiving Intuitive Images, Recognizing Intuitive Messages

| Subconscious Channel: | Receives Image By: |
|---|---|
| Auditory | Hearing songs, music, stories |
| Visual | Seeing a vision, a new perspective |
| Kinesthetic | Feeling an energy shift, an idea of what to do, a desire to act |

| Conscious Channel: | Recognizes Message By: |
|---|---|
| Auditory | Talking to someone about it |
| Visual | Writing or drawing it (with non-dominant hand) or describing it as a visual metaphor |
| Kinesthetic | Experimenting through taking action, noticing the effect; moving toward something |

# How Different Perceptual Patterns Receive and Understand Intuitive Imagery

**V–A–K**  Feel yourself searching; notice songs, phrases or stories which may pop into your mind. Write that down, or draw it, to help you clarify the message.

**A–V–K**  Feel yourself searching; notice vision or flash of an idea, or a new perspective of something you could do. Talk to someone about it so you will understand how to integrate the message.

**V–K–A**  Notice feelings which you experience in your body after you ask the question, or desire to take a specific action, or to move in a particular direction. Put a pen in your non-dominant hand and transcribe those feelings onto paper, or a drawing, to clarify their message.

**K–V–A**  Notice the visions or flash of an idea or new perspective that come to you after you ask the question. Walking or moving with them will help you know how to put them into action.

**A–K–V**  Be aware of the feelings or impulses to take action that come after you've asked the question. Find someone to talk about these with, so you can integrate the message.

**K–A–V**  Be aware of the songs or stories which pop into your mind. Walking or moving with them will help you get a grasp on how to put them into action.

*Exceptions are the rule*! People who spend a great deal of their time out on the circumference of their minds—meditating, creating, in solitude or doing hypnosis—are much more likely to be aware of the image when it first arises from the unconscious state.

Conversely, people who spend a great deal of time "in their head," "climbing that ladder" and functioning in a linear state of consciousness, may not pick up the image until it reaches their conscious mind. If that is visual, they may have transparent flashes of a vision, or find an idea emerging while they are doodling; if that is kinesthetic, they may recognize the image when they are relaxed, and have an idea of something to do or a "gut" feeling; if that is auditory, they might find the idea coming out of their mouth, while they are in conversation with someone or humming.

*"Our error is not the outer directed confrontative mind itself, but over-emphasizing it."*

*–Carla Needleman*

## Collaboration, Not Control: Entering Into A Healing Dialogue

I probably should have told you this right from the start. I have a lot of biases, as far as working with imagery is concerned. Here they come.

There are many ways of working with imagery. I'm biased in the direction of indirection. I don't believe in the conscious mind bossing the unconscious mind around. In the traditions of wisdom I have studied, you inquire or you advocate, but you don't give linear directions to a non-linear mind. Milarepa did not order the demons he faced to go away. Aikidoists don't force their opponents in a specific direction. Milton Erickson did not control people into healing trance states. They all used their influence indirectly and creatively, which is how the unconscious mind works naturally.

I am very loyal to, and in awe of, the power of revelation from our unconscious minds. Rather than guide your mind from the outside in, I'd like to teach you to dance with it, to work with it from the inside out: symbolically and indirectly through fantasy, story, ceremony, and craft, as cultures have all over the world. This is an organic way to reach the deepest level of understanding possible, to break down compartments and create healing relationships within you. It respects the individual uniqueness of your own symbolic system, and enables you to be guided and activated by your most profound wisdom. It brings you into integrity and into alignment with yourself.

This doesn't mean you have to just sit there and let your imagination do with you as it will. Instead, since this is the land of relationship, you learn to dialogue, to go back and forth, to hold inner conversations instead of just issuing edicts. A healing dialogue is about exchange: asking for input from your unconscious mind, receiving it, and then communicating the information to your conscious mind, advocating on your own behalf.

Unfortunately, a lot of what is called "guided imagery" and creative visualization is old-fashioned and clumsy at best, ineffectual and insulting at worst. (The inner mob of voices in my mind are screaming at me to change that last sentence. They want me to be nice, polite, and avoid controversy. They are showing me flashes of the thousands of books that are written, the hundreds of lecturers and healers who have made a fortune teaching directed affirmations and visualizations. Like Milarepa, I bow to them, and promise them a song as soon as we're done with this section.)

I don't think all of the teachings about directing, guiding, and controlling are wrong. I just think they are incomplete, and come mostly from people's conscious minds—which is where the problem exists. Linear minds acting like despots in a non-linear terrain.

*"What is esteemed in human relationships is the just estimate of another's inborn nature, and helping him to realize it. When you see a straight piece of wood, you don't want to make it into a wheel, nor do you try to make a rafter of a crooked piece, you don't want to pervert its inborn quality but rather see that it finds its proper place."*

*–From 3rd century China as quoted by Carla Needleman*

*"All theoretical state-
ments are really
autobiographical."*

*–Bruce Chatwin*

As an example: A few years ago, I sat in a lecture given by a very charismatic and famous doctor. He gave a brilliant and inspiring speech to the audience. Then, to my dismay, he had the lights lowered and proceeded to read a guided fantasy. It was written and spoken by his conscious mind to the unconscious minds of the thousands of us in the room. Up until that time, I would have followed him anywhere; but for twenty minutes I squirmed and clutched the edges of my brown metal chair. His words and phrases had one conscious meaning, but many of them had a completely different significance to the unconscious mind: "You can go . . . *DEEP IN* . . . relaxing completely, listening to . . . *MY WORDS* . . . you don't have to worry about *CONTROLLING* anything . . . *YOU* can allow . . . *ME* to talk as you are  *ENTERING DEEPLY* . . ."

Without realizing it, because he was in his logical mind, the good doctor was giving what is called an embedded message to all of the unconscious minds in the room. I have spent years working with people who have been traumatized by sexual abuse. If you read just the words that are capitalized, you'll understand why I could barely keep myself from choking the doctor with his stethoscope. For those of us who have been violated from the outside in, we do not need to have our minds invaded in a similar fashion. I'm sure that was not his intent, and had he been in an expanded state of consciousness himself, I believe he would have known better. Of course, it would have taken a great deal of trust on his part to not plan ahead of time what he would say to all of us in that twenty minutes; but then trusting yourself in the unknown is what working with the unconscious mind is all about.

Understanding how to be guided by, and to express the natural messages that come from your own source, and exploring effective ways to influence it will enable you to do any form of guided imagery much more effectively. I once worked with a woman who was going blind because of a tumor which was filling up her brain. She had been listening, for almost a year, to a healing visualization tape made by someone she had never met. I asked her to listen to her own pain as faithfully as she had the tape, and to make room enough in her life to see deeply into her tumor and notice the messages that it had for her healing. Then she made her own tape, with her favorite music and messages that she had deciphered directly from the growth in her brain. It was entitled "*To More* Room in My Own Life!"

A few more guidelines:

*Negative imagery doesn't seem to work*. Think of a sign that says "Don't touch the wet paint." Everyone reads it and walks away with yellow fingertips. As far as we can tell, the unconscious mind does not make negative images. If you send it a message that says "Don't eat that chocolate cake. I'm getting fat as a pig," your unconscious mind will make an image of a delightfully fat and happy pig eating a piece of chocolate cake. This will be as strong and impactful as the image of the rattlesnake in the desert (or is it dessert?). Anyway, you'll begin to salivate and reach for that piece of cake, while your conscious mind will do the negative part by trying to cancel the image. It's far more effective to just make an image of a lithe and limber you dancing naked in a field of flowers, or to give the verbal message "What is it I want much more than any old chocolate cake right now?" Or give yourself a foot rub or . . . You get the idea—positive images of what you are moving toward.

*The more multi-sensory your imagery is the better*. For example, my images of finishing this book include a vision of me bowing and offering it to Milton, Sensei Kuboyama, Thich Nhat Hanh, Andy, and you—the reader. I can also hear the conversations, feel the welling thrill in my body, smell the lemony air, taste the excitement on my tongue, etc.

> "Miracles are mundane happenings that an awakened eye can see in a fantastic way."
>
> –Natalie Goldberg

*Imagery is most effective when it is combined with awareness and compassion.* For instance, directing your awareness into your body *while* guiding your imagery in some way, and opening your heart to whatever pain, frustration and sadness may arise is the most powerful way to use your mind. Or being aware of the medicine you are taking, while empowering each pill with your imagery to do what you want it to, and being compassionate with your fear that it might not follow your direction.

*Stay open to the unexpected.* Receive whatever comes, without analyzing it or judging it. Honor your initial impulses. Imagery is not about right or wrong, good or bad, better than or worse than, pretty or ugly. It is about finding what is true.

## From A Grain Of Sand

In every injury, there is the potential gift of healing. What follows is a personal description of how a gift of healing can build itself around a wound. It rolls all of my biases and beliefs about using multi-sensory imagery into one small jewel.

*"True love and prayer are learned in the hour when love becomes impossible and the heart has turned to stone."*

*–Thomas Merton*

There is a shelf in my office where my eyes go to absorb inspiration when the blank computer screen burns a hole in my brain. Each object or book there is a symbol for a turning point in my life. The little willow tree that helped me finish *The Art Of the Possible* is next to a picture of my grandmother. To her left is an oyster shell my father gave me years ago.

He was a traveling salesman before I was born, driving the back roads of New York and Connecticut in a Model T Ford, or maybe a Model F. He sold precious stones to jewelers—jade and coral, lapis and tanzanite. And he sold pearls.

When I was thirteen, he gave me this particular half-shell with a forming pearl embedded in its side. He explained that this bit of preciousness began as a grain of sand—an irritant, an annoyance—that the oyster could not get rid of; and he explained how it began to incorporate the sand into itself by layering mother of pearl over it, around it, surrounding it in the iridescent stuff until it was complete and separate. Folding my fingers around the gift, he told me that a pearl couldn't acquire what he called luster until it touched warm skin.

I treasured that half shell, trailing my fingers over the iridescent surface a thousand times, so that even though it would never be fully formed it would still have luster. In exchange, it brought me comfort through the pimpled turbulence of puberty.

Fifteen years later, when I felt a lump in one of my lymph nodes, it was surprisingly like that pearl. After the cancer was diagnosed and I was in my "trying everything stage," I went to healers who told me that I had created the lump with my mind. That was supposed to help me believe I had the power to make it go away by doing healing visualizations.

I did believe I had the power to hurt myself but, to be honest, I couldn't make the necessary leap to believing I had the power to heal myself. Nonetheless, I visualized three times a day. Since my mind uses the V-A-K pattern to think, my conscious mind saw the enemy cells being destroyed by the various treatments. Unfortunately, as I've subsequently discovered, my conscious mind had little or no effect on my immune system. It all went "in one eye and out the other."

On my own, I decided to add stories to my visualizations, so that I could involve more of my mind. I also shifted to symbolic visualizations of bad crabs being bombarded by power ray guns. That seemed more interesting at least. Then one night, while I was dusting things in the little two-

"An image is a vehicle for mental processes that reaches deep into the cell structure and alters the intelligence of the cell."

–Jeanne Achterberg

179

room apartment on Poverty Lane where David and I lived, I picked up that half oyster shell, and began to touch its embedded pearl the way I had touched it growing up, giving it some of my luster. This kinesthetic input triggered my mind to expand its wings. Up, up and away. Stories naturally formed full blown in my mind about how the pearl was finally released from its entrapped state and became a medicine necklace.

Those three-dimensional, multi-perceptual imagery experiences seemed to affect my immune system in a significant way that just "visualizing" didn't. I leave proof to others whose interest and training so directs them. But my cells are sure. The ones that were growing crooked have been going straight for a long time now. And my immune system seems to have learned from the deepest ocean floor of my mind how to deal with a variety of irritants.

## Guided By A Song

Jack Kornfield, spiritual teacher and author, tells of a tribe in Africa that uses song as guided imagery. When a woman first thinks about getting pregnant, she waits until a song comes to her. She teaches it to her mate and they sing it at conception. She teaches it to the midwife and it is sung during the pregnancy and at birth. The song is taught to the entire tribe, who sing it at every rite of passage the child goes through from puberty to marriage. When the person dies, the song is sung by the community for the last time.

*What would be the song or chant that was meant to companion you from birth to death? It may or may not have words. Experiment with what would make an awareness of it more apparent to you: going for a walk, doodling, drumming on your knee, etc.*

*"Imagination is more important than knowledge. It is the preview of life's coming attractions."*

*–Albert Einstein*

# 9 Learning From the Wounds:
## Using Disconnective Imagery

"If we could read the secret history of our enemies, we should find in each person's life sorrow and suffering enough to disarm all hostility."

–Longfellow

A turning point forces you to notice where you've been, where you're going, how you've gotten from then to now, and how you want to get from here to there. The answers seem to get smaller and farther apart and the questions grow bigger and closer to each other. We're ready now to discover two ways to use your imagination to live between those answers and inside of those questions.

For this part of the journey, we'll be traveling on a river, your subconscious mind, into a dark pool that reflects all of your memories, your unconscious mind. If your healing requires finding a new way to relate to the memories and events that haunt you, then how are you going to do that without re-experiencing the pain that those events caused you? Won't remembering dismember your peace and sanity? Why not just let sleeping dogs lie, and the past be passed? Is there really a way to learn from the violations we've experienced without having to pull the scab off again and again?

This chapter will help you build a raft to navigate in these challenging waters. It shares the first of two processes for using imagery to find new ways to relate to your enemy and the debris of your life, ways that produce learning rather than pain.

*"The image is the world's oldest and greatest healing resource."*

*–Jean Achterberg*

## Disconnecting In Order to Reconnect

The process of transformation we will be using takes a bad joke and turns it into a good one. I mentioned earlier that one of the difficulties many of us who face turning points experience is that we have become disconnected or dissociated from much of our ability to experience being alive. None of us, of course, chooses to be disconnected from life. We become walled off from ourselves as much as we are from anyone outside of ourselves. It is as if, when children, we made bargains to give up chunks of our openness in order to get by with a minimum of pain. As we grow, these bargains become barricades so no one else can get in to hurt us; but ultimately it is only ourselves we keep out. These walls leave us stranded—on the outside looking in.

Some wounds deepen as they heal. When a woman is raped, for instance, that violation can be re-experienced every time her body is horizontal, or at every dark corner she turns. To protect our souls, many of us disconnect from our bodies. We barricade our souls in the wall, watching everything from a remote camera. My soul never got raped, but it was outcast from the rest of the vividness of life as well.

Turning points shake our barricades fiercely. Physical illness challenges the walls between you and your body, addiction between you and your spirit, abuse between you and your emotions and troubled relationships between you and your heart. In order to heal, those barricades must be replaced with boundaries that protect us, without requiring that we withdraw from life.

In my experience, many people who have survived childhood trauma tend to make connected images of pain, and disconnected ones of pleasure, when they become adults. Experience the difference, for a moment:

*Imagine yourself in the front seat of a roller coaster. Connect to that image; step into it; get subjective; be in the scene; wrap it all around you. Now, disconnect by allowing one aspect of yourself to step out on the ground and witness another you in the front seat.*

Which way did you experience more sensation? If you are like most people, it was when you were connected to the roller coaster by a seat belt and the seat of your pants.

*"When you face pain directly she will give you an ointment so the wounds don't fester."*

*–Ruth Gendler*

Thus, connection increases your sensation of an experience—you feel more; disconnection diminishes sensation of an experience—you feel less. The brain is capable of thinking about anything from either of these two perspectives. That is its resource. Unfortunately, many people don't know how to use this tool. When they remember painful situations, it is as if they are still experiencing them. They are up on the movie screen. They are in the experience. They step into the room where their mother is still yelling at them, the kid down the block is beating them up, the car is running over their dog, while they watch all of it, helpless as when it first happened. This is the mechanism that creates "I am the problem." But when something pleasurable happens, that same person automatically climbs down from the screen and sits in the plush velvet seat objectively observing the whole thing as if it's happening to someone else, feeling nothing at all!

Fortunately, a sock can be turned inside out. The mind can be taught quite effectively to shift from a connected image to a disconnected one. Or vice versa. Thus, we can re-learn to connect to pleasure and disconnect from pain. If the painful experience is happening, out there, to him or her instead of to me, it makes learning much less difficult. It makes it possible for you to begin a dialogue with it, to re-view and re-do the ways you have been relating to it.

A woman I worked with, whose mind used the K-A-V pattern, felt overwhelmed by all the images of past suffering that filled her thoughts with fear of dying, suffocation, and chest pains. When she explored those images, she found they were being generated by old unconscious movies that she starred in, but couldn't see. What she heard was a continual flow of internal words telling her that she was always wrong and that her pain never mattered.

Once she found the images her mind was connecting to, she could step out and create a multi-screen theater with a grand piano up front. Sitting at that beautiful

*"If the only tool you have is a hammer, you tend to treat everything as if it were a nail."*

*–Abraham Maslow*

185

instrument, she could watch each film go by with a younger self in it and, as the adult self, could play what she felt in her body as a response to the situation and the child.

A misconception commonly held is that being disconnected is bad. The truth is that it is a skill—a talent—when used in the right context. In a dental chair, for instance, I'm thrilled to know how to disconnect from my experience by floating above it all, hanging onto the fluorescent fixture while Dr. Mooney does a root canal. Who needs Novocaine?

Some of the most successful people in the world "disconnect" as a way of problem solving: they step out of the situation they are thinking of, and "get objective," i.e., they observe another "self" doing it. A dynamic 75-year-old aikidoist from Maui, Suzuki Sensei, calls it contemplation. He describes the process as taking a problem and suspending it in front of himself, where another self is working on it. He just sits there, breathing in and out, and lets it dangle. "The solution comes to me eventually. Why should I worry it? Better to contemplate it."

One of the uses of disconnecting is to create space. Having the ability to establish distance in any relationship when you need it, including the one with your enemy, helps you to reconnect with your own values and resources; thus, it makes it more possible for you to come close to the other in an intimate way.

*"In the diary I can keep track of the two faces of reality."*

*–Anais Nin*

## Out Of the Frying Pan and Into the Fire

I'd like to share a story with you as an example of using disconnective imagery to find a healthy way to think about an unhealthy situation. Within minutes of meeting Mark (V-K-A), I felt as if I'd known him forever. By the end of two hours, however, I felt as if I didn't know him at all. He was a man in his late thirties, with wavy prematurely gray hair and even, perfect features. He dressed in "studied casual." When he spoke, the only animation was in his hands, which seemed to pull his words out of his mouth. For some reason, he made me think of a canyon, an abyss.

"I guess I'm supposed to spill it all, so here it is. I come from an alcoholic family and I am an alcoholic. I've been in recovery for seven years. I grew up taking care of my mother. Neither of my parents enjoy me very much for who I am. I was a disappointment to my father right from the beginning. He was a famous author and politician, and I was not exactly brilliant in school. My mother was, well . . . I guess the term is controlling. But she didn't have too much to do with me either. I was raised mostly by house-keepers. Recently, I've remembered that one of them . . . mm . . . sexually abused me; but that's not what I want to work on. I don't want to know any more about that."

His face was closed tight as a fist. "I seem to draw women to me easily enough. My first wife was an alcoholic and we've been divorced for four years. I want to be in another relationship; but I withhold myself from any real intimacy. There's no place for anyone else to live inside me. I keep disappearing whenever the good stuff is around for me and appearing whenever the shit hits the fan."

I was nodding as he spoke, but Mark seemed unaware, as he stared out into some place I couldn't see. "I don't have trouble getting close to women. That's not true. I don't have trouble letting them get close to me. It's like they're instantly there, in my center. It's as if they become an island in my boundaryless ocean. They slip in and I have no choice about it. Boom! We're intimate. But then I go on the outside and begin to look in on the whole thing. I begin to live outside myself, as if there is a vacuum between me and me. I have no sense of the space between near and far. Everything becomes either/or."

Mark's hands twisted spirals in the air as he spoke. His

*"There are some who participate in life without observing it and some who observe life without participating in it."*

*–Jim Rohn*

187

voice got flat; the pupils of his eyes dilated, and his body began to rock back and forth. "I don't know where middle is. She, any woman, is inside of me immediately. I never give her permission. I can't. I'm off some place watching. It all happens automatically. She enters my space without asking and then I know she has no boundaries either, so I enter hers. There is no middle. I can't keep her out and she can't keep me out. There is just this awful, unwanted closeness. She begins by thinking she can control me, but I prove I can control her. It all happens automatically. That's the hardest part. I have no choice."

His breath was rapid now, but I was sure he had no awareness of breath or body. He was a satellite in orbit, watching himself tell me, watching the violation of years ago, watching himself attract other women to violate him in similar ways.

"I've tried to keep myself away from her—from them—but it's no good. I attempt to maintain a distance from all women, but it's not so much to protect me from them, as it is to protect them from me. I live at the edges of both polarities. I am totally withdrawn and isolated or enmeshed. They are inside of me. I want a middle ground. I want to have a chance to choose, to consent. I want boundaries.

"My former wife oscillated between consumption and isolation. In the beginning, whenever I wanted her, she'd become unattainable. I became consumed with wanting to invade her boundaries. But when she would finally let me, I just couldn't. . . ."

Mark's face was a prairie. There were no contours in his voice. Only his body moved rhythmically, back and forth—like a metronome. "I became impotent. She became scornful, verbally attacking me. I withdrew."

He shook his head, rubbed his forehead and refocused his blue eyes. His hands had left damp patches on his gray corduroy pants. "We've been divorced for some time, but

*"If the dead be truly dead, why should they still be walking in my heart?"*

*—Winneap Shosone, medicine man*

things aren't much better with other women. That's what I want to work on. The impotence I mean. I want to be able to include someone else in my world by *choice*. To make friends with her first. To be a separate self and still include another person. Is that possible?"

I didn't answer him for quite some time. I just let the silence rest between us. Then I told him there were many layers to the learning he was ready to do, and we could move through them one at a time as he was ready.

I invited him to go for a walk. He seemed to ease up a great deal when he was moving, and centered in the process. We paused on a small bridge. As I listened to him describe his first marriage, I realized that he was stepping into the memory of it and re-experiencing it in that moment. His face flattened; his movement became stilted and minimal; his voice got monotonous. He described his fights with his wife as if they were still happening. "She starts yelling at me and I just freeze. I feel like such a fall guy, but I can't move. I'm terrified."

When I asked him when he had last seen her, he told me it had been two years. I asked him to describe in detail what the images were like in his mind when he was about to make love with a woman. I explained that I wasn't particularly interested in the content of them, just in *how* he was thinking them. His response was a perfect example of disconnected imagery: "I never thought about it before, but I guess I'm on the ceiling watching another me in bed with the woman, giving him advice and commenting on what he's doing right and wrong."

When I asked for the tone of the comments, he said it sounded like his father or a critical football coach commenting negatively on everything he did or said. He was staring into the stream below, carried by the current of the memories he was reliving. I invited him to see the younger Mark who was being scorned by his wife reflected in the surface of the stream. I suggested he give him advice from

> *"Symbols have the capacity to touch us not just on an intellectual level but on behavioral and emotional levels as well."*
>
> *–Albert Einstein*

189

his now wiser perspective.

With a wry smile on his face, Mark spoke articulately and compassionately to his married self. "Breathe man. It'll be over soon, water under the bridge. You'll survive it. I'll be here for you."

I reached over and lightly touched his interlaced hands. "Yeah man, like this. You and me, like this." He held them over his head and laughed the moment clean.

When we got back to my office, I congratulated him for stepping out of his past and being able to see from that perspective what he had needed back then in that painful relationship with a woman. I asked him to consider what he thought would happen if he stepped into his pleasurable experiences with women by crawling behind his own eyes and ears, back inside his own skin rather than viewing from the sidelines. His response was halting at first. "I'd see the way the light touched her, and the way my hand touched her . . . and I'd see her eyes and how they'd get soft and . . ." When his mind caught on, he laughed that laugh that always comes when an unconscious mind discovers that a bad joke can turn good. Quite good as a matter of fact.

Mark and I both knew he had a lot of learning left to do before his relationships with women could be nurturing and safe. We also knew that they could now be pleasurable as well.

*"In exercising imagination, we can begin to imagine different economic, political, educational relationships and ways of worship that will do us justice instead of bringing more pain. . . . This makes our time very exciting to live in. It's like boiling water. It doesn't look like a lot is happening until it moves that crucial degree or two. I think underneath, there's a lot of water boiling in the human psyche today."*

*–Matthew Fox*

## Such A Simple Step

So few people seem to know about using disconnective imagery in this way. I was driving to Keeler's Bay market the other day and listening to a tape I had bought about journal writing. The woman who made it was articulate, creative, and very experienced. She offered wonderful ideas for using journals to increase self-knowledge, until—I almost drove the car into the lake—the voice coming through the grilles of the car's speaker was telling me to think of the worst thing that had ever happened to me, and to revivify the memory. "Make it come alive as if it were happening now. Step into it; smell the smells; feel in your body what you were feeling then; hear the sounds around you. What are you wearing?"

I remembered a woman I had worked with years before who had gone hysterically blind after a workshop leader had done a similar exercise with her. She was catapulted back to being two years old and jumping up on a stove when her nightgown caught on fire and seared 80 percent of her body with third degree burns! No wonder her unconscious mind didn't want her to see!

I almost slammed into the big green dumpster in the parking lot before realizing that I'd better step out of that memory. I promised myself that I would write a letter to the woman who made the tape and explain as gently as I could about how stepping out of a painful memory can make learning more effective, and comfortable, without losing any of the details.

Let's call the practice that follows the mental Texas Two-Step, and think of it as a dance. Let's use it to step in and experience the pleasure in our lives as big as life, and to step out onto a big prairie with the suffering of our lives out there on the horizon, where we can get a fresh perspective on what it was we needed and didn't get.

*Bring to mind any memory that gives you pleasure. Perhaps it will be one from last week, or last year, or the last time you thought of yourself as a child.*

*Step into the memory, if you're not there already. Connect with it as if it is wrapped all around you, happening now. Notice how that feels, looks, sounds, smells, tastes.*

*Bring yourself back and center. Make your body very com-*

*"If I could paint the flower exactly as I see it no one would see what I see because I would paint it small like the flower is small. So I said to myself–I'll paint what I see–what the flower is to me but I'll paint it big and they will be surprised into taking time to look at it."*

–Georgia O'Keefe

191

> "What happens
> when I look in my
> [mirror] is that I, who
> am nothing here,
> place myself there
> where I am a man,
> and project him back
> upon this centre . . .;
> my glass does for me
> what my friends do,
> only with fewer
> complications. . . .
> Between us, the glass
> and I achieve a man."
>
> –D.E. Harding

fortable and easy. Perhaps hold onto something that makes you feel safe, or sit in your favorite chair, or pace around the floor as you proceed.

Now, bring an unpleasant event in your history to mind. It doesn't have to be traumatic or gory, just definitely unpleasant. Practice stepping out of that image, allowing it to go on and happen to a younger you, while the present self just notices it and continues to be grounded in the safety of the present moment. Notice the effect of doing that on your sensory awareness.

You can shuttle back and forth at a rhythm that's comfortable for you, stepping into the pleasant memory, and out of the unpleasant one, until you can do the dance with ease.

Bring an image of your enemy to mind. Step out of it and notice the way it relates to a younger you. From this new perspective, what is there you can learn?

## Establishing Safety, No Matter What

Here's some guidelines to establish and re-establish safety as you work with your imagery:

> "Humankind cannot
> bear too much reality."
>
> –T.S. Elliot

First, center. Sometimes, if you lose it while thinking about your pain or struggle, all you need to do in order to regain your center is to take more physical space from your enemy. This can be accomplished in many ways. Alter the environment: Put a glass window or door between you and the representation of your enemy; take it outside to someplace in nature you love. Put yourself in a situation where you physically know, in every cell of your body, that you are safe—a warm bathtub, or in the arms of someone you trust.

If you're working with an image in your mind that's very frightening to you, you can imagine you are holding a remote control button like the kind you use for a TV set. Keep one finger on the stop button; be able to locate the mute button in an instant—likewise rewind and play. If you sense you're "losing it," push the pause button, center and breathe. Do whatever will help you feel immediately safe and then proceed. I've asked some people to imagine their enemy or wounding on a tiny postage stamp size screen—or to listen to it on a wrist radio—or from the back seat of a movie theater, while holding the hand of someone they trust—hugging a stuffed tiger, a favorite rock—getting a foot massage. What's important is that *you feel your body in the present moment, safe and comfortable.* Your kinesthetic channel is going to stay in the now time, even if your eyes and ears are going to be looking and listening back in the then time.

Please do not underestimate the importance of feeling safe. If you don't feel safe, your intuition will withdraw behind every wall, barrier and barricade in your entire mental landscape. Creating space, centering; increasing awareness; choosing how, when and where you perceive something, are all part of establishing boundaries. And, when you have good boundaries, you don't need barriers.

One way you can know when you're safe and have boundaries intact in the present moment is to notice if you can see with your peripheral vision, or if you can hear the sounds around you, or whether you can feel all of your body and the energy in the whole room.

You've been discovering that there is an unlocked doorknob on the cage. The choice to turn, and step out, so you have the freedom to learn from your wounds, is now yours.

*"If one cannot change a situation that causes his suffering, he can still choose his attitude."*

*– Victor Frankl*

*"Those who cannot remember history are condemned to repeat it."*

*– Santayana*

# 10 Giving Pain A Home:
## Using Creativity To Externalize

"A story is a medicine that greases and hoists the pulleys, shows us the way out, down, in and around, cuts for us fine wide doors in previously blank walls, doors which lead us to our own knowing."

–Clarissa Pinkola Estes

Orienting on a long journey is a lot easier if there is a place you can go to that will give you an overview—a tree or mountain to climb so that the whole landscape becomes apparent. In a similar way, healing is facilitated by being able to take the enemy, the *uke*, out of isolation and return it to the larger framework of your life, where you come to realize you are bigger than the problem.

If you change the context in which you are thinking about something—get off the ground and up into a tree branch, for example—you can change your perspective. If you change the way you are perceiving something, you can change the way you're thinking about it, experiencing it, and relating to it. Change the context; change the perception; change the experience; change the response. Instead of going around and around in the same damn struggle, your mind opens to new possibilities.

*"Before we can move into a new arrange-ment, we must first go through a period of de-rangement."*

*–M.C. Richards*

You may have guessed by now that this book is not going to be very much help in getting rid of your enemy. What can change, however, is *how you relate to that enemy*. And that can change everything.

Sensei Kuboyama often tells us, "Dealing with *ukes* on the outside is easy. It is the inner ukes who can most easily defeat us." Inner or outer, he teaches that we don't run from *ukes;* we don't ignore them and we also don't try to destroy them. We have to be flexible enough to create the space necessary to make choices about how we respond. Given this space, we can choose how to use and redirect the opponent's energy, in the same way that an outfielder catches a baseball by backing up and going in the same direction as the ball is flying, before redirecting it to the infield.

The following practice, which Sensei Lloyd Miyashiro calls "Butterfly on Wrist" is filled with lessons that helped me learn how to respond, instead of re-act to a force which appears not to move. It makes it obvious how much choice we do have when we give ourselves the space we need to be curious, and learn rather than control and defend. It also gives a model for a powerfully tender way to explore the wounded history that hides within every closed fist.

*Allow one of your hands to be extended rigidly in a fist. (Or, even better, have someone else extend their hand, if they're willing to learn with you.) With the other hand, try to push it to the side, or up or down.*

*What happens to the fist? For most people it gets even more rigid, as if its life depended on staying exactly where it is. Many of our enemies are just this stubborn in their refusal to be changed or controlled.*

*Now, try a different way: Center, then expand your mind as if it had wings. Place the thumb and middle fingertips of your second hand on either side of the extended wrist, AS LIGHTLY AS A BUTTERFLY. Receive the fist. In other words, feel how it is already moving minutely as you breathe.*

*Move with it, ever so lightly, and then notice where you can influence what is a natural movement. Give yourself lots of time and space. Keep playing. Have no goal. Just be curious where there is already movement that you can extend and influence.*

*How is the effect on the fist different than it was the first time? Most people find that the fist gets tired and doesn't want to hold itself rigid when there's nothing with which to struggle.*

Being this gentle, with your power centered, flexible, receptive, and patient, encourages an alliance with, instead of a struggling against. In other words, it announces to one aspect of yourself, your inner enemy, that you are an ally and will not violate it further in an internal civil war.

To integrate this lesson, spend a few minutes using the power of your mind to transfer it to how you are relating to your enemy. If you were feeling like the butterfly, how would you talk to yourself when you got frustrated with your enemy? How would you think about the woundings of your history?

In the pages that follow, you'll be using the power of

"To be able to learn is to be young and whoever keeps the joy of learning in him or her remains forever young."

–J.G. Bennett

198

personal creativity to change even further the context in which you are learning. This chapter will teach you how to move from an identification of "I am the enemy" to externalizing, "I have the enemy in my sensitive and firm hands, where I can begin to relate to it in a more effective way." This will enable your mind to reverse the flow of swallowed events, be they wounds or disconnected aspects of body, mind, or spirit. When they are at your fingertips, rather than behind your back or hidden in the core of your mind, and once they are out in front, you can work with them.

*"I began to draw looking for comfort within an imagined world. But this time my inner voice was saying: 'Reach out to people. You don't need to do this all alone.'"*

*–Laurel Burch*

## Using Personal Creativity to Learn

Milton Erickson expanded the use of symbols, stories, analogies, and ceremonies for healing. He taught that indirect learning is powerful, because it changes the context in which someone thinks about a problem. A simple metaphor expressed through stories, poems, carvings, photographs, dances, songs, weavings, or drawings can shift entrenched patterns and create conditions for change. It is an idea disclosed in a special way that takes what has become familiar to you—"the same damn thing over and over"—and helps you think about it in a strange new way. A metaphor can accomplish that because it communicates on many levels at once. It helps untie the knots in our minds, because it loosens our fixed ways of thinking.

*"Art and poetry have always been altering our ways of sensing and feeling–that is to say, altering the human body and the human mind."*

*–Norman O. Brown*

Thus, giving inner experience an outer form shifts us to the symbolic languages of the subconscious and unconscious minds, where detailed linear analysis is translated into comprehending a web of ideas. There is a mental alchemy at work, which turns suffering into sculpture or music. In that new form, the chances of your message being received, by you and others, are greatly increased.

*"Our bodies are garbage heaps. We collect experiences and from the decomposition of the thrown out eggshells, spinach leaves, coffee grinds and old steak bones of our minds come nitrogen, heat and very fertile soil. Out of this fertile soil, blooms our poems and stories."*

*–Natalie Goldberg*

Our culture has taught us that the *products* of our creative process are what counts. For the purpose of healing, the products are irrelevant. It is the *process* that counts. It is, in essence, a way of wondering, where you enter the darkness and move through it, getting the images out—on paper or film, in clay or fabric—to release the terror and give it shape, form, grace and renewal. The purpose, as we use it here, is to explore the act of creation as a healing practice and as a way of awakening to your truth.

Humans are the only creatures on the planet that can, as Alice Walker describes, create poems from our "leftover loss, leftover grief, leftover love." Yet, in our culture, art and creativity have been relegated to performance. We are taught that only a rare few people are born with "talent," and therefore the rest of us should become an appreciative audience. In addition, the conventional methods of psychotherapy block the creativity of therapists as well as their clients. Over the centuries, however, many primal cultures have developed metaphoric ways of teaching people to move through darkness, to embrace and transcend pain— ways that are gentle, celebrative, and truly community building. In Bali, for example, everyone has a job, be it cleaning fish or planting rice. In addition, each person has some form of creative outlet, be it through dance, batik or sculpture. Creativity is considered a necessary strand of reality, a binding together of spirituality and daily life.

What if one person doesn't have more talent than another, but simply allows him or herself to sense more of what is in the world and express it? Illness and abuse brought me face to face with the possibility of being destroyed. Addiction brought me to my ability to destroy. Healing from all three involved reclaiming my capacity to do the opposite—to be part of the generative process of life.

If you go deeply enough into any person's mind, you will find the place that creates. Dreaming is creating. If you dream you create. Worrying is creating. If you worry, you create. I once worked with a group of women who all had extremely high blood pressures. The youngest woman was sixty-two. At first, I thought I'd help them to dance and draw, to relax and bring down their blood pressure; but they laughed at my suggestions and went on with their community of complaints. Every afternoon, they'd sit in the lobby of the nursing home, swapping stories about whose children were the most negligent, whose grandchildren were most likely to end up dead in a drug war, and which of them was next to be delegated to the charity wards for the terminally ill.

I asked the nurse to take their blood pressure before and after these sessions for one week. Sure enough, in every case, medication or not, the collective blood pressure of the group was higher after all of this complaining. It became obvious to me that under all these tales of misery and woe were some serious worries done by experts. And under the worries was an untapped pool of creative energy.

I told the group about my son David, who was ski jumping at the time. I explained how he was taught to train by seeing movies in his mind, and telling himself stories about going off that 90 meter jump with grace and success. I explained in detail how he would stand way up there, breathing and waiting until his imagery body leapt off; then he allowed his real body to follow. At once, the women all began to worry about poor David falling off, poor David splattering blood all over the nice clean snow, poor Dawna crying at David's funeral.

I explained that their worries were the same as David's— imagery, only with miserable endings. They produced bad feelings in their bodies—knots and high blood pressure— instead of good feelings. I chastised them for being lousy worriers, and told them that if David couldn't imagine the leap, he wouldn't be able to do it. I suggested that they

> *"The cinema like all other manifestations of creativity, ought to be in a state of combustion, a metabolism of the unconscious, a journey toward the center of ourselves and the world."*
>
> –Fredrico Fellini

201

practice worrying well, so that each story would help them "take off." They left, worrying about whether they could learn to worry better. By the next session, their worries had transformed from soap operas to success stories. If one woman got stuck, the others would prod her on by nagging, "Jump Ethel. Jump! How could your granddaughter Marcy be happy, even if she does marry that jerk?" "Tillie, what if your son loses his job? But then something terrific should happen, like . . ." The nurse called me the next week and reported a remarkable *drop* in the blood pressure levels of every woman in the group!

The goal of using personal creativity is to reclaim choices in how you relate to your enemy, to understand at a deeper level what motivates it, to reclaim your sense of wonder, and appreciation for being part of a larger whole.

Lisa (V-K-A) experienced severe depression in the dark months of every winter. I noticed that she carried a canvas bag of knitting with her to every session. One day I asked to see it. (I'm very nosy at times.) She was knitting a pastel cardigan from a standard pattern. At the end of our session, I suggested she center, turn in and, from that place, design and knit herself a "medicine sweater" that expressed her whole history of darkness, the pain she had experienced as a result, as well as how she would like to be relating to the pain. That was in early fall. I saw her six months later and she was wearing what she had crafted: the story of her healing in an ankle length coat, made in over seventy different shades and textures of darkness and light. It was a cloak, a cave, a warm home for her fear. She wore it proudly every day of that dark winter, instead of her depression. Instead of being an object to whom things happened, she made the darkness a quality with which she could create.

Creativity is the identification and expression of uniqueness. When people are taught not to assert this basic essence, what they do is to become different. We become

> *When we can be dumbfounded at what comes out of us or what others are capable of disclosing, we are growing persons."*
>
> *–Sidney Jourard*

> *"Give me everything mangled and bruised, and I will make a light of it to make you weep, and we will have rain and we will have begun again."*
>
> *–Deena Metzger*

different instead of daring to make a difference. My own assertion of "different-ness" was a terminal illness, where my body produced internal growths that no one could cure. Underneath that was my need to turn inward, to create in a way unique to me, and to express that creation outward. I have worked with people who assert their differentness by being grossly overweight, by being "the only one who . . ." (e.g., can't be healed, can't understand, doesn't deserve love, etc.), by being isolated and separate. Being different is the closest some of us can come to acknowledging our uniqueness.

Nancy (A-V-K) was tormented by dreams of being a lesbian, who was suffocating under a huge fabric canopy over a bed. She was newly married and deeply in love with her husband. The dreams left her confused and tormented. I asked her to draw the fabric on a large sheet of newsprint. She covered the paper with an intricate pattern—in turquoise, red, and orange with a very small brown spot near one side—then carefully drew borders around the edges. We hung it on the wall, and I asked her to step back and describe herself as the drawing. Her words were: "I have an underlayer of connecting membrane. What you see depends on that membrane. I have a lot of colors and passions, things to say. I have a border I can trust. I am willing to let myself explore and I can just enjoy that. The feelings that are hardest for Nancy are only that one small brown spot in the middle of all of the rest of me. Some day she'll understand that spot too but, for now, all she needs to remember is the whole fabric of herself."

I suggested she frame the drawing and place it in just the right place in her bedroom, where it gave her comfort and made her feel safe. She began drawing on a regular basis as a way of exploring both her sexuality and individuality. Each work she created revealed the deepest, underlying truth of her heart, and gave a broad context to frame the confusion of her life.

## Guidelines For Reclaiming
## Your Creative Capacity

It's helpful to give yourself as much privacy as you need, so you can abandon the image of who you are supposed to be, and release all outcomes of what you're supposed to do or produce.

Since what we produce in this reconnective process doesn't matter, everything we create is all just practice. If you feel awkward or "self-conscious," recognize that as the signal that some subtraction may have to be done. Maybe Mrs. Treblecleff from third grade choir still is alive in your mind; perhaps your aunt Lydia or camp counselor Acres. If one or all of them appears, just recognize them, "Hello Mr. Fartfellow. I notice you're here." No need to scream or pound a pillow. Just "Hello Mrs. Treblecleff. You're still here. Well, I am too. This is my moment and I want to enjoy it."

Begin by imagining what it would be like to dance, move, draw, sing, sound or write without thinking about whether it is good or bad, or if it could be better or worse, deeper or more meaningful. If you can conceive of it, you can create it.

I often begin with a timed warm-up ("I will do this for eleven minutes") I learned from Natalie Goldberg, author of *Wild Mind* and *Writing Down the Bones* and expanded to: I write the worst junk in the world for eleven minutes, or draw the most ugly picture, or dance in the most awkward way, or play with clay in the most uptight way I can for eleven minutes. I time it on a watch. After three or four minutes, the critical voices seem to get quiet, but I insist on the predetermined time. "You wanted space and attention, I promised eleven minutes so you get that." It will not take longer, in fact, because after the eleven minutes, you will all be going in the same direction, rather than

*"Inspiration may be a form of super-consciousness, or perhaps subconsciousness–I wouldn't know. But I am sure that it is the antithesis of self-consciousness."*

*–Aaron Copland*

sabotaging yourself at every other thought.

When you are creating, and after, the most relevant question to ask yourself is "Is this true?" or "How can I make this more true to what I experience inside?"

## Finding Your Own Way: How Various Patterns Externalize An Enemy

To externalize your enemy by putting it "out there" in some imaginative form, you'll need to find a sequence that is the most effective for you, reviewing what you've learned in previous chapters. The comments that follow indicate how people I questioned in our advanced study groups externalize their enemies. But some people like to decide as they go. You also might like to experiment with one channel today, one tomorrow and one next year. That's fine.

Overall, most people (but not all or not always) I interviewed spent a lot of their creative time in their subconscious channel. Thus, after centering and turning inward as described in previous chapters, V-A-Ks and K-A-Vs worked mainly through songs, stories, dialogues or sounds; K-V-As and A-V-Ks created scenes, drawings, written material or photographs; A-K-Vs and V-K-As tended to create sculptures with their bodies or clay, using objects, movements or experiences. To be more specific:

*"Human beings need to express themselves daily in a way that invites physical and emotional release. Musical self-expression is a joyful and healthy means of communication available to absolutely everyone."*

*–Music For People*

### K-A-V

"First I have to notice what I'm feeling in my body. Walking or moving helps me. Then I get to a piano and make sounds that match the feeling. Or, I make the sounds on my body or on the floor. Sometimes I sing them."

"I give myself a foot rub, or a massage, and then sculpt

the enemy or what I'm feeling about it. I need to find somebody to talk to then about what I've learned. Sometimes I write a story about it, but it's hard to read it afterward."

"I just dance. Stories come into my mind while I'm dancing, if the music is wordless. From time to time, I draw whatever comes to me after one of these sessions."

## K-V-A

"A very powerful way for me is to move the way I am feeling and watch myself in a mirror. Then I sit down and write in my journal, or find a good friend to listen as I describe what I saw."

*"Write hard and clear about what hurts."*

*–Ernest Hemingway*

"I like to sculpt, or draw the enemy out of clay, and I put it as far away as I need to in order to look at it and write about it."

"I go for a walk and find something in nature that reminds me of it; then I look at it and describe it as if it were me ('I'm dried up, and hollow in the middle . . .') Sometimes, I take a camera with me, and when the roll of film is developed, I lay the photographs out on a table and listen to what they're telling me."

## V-K-A

"I write myself letters as if the enemy were writing to me."

"It helps me to find a symbol for the enemy, and walk around holding it, listening to it, asking it questions. Sometimes I'll see something that just represents the issue, and then powerful feelings come up which I release by writing."

"I like to find a mirror and 'become the enemy,' sculpting my body into it and watching it as I move. Sometimes, I just look in the mirror and ask myself questions."

## V-A-K

"I draw a picture with my non-dominant hand and then write whatever story comes to me while I'm looking at it. Inevitably, I'll have to find someone to tell that story to or to tell what I've discovered."

"I just stare at my hand and then begin to make it look like what I think the enemy would look like. I do a kind of puppet show with it, bringing a voice from my head into my hand, so I can dialogue with it."

"I give the enemy a separate name and then write myself a series of letters from it to me and me to it."

## A-K-V

"Well, I talk to other people about it. No surprise. But I need enough time to talk into the nooks and crannies. It helps alot if the person asks really curious questions."

"I like to talk as if I am the enemy and talking to someone who will listen. If no one's available (not unusual), I just tape record it; but I don't always listen to the tape, unless I'm walking or driving."

"I like to work out a physical model of it after having described it to someone. I make them out of anything— toothpicks, wood, napkins at a dinner table."

## A-V-K

"I talk, talk, talk. Describing the enemy in another language helps. Or, after talking it out on the phone, writing about it allows me to explore it. If I draw it, I begin to feel it, or feel something, anyway."

"Chanting sounds that describe it while I sit still and stare at a wall really brings up a lot of images, which I then write down."

"I just make up a song about it. Sometimes the song is from it to me, and sometimes from me to it."

"After talking about it, I imagine I'm holding a book

*"A man wanted to know about mind, not in nature, but in his private large computer. He asked it (no doubt in his best Fortran), 'Do you compute that you will ever think like a human being?' The machine then set to work to analyze its own computational habits. Finally, the machine printed its answer on a piece of paper, as such machines do. The man ran to get the answer and found, neatly typed, the words: THAT REMINDS ME OF A STORY . . ."*

*–Gregory Bateson*

that's written to me. In my mind's eye, I can see the pages, and as I flip through them, read the messages it has for me."

## Externalizing Your Enemy

Creativity cannot be taught, but it can be released. The purpose of using it here is to create an external representation of your internal struggle, so that you can retrieve those parts of yourself that are lost or unremembered, reconnect to them in order to understand the unmet needs that motivate them.

There are as many ways to do this as there are people, cultures, and books. What I am going to share is a process I've used in workshops for the past five years. It is multi-modal, giving you the opportunity to explore in all perceptual channels, so that if one channel is stuck or shy, you can learn through another. Feel free to experiment and make this yours. Change the sequence; omit what you will. To begin, we need to create an external representation of your enemy. Some people find having a time limit—say, ten minutes—makes it easier. Some people like to play music while they do this, to occupy the critical voices in their minds. And, of course, begin by centering.

*Art is the lie that tells the truth."*

*–Pablo Picasso*

*Find some colors to draw with. Oil crayons are wonderful, because they're inexpensive and you can smear them or blend them or layer them; but crayons or pencils or magic markers will do just fine, as long as they intrigue you. Make sure you have large blank pieces of paper. If you want to work in three dimensions, get some inexpensive clay to form into your enemy. Or, you can choose instead to go for a walk, and find an object that would be a good representation of your enemy.*

*Or, get a pair of scissors, a pile of magazines, and some tape or glue. Start cutting out words and pictures to make a montage— a kind of collection of jigsaw pieces that make a whole, which* represents that enemy. What's important here is that you give it a form, out there at arm's length.

Once it's finished, place the visual representation you've made of your enemy, or a symbol of it, some place where you can choose to be a distance away from it. Give yourself enough space from it so that it seems "out there," where you can perceive it but not merge into it. Some people need a window between themselves and the enemy to accomplish this. I hope you won't need thousands of miles, but give yourself permission to do whatever you need, so that you are safe enough to feel at least curious about this enemy. Asking for loving at this point would be premature. Curiosity will be fine.

I'd like to invite you now to receive that representation or symbol in the way you learned to receive your hand. Breathe in, imagining you could inhale through the pupils of your eyes, all the way to your center. Exhale curiously. No figuring out, judging, comparing; just for a few minutes, receive that enemy as you would a red frog or a 1976 turquoise DeSoto or the fossil of a reptile.

> "Help us to be the always-hopeful gardeners of the spirit who know that without darkness nothing comes to birth, as without light nothing flowers."
>
> –May Sarton

## Externalizing Through Storytelling

It would be possible to deepen and expand your awareness of this enemy in many ways; but I'm going to suggest you use storytelling, because it's the art form with which most of us are familiar—we tell ourselves stories all the time.

> "The universe is made of stories, not atoms."
>
> –Muriel Rukeyser

With pen or tape recorder in hand, begin to tell a story inspired by the visual representation or symbol of your enemy. The more removed it is from your life, the better. For instance, instead of "Once upon a time there was a woman who . . .," go for "Once upon a time there was a green warted tree frog who . . ." The more you change the context, the more you'll change how you perceive the enemy. You can forget trying to make it good, and just let the story tell itself through you. Let the pen or *your mouth move itself.*

*Allow it to come to the present, not to an end. Perhaps it will just come to a pause. That's fine. Then put it away for at least a day. Let it cook, like yeasted bread dough rising in a sunny window, like soup on the stove in winter. When you get curious about it again, you can read the story out loud to yourself or listen to the tape.*

Please remember this story comes from the part of your mind that does not function in meanings. It will not mean anything, any more than a map of Topeka means anything. It has a message, a purpose; it can help you get to your next step, but it has no meaning. Allow yourself to just receive the story without trying to figure it out.

Creating releases a vital force, which is an essential part of being human, without which we can survive but not thrive. It taps into that force as if it were a water table, a source that is ancient and yet always new.

By putting your enemy "out there," in hands that are merciful and aware, you have given it room to float in your consciousness, instead of drowning or overwhelming you. You have created a safe and respectful space, a perspective from which you can find out what the unmet needs are that motivate this obstacle.

*"To begin writing from our pain eventually engenders compassion for our small and groping lives. Out of this broken state there comes a tenderness for the cement below our feet, the dried grass cracking in a terrible wind."*

*–Natalie Goldberg*

# In the Mouth Of the Demon:
## Bringing Compassion Home

"Though hard to bear, the sorrow and the shame, the anger, the fear and fatigue— each is a gift. For each can bring into focus our deep, invisible interconnection in the web of life. And lift us out of our narrow selves, and bring us into community across space and time. Each can open us to the boundless heart. Though found in pain, that boundless heart is real, and the ground of all healing."

–Joanna Macy

There is a central concept in Chinese medicine represented by the word, *hsin*. In Japanese, the equivalent word is *shin*. In both cases, it means the mind which is in the heart. Here is the source of compassion.

Having externalized your enemy does not mean it's time to discard it. But what do you do with it now? What are you supposed to learn from it? Why have compassion towards the enemy instead of toward the rest of yourself? What makes all of this worth it?

Thus far on this journey, we have used our bodies and imaginations as vehicles for learning. Now we are at an intersection where only our hearts can assist our travel. Learning from here requires that we witness the pain of our present condition, bearing the grief of it with tenderness and mercy. It insists that we come to understand the aspects of ourselves that have been lost and separated, and bring them home. Ultimately, our hearts yearn for an end to isolation and fragmentation. They long for reconnection with the enemy, with meaning, with intention, and with community.

Turning points break our hearts. Break-downs, break-ups, break-aparts. We rant and rail, "Why me?" We rant and rave at God, our unhappy fate, our miserable helplessness. We search for meaning in any dark corner we can find. We grasp at the first answers we can find, assuming our suffering is punishment and retribution, "It happened because I'm too much, not enough, because I never . . . because I always . . ." We seal ourselves off with cynicism, and the searching stops. One of the greatest crimes people can commit against themselves is this trivializing of their own pain.

But turning points also provide us with the opportunity to use our wounds as a doorway to reconcile with our pasts and realize our futures. If we allow it, our hearts can break open, break through, break away from blame and shame, and easy answers. The wound can become a birth canal for

*"Pathology is not a problem to be solved, but the soul's way of working on itself."*

*–James Hillman*

the seeker in us—the one who searches for meaning. This is the one who will stick his or her head in the belly of the demon to find its motivating force, the one who will find a way to perceive what has been experienced as a path to wholeness.

Having compassion for yourself is often wiped away with the phrase "self-pity," but pity involves touching one's pain with fear. Compassion, on the other hand, involves using the fearless capacity of one's heart to embrace pain with awareness. It involves establishing a respectful relationship between the *source* of your problem (the enemy) and your inner *resources* (your wisdom). In other words, you need to make room for this enemy in your life without allowing it to control you. At the same time, the concept of yourself needs to expand: you are more than this disease, more than this fear, more than this abuse; you are, in fact, all the resources you have gathered in a lifetime of experience.

When I was in the hospital, the one person whose presence I welcomed was a woman who came to sweep the floors with a large push broom. She was the only one who didn't stick things in, take things out, or ask stupid questions. For a few minutes each night, this immense Jamaican woman rested her broom against the wall and sank her body into the turquoise plastic chair in my room. All I heard was the sound of her breath in and out, in and out. It was comforting in a strange and simple way. My own breathing calmed. Of the fifty or so people that made contact with me in any given day, she was the only one who wasn't trying to change me.

One night she reached out and put her hand on the top of my shoulder. I'm not usually comfortable with casual touch, but her hand felt so natural being there. It happened to be one of the few places in my body that didn't hurt. I could have sworn she was saying two words with each breath, one on the inhale, one on the exhale: "As . . . Is . . . As . . . Is . . ."

*"Let no man sleep on another man's wounds."*

–Ernie O'Malley

On her next visit, she looked at me. No evaluation, no trying to figure me out. She just looked and saw me. Then she said simply, "You're more than the sickness in that body." I was pretty doped up, so I wasn't sure I understood her; but my mind was just too thick to ask questions.

I kept mumbling those words to myself throughout the following day, "I'm more than the sickness in this body. I'm more than the suffering in this body." I remember her voice clearly. It was rich, deep, full, like maple syrup in the spring.

When the nurse came with my shot of morphine the next night, I refused it. I wanted to find out if my nighttime angel was real or not. An hour or so later, I heard the sound of her broom brushing against the marble hall floors. Her body filled up the whole doorway, and cast a long shadow on the floor of my room. She sank into the chair. The pain I was feeling was intense. She breathed loudly and said, "You're not the pain in that body. It's there, but you're more than that pain."

I reached out for her hand. It was cool and dry. I knew she wouldn't let go. She continued, "You're not the fear in that body. You're more than that fear. Float on it. Float above it. You're more than that pain." I began to breathe a little deeper, as I did when I wanted to float in a lake. I remembered floating in Lake George when I was five, floating in the Atlantic Ocean at Coney Island when I was seven, floating in the Indian Ocean off the coast of Africa when I was twenty-eight. Without any instruction from me, this Jamaican guide had led me to a source of comfort that was wider and deeper than pain or fear.

It's been fifteen years since I've seen the woman with the broom. I've never been able to find her. No one could remember her name; but she touched my soul with her compassionate presence and her fingerprints are there still.

The space between the source of your pain, fear, or confusion and your resources can be filled with respect

*"I never asked a wounded person how he feels; I myself become the wounded person."*

*–Walt Whitman*

that acknowledges and agrees to the existence of the other. It is a simultaneous recognition of being wise and being frustrated, of being in pain, vulnerable or empty.

The word respect means "to see again, to show consideration for, relate to." In this case, it means respecting your enemy, by being willing to consider what its needs are and to see it in a new way; it means respecting the pain you've experienced from your enemy, by putting boundaries around it. In aikido, this is called creating *ma-ai* which, roughly translated, means a safe mental and physical distance. You make sure you always have enough room between you and your opponent so that his or her extended arm or leg cannot reach you. Because you have made this space happen, you are safe enough to be curious about your challenger. You don't need to interfere or manipulate, to try to control the opponent; you have enough room to maneuver so you can't be controlled.

With an inner challenger, what we are calling the enemy, you need to make this room inside you. If centering is condensing the universe into your belly, then this process is expanding your center out towards the universe. A woman I worked with, for instance, whose enemy was the desire to cut herself, had done everything in her power to try and control or get rid of the enemy, to no avail. I gave her a stuffed doll, similar to one she had loved as a child, and told her that when her enemy told her to cut, she could cut the doll, and then sew it up. This gave her the chance to make room for that enemy so she could learn from it; but, at the same time, it allowed her to contain the enemy in such a way that demonstrated respect for its potential danger. In the space that had been occupied by the enemy, she created a healing self, who developed an alliance with the mutilating self.

Because I have been wounded and am healing, I know there is inherent within each of us a natural life force struggling to assert itself—a flame seeking, at every mo-

"Great pain, when it is honored from the heart, opens into great understanding."

–Jack Kornfield

ment, to rise upward. Learning through the heart is a birth process, an emergence from in-valid victim to veteran to venerated teacher. In the chapters that follow, the hardships you have experienced will rest in a heart softened with understanding and forgiveness, strengthened with wisdom and commitment. In the process, your innate desire to learn, to cause things, to reach beyond the known edge of yourself, to serve others, can awaken.

*"In the end we can see this either as a world where we all eat and are eaten or as a world where we all have an opportunity to feed one another."*

*–Jack Kornfield*

# 11 What's Right About What's Wrong:
## Finding the Unmet Needs

*"Each disease bears its own remedy within itself. . . . Health must grow from the same root as disease."*

–Paracelsus

When I was in private practice as a psychotherapist, almost everyone would begin their sessions telling me what they wanted to get rid of. "Dr. Markova, please help me get rid of my fear, my shyness, my cancer, my addiction, my rage." But true to my grandmother's teachings, I knew that underneath all of that garbage was something too valuable to throw out—an unmet need waiting to be filled.

Carl Jung frequently used a word I have come to love: *teleology*. It comes from the Greek, and means to focus on the ultimate purpose in natural phenomenon. Our symptoms are not random. They fill some need, some function. There is a force that drives them.

As I mentioned in the very beginning of this book, needs for nurturance and protection that have waited to be met from childhood do not go away. Whether we know it or not, they push, prod, urge us toward wholeness. They are at the core of our longings, at the depth of our yearnings. Each of us needs to be listened to, seen, touched with acceptance, whether we allow ourselves to be aware of it or not. Each of us needs to come home into the compassionate embrace we may never have experienced.

In this chapter, you'll be digging in and through the surface debris to discover how your enemy has affected you, and how to receive your own pain tenderly. You'll be exploring behind the shadows for the force that has been driving this demon, the unmet needs it has hidden in its belly.

> "Without suffering, happiness cannot be understood. The ideal passes through suffering like gold through fire."
>
> –Fyodor Dostoevsky

> "Like everything else in life, I mean all suffering . . . we have to find the gift in it. We can't afford to waste such an expenditure of feelings; we have to learn from it."
>
> –Katherine Mansfield

## Receiving Your Pain With Compassion

Many people who are in the process of healing their histories of abuse have discovered "the inner child." Unfortunately, too many have *become* that child. In my experi-

*"There are so many things in human living that we should regard not as traumatic learning but as incomplete learning, unfinished learning."*

*–Milton Erickson*

ence, the wounded child needs a competent and resourceful adult who will take care of him or her, not a large child who is carrying around a teddy bear. It's necessary, therefore, to establish a respectful relationship with that child where you can receive his or her pain and give what has been needed all along—someone to be in charge. You're the someone, and because of the wisdom you've earned in your life, no one could do it better than you can! Creating this inner spaciousness opens up possibilities for a relationship so deep that you tap into a larger whole, a force greater than yourself.

Norma was a woman who attended one of our weekend workshops and was courageous enough to do exactly that with her wounded history. She was about to go to the Philippines to teach hearing impaired children. She had been in therapy for twelve or thirteen years, and described herself as "borderline." I told her I wasn't really interested in thinking of her that way. She narrated all the forms of treatment she had experienced and, I must admit, the list was formidable.

My father used to be a salesmen and he often talked about people who were "all show and no go," professional shoppers who never buy. They'd keep you busy, but no sale. For four minutes or so I told myself, "This is a professional client—she'll keep you busy, but never change." I told myself I didn't have to do anything to fix her, just make room enough in my mind to be curious about her.

She tearfully told me how she couldn't get away from her pain. She kept drowning in it, no matter how far away she went. As she described her pain in a thin, nasal voice, it was as if she created a vacuum, drawing everyone else in the group into it. It was the first time people in one of our workshops began to shout out suggestions. They started jumping in, trying to rescue her with Kleenex, offering to get her water, patting her on the back and giving advice. She said she had been ignored and abused by her parents as a child. Every time someone made a suggestion, she pulled the sleeves of her purple chenille sweater down over her hands, nodded and responded, "Yes, but . . ."

While everyone else was trying to rescue her, Andy and I just sat there. I tuned out the content of her words and noticed instead the energy that was beneath the surface. Andy mirrored the movements of her hands, memorizing them. Occasionally I said, "I'm still here."

She got hysterical. I breathed, centered and asked myself, "What's right about all of this? What needs are being served by this hysteria? "As long as I remembered that I didn't have to do anything but receive her, I didn't need to pull away or ignore her. I kept wondering, what could be right about never being able to get away from your pain? No answer came so I said, "I'm still here."

Norma squeezed her eyes shut, pulled her shoulders around her ears and yelled, "Yeah, but you'll get tired and leave me, they all do!" I breathed loudly again and said, "That's right, I will." She opened her eyes and dropped her shoulders. I leaned in towards her and went on, "That's why your pain is so lucky to have you be so loyal. Fortunately you don't get worn out by it. You've always been there for it. Much more loyal than I could ever be."

We went through seven or eight minutes of this, and then quite suddenly, she said, "This isn't working." I nodded.

She stood up and walked into the center of the circle. It was the first time I had noticed her thin and agile body. Turning to face the place she had just been sitting, her eyes were watery behind rimless glasses. "Now what do I do?"

Everything changed suddenly. The energy shifted as if a thunderstorm had blown through a muggy afternoon, washed it clean and passed on. Her pain was there. Her wounding was there. Andy stayed there, his hands continuing the movements she had made. However, she was at the turning point. Rather than circling around and around

*"If there is a meaning in life at all, then there must be a meaning to suffering."*

*– Victor Frankl*

223

in the revolving door, she was ready to move on.

I taught her to center. Then I reminded her of one of her resources, by talking about how she could read the faces of the children she worked with, even when they couldn't speak to her. I asked her to look around the circle at the other people and read what was on *their* faces. She scanned the circle slowly, chewing nervously on her bottom lip. The next thing she said surprised me. In a soft but clear voice, her words were, "There's no end to this. I see caring. They're curious and they're here. This isn't going to end."

For the next few minutes, she watched Andy's hands, transfixed. She said, "If he knew sign language, Andy would have just said, 'Don't give up on me'. I asked her to imagine her wounded self sitting across the room next to him. "Sign to her what you've seen in this circle and in Andy's hands."

Norma's thick black hair fell over her face as she looked at her own hands, nodding slowly. In the next moment, her fingers suddenly became birds, dancers, willow branches, flying in the air, arcing, looping, as if pulling invisible threads of light out of nowhere. Her lips followed the movements, but no sounds came out. I asked her to speak as she signed.

Each phrase followed a sequence of movements. "I care about you. I'm curious about you." Her voice was steady, filled with rhythm and feeling. "We're not done yet. We'll never be done. Don't give up. I'm still here. You don't have to work so hard." Her words and hands came to stillness together and tears punctuated the moment.

The whole group moved as if with one mind and pulled up into a clump of support around her. I suggested they could imagine a wounded self of their own over there. Norma continued to sign and speak and we all joined her, learning from her. "I care about you. I'm curious about you. We're not done yet. We'll never be done. Don't give up. I'm still here. You don't have to work so hard." In that

"As long as you are trying to be something other than what you actually are, your mind wears itself out. But if you say 'This is what I am, it is a fact that I am going to investigate, understand,' then you can go beyond."

–Krishnamurti

"Perhaps everything terrible really, in its deepest being, is something helpless that wants help from us."

–Rainer Maria Rilke

moment, each of us fully received our own pain and unmet needs. A wave of compassion was conducted through us the way water allows an electrical current to complete its circuit. Norma was glowing as if she had conducted an oratorio in a human cathedral.

At first the participants in this particular workshop responded to Norma the way their parents had responded to them. They approached her pain with fear, which resulted in pity. They tried to fix her, to make what she was feeling go away. She was equally afraid of her own pain; what resulted was self-pity. What Norma needed, what most all of us need, is to simply be received as we are, wounds and all, to touch our pain with love, which results in mercy.

## What's Wrong About What's Wrong

Before you can understand with compassion what's right about what's wrong, it's necessary to become fully aware of what is wrong and how it's affected you. As long as you keep your pain and suffering unconscious, you'll act in ways that continually defeat the best of your conscious intentions. It's not the wail of pain that maintains suffering; it's the whisper of fear about becoming aware of the pain. You need to validate the pain you have experienced, notice the effects of your experience, *in order to learn from it and make the necessary changes in your life that your healing necessitates.* You must, therefore, allow the pain you have experienced to inform you. In essence, what I am suggesting is that it is important to identify your pain, but not identify *with* it.

Please consider the following as specifically as possible, writing or recording your responses in some way:

*"The truth is more important than the facts."*

–Frank Lloyd Wright

225

*How has this enemy influenced you in your life? How has it affected your attitudes, your body, your emotions, your actions? How has it worked against you? How has it blocked you from getting your needs met? How has it affected your relationships with others?*

*What does your present self need that will help you relate to the enemy? What would be supportive?*

## Expressing Your Pain

Relationship is a circuit, a flow in and out. In order to make room in you for new possibilities, it's necessary to release what's been stuck inside. The practice that follows, which I call creating a "damage report," does just that.

*It's my suggestion, therefore, that you document how this enemy has been affecting you in some way, writing letters to the people in your life (that you may or may not send), making an audio or video tape, finding objects that symbolize the suffering you've experienced as a result, drawing, moving, photographing it as specifically as possible.*

Please save whatever you craft. We will be using it in future steps on this journey. For now, allow it to float in the river of your mind. You are more than that suffering.

*"The secret of life is in the shadows and not in the open sun; to see anything at all, you must look deeply into the shadow of a living thing."*

*–Ute saying*

## Having Compassion For Your Enemy: Your Unmet Needs

Your healing will go as deep as you allow your understanding to go. If you hold a smooth stone in the palm of your hand, it seems solid and impenetrable. But if you examine a slice of it under a microscope, what you will find is a crystalline structure with space between the molecules, as if you were looking at the constellations in a night sky.

Thich Nhat Hanh says that it's necessary to learn to understand deeply, so that when we see garbage we will also be able to see the flowers that are in it. When I heard him say that, I immediately thought about learning to compost when I first moved to Vermont. You take "live garbage" such as banana peels and coffee grounds, pile it up on the ground with spoiled hay and horse manure and let it freeze over the winter. In the spring, you turn the whole pile over to reveal thick, rich black dirt that fertilizes the peonies and begonias of spring.

My grandmother didn't believe in wasting anything. She used to tell me to kiss my tin foil gum wrappers before I threw them away, so I would think about the value of things before I got rid of them.

She also didn't believe in aspirin, but for different reasons. She had magic paper instead. (Well, it probably wasn't magic to anyone else but me.) When I had a headache, for instance, my very rational American mother would give me something to swallow, an aspirin or a malted. She believed in curing, and curing began with one's mouth. To my intuitive, immigrant grandmother, curing was something one did to pickles or meat. She believed in healing, and healing began with one's mind and a kind, clean pair of hands.

Her treatment for my headache was as follows: she wiped her hands on her white apron and sat down, patting her lap. My head was drawn to her lap as a kitten would be to a saucer of warm milk. She rocked back and forth, stroking my forehead, and humming in a throaty voice something with lots of "loo loos" in it. Her hands were cool and dry.

She then cleared off her kitchen table, which was covered in red oilcloth, and put out a large piece of plain

*"I know of no trouble in life which does not stand as a counterpart to some positive capacity."*

*–M.C. Richards*

227

*"An ulcer is an unkissed imagination taking its revenge for having been jilted. It is an undanced dance, an unpainted water-color, an unwritten poem."*

*–John Ciardi*

brown wrapping paper. I knelt on a chair and she told me to let my mind go wide, like a pigeon's wings; let it go to the dark place, the deep place inside all of the layers, the place where no one could bother me. She told me to let my eyes rest patiently on the blank paper. Soon, soon, some-time soon, the paper would show me what my headache needed to heal.

An image emerged as if it had been drawn with lemon juice and then held over a candle. I saw Diane and Betsy. They had been my best friends until a few days before, when they told me I was a baby and they were ashamed to be seen with me. When I told this to my grandmother, she had me take off my shoes and socks. She rubbed my feet tenderly, saying, "I'm so glad you still have these."

A strange thing happened then. My head emptied of the ache and my feet filled with heat. They sizzled. I jumped up and stomped on the paper chanting, "I am not a baby. Ouch! Ouch! Ouch! I don't want you to be my friends anymore." What was getting satisfied was a red hot anger, a fury. Call it what you will, but I *needed* to express my pain, to reject that shame, to give back that identity. I had literally been "putting the lid on" all of that need. Then we burned the paper with her candle, letting go of the garbage. But the jewel I kept was a fiery power I had deep inside of me.

My grandmother was teaching me the same lesson as Thich Nhat Hanh—to understand deeply. This is crucially important when it comes to developing a relationship of compassion and respect with your enemy, since it's neces-sary to understand that it does indeed fulfill some function for you. All behavior is purposeful. Your unconscious mind is always working on your own behalf. More than anything, it wants to help you survive, heal, and get your basic needs met. It does not care about anyone else. Its ways of meeting your needs may be very unsophisticated and limited, but once you understand what it is trying to do, it is very willing to learn healthier and more effective ways to

*"What is meant by light? To gaze with undimmed eyes on all darkness"*

*–Nikos Kazantakis*

meet those needs.

Abraham Maslow, a remarkable psychologist, describes what he calls the basic hierarchy of human needs: fundamental survival—food, water, shelter; emotional warmth and connection; belonging; meaning—making a contribution; and self-actualization—the development of one's full potential.

To be protected, nurtured, communicated with; to be looked at, listened to, and touched without judgment; to have choices about contact; to express ourselves and to have boundaries which differentiate us from the rest of the world: these are fundamental psychological needs. If children are not touched with love, for instance, they do not develop normally. Their essence is damaged; their souls are wounded.

The greatest human motivation is an unsatisfied need. Like a shadow, it never goes away. It has density and a powerful magnetic pull which follows us, drives us, seeking, craving fulfillment. An unmet need will attract you to opportunities to do the work your soul needs to do and learn what must be learned for your own actualization.

Like all children, I had the need to be protected. I was protected by my father, but not from him. When I grew up, I looked to other men to meet this need, but I kept finding myself in situations where the men I turned to for protection were the men from whom I needed protection. My unconscious mind wanted me to complete the needs I had carried for so long: to protect myself by establishing boundaries and safety with a man, as I had never done with my father. If I was dependent on someone else to fill my needs for me, I knew I'd lose him eventually and then be totally without protection. It was like giving someone else the only key to my safe deposit box.

When I chose to avoid men in an attempt to get away from abuse, I began to abuse myself through drugs. It was only when I allowed myself to externalize that abuser, and

*"There is enough for everybody's need but not for everybody's greed."*

*–Gandhi*

229

notice how deeply I was wounded, that I made space to give myself what I had really needed since I was a child: comfort and protection.

## What's Right About What's Wrong

When Andy and I teach people to shift their level of thinking beneath their symptoms to the level where the current of unmet needs flow, we play a kind of psychic detective game called "That's Right." Here's how it goes:

One person, X, acts out the most difficult behavior of any person they've encountered during the week. The other person, Y, is only allowed to say, "That's right." The pair knows that at any moment Andy or I will come up behind them, place a hand on Y's shoulder, and say, "What's right?" At that moment, Y will have to describe what could possibly be right about the behavior X is exhibiting.

For our purposes, I'm going to describe briefly some people I've worked with recently, and then share the underlying needs of their symptoms that they discovered. Then I'll give you a few more to think through on your own.

A woman is terrified of being alone. She is fine if she is alone in her car or in her office, but when she is home alone, she gets more and more anxious. "I just feel lost and afraid. As if I'm in danger. That's it! When I was a kid, I always used to get shut up in my room alone. All I could hear was my drunken mother screaming she wanted to kill me, and then silence when she passed out. Now I have that screaming voice inside my head, and when I'm in a silent house I get scared she'll burst in any minute and try to kill me. What I always needed was my father to come home and talk to me and explain what was going on."

A man describes himself as suicidal and wanting to end

it all. "What I'm beginning to understand is that my unmet need is to end being who everybody else wants me to be. I'm going through a major transition in my life, a divorce. One part of me is dying, while another part is ready to be reborn. I think it's time for a particular way I suffer to die."

A man is extremely self-critical whenever he begins to create. "I just found out that my name means 'guardian.' I'm learning that the critical voices in my mind were guarding my unconscious mind, like demon statues standing guard outside a temple. If I criticize myself enough, no one else will be able to do it any worse, and I'll never have to be surprised like when I was a kid. I always needed the space to explore without being humiliated."

A man was aging. He had been married fifty-five years. He was deaf in one ear and would drift off when his wife spoke to him. His wife developed a muscular weakness from the edges of her body inward. "My unmet need is going deaf? To listen to my own inner voice. At my age, it's time to pay attention to it. I figured out my wife's, too, but I know I'm not supposed to tell her. Her body is making sure she gets her needs to pay attention to herself met by not being able to run around and wait on everybody else, 'hand and foot'. She needs to receive attention. She needs to feel herself, which she never did when she could run around like that."

A woman found herself having what she called temper tantrums, right before dinner. She hated her entire family and fought with everyone. This frequently led to her stomping out of the room, slamming the door, and sulking. With flushed cheeks, here's what she discovered hiding under the enemy tantrums: "I needed to be alone. It's as simple as that. I feel mortified to admit it, but hating everyone else was the only way I could allow myself to be alone. When I was a kid, my parents used to send me to my room when I had temper tantrums. I loved it! I got to read and be undisturbed in the quiet. I guess I was still using the

> *"Nothing human is alien to me."*
>
> *– Voltaire*

231

same solution."

Here are some examples from people I've worked with in the past week: to have an individual identity acknowledged; to be taught and guided with encouragement; to be supported to rest; to become conscious of and nurture one's own feelings, to express one's pain; to be enjoyed; and to enjoy accomplishments with satisfaction.

## Practice: Finding the Rose Among the Thorns

*"What is a weed? A plant whose virtues have never been discovered."*

*–Emerson*

Time to do some on your own. What we're doing is learning to understand *teleology*, the force that drives symptoms, the unmet needs that lie beneath the surface of symptoms.

Let's start off with something very simple. You and I are sitting facing each other and I keep running my fingers through my hair. Andy taps you on the shoulder and whispers, "What's right about that?" You say . . .

"Maybe she's trying to increase the circulation to her brain; perhaps her mother used to stroke her hair when she was worried; perhaps she needs some kinesthetic stimulation to help her words flow; perhaps she has dandruff!"

Try this one. A woman who was sexually abused as a child is bulimic. She gorges herself with food and then goes into the bathroom and vomits. What's right about that?

Perhaps as a child her parents controlled her very strictly, so this is her way of meeting the need to parent herself—by feeding herself whatever she wants and then controlling what she digests. Perhaps she's demonstrating that when she was young, she couldn't keep things out of her that were forced on or in her, but vomiting is her way of meeting the need to get rid of them. Perhaps it's a way of un-swallowing her rage at someone who abused her.

A man develops food allergies. He can no longer eat or drink anything made of grain without going into shock. What's right about that? Perhaps he needs to be very careful about the way he nurtures himself. Maybe his mother was an alcoholic and he suffered as a result. He may need to make sure he doesn't drink substances made of grain—liquor—so he will nourish himself in a way that isn't toxic to him.

*"If the oyster had hands, there would be no pearl. Because the oyster is forced to live with the irritation for an extended period, the pearl comes to be."*

*—Stephen Nachmanovitch*

## Personal Exploration: Finding your Unmet Needs

So what's right about what's wrong with you? I'm not going to ask you to kiss the garbage. What is important in this practice is that you enter into an intuitive conversation with your enemy about its needs; braille your way through, deep into the center of it; embrace it, jiggle it in your arms, walk with it, making cooing sounds the way you would with a baby that you loved until you could sense what she needs.

Some of the questions that may guide you are: What is the enemy asking you to let go of? What is it asking you to hold onto? What lesson is it trying to teach you? What suffering has resulted from how you've responded to it? What is its hidden value?

It is possible to do this practice through holding the disconnected image of your enemy at a safe distance in your mind, or by placing the representation you made of it in the last chapter at a comfortable distance from yourself.

Here are several different ways of learning about its unmet needs:

*"In order to grow beyond an old myth, it's necessary to accept the role it played in your life, understand the reasons you at one time needed it, and appreciate the valid messages it still holds."*

*—Stanley Krippner*

233

"Perhaps everything terrible in us is in its deepest being some-thing helpless that needs help."

–Rainer Maria Rilke

Imagine it is having a conversation with you and tape record the spoken dialogue.

Put a pen in your non-dominant hand and have it write you a letter, or create a visual dialogue by writing your questions in your dominant hand and allowing the enemy to respond with your non-dominant hand. This hand is untutored, uncontaminated, untaught and thus what results from it, although it doesn't look neat or polished and is awkward, is often raw truth, original uncensored thought. I hear people say all the time, "On the one hand . . . on the other hand . . ." So you can give your conscious mind one hand and your unconscious mind the other.

Take yourself for a walk—your hurting self, your shadow self, your internal enemy. It can be around the block or to the other side of town. Pretend that self is next to you instead of inside of you, or in front of you, if that feels more comfortable. I'm not asking you to have a major relationship at this point. Just make space enough inside your mind to be curious. What would it be like to breathe with this self, to listen to this self? What tone of voice would it use? What would its movement be like, its rhythm? How would it see the world? Just have the experience of being on the same side as you amble in curiosity. As you would with a friend, notice how you could draw out what needs wait to be met.

Allow yourself to feel the energy and rhythm of the enemy, and let it dance to you, sound to you, or play what it needs on a drum, a guitar, a keyboard.

Go on a lazy walk and notice which objects in the natural world pull on you as representatives of your unmet enemy needs. Photograph them or bring them home and describe them in your journal, using the words "I am" instead of "It is." The last line of your description could begin, "If you want to treat me well, know that I need. . . ."

Go through a pile of old newspapers and magazines and cut out words, phrases, images which leap out as representative of your unmet needs. Do it quickly enough that your linear mind won't get in the way.

"Beneath every conflict is a desire to connect."

–Dannan Perry

An example from the nearest mind around: Here's the letter my non-dominant hand wrote to me from my top favorite enemy of the month—the aspect of myself that would rather put off until tomorrow whatever is needed urgently today–Inertia!

*Dear Pressuring Present Dawna,*

*I know you think I'm a space cadet and that I blank out on you whenever you need me. I also know that you think I'm lazy and procrastinate. Well, I'd like you to know that I have needs too. I need to dream sometimes and I need to buffer your relentless demands to produce, produce, produce. I think around in circles and I want respect for my unique way of operating in the world. And while we're at it, I need to play. You took away all the destructive ways we used to play. Now how are we going to play?*

*Sincerely, very sincerely,*
*In Her Shell*

## Receiving Your Needs With Compassion

Have you ever heard anyone say, "I don't want to appear to be needy, but . . ."? Have you ever said, "I don't need anybody!" I remember saying that a few months before I got sick. Then I took a fourteen-year refresher course in how much I really do need. The less aware you are of your needs, the more enemies will lurk in the shadows of your mind.

If you have been trained to ignore what you need, one way to reclaim your awareness is to notice what you're giving to those around you. Inevitably, we give to others what we most need to be giving to ourselves.

The following practice is a simple one, the purpose of which is to enhance your ability to receive your needs with compassion:

*"The harder we look at our aches and ailments, the more we will be startled by the painful truths they are trying to convey about our dangerously disembodied way of life."*

*–Marion Woodman*

"Break a vase and the love that reassembles the fragments is stronger than the love which took its symmetry for granted when it was whole."

–Derek Walcott

*For a week or so, just simply notice how you experience needing in your body. What causes it to arise? Is your awareness of it in one channel or multi-modal? Do you contract energetically or expand when you become aware of it? What is it like when your needing stops? What follows it?*

In every wounding, there is the potential of a gift for healing. You will begin to sense that when you are willing to listen to your enemy through your heart, when your eyes see it through the light of compassion, when you allow yourself to touch it with mercy. When you reach to understand the needs of the wounded warrior and helpless healer within, when you give the seeker the freedom to search for meaning in the darkness, your journey to wholeness has turned a corner and is inclined toward the light.

# 12 What You Need Is What You Got:
## Recognizing Internal Resources

*Hold on to what is good
even if it is a handful of earth.
Hold on to what you believe
even if it is a tree which stands by itself.
Hold on to what you must do
even if it is a long way from here.
Hold on to life
even when it is easier letting go.
Hold on to my hand
even when I have gone away from you.*

—Pueblo Blessing

Before you journey further, we need to stop and rest for awhile. Any expedition needs a base camp of some sort—a place to hunker down with all the stuff that protects and nurtures you, a place to leave the struggle out there and rest, recoup, restore, reconnect with your supply lines.

That's exactly what we're about to do now. Thus far, we've been learning by "sourcing," traveling on an inward journey, using intuition and imagination as fuel. The enemy rests outside in compassionate hands. Now it's time to stop and learn by resourcing, re-engaging our intellects to open up the realms of what we think is possible. This requires a mind that is powerful, with a flexible curiosity rather than a rigid certainty. Instead of focusing on the enemy, in this chapter, we'll be learning to recognize your inner resources, the assets and life experiences you have to meet the needs of that problem.

But what if you don't have any resources that you know of? Or don't have the vaguest idea of how to find the ones that would help you with this struggle? The word *resource* comes from the Latin, meaning to rise again. And the root of recognize means to know in a different way. So you are in effect going to be learning how to know in a different way, in order to rise again.

*"Your inner opponent's greatest advantage is your lack of belief in your ultimate triumph."*

*–R.L. Wing*

## You're More Than Your Enemy: Developing An Asset-Focus

When I was in fourth grade in Chicago, Illinois, one of my favorite places to go after school with Bob Newton, my boyfriend, was the Mayflower Doughnut shop. I don't remember whether my favorite doughnut was maple glazed or cinnamon, but what glistens in my memory is a sign painted on a piece of pine that hung over the green wall behind the cash register. It read: "As you wander on through life, whatever be your goal, keep your eye upon the doughnut, not upon the hole."

In graduate school, I was trained to notice the hole, to define and categorize every shape and sort of deficit. Milton Erickson, however, was a doughnut master. While my clinical supervisors exhorted me to uncover the patterns of every patient's misery, Dr. Erickson believed it was necessary to discover and re-cover the patterns of their happiness. He switched the issue from how well someone was to how they were well. As I was memorizing the rules of pathology, he was teaching people to notice the exceptions to the rules: When wasn't this person, who was diagnosed as being paranoid, afraid? Under what circumstances *did* this person, who was diagnosed as being catatonic, move? He taught that people had problems because, in their current context, they were unable to access or use the resources and abilities available to them. It was as if their resources were locked up into tiny separate compartments. The challenge was to find a way to take what people have and move it to where they needed it.

It's so easy to be oriented toward what isn't working and what hasn't worked. We are tracked into our deficits at an early age. Our entire educational system is organized around how many things we get wrong. It is no wonder we have such a loyalty to our problems. Alice Walker describes it as loving what is scarce instead of what is plentiful. Our culture is now filled with groups magnetized by their pathology. We are trained to both label ourselves *as our problems*, "I'm an incest survivor," and label ourselves *as the cause of our problems*, "I broke my arm yesterday. I guess I should have been paying more attention to what I was doing."

There are obvious benefits to be derived from identifying ourselves in that way. We no longer have to be isolated and alone with our problems; we can be connected to a community of others, a subculture within the "normal"

*"I work as my father drank."*

*–George Bernard Shaw*

culture. There are also dangers: "I'm an alcoholic so I couldn't help it if I beat her up."

However, if you are only interested in your problems, in what you cannot do, you will think of yourself as inadequate, and seize your brain into that pattern of stuckness. On the other hand, if you are first compassionately aware of your problem—as we have been learning to do—and then interested in the wide horizon of your experiences—the coping strengths and patterns of success you've already earned in your life—you will feel empowered. Your self-esteem and sense of competence will be increased as you become reacquainted with your natural patterns of health, enabling you to bring this innate wisdom to your problem.

I had a wonderful dream that taught me about how much more free I was than I allowed myself to know. It began as a recurring nightmare: A woman is in a prison cell. Someone is shooting at her. She wears shiny, impenetrable power bracelets that deflect every shot. But the bullets keep on coming, faster and faster. She enjoys the triumph of surviving the onslaught—at least at first. But it is exhausting and, after awhile, meaningless. Her arms begin to feel leaden. She mumbles listlessly, "Why bother?" Just as she is about to drop her hands and let one of the bullets make the decision for her, I wake up.

Relentlessly each night, the dream haunts my sleep. Months later, the bullets are still flying, bracelets deflecting. But this time, in her exhaustion, the woman leans against the cell door for support, and notices that something is poking in her lower back.

I am jarred awake, the dream still unfinished. By the next night, I am fiercely curious about this dream and determined to complete it. Shortly after falling asleep, the woman is again frantically fending off flying bullets. Leaning back against the cell door, the poking object is still in her back. Reaching one hand behind her, while deflecting

> "You can't escape certain parts of your makeup. . . . They may have been installed early without your knowledge or permission. Sometimes the equipment is very good and useful. Other times you'll end up in a ditch sooner or later. Either way, you pay the devil trying to get rid of any of it."
>
> –David Small

241

twice as fast with the other, she feels ... impossible! ... she feels a *doorknob* ... a smooth, metal doorknob! Shocked, her hand automatically turns it and, as she does, the cell door opens outward.

Whirling around, there is a vast landscape spread before her, a magnificent panorama that rolls unimpeded to the horizon! Overwhelmed, she tries to cringe back into the cell, but the wind sucks her out. Curling her body in on itself, she becomes a stone falling into the center of everything. A voice from somewhere shouts, "Let go. Let go ... and live!" She does exactly that, though it's not really a doing, more of a wild releasing. Her body spreads wide, like a kite or parachute. Falling becomes floating, which in turn becomes soaring and laughter, unlimited, unrestricted, outrageous, laughter!

*"Wounding opens the doors of our sensibility to a larger reality, which is blocked to our habituated and conditioned point of view."*

*–Jean Houston*

## It's All There

A Canadian neurosurgeon, Wilder Penfield, discovered in the 1950's that electrical stimulation of areas in the temporal lobe of the brain caused patients to vividly experience memories of seemingly everything that ever happened to them when they were five, then thirteen, then twenty-four, including things that they were not aware of at the time.

In other words, the five-year-old who doesn't know you've grown up, the needy teenager, the confused young adult are still alive as whole beings someplace in your mind, *as are their qualities and capacities*! We know so much more than we know that we know! To use the full power of our minds is to tap into those resources—be they as simple as chopping onions or as complex as painting a jungle mural—and use them to change how we relate to our histories, the problems in our present lives, and the way we design our futures.

Here's an example. Andy and I worked with a former minister (K-V-A), who was very respected, but miserable. He had always wanted to paint, but he told us the most significant artistic thing he ever got to do was to perform marriage ceremonies. He finally left the church, but he was so overwhelmed by guilt that he couldn't paint. I asked him to imagine seeing his left hand filled with his intuitive, creative self, and his right with the respected "out in the world" self. He sat for awhile, with his palms facing upward, balancing one against the other. He reported that the position was an accurate representation of how he felt stuck in his life. I told him to marry his right hand to his left. He looked dumbfounded, and then threw his head back and laughed. In the moments that followed, he recited the entire wedding vows and performed a ritual marriage of wholeness between those two aspects of himself.

There are four compartments of resources that you may not have recognized, or known how to access and use in relation to your enemy. The first contains the talents and skills from other realms of your life, like the man who performed wedding ceremonies. The second holds the moments when you were not blocked by your enemy. The third includes a collection of skills that have been mis-perceived because they have been used in the wrong context, and the last houses qualities and aspects that may have been not used to the fullest. We'll explore them one at a time.

*"Through the resource of power we are able to show up. Through the resource of love we are able to pay attention to what has heart and meaning. Through the resource of vision we are able to give voice to what we see. Through the resource of wisdom we are able to be open to all possibilities and unattached to outcome."*

*–Angeles Arrien*

## Noticing Where You're Free: Recognizing Your Assets

Most of my teachers trained me to put my center in the stuck place, in the struggle. Then, one day, Terry Dobson, the brilliantly simple aikido master, stood in my kitchen and grabbed my wrist with his large, calloused paw. I, of course, responded habitually. First, I tried to pull free by getting rigid. Then I collapsed and tried to ignore him. With his eyes glittering out from the cave of bushy gray brows, he said, "You're noticing where you're stuck. Shift your attention to where you're free!" Instantly I realized that about 98 percent of my body was free to move, to bend, to twirl around and put the free arm over his shoulder and hug him!

When you are struggling with a problem, fighting to fend off the bullets, you forget about all the experiences, resources and wisdom you've been collecting all your life. It's so easy to lose the sky of your mind and become stuck in that one single storm cloud.

An asset-focused way of thinking is based on the assumption that you already have the inner resources to construct a way through, that is uniquely your own and highly effective for you in other situations of your life. As I have said before, this approach is very different from what most of us have been taught to believe. And it is the difference that makes such a difference.

I had just three sessions to work with Rena (V-K-A). She was very clear about that condition. She had a mane of hair the color of an angry sunset. She also was struggling with cervical cancer, had just had a hysterectomy, and was about to begin chemotherapy. She wanted me to do hypnotherapy with her to assist her through the pain. She explained right off to me, in a high fast voice, that the man who drove her to my house (she referred to him as "My Old Man") was a marijuana dealer. I turned and examined the bearded man sitting in the red 1975 Ford pick-up truck outside the big bay window of my office.

"He beats me up too. And I know I have to leave him; but I can't handle it right now, not till the chemotherapy is over." She put her long white fingers over her eyes. I noticed blue stains under her fingernails. Her voice was

*"There is a vitality, a life force, an energy, a quickening that is translated through you into action, and because there is only one of you in all time, this expression is unique. And if you block it, it will never exist through any other medium and be lost, the world will not have it."*

*–Martha Graham*

exhausted. It made me think of worn slipcovers.

"Do you paint?" I asked.

"Yeah, I do—as a matter of fact. Well, I don't paint exactly . . . well, I do. What I mean is, I paint tee shirts and sell them. That's how I make my living."

I just nodded and breathed. No questions came to me. If the truth was known, I was a little intimidated knowing I was being watched by an abusive pot dealer. I sat up a little straighter.

Words tumbled out of her throat. "In some ways, I guess I know he loves me; but he's rough on me. It's been like an exchange, a trade-off; except, now that I'm sick, he's scared. I'm using him. But I don't want to talk about that. I want you to do trance work with me to help me with the pain and so my hair won't fall out. He's paying for these three sessions."

I sat back against my brown corduroy pillow. "I can't do that, Rena."

Her mouth dropped open. I've read about that happening to people, but I'd never seen it before. "But you're a hypnotherapist."

I explained in slow, simple sentences that most people wanted to use hypnosis to stop things . . . things like smoking or overeating or nail biting. I told her that I didn't think it worked real well for those things anyway, and that since hair loss was a result of the toxic substances it was necessary to use for chemotherapy, there was nothing anyone could do about it. I stood up.

"So, I don't think I can help you, Rena. I don't want to waste your time."

She pulled on my wrist. I couldn't avoid her eyes. They were immense and watery green. "Wait. Just listen. I'm really scared. _You_ got through this. And you're a woman. All my doctors are men. I need a woman to help me. Please help me."

I sat down, placing my other hand over hers.

_"To be an artist is to fail as no others dare fail."_

_–Samuel Beckett_

245

"You've got my attention, Rena. I *am* a woman. I could care very much about you and what you're going through. Too much, maybe, to help you. I also haven't 'gotten through this'. I never had chemotherapy. I don't have the vaguest idea how to heal you. You're living in a toxic situation."

I tilted my head toward the red pick up truck. "You're about to go through another toxic situation. How can I possibly help you?"

She curled in on herself, sobbing, a tiny boneless creature. I placed a hand on her back and breathed in and out, in and out. We stayed like that for many minutes. Finally, she was breathing long and slow with me. Her cheeks were streaked with black mascara.

"I . . . I'm sorry. I didn't think I'd do that. I . . . I'm terrified and I needed to say that to a woman, I guess. My mom died when I was a kid. I'm furious too, really angry . . . and, well, thanks anyway." She walked over to the mirrored wall at the other end of the room, where she began to clean up her face with a Kleenex.

I followed her. "Rena, what I *can* do is accompany you, and maybe I can help you find some choices you might not be aware you have in all of this."

She looked at my reflection in the mirror, and stopped mid-wipe. "What do you mean?"

"Well, what if your terror is just excitement waiting to happen? What if your fury, your anger, is energy demanding motion? That's what I think all emotions are—energy demanding motion. What if that energy is trying to signal you that change is necessary, that you have to grieve and let go to make way for what can be?"

The words were pouring out now. I paused to breathe and put my hand on her shoulder. "What if, just suppose now, that instead of thinking of yourself as a victim to whom this all is happening, what if you thought of yourself as a noble warrior, facing the barriers to your own truth?"

*"A person is his own worst enemy. . . . Ten enemies can't do what a person does to himself."*

*–Isaac Bashevis Singer*

"Here's an example of what I mean." I left her standing there and walked out of the room. I came back in three or four minutes, with my arms full of stuff, which I dumped at her feet.

"You don't have to let this happen *to* you, Rena. You can choose to use the talent you have and make the whole thing your work of art." I spread out scissors, an electric razor, six little jars of tempera paint, three sable brushes, and a large white towel on the bare floor.

She looked at the stuff. She looked at me, then in the mirror, shaking her head. "Do you mean I should shave off my own hair?"

"I mean more than that, Rena. I mean you should create this event as a rite of passage, which includes shaving off your hair, then painting your own bare scalp with images that symbolize healing and power to you."

Her face went through seasons of emotions in two minutes—from amazement, to fury, to grief, to wonder. She turned to face the mirror and began to run her fingers through her hair. "Say it again, that warrior stuff."

"Rena, you are not a victim to whom things happen. You are a splendid warrior, a noble artist, called to go through a rite of passage now. Your anger calls you. Your terror calls you. Your life calls you. You will be going through a healing process that will be destroying cells. You have chosen some ways of living that have been destructive to you. You can release those now. You can create from them."

She kept stroking her hair. I breathed. A voice in my mind began screaming, "*Markova are you crazy? What is he going to think if she walks out of this house with a painted bald scalp? He's paying for you to save her hair. Markova, he is a very large and dangerous man!*"

I was about to interrupt her reverie to tell her she didn't have to decide now, and maybe she should consult with her old man, when her back lengthened and she squatted

*". . . If you want to get rid of something you must first allow it to flourish. If you want to take something, you must first allow it to be given."*

*–Lao Tzu*

247

down on the floor, wrapping the towel around her shoulders. "Aren't you going to sit down next to me, Dawna? Hold up that hand mirror so I can see the back too." I collapsed down on the floor immediately, and followed her instructions. She reached for the scissors.

I'm not sure how long it took. I just breathed. In and out. At some point, she turned to face me. "You can look now, Dawna."

How do I describe that moment? Her head and neck were covered with a jungle, screaming in the hot sun with parrots, vines, frogs, zebras and alligators. She was luminescent, as if she had swallowed summer.

*"Discover their patterns of happiness."*

*–Milton Erickson*

In the weeks that followed our session, several people told me about the beautiful woman with the painted head they had seen. She made quite a splash walking down the main street of the little Vermont town in which she lived.

"I did what you told me," she said proudly at the beginning of our next session. She stretched her long legs out on the cushions of the window seat. She was wearing dungarees and red leather high heeled boots. She wore no make up, but her head definitely was painted . . . a riot of images—cats this time—panthers and leopards, tigers with bloody teeth. In the center of her forehead was one fluffy black and white kitten. It was connected to the rest by a black web. I was so fascinated that I was speechless for several minutes.

"I've been using my head as a kind of journal. Instead of drawing my disease in my journal, and what it needs and what I'll be like when I'm healed, I've been painting a different section on my head each day."

I looked nervously in the driveway. There was the red pick-up and her old man—smoking his Camels. This time, though, he was staring straight in the window.

"How has your old man responded to all of this?" I asked with great trepidation.

She leaned back and laughed softly. "Well, it's weird.

When I got in the truck last week, all he said was, 'Sheeeeit!' and I said right away, 'Don't fuck with me!' I never have talked to him like that, you know; but I just centered like we did here and those words came right up from my belly. She pointed a thumb toward the red pick up truck, "I think he gets off on my head or something. Anyway, all week, I've been finding myself saying 'Don't fuck with me' to alot of people. I decided I don't want him paying for these sessions, either. I want to pay you in tee shirts. Is that OK with you?"

Not only was it all right; in answer, I turned toward the window and pulled the cord which hung at the corner, slowly letting the thin silver venetian blinds come down over the glass.

"All right! It's you and me now, Rena."

Thich Nhat Hanh tells us that in times that are chaotic, it is most important to notice what is stable in our internal and external worlds, what we can count on no matter what, when all else is changing. Rena was going through a storm in her life. It was not helping her to try to hang on to the branches. By turning to her art, which was always there for her, she crawled down to the stable trunk where her wisdom could help her explore the roots of her healing.

> *"Therapy is a matter of tipping the first domino. All that was needed was the correction of one behavior and if that was corrected. . . ."*
>
> *–Milton Erickson*

## Recognizing the Doughnut

This is not the same as "positive thinking" or doing affirmations. The point is not to deny your suffering, or affirm that the world is the way you wish it would be. Your enemy gets full attention, and then you *also* notice the exception to your enemy's rule. Because change is constant, at some moments we are happier and more effective than at others. What I'm suggesting is that we learn to study the choices we make in *those* moments, how we think and respond, track our successes, our resources, our assets—so we can use them to meet the needs that are embedded in our problems. This is what William James, in the *Varieties Of Religious Experience*, called "healthy mindedness."

I worked with a man (V-K-A) who had very severe asthma attacks. He wanted me to use hypnosis to assist him in getting over them. I explained that I couldn't do that, since I had never had an asthma attack. He went into an immediate state of confusion. I then explained very slowly and rhythmically, so his unconscious mind would hear me as his state of consciousness expanded, that he, in fact, was the expert on getting over an attack, since his system had overcome hundreds of them. As his eyelids fluttered and his body began to rock back and forth in time to my words, I requested that his unconscious mind utilize everything it knew about getting over asthma attacks, and apply it exactly one minute after an attack began.

When he returned two weeks later, he told me that I was a failure, because he had the same number of attacks as before our previous session. But then he winked, and said that he was a success because each attack was over before he could take his inhaler out of his pocket!

Let's rummage through this compartment of your experience of what you do know about dealing effectively with what's "wrong" with you.

*Think of one time when you were successful at influencing your enemy, if only for a minute. If nothing comes to you, then think of a time in your life when you were successful at doing something you really wanted to do.*

*Let that go and switch to thinking of a time when you got stuck.*

*Go back and forth between the two, until you can identify one or more things you did that made a difference (i.e., In the successful time, I was walking outside and in the stuck time I was sitting at a desk. In the successful time I was seeing things through*

"*Our deepest fears are like dragons guarding our deepest treasure.*"

–*Rainer Maria Rilke*

*my own eyes and in the stuck time I was looking in on myself as if from a surveillance camera.)*

## Researching Your Resources

What follows is a list of questions, some of which may be helpful in recognizing where and when you are already free of your enemy. Many of them were inspired by the work of Stephen de Shazer at the Milwaukee Brief Family Therapy Center. You may want to write the answers in a journal, talk them into a tape or go for a walk, as your brain mulls them over. You may need to do some research for awhile and just notice the answers to the questions over a week or so:

*How will you know when you're beyond this? ( Be as specific as you can.)*

*What was one time in your life when it seemed as if everything fell apart and you wanted to give up, but didn't do so?*

*When doesn't your enemy bother you? When is it less difficult?*

*What specifically do you do at those times? How do you decide to do what you do? What resources and attributes do you drawn on then?*

*Can you imagine what it will be like when you are no longer struggling with this enemy? If not, imagine a miracle has occurred and you wake up without it anymore. How will you know you're beyond it? What will be different for you and those you love?*

*When the enemy is not bothering you, what are you feeling in your body? Can you imagine what will happen in your life when you are feeling that way in the future? Are any of those things happening now, even a little?*

*What are the resources of that enemy? (i.e. stubbornness/ determination, loyalty, protection, etc.)*

*Think about a time in the past before you experienced your enemy, no matter how far back you have to go. What abilities or*

> "Error is just as important a condition of life's progress as truth."
>
> –C.G. Jung

251

*"There is only one real deprivation, I decided this morning, and that is not to be able to give one's gift to those one loves most. . . . The gift turned inward, unable to be given, becomes a heavy burden, even sometimes a kind of poison. It is as though the flow of life were backed up."*

*–May Sarton*

*resources did you draw on then?*

*How have you already begun to heal this? What will be the very first sign that things are getting better?*

*What will you be thinking about in the future when you are beyond this?*

*Who in your past has been really supportive of you, in some way? What difference did their support make?*

*Who has been an inspiration to you: historic or current hero or heroine? What animals have been allies to you?*

*Who and what are the people and things in your current life that are important to you and you would like to continue?*

*What habits or routines do you have in your life? Is there any way you could use those to help you with this situation?*

## Utilization of Psychic Discards

Most things of worth begin as mud. The challenge, of course, is to take that mud and make pottery. The resources of your enemy and life are waiting to be re-shaped into something useful. The only thing that's required is that you take them out and use them in a different way.

I worked with a woman who told me she always felt rejected. As we plunged into therapy she discovered, in fact, that she was an expert in rejecting and abandoning herself. We decided that could be used as a valuable resource, if she would begin to reject her self-doubt. Since she abandoned herself regularly, we decided to put that to use by having her experiment abandoning self-criticism. We both began to really enjoy these bad jokes turned good. I practiced with her and began to procrastinate criticizing myself, playing with having a lack of confidence in the ways I was doubting my own abilities.

Inspired by my tales of this experience, a man I worked with who was always "yeah . . . but-ing" every desire he had

("I want to learn to fly a plane. Yeah, but I don't have enough money.), decided to turn the "buts" inside out, using them to keep out unwanted interference from people when he was selling an idea at work. ("I know you don't think this will work, but that's not helpful for me to hear right now.")

Here are some more examples of using the mechanism of the problem to work *for* you. Thich Nhat Hanh uses the things that are irritants to most of us as signals to breathe and gather stillness. He suggests, for instance, that every time the phone rings, we notice three breaths before picking it up. Likewise, before making a phone call, notice three breaths. For some of us, that means many opportunities during the day to calm our minds. He also suggests using red lights and traffic jams in a similar fashion. I realized that when I smoked two packs of cigarettes a day, I unfailingly gave myself the chance to notice my breath forty times a day for seven minutes each time! So, there still is time in every day to "meditate" on my breath at least forty times.

Another one that makes me smile to think about is the man who was driving himself to be the best in his work, because he wanted desperately to be special. At the same time, he realized that he wasn't enjoying his life at all. It was just happening to him. As he began to notice his process, he discovered that there was a voice in his mind that was frequently whispering to him that what he was doing was really ordinary, not special at all. It was also pointing out examples of how this was true. We began to explore the uses and virtues of "ordinary" together, and discovered that it could enable him to take simple pleasure in his life, to open with wonder to the little things, to feel peaceful and easy in every situation, and to just receive what was around him.

In a slightly different vein, here's a compartment that leaves you feeling fuller, wider, more alive every time you poke into it:

*"The only real liberation is that which liberates both the oppressor and the oppressed."*

*–Thomas Merton*

253

*"It is not by one's sins that you know some-one but by what the person celebrates."*

*–Rabbi A. Twersky*

*You access this resource by making a list, written or verbal (out loud). The list is entitled, "Ten Things I Greatly Love." Just before you start, imagine you're in prison and these are things you miss. Or, imagine you're on your death bed and these are the things you'll be really sad to leave. They can be little things like the Sunday newspaper, or bigger things. Whatever comes to you.*

*Give yourself a short time limit, such as four minutes. This makes it difficult for your linear mind to get in the way.*

*Then, make a list of three times in the last month you made a difference. Small or large. It can be as simple as, "I took care of my cat and kept her alive for a month."*

For some people, these are challenging. Just keep practicing—like a path in the forest that becomes yours only after you walk it many times, acknowledging them helps your resources get clearer each time.

One last one. Let's find out what resource your unconscious mind thinks would help you meet your enemy's needs in a new way:

*Please center. Expand your state of mind, and access your intuition in whatever way you have found comfortable and effective.*

*Wonder with the question, (stated in your own words), "What resource would most help me meet these needs? Please give me a symbol."*

*Then, allow your mind to wander wherever it would like to go. At some point, a symbol of a resource will make itself known to you. Perhaps now; perhaps later. When it does, ask where in your body would be the most effective place to keep that resource. Whenever a response comes, imagine rooting or nesting that symbol in that place, a kind of sacred safe deposit box, if you will.*

## Putting Needed Qualities At Your Fingertips: Metaforms

Albert Einstein said that the problems we face can't be solved at the same level of thinking we used to create them. We need to step back, widen our periphery, expand our awareness, shift the context in which we're thinking about them.

When I was in recovery from an addiction to marijuana, I found myself retreating daily to a brand new handmade macrame hammock I had bought, without really understanding why. I often didn't even lay in it, but I used to love to run my fingers over all the knots and in and out of all the spaces between them. I'd pull on one end until the strings were stressed so tight that I'd bounce right out if I'd tried to sit on it. Then I'd let out all of the slack until it lay limp on the ground. Finally, I'd find just the right amount of stretch and give so that when I climbed in, it was like a womb I could surrender to, feeling completely supported and safe.

Going through this hammock ritual became crucially important to me. It was months before I understood that I was using a concrete object as a metaphor to teach me a whole new way to relate to myself—with brand-new "nots" and space, and just the right amount of stretch and give. I'm calling objects that we can use in this way "metaforms."

A metaform helps your unconscious mind make the walls between compartments permeable. It creates or reveals relationships. Here's an example. A man I worked with had been taking anti-depressants for years. He felt he was dependent on them, and wanted to stop, but he was terrified he'd crash into a perpetual dark hole. So he decided to hold one pill up each morning and imbue it with his own power by declaring, "I give you the power to help me feel vital and alive." After several weeks of this ritual, he

*"There is no such thing as a problem without a gift for you in its hand."*

*–A Course in Miracles*

*"All things are connected like the blood which unifies one family. Whatever befalls the earth, befalls the children of the earth. People did not weave the web of life; we are merely a strand in it. Whatever we do to the web, we do to ourselves."*

*–Chief Seattle*

began to shave each pill, saying "I take on this much responsibility myself for feeling vital and alive." Within three months, he just looked in the mirror and said those words, carrying his empty pill bottle in a pocket as a reminder that the power was all his own.

Here's another example, on a more mundane level. Since Andy and I are "on the road" so much teaching, we often miss our home. So we started carrying little pieces of it with us. I think it all began with pillows, then a rock from the nearby lake, then a little piece of cedar from the nearby woods. Our pockets usually hold at least one such treasure, the dresser in hotel rooms another, the room where we work, another. It's a way of making home wherever we are. Objects can also serve as metaforms for resources we have, but might otherwise forget to use. They are kinesthetic triggers to help associate chosen qualities, abilities, resources. A small stone can help you find your steadiness; a piece of elastic can remind you to be flexible; a lock of your child's hair can help you access your tenderness.

Now it's your turn to collect some metaforms that will help you access resources you'll be using in the next chapter, to meet the needs you discovered in the last.

*Go on a lazy walk in or outside your house and find four objects that seem in some way to represent four qualities or aspects that would help you meet the underlying needs you discovered in the last chapter. One that I usually suggest is something to stand for safety. Some others that people have used are creativity, power, clarity, compassion, healing wisdom, etc.*

*When you get back, take a few minutes to jot down a description of each, using the words "I am" rather than "It is": "I am smooth and round. I can be thrown, but not destroyed. I was found under a garbage can, but that's not where I'm from," etc. (This is, by the way, another way of using the mechanism of the problem—projection—as the mechanism of the solution—creative projection.)*

*Save your objects for our next step.*

## Doing, Not Being

When you realize you are *doing* a problem, instead of *being* it, you can also realize there are other things you can do as well. Your loyalty can shift to your assets and resources, to a place from which you can maneuver through many choices, instead of continually trying to manipulate the problem. With this change in allegiance, the questions you're asking yourself change from "Can I do this?" to "How can I do this?"

I've asked you to reconsider your original nature as something wider and deeper than your problem. I've asked you to shift the level at which you think about yourself and your assets. I've suggested that you can be faithful to your individuality, by recognizing your own wisdom as completely as you do that of external authorities. Recognizing—as in knowing yourself in a different way.

With awareness, imagination, and compassion, we've been exploring how the thought patterns which generate suffering can guide us toward wholeness. Alice Walker writes that in Yoruba, the word *aché* means "the power to make things happen." So *aché*! It's time to braid all you've been learning together and do exactly that.

"A final comfort that is small, but not cold: the heart is the only broken instrument that works."

–T.E. Kalen

"Attend me, hold me in your muscular flowering arms, protect me from throwing any part of myself away."

–Audre Lorde

# 13 Braiding A Possible Future:
## Integrating Through Symbols and Ceremonies

*"Suddenly I saw myself standing on the platform of a well-lit and pleasant lecture room. In front of me sat an attentive audience on comfortable upholstered seats. I was giving a lecture on the psychology of the concentration camp! All that oppressed me at the moment became objective, seen and described from the remote viewpoint of science. By this method I succeeded somehow in rising above the situation, above the sufferings of the moment, and I observed them as if they were already of the past."*

–Victor Frankl

It's time to build bridges across the valleys and chasms that exist between the resources at your base camp—the territory we've been exploring—and the path that lies ahead. It's time to turn a corner and move from disconnection to re-connection, from degeneration to regeneration. In essence, you'll be uniting the needs represented by your enemy with the context of competence represented by your resources. From that place, we'll turn and orient toward what can be. The goal of this chapter is reconciliation with the past and realization of a possible future.

Is that really feasible? How do you bring the present and the past together, and how do you go on from here?

Let's use an image to hold those questions. There are things that stop time for me. Watching a woman braid her very long hair is such an event. It's a simple thing really—those hands dividing that hair into three separate hanks. Those fingers carrying the outside over the middle, which becomes the outside and then is crossed over the middle. On and on, in an ancient rhythm, until there is one strong and shining plait.

You've held a strand, representing your enemy, in compassionate hands. You've held the strand of your resources with curious fingers. You are about to cross one over the other and then tease out the last hank—that of your future self. Building passageways between things such as this is best done using the language and symbolic thinking of the navigating, unconscious mind.

*"There lives in you a 'sense of the possible,' a yearning to move forward to embrace life in all its fullness."*

*–Danaan Parry*

## Reconnecting Resources and the Enemy

I read that Antonio Stradivari made some of his most beautiful violins from a pile of broken-down, waterlogged oars he found on the docks of Venice. He was willing to connect his resources—creative vision and skillful hands—

261

with the raw junk life offered him. From break-down, he crafted persistently until he had a new pattern: break-through.

My son, David, used to play for hours with red and white plastic Lego blocks. He'd spend an hour combining them together, until he made a tank. After a bowl or two of Fruit Loops, he'd return, disconnect the old pattern into a huge pile, and then spend another hour reconnecting the red and white blocks until they became a space ship. Both Antonio and David were using the very natural process of the unconscious mind to create new patterns, by disconnecting and reconnecting resources and experiences.

Max (K-V-A) was a sculptor who suffered from chronic back pain as a result of an automobile accident. He was a guide in a fine arts gallery. His job included taking customers on tours, pointing out the virtues of the works on display. He said this was often a challenge, since he didn't like a lot of the art that was being sold; but he had learned to use the abilities of his subconscious visual channel to see it from many perspectives, including that of the artist and the customer.

I offered him a large pad of newsprint and some markers, and asked him to draw a quick sketch of the pain in his back—the enemy. Next, he drew another of the feeling of comfort he remembered from before the accident, and a third of the safety he felt while being held by his wife. The last resource that he drew was the power of his imagination that had been an asset to him since childhood.

We decided to imagine the room we were in as the gallery, and I asked Max to "hang" a show, by placing his enemy portrait on one wall and the resources on the opposite one. He offered to give me a typical tour, beginning with the three sketches of his assets.

As he stood in front of each resource, I suggested that Max look at the enemy portrait and describe its virtues, needs and function. The comfort perspective revealed that

*"Go to heaven for form and to hell for energy, and marry the two."*

–William Blake

the pain was trying to get him to "back off" and stop trying so hard to impress everyone. It was trying to make sure he stayed "back home" in his body.

From the perspective of safety, Max saw how he forced himself to take a lot of risks in his life, and put himself in positions where there was no way for him to "back out."

Finally, as his child-like imagination, he saw that the chronic pain kept him from becoming a production artist, making things from a marketplace mentality that would block him from feeling the simple joy of experimentation and surprise he so needed in his life.

Needless to say, the show was a smashing success and acclaimed by the local critic! Max learned that, though his body had been the battlefield for the conflicts he had been having in his mind, it was also possible for it to be what the ancient Greeks used to call temenos—the sacred place where extraordinary events could happen.

*"You can't stop the waves but you can learn to surf."*

*–Anon.*

## Integration: Enemy and Resource

Integration is a natural process for the unconscious mind, which creates and recreates patterns of relationships. It connects individual bits of data into a whole by use of stories and symbols. A simple example is binocular vision. Each of our eyes gives us a description of the world. When these two are combined in our mind, a new, deeper perspective of reality occurs.

Thus, we'll be using two symbolic processes to integrate your lost self back into the web of wisdom that resides in your unconscious mind. The first uses the objects you collected in the last chapter and the one you made or found for the enemy to create a story that connects your enemy to your resources. The other uses your imagery and body to create a wholing.

## Bringing Your Enemy Home

*Holding each object that represents a resource, one at a time, bring vividly to mind a time when you experienced that quality. Step into it, associate to it, wrap it around you. Become as completely that quality as possible; then turn your mind to the symbol of the enemy. How would you perceive it as that resource? How do you perceive that it could work for you?*

*When you have finished, arrange all the objects around the enemy as if you were creating a landscape. Give thought to how they relate to each other in space. You may want some to be close, some far apart, some nesting, etc. Arrange them until you find what intuitively is "right" to you. Walk around the whole landscape with curiosity.*

*Keeping the landscape in your mind, expand your state of consciousness. Allow a story to come to mind. Begin with the struggle with your enemy, and let the story work its way through an introduction of the resources to a possible future. At any point that you need to, pause and let your eyes just "read" the landscape. Find a way that is comfortable to record the story—videotape, journal, tape recorder, etc.*

*Whenever you wish, play or read the story back to yourself. There is no expert or authority in the world who could create a more potent "visualization" or "affirmation" or "guided imagery" for you than this one. You are the author of your own experience. You may want to leave the symbols on your desk or in a special place, and rearrange them every once in awhile, allowing your mind to drift through the landscape.*

## Wholing: Integration Through Physical Imagery

Andy and I use variations on the wholing process with most of the people we teach. It is a simple way of asking the computer of your mind to combine two "files" and make that new information available to you when you most need it.

People develop their own ways of doing it. Sometimes they just listen to the description of how to do it and never find an object or draw or write, but while they are driving across the George Washington Bridge or raking leaves, they find their mind just "thinking about doing it." One woman discovered she was doing the wholing process while she made a quilt; another did it in her dreams.

*After centering and widening your periphery, please extend one hand comfortably in front of you. Imagine as vividly as possible that you hold the energy of your enemy and its needs in that hand. Allow whatever images and sensations to emerge while you notice your breath.*

*Extend the other hand and imagine the energy of the resources you chose filling it. Again, notice the sensations and images that come to your mind while you notice your breath.*

*Turn your hands so that the palms face each other about two feet apart, with your elbows softly bent and your shoulders hanging easily. Feel the magnetic-like attraction that is between your two palms. While you breathe, find an image or story that seems to increase this attraction, until your hands begin to actually approach each other.*

*When your hands have made contact, allow the feeling of resolution to move up through your arms and your entire body. Describe it to yourself in some way.*

> "Conditions don't overcome people, people overcome conditions."
>
> –Oprah Winfrey

## Orienting Toward A Possible Future

> "Argue for your limitations and they're yours."
>
> –Richard Bach

A great deal of time in healing is spent on working with the traumas of the past, but relatively little is directed toward creating the possibilities of a future. So much time is spent teaching about the crucifixion; so little on the resurrection. We have to give our minds a horizon to reach toward. We all need a vital passion, a desire to extend, an internally-driven purpose to carry us like a tiger, or a strong wind, across the abyss we encounter at a turning point.

When I first went into psychoanalysis to untangle the knots of my unhappiness, Dr. Freudenfarkle focused on resolving the conflicts of my past that were responsible for creating my neurosis. Fifty thousand dollars later, I was still "neurotic" and miserable, but I could discuss the "whys" and "becauses" at cocktail parties with other graduate students.

Then I came upon the psychotherapy movement of the sixties and seventies, which focused mostly on the present. My past may have predisposed me to my problems, but what became important was what I was doing in the here and now to maintain them. This was far more effective in creating change, although it generated less interesting conversation.

When I approached my first major turning point, however, no amount of pounding on pillows or sitting in hot seats could help. As far as I know, Dr. Erickson had no theory of why people had problems. Instead, he had a theory of intervention—what to do, and an orientation toward the future. The past was only relevant insofar as it pointed toward the present and solutions that would evolve into a better future. He was famous for always being able to tell people what he was "looking forward to" in his own life.

This was very difficult for me when I was sick, since I didn't think I had much of a future. But I was inspired by the fact that he had been in almost continual physical pain for much of his later life, and was challenged in more ways than I could count; still, he lived fully in the present and was looking forward to a delightful future, which he seemed to create. He didn't try to fix the past. He worked with people on meeting their present needs and cooperated with them toward generating futures that worked.

"All men should strive to learn before they die what they are running from, and to, and why."

–James Thurber

"I wish I could have know earlier that you have all the time you need right up until the day you die."

–William Wiley

It seems quite possible that we are as capable of having cellular programs of future pleasure as we are of having cellular memories of pain. And since cellular trauma can keep forcing us backward in time, it also seems logical that those future programs can serve as a powerful current, moving us forward. Victor Frankl was a pioneer in doing this, and it helped him survive the agony of years in a concentration camp.

## It's Not Only What You Think, But How You Think It

To think about the future, which you have never, of course, experienced, you need to use your mind in a way that creates new patterns. What seems most natural would be that your linear mind would think about the past. It was, after all, a step-by-step progression. However, when I was in private practice, I studied the patterns that many people, particularly those who were suicidal or depressed, used to think about the future and found the reverse: *their creative minds think about the past and their logical minds think about the future.*

Thus, in the magnifying lens of the creative mind, last year's spat with Marvin becomes a major mud wrestling match. One woman described her life as a "relentlessly sad history." When we explored her memories, the images were all literally colored blue!

In addition to thinking about their pasts with three-dimensional Disneyland maps, these same people have often been taught to think about their futures with a map that resembles a thruway ticket. But since the conscious mind cannot conceive of something that has not been, it just gives a reasonable facsimile of what has already happened, or what someone else predicted would hap-

*"It's not how much we do but how much love we put into what we do."*

*–Mother Teresa*

267

pen. ("You'll end up just like your father.") The thoughts, therefore, are bleak, dark, silent, black and white, still, hard and cold, somber (Just the facts Ma'am). They said things like, "*I can't even imagine* what I want, where I want to be six months from now, what will be going on next year." Or "I'm beyond my belief system and I'm scared. It's all a big black hole in front of me, like when the pavement runs out and you get to the end of the road."

I don't believe it is an organic function of the brain to twist the way we think about our destiny like this. I choose to believe that in our soul, each of us is an artist, a dreamer, a poet. We are butterflies who have been taught to become caterpillars. "Don't be such a dreamer. You'll waste your life. Just put one foot in front of the other. The world is a cold, cruel place. You can't have your cake and eat it too. Be practical."

What our brains are *designed* to do is use our creative minds as the map maker and navigator, since it is the generator of new patterns and possibilities; the conscious mind is then the chauffeur. Let us re-learn to drive through the countryside of the past as it was, and dream our way into our futures.

Di (A-V-K) did just this. She grew up with fear as a continual background noise. She shared her tragic history in a weekend workshop. Her mother had tried to commit suicide by slashing her wrists. Fourteen-year-old Di was the one who found the comatose body, called the hospital and had to take her role in the family, caring for a younger sister. Her father was an alcoholic who sexually abused her. When her mother returned home a year later, she was still hallucinating. When Di went to college at eighteen, her sister hung herself.

Di told us she needed to be able to find words to describe what she wanted in her life. Although she usually had no trouble speaking, when she tried to talk about her future, she went "dumb." All she could do was think of

*"One discovers that destiny can be directed, that one does not have to remain in bondage to the first wax imprint made on childhood sensibilities. Once the deforming mirror has been smashed, there is a possibility of wholeness. There is a possibility of joy."*
–Anais Nin

dead ends; becoming a woman meant death and destruction to her. Di had done years of therapy working on her sexual abuse, on her mother's attempted and sister's completed suicide. When she thought about the past, it seemed now to be in a rational and logical way. But she had no creative way to talk to herself or anyone else about a future. She told us about a recurring nightmare she had where she was holding a baby who turned cold and blue in her arms. I noticed that when she sat in the group, Di often drew cartoon figures. I decided to attempt to get her creativity engaged in her future by using this resource. I asked her to sketch a very colorful future self, who was the kind of woman she wanted to become. She drew an image of brightest light.

We placed that in front of her, and in the stillness of the next moments, we asked her to listen to the Di of the future sing to her about all the possibilities that were waiting in the light of a new future. With that song in her mind, we asked her to turn around and reclaim both the teenaged Di who was holding the infant, and the Di who found her mother. She wrapped her arms around herself and, as the guiding angel sang to all of them, and us, about the future they would have in the light, the group echoed her song back to her.

Some people can use their creative minds to think about the future, but they create what Sheldon Kopp called "neurotically hopeful" fantasies, instead of an attainable future image. I think of them as the balancing forces on the other end of the see-saw from those who can conceive of no future. Neurotically hopeful says, "Some day I'll win the lottery" while neurotically fearful intones, "Some day I'll be a destitute leper."

Both sides co-exist within us. One usually represents the force of growth and the other the force of safety. One a "no," and one a "yes." Thus, my hopeful image of winning the lottery is trying to get me to expand and my fearful

> *"Our life is shaped by our mind. We become what we think."*
>
> *–Dharmapada*

> *"No bird soars too high if it soars with its own wings."*
>
> *–Michael Jordan*

image that I'll go broke is trying to encourage me to get a hold of myself by creating some boundaries.

The image of the future you will be developing goes beyond either polarity by incorporating and integrating the functions of both into a more developed self. An example of the resolution of the above might be in allowing myself to be rich in time, and prosper by enjoying every aspect of being alive, including rest.

It is time now for you to reap a single guiding image that will point you toward a meeting of your highest possibilities. It is time to go beyond mourning what you can no longer be, so that it doesn't obscure what you can become.

## Developing Imagery Of a Possible Future

*"What is now proved was once only imagined."*

*–William Blake*

In the 1950's, Dr. Erickson frequently had people vividly imagine a crystal ball while in trance. He asked them to find a future self who was wiser and older and healed from whatever symptom with which they were struggling. Then he asked them to walk backwards and look in another crystal ball, where they would see a scene of him treating them so effectively that it led to that healing. They would then tell him what they had seen in the ball. He ended the session by talking endlessly about how people forgot things in many different ways. Upon their awakening from trance, he would prescribe whatever treatment they had reported to him!

I happen to have an unlimited supply of leftover crystal balls he never got to use. As a matter of fact, there's one tucked in the pages of this book, with your name on it. Shake the book in your lap and, as you hold it in your hands, you can notice that older, wiser self, who has been successfully treated by the brilliant Dr. Erickson:

*How are you different? How is your posture? How do you move? How do you look out at the world? How do you speak? What do you say? What do you know then that you don't know now?*

## Using Ceremonies To Bridge Past and Future

The final connection to be made crosses the strand you wish to carry forward from your enemy, with the possible future you are reaching towards, developing a relationship between what was and what can be. One way to do this is by creating a ceremony or rite of passage that has symbolic importance. It can be the passageway to carry your inner learnings into your outer life. It can also nourish what is known as *hambre del alma*, soul hunger, by cultivating depth and sacredness.

All my teachers seem to be short in stature, big in soul, and masters of ceremony. My grandmother carried out ancient rituals that turned something as mundane as cleaning the kitchen drawers into a rite of passage. Sensei Kuboyama begins and ends every class with centering rituals. Milton Erickson pioneered the use of symbols, stories and rituals to pursue therapeutic goals.

A ceremony, no matter how simple, creates a pattern that connects disparate parts into a whole. It is a conduit between cultures, generations, genders, and different aspects of our minds. In the summer of 1991, for example, Thich Nhat Hanh conducted a retreat for Vietnam veterans and Vietnamese refugees in upper New York State. After a meditation, he addressed the veterans in a tender voice. "You are the hand that grasped the fire, but the order to do so came from the whole body, and the whole body suffers as a result." On a paper altar cloth, wreathed in flowers,

*"Positive images of the future are a powerful and magnetic force. . . . They draw us on and energize us, give us courage and will to take important initiatives. Negative images of the future also have a magnetism. They pull the spirit downward in the path of despair [and] impotence."*

*–William James*

*"Ritual and myth are like seed crystals of new patterns that can eventually re-shape the culture around us."*

*–Starhawk*

271

participants pinned notes inscribed with the names of those they wished to remember. It was not possible to read them without being profoundly moved. One, for instance, read, "In memory of all of those who died under my guns." Next to it was another that said simply in Vietnamese and English, "In memory of my brother who was killed."

After a silent walking meditation in the dark, several veterans stood holding the paper altar cloth. Standing under the stars with each person holding a candle, the cloth was burned and the ashes scattered on the lake, as people sang both Vietnamese and American songs deep into the night.

I think of healing ceremonies as initiations into wisdom. They shift entrenched habits, give form to a chaos of feelings, and become an island of clarity from which new patterns can emerge. There are many kinds of rituals and ceremonies, but the ones we are speaking of here have as their purpose actualizing or revealing the complete person.

There are quite a few books these days with rituals which have been designed by someone else for you. For our purposes, it is important that the rite of passage be developed *by* you, because it is necessary to use symbols that have specific connotations to your unconscious mind. In a recent workshop, one man chose a piece of a net for his ceremony as a symbol of safety; to someone else, that net could have represented entrapment. The goal here is to connect you to your world, to validate something important that is happening, to quicken your heart to its potential, and to prepare the ground of your life for change.

These ceremonies do not have to be intricate or ornate. A man called me on a radio show last week wanting to know whether it was worth spending a thousand dollars to have hypnosis so he could stop smoking. He said he wasn't really sure he was ready to stop. I told him I really understood his difficulty, since I smoked for thirty years, and have a great deal of expertise in stopping. I stopped at least twenty times!

I told him that I knew, finally, that I was ready to stop "for good," when I was willing to do a ritual burial with my friends, Robert and Peggy. We went up on a hillside, smoked one last time, inhaling furiously and choking on purpose with every exhale. Then we buried everything we owned that was connected with smoking. Each of us named all the needs that had been met by smoking and the new ways we intended to meet those needs. We declared that we had been loyal to our substance, going out in the middle of the night, if need be, to acquire it; but we had betrayed our own bodies. We said good-bye to these old abusive friends at the grave side and shed tears at their demise. From the ending of the old, we declared our intention to flower a new start, where we were loyal to ourselves and embraced a future that was free. We could use the resource of betrayal by turning it against all that was toxic to us.

The man on the phone was silent for a moment. Finally. he said he wasn't the type of person to do a ritual. I suggested to him that the act of smoking itself, of procuring his cigarettes, arranging them just so, gathering his symbols—ashtray, matches—doing things in a ritualized way, placing the pack on the desk by his right hand, lighting with his left hand, selecting sacred places—his car, the hallway behind his office—was a ritual. Indeed, it was a very complex ceremony.

He didn't have too much to say about that, but he did reply, "Well, if I were ready to do what you guys did, I wouldn't need to pay $1000 for hypnosis!" There was no arguing with that.

The physical act of doing something symbolic seems to work when talk and reason fails. Preparing the ceremony, thinking about it, enacting it, and remembering it all

*"Do you know that disease and death must needs overtake us, no matter what we are doing? What do you wish to be doing when it over-takes you? If you have anything bet-ter to be doing when you are so overtaken, get to work on that."*

*–Epictetus*

273

*"The mind aware of itself is a pilot."*

–Marilyn Ferguson

contribute to its meaning. Most people don't need to be told how to develop a ritual. They just like to hear about what other people have done. They seem to understand the underlying principles and to adapt them to their own purposes.

The story that follows describe the integrating ceremonies of one of people you've been reading about; it may lead you to your own.

Remember Rena? Her third and last session we had together took place almost three months later, after she had completed the first phase of chemotherapy, as well as some powerful healing of sexual abuse she had experienced in her childhood. Her head was covered with less than an inch of rambunctious red fluff. In my driveway was a small yellow Volkswagen, covered with wild jungle cats and butterflies and even a kitten crouching on the front hood.

She told me that she had left her "old man" and was taking off for California, where she intended to learn about massage and herbs and good nutrition. She placed a blue plastic bag on the cushion between us. I looked inside and there was all of that angry hair from our first session. She said, "I want to do something with this, to finish in some way, to feel complete with what's happened. After our last session, I realized that since I was a little girl my body has been asking me to be a woman who could say 'Don't fuck with me'. I think that's what the cancer has been about. That's what my body's been trying to say. It didn't want to be a woman. It felt dirty. Will you help me find a way to complete all this?"

I nodded and went to my desk. On a shelf above it was a pale green wine cup made out of soapstone. I carried it and a pitcher, and told Rena to bring her bag of hair and the shovel she'd find leaning against the barn. We left my house and walked to a big old maple tree that stood on the crest of the hill. I suggested she create a ceremony of

274

closure. She looked out over the landscape for a few minutes and then began to dig a hole at the base of the tree. When it was knee deep, she threw the shovel down and began to sift her hair into it, mumbling words I couldn't hear. When she was finished, I poured the goblet full of water and added some dirt. I offered it to her with these words:

"You were abused and you are no longer. This goblet is a symbol for the woman that you are. It can contain anything, but it is much more than what it contains. Its power is that it gives shape and form to its contents. She can give itself to hold those contents and then spill them out, taking herself back, free once more."

Rena's hand reached out slowly to grasp the goblet. It moved intermittently, as if pulled by a string. She looked at the dirty water inside and then slowly, ever so slowly, poured it into the hole with her hair. I lifted the pitcher towards her and she extended the goblet toward me.

I filled it with clear water. "What do you want to contain now?"

The lines that formed parentheses around her mouth deepened. She said, "How about some self-respect for starters? Yeah, I'm ready for a future where I feel full of self-respect."

"This is the beginning of self-respect and the ending of terror."

Rena held the cup poised in the air for a moment, and then toasted, "Here's to a new beginning."

I expected her to gulp it down, but she didn't. She savored it, drank it sip by sip, as if it were vintage French wine. At the end, she poured the last drops into the hole and filled it in with her foot, pushing the dirt over her hair, her wounding, her history. I patted the rough trunk of the maple tree and, said "Use it well." It was what my parents used to say when they gave someone a gift. Rena looked up at the blazing branches and laughed, "Yeah, old tree, use it well."

> *"The time you have is as long as you're alive, and not one minute longer."*
>
> – W. Edwards

> *"The wonder, the terror, the exultation of being on the edge of being."*
>
> –Anatole Broyard

## Creating A Reconnection Ceremony

The practice that follows is a "yeasting" meditation to encourage ideas for the creation of your own ceremony to rise to the surface of your mind:

*In one hand, feel the energy that represents the needs of your enemy. You may want to look at its representation or object. In the other, imagine the energy of your future self, as vividly as possible.*

*Allow each sensation to spread to a different side of your body and explore the differences. Is one warmer? Heavier? darker? How are the textures different?*

*You might like to bring to mind examples of harmony, blending, integration: singing, dancing, weaving, building bridges. As you do that, you can allow your palms to turn and face each other and feel the magnetic pull that exists between them.*

*When your hands approach each other, merging the energies you feel in your body, you can find an image or story that represents this blending to you.*

*You may want to ask your unconscious mind directly to allow this mating to go on in your life. One way of doing this is by imagining your enemy and your future self walking down separate paths that are destined to meet at a common point. Some people would do this by using words, others would visualize and others would just get a feeling for the movement. Bring this image to mind before you go to sleep and first thing in the morning.*

*"The thing I will be most proud of is that toward the end of my life, I became what I always should have been–a decent gentle man."*

*–Stan Getz*

## Creating Your Own Ceremony

I leave this final symbolic act of endings and beginnings, of braiding all of who you are and can be, up to you and your imagination. Remember that rituals can be quite simple or complex, but mostly they are by you and for you. Take all the time you need to get clear on the intention of the ceremony, and what you want it to do for you.

Some other things to consider are: Where would you like this rite of passage to be? Would you like anyone else to be there as witness and support? What do you need to do to prepare? Is there a poem, prayer or invocation you'd like to include that will help you in your determination to move on?

This rite of passage is a living enactment of your intention to enter into a new intimacy with yourself and your world. You will emerge from it more ripe and ready to inhabit your life.

You have been weaving the supple connective tissue of an awakened presence, a creative mind, and a compassionate heart around your lost self. In this cocoon of understanding, fear can become transformed into wisdom and sorrow into forgiveness.

# 14 Let Our Wounds Be Our Teachers:
## Making and Enacting Commitments

*"Free from clutching at themselves, the hands can handle; free from looking after themselves, the eyes can see; free from trying to understand itself, thought can think."*

–Alan Watts

Transformation is one part inspiration and one part realization. The last stage of this journey, the open moment, brings us out of the dark wilderness we've been traveling through, and back to a place we never really left—our daily lives, our family, community, society. In the open moment, you no longer are looking for answers; you have to *be* the answer. This place where internal and external landscapes merge is, perhaps, the most rugged terrain of all. Here, we shift from allowing things to happen to making them happen, from receptivity to actively creating the kind of life that enhances our healing.

It is on these edges that the soul can manifest itself. It is also on these rocky shorelines that we carry scars from the battles and invasions of our past. Thus, it is on this place that we must prowl amongst the driftwood of our needs to ignite the signal fires of our commitments and boundaries. It is here we build rafts and bridges from our genuine "yeses" and uncompromised "nos."

Many travelers do not make it through this last intersection. They stay identified with the worst times in their life, with their suffering; the shell breaks open, but the seed will not push through the surface of the soil and reach toward the light. I worked with a woman who was struggling with cancer. She said she'd do anything to heal. But, by the way, I shouldn't ask her to change her relationship with her husband, or the place she lived, or her job, because that would be too much, and she had worked too hard to get there. "I'd rather die than be poor again." And she did.

Suffering is the soil of renewal. The burden and responsibility of learning your way through the "sacred catastrophe" that is a turning point is that you must change the way you are living your life—deep, fundamental changes of the entire system. Often these are made in very small steps, but still they require great strength of heart. Our soul is asking nothing less of us than that we reassert the truth of our full potential.

*"What you will be is what you do."*

*–Buddha*

*"Our own life is the instrument with which we experiment with Truth."*

*–Thich Nhat Hanh*

281

This chapter is about enacting and fully inhabiting the learning you've been doing thus far, about *rooting* it so you're creating the kind of life that fertilizes the work you need to do. We'll be building boundaries around the tender edges, making pathways of forgiveness, and constructing commitments that guarantee there will be tending, caretaking, and support for your ability to grow in all directions.

We'll continue to use creative thinking to make unconscious wisdom available to the conscious mind, but as we move through the final stage in this learning process, we will be depending more and more on the conscious mind as the bow with which you can aim the arrows of inspiration you've crafted.

*"Let the beauty we love be what we do."*

*–Rumi*

We begin, of course, with a story. Well, to be truthful, there are several stories here, different chambers of a single heart. Or perhaps, embedded inside each other, they are like a series of Chinese nesting boxes.

## Tenemos las Manos Limpias, Somos Màs

Alice Walker has said that we are all telling parts of the same story. But this is a story that I'm afraid to tell you. I'm much more comfortable telling you stories about how I was the victim than how I was the violator. However, it's not enough for me just to teach. I need to be informed by what I teach. And it is my own wounds that are my greatest guide.

This story begins with Amy Davis sitting in a circle of people during an evening session of our Madison study group. She asked for time to tell us a story. One of her hands floats up to her throat; the other rests in the center of her chest, like a lily.

"I want to tell you about this woman I heard speak

yesterday. Her name was Isabel Letelier. She was the wife of Orlando Letelier, the Chilean ambassador to the U.S. who was assassinated a few years ago in Washington."

Amy's voice is raspy. She pauses, as her hands began to twist the fur on the edge of her slippers. She rocks back and forth slightly, and I think of all the blue-eyed dolls I played with as a child—dolls with moon-shaped eyes that slid open and closed as they were moved.

"She was talking about what's happening in Chile, about the abuse of human rights. One of the stories she told stayed with me. I can't forget it; I hear her telling it over and over in my mind.

"At noon in the capital city, when most people are out in the plazas, the university students frequently surround a detention center and begin to shout, 'This is a torture house. They are murdering people here!' When the soldiers and police attack, they link arms, hold up their hands and chant, 'Tenemos las manos limpias. Somos màs!,' which means, 'We have clean hands. There are more of us!'

They disperse in the crowd if they can. If one of them is caught, the rest link arms and chant, 'Tenemos las manos limpias! Somos màs!,' forcing the soldiers to arrest them all, and carry the group as a whole into the torture house.

"The chant has spread all over Chile. After concerts, instead of applauding, the people stand silently, linking arms and holding up their hands. When buses pass a soldier beating someone in the street, the passengers press the palms of their hands to the windows. 'Tenemos las manos limpias! Somos Màs!'"

Amy's hands come to rest with her palms raised, facing the center of the circle. Her chin quivers, then sets firmly as she lifts it slightly. The silence in the room has a weight to it, a shape, a pulse. Within a minute, as if orchestrated by an invisible conductor, the other people in the group link arms, and raise their hands. As if of one voice, they

*"Do you know what astonished me the most in the world? The inability of force to create anything. In the long run, the sword is always beaten by the spirit."*

*–Napoleon Bonaparte (at end of his life)*

chant, "Tenemos las manos limpias. Somos màs!"

Tears track slowly down Amy's face. I reach over and put her hands in her own tears. She looks down at them and then slides one palm upon the other as if she were washing them clean.

As I watch Amy and hear the chant, an image rises in my mind and cuts through the moment like a blade; a wound from a blade; both.

"Even when the obstacle of myself seems endlessly unsurmountable, I continue."

–Carla Needleman

*David was standing in front of me—David of seven or eight—David, the life that sprang from my body. David, child of my heart. David was standing in my mind, his dark eyes flashing fire, his small red mouth screaming words at me. "I hate you Mommy! I really hate you!"*

*There was a raw wild bruise on his peach fuzz cheek. It looked like a brand in the shape of my hand. His hands were frozen closed, clenched in the air, shaking. His voice was ragged, loud. "Why can't I hit you, Mommy? What stops me from hitting you? Someday I'll do it. I'll hit back and then you'll be sorry."*

*For a brief moment, everything gets dark. Then a bright thread pulls me through a tumbling ribbon of years. I see a young girl with long fiery hair, too unruly to be contained in the braids hanging down her back. She is tugging at a man's hand with a gold ring on the pinky finger—a ring with two faces carved in it, one laughing and one ferocious, and a green stone like an eye between the two faces. It was the hand that was supposed to guide her, to protect her, the hand she trusted beyond any other. The hand pulled away sharply.*

*She reached for it again, but this time it leapt up against the sky, and then fell toward her. Wrapped around it was a brown alligator skin belt with a shining golden buckle. The girl saw the knuckles of that hand covered with little fiery hairs, just like hers. The belt . . . moving down . . . fast. Wild lights flashing, toward her. She could not move. She twisted inside herself instead . . . the buckle cut, carved her open, spilled her out. She floated above the belt, above the hand, above her own body, which was frozen behind a shield of silence.*

*She floated to where her heart could not get hit. She*

*promised herself she would not cry...would not let him know he was hurting her body. She screamed, "I hate you! Some day I'll hit you! I will someday. I'll hit you back and then you'll be sorry. But I'll never hit my kid. Never, never, never!"*

I feel as if I've been shredded. A big hole has been blasted in my belly, tearing my breath away. Time unravels as I find myself back in Madison. I look down at my woman-sized feet, stockinged against the wooden floor. I whisper, "I'm here now. I've made it. I survived. Hurt people hurt. Healing people heal. I am remembering so I can learn. I learn so I can heal."

Then through the hole, as if carried by a wind, words come from my mouth, bruising the immaculate silence of the circle, "I can't say that chant. I'd like to join you all. I'd like to pretend that *these* hands are clean." My throat tries to clamp shut. I force the words through.

"The Chilean soldiers are not the only ones with dirty hands. I cannot just say the words; somehow I need to inhabit them. I have to remember the times my hands have violated others—my son for one—and learn from those memories. I have to remember and learn from the times I've been violated by other's hands. Until that happens, my hands aren't clean."

It seems like a very long silence until Andy speaks. He says quietly that what I was experiencing might be true for other people in the room as well. He suggests we sit back to back in pairs, supporting each other. His instructions are, "In the still safety of the next few minutes, perhaps each of us can find a time in our histories when our hands have violated another, or when we've been violated by the hands of another. This silence can be our moment to clean our hands."

I can feel his back expanding and contracting with each breath. Such simple comfort. I place my hands on my belly, and feel my feet on the bare wooden floor, trying to find

*"There are always hungry people to feed, naked people to clothe, sick people to comfort and make well. While I don't ask you to save the world, I do ask you to love those with whom you sleep, share the happiness of those you call friend, engage those among you who are visionary, and remove from your life those who offer you despair and disrespect."*

*–Nikki Giovanni*

285

root. Time begins to widen. As my eyes close, I notice Amy sitting back to back with Gena, Joanne with Lee, Will with Jackie. I feel a warmth spread in the center of my chest as I realize there is a common pulse in the room deeper than my own.

I ride back on the coils of time to the child with fiery hair. Reaching to her, I whisper, "You will make it. You will survive. I promise." She backs away from my outstretched hand.

"I'm your future, little one. I know. Never again will I allow anyone to beat you up. I'll give you the protection you didn't get. And I'll scream the pain for you, scream 'Ouch!' I'll let him know how much he is hurting you. Never again will I allow someone to abuse you like that. Never again will I allow you to cut off the sounds of your own pain. Child of my history, never again will I let you abandon your body, and never again will I abandon you!"

She begins to sink into and through me, as if I am absorbing sunlight and mist. My father's image rises in my mind. He is standing alone in a room, the alligator belt lying limp at his feet; his eyes are watering. He has retreated into a shadowy corner inside himself, his own body the battle-field, his own life the challenge. Out of my broken heart grows a compassion for all things broken, like a tree root forcing its way through pavement. Finding forgiveness for him seems possible, now that I know I am safe.

"You were doing the best you could at the time, weren't you Dad? No one taught you how to make your mind strong so you wouldn't need to use your hands as weapons. When you struck out at me, Dad, you were violating your own innocence and purity. I won't ever again allow anyone to do to me what you did. Knowing that, I forgive you."

Grief is a tide running through my blood. Grief and love and the need to absorb all that sorrow. It carries me to the memory of David's face contorted with hatred.

*"The world breaks everyone and afterward many are strong at the broken places."*

–Ernest Hemingway

I am outside, witnessing myself as a young mother in that living room with David—a confused and unknowing woman, a burdened, trying-to-raise-a-son-alone woman, a woman who is numbed by her nightly vodka and tonic.

I whisper fiercely to her, "Never again. Never again will I allow your hands to be weapons of your fire. Never again will I allow your hands to violate another human. Never again will I allow you to numb yourself so you lose awareness of what effect you are having on other people. I don't know if David will ever fully forgive you; but knowing I will keep these commitments, live within those boundaries, I forgive you for abusing your own child."

Once again, grief and tenderness flow through the chambers of my heart. A hard and closed place, that I hadn't even noticed, softens and dissolves; a doorway opens. I am flooded with an awareness of my father. Not as I knew him when he was alive, but of his essence. In that one still moment, his love is a vivid presence running through me. I can hear light, smell it, taste it in the places in my mouth which had only tasted bitterness.

My ears bring me back to the circle. All around the room, there are voices intermittently whispering, thundering, chanting, "Never again . . . I forgive . . . never again will I allow my body to be violated . . . I forgive my sister . . . my uncle. . . . Never again . . . I forgive myself." I look down at my own hands, bring them to my cheeks as I had done to Amy's. As I wash them in my tears, my words join the chorus, "Never again, nunca màs, will these hands abuse another. I forgive these hands. Never again will I allow myself to be silently abused. I forgive my silence. Nunca màs!"

It is too close a moment to hug. We move as individuals within a larger whole, luminescent fish in a current of warmth. We form a circle, linking arms, and hold up our wet hands.

"Tenemos las manos limpias. Somos màs."

*"The reality is that healing happens between people. The wound in me evokes the healer in you, and the wound in you evokes the healer in me, and then the two healers collaborate."*

*–Rachel Naomi Remen*

The words are a chorus in my heart, voices in a vaulted place, a human cathedral.

"Tenemos las manos limpias. Somos Màs."

## Defining Your Boundaries: The Sacred No

*"At the boundary, life blossoms."*

*–James Gleick*

A boundary is a region, not a line. It has the effect of defining what is included, as well as what is excluded. In fact, it is a place of meeting and connection, for it's where your edges meet mine.

We don't know much about boundaries. Most of us have been taught to withhold ourselves behind invisible barriers. This results in a contracted sense of our selves and often leads to projection. Instead, what we need to do is to find our edges and expand our awareness, to go deeper in our bodies. This doesn't mean shutting someone else out. It means letting your needs in, making them explicit, teaching other people how to treat you well. It means individuation rather than separation.

A woman I worked with didn't want to be consumed by her mother, who was extremely controlling. She kept walking out on her, hoping to make it clear that she wouldn't stand for that kind of treatment.

She had been doing it for a year, and the only result was that she missed a lot of dinners. Her mother went on doing what she had always done. Finally, the woman decided to declare her boundaries as follows, "Mom, I'm leaving because I don't like how I feel or how I'm responding to you now." She walked out with her sense of self intact, unenmeshed from her mother, needing nothing from her. Her mother was totally confused and called her up to tell her she shouldn't feel that way, etc.; but the woman felt amazingly clear and "unhooked." Her loving was freed up to be expressed to her mother, who therefore controlled her less and less.

The practice that follows is adapted from one that was taught to us by Sensei Lloyd Miyashiro. It will help you experience a cellular "no," and get a feeling in your bones of the difference between defending yourself by building barriers and protecting yourself by establishing boundaries.

> "What you do every day is as important to the soul as what your parents did to you."
>
> –James Hillman

*As you stand centering on your own two feet, imagine there is a tender and fragile infant clinging to your chest. Shake out your arms and release your shoulders. Raise your arms so that they are straight out in front of you. Grasp the back of one hand with the palm of the other hand. Your arms make a barrier around the space in front of your chest.*

*Now lock your elbows and tense up your shoulders. Ask a person to stand in front of you and push against your hands. (If you'd rather do this by yourself, vividly imagine someone pushing you.) Notice what else goes on in your body and mind as you go rigid to defend yourself in this way.*

*At some point, you will get too tired to be rigid any longer. At that point, just let your arms get limp—like cooked pasta. This is the posture of collapse, so that the challenger can just push right through your arms and be able to invade the sacred space that to which the infant is clinging. Some people call this accommodating or being a "push-over."*

*Now for another way. Re-center and shake out your arms and hands. Notice three breaths, lifting your shoulders slightly with each inhale and releasing them with each exhale.*

*Imagine that your arms are like those huge canvas fire hoses that are flexible until they are filled with water. Bring them in front of you, with your hands in the same position as before; but this time allow your elbows to be bending. Imagine that you are drawing energy up through your legs, from the ground, up through your heart, then round and out your hands—as if it were water flowing from a hydrant, round and round in the circle of your arms. Thus your arms, supported by all of this energy, form a safe and sacred place for that infant.*

*When the challenger pushes, imagine your hands just*

absorb the energy and run it round through your flexible arms as well. They may bend a little and give, but they won't give up or collapse. If the pressure gets at all uncomfortable, you can pretend you are a glass revolving door and just allow their push to turn you on your axis. This is the way protecting feels.

To make this more real, imagine it is your enemy challenging you. What boundaries would you make explicit? ("No I won't allow you to drink a fifth of bourbon." "No I won't allow you to throw that chair at her." "No, I won't let you use your words to cut him to shreds." "No, I won't let you eat whatever you want." "No, I won't let you pay attention to everyone else's needs and ignore your own." "No, I won't let you ignore your own inner life."

You may want to imagine another person or situation from your life while you do this, and speak your boundaries aloud. ("No, Work, I won't let you take all my free time away." "I won't be treated like that. If you continue to scream at me, I'm going to find some quiet space." "No, it is not alright for me to not know where you are for two days," etc.)

> "People are always blaming their circumstances for what they are. I don't believe in circumstances. The people who get on in this world are the people who get up and look for the circumstances they want and if they can't find them, make them."
>
> –George Bernard Shaw

It is also possible, and often very moving, to do this with people from your history—imagining the younger you, clinging to your chest, and someone who invaded or violated you, pushing against your hands.

Boundaries are not made *at* people; they are declarations *for* yourself. After doing these practices, it is often very useful to sit down and create a list that is entitled, "If you want to treat me with respect . . ." which makes the boundaries you discovered explicit, so you will have a readily available teaching tool for the people in your life. It is also quite powerful to stand in front of a mirror and read the list to yourself. Risk it.

## The Practice Of Forgiveness: From A Bounded No To An Unbounded Heart

To forgive without learning from your wound will cause history to be repeated; to learn without forgiving will bind your heart in bitterness.

In the days when I was learning Gestalt psychotherapy, it was common practice to pound on pillows and scream at people who were invisible to anyone except oneself. In one workshop I went after my father, who was hidden inside a red corduroy pillow with an old wooden tennis racket. I whacked and screamed in a way I never could on a court, "I'll never let you hurt me again, never, never, never." A wave of fire spread through the dry tinder of my pelvis, and was followed by soft waves of expanding tenderness in my chest. When I reported this to the therapist, he said I was afraid of my father and wimping out. Following his instructions, I pounded and shouted again. Once more the passion was followed by compassion. I left the workshop convinced that I was an emotional wimp.

*"All our final resolutions are made in a state of mind which is not going to last."*

*–Marcel Proust*

What I've come to understand is that extracting lessons from your suffering, and setting boundaries, makes you safe enough to release the bindings that hold you attached to what was. The shell falls away and the seed can expand toward the light. "Never again" are the words that make "I forgive" possible. Wisdom is the companion to compassion. Forgiveness, that widening warmth I felt in my chest, was my heart softening, reaching, protected enough to connect. It is as natural as a sunrise following a sunset.

Forgiveness in no way justifies the actions that caused your wounding, nor does it mean you have to seek out those who harmed you. It is simply a movement to release and ease your heart of the pain and hatred that binds it. It is the harvested fruit of a season of darkness, followed by a season of growth, and very hard work.

291

*"Spiritual maturity is
an acceptance of life
in relationship."*

*–Jack Kornfield*

The practice that follows, heart releasing, was inspired by a meditation taught by Jack Kornfield. You may want to do it while walking in nature, resting in a bathtub, or sitting someplace where you are very comfortable and feel safe:

*Bring your awareness to your center in whatever way you have found successful. Allow your mind to expand by widening your visual and auditory periphery. Feel the whole of your body in the present. You may want to continue with your eyes opened or closed, in silence or with music.*

*Move your awareness to the center of your chest. You may want to imagine you can inhale from there and exhale curiosity. As you do this, invite yourself to notice any tightness, tension, holding, or barriers that are there, because you haven't forgiven yourself and/or others. You can ask yourself to notice if you have been keeping your heart closed. Continue breathing and expanding your awareness around this place.*

*When you are ready, bring your enemy to mind. Imagine it at any distance that feels comfortable. There may be words you need to say to express the pain you have experienced as a result, the lessons you've learned and the boundaries you are making to prevent further suffering. If you are ready, find the words that will release your heart in forgiveness.*

*This can be followed by noticing the ways you have hurt, wounded or damaged the enemy. If this is appropriate, find the words that will express what you've learned, and what boundaries you intend to keep as a result. This can be followed by a request of forgiveness from the enemy.*

*Lastly, if it seems right, you can put yourself in front of you. The self that has been harmed by you. You can allow yourself to become aware of the sorrow you have carried as a result. As you extend forgiveness to yourself for each of these, you can also release your heart from the guilt and shame in which you have been bound.*

Like new shoots of grass, forgiveness cannot be pulled out of you. It takes time, tilling, the fresh rain of warm tears and much turning toward the sun. This practice can be repeated daily, allowing the images to work like balm into the crusty shell that has bound your wound.

## Making and Enacting Commitments: Establishing A Cellular Yes

There is a Japanese story told of two great samurais who came together to determine who was the greatest in all of the country. One morning they stood facing one other, hands on swords which were sheathed at their waists. They were surrounded by a huge crowd, all silent, waiting in the sunrise for the great battle. They waited. And waited. The minutes turned into hours. Neither samurai moved. Finally after three hours, one man fell to his knees, bowed and walked away. Defeated. Though neither sword had been draw, the warrior who won was the one with an unbendable intention.

Our energy drives our bodies, but our intention drives our energy. What's necessary is holding the aim of your intention true, while at the same time maintaining a full awareness of your current reality. You don't need to concern yourself with how you will bridge the gap between the two. That gap is called creative tension, and it can best be filled with faith. You become more and more aware of where you are, and more and more aware of where you want to go.

Choice is the basic expression of who you are. What commitments could you make to yourself that will help you live what you have been learning from your enemy? Which choices can you make that will increase your own well-being and that of those around you? What choices will protect your soul, meet the needs that have been calling to you, and also allow that circumference of your self to stretch and expand? Document your responses in some

*"What soap is for the body, tears are for the soul."*

*–Hassidic proverb*

*"I have been blessed to believe passionately, to love deeply, and to be able to work out of those loves and beliefs."*

*–Audre Lorde (after learning the cancer in her breast had metastasized to her liver)*

way: tell someone, write them down in a prominent place, tape record them, make them concrete. Make sure your commitments are specific and attainable. Make them small enough and deep enough that you will live them. No matter what.

We all need very simple and specific things we can do on a daily basis to help live out the commitments we make to ourselves and foster the factors that strengthen our own evolution. Since very few of us have been taught self-loyalty, here are several examples of the kind of pledge I'm talking about: One woman who had to work at a job she hated, to make money, committed to herself that she would give herself an hour a day before she went to sleep to dream and plan how to make a "jail-break," so she could prepare for a future that would nourish her. A man committed to ask himself what he really wanted every time he had a craving to smoke. Another person I worked with committed to ask himself what he wanted every time he asked his lover that question. A woman chose to stand in front of a mirror naked, repeating her promise to consume only what nourished her before she ate any meal at home. A man bought a "freedom" pen that he kept in the same pocket where he used to keep his cigarettes, and reached for it to re-write his commitment to be free of addiction each time he felt a nicotine craving.

Since becoming paralyzed and speechless are old ways I used to try to defend myself, my commitment is to engage and channel the fire I need to protect myself by walking, stomping, going for a run, vacuuming every dust bunny I can find, shouting in gibberish at the top of my lungs, going to the landfill and throwing bottles into the green dumpster, driving my car on an interstate and singing absurd songs as loud as I want, taking a huge chunk of clay and letting my passion sculpt. In other words, I find a way to externalize my fire until I can decode how it is trying to protect me.

*"There are two ways to live your life. One is as though nothing is a miracle. The other is as though everything is a miracle."*

*–Albert Einstein*

A man who made a commitment to maintain his own sense of autonomy when he got married, stood in front of a full length mirror, stated his own wedding vow, and gave himself a ring to wear on his right hand. A woman I worked with discovered that her enemy, which she labeled Pathos, needed to be supported when she was sad. Her mother used to ridicule her, trying to get her to pay attention to something else. In her commitment to Pathos, the woman promised to wear a silver pin with a spiral knot carved on it whenever she felt Pathos pulling on her. It was a friend to her sadness, and a commitment she was "knot" going to humiliate her.

Now it's your turn. The following two practices will help. The first, called "Moving Forward From Center," taught to me by Sensei Richard Kuboyama, will help you develop a cellular feeling for having a future orientation, as well as increasing your awareness of moving toward what you want—that one hundred percent genuine yes.

> "A fine wind is blowing the new direction of time through me. If only I let it bear me, carry me."
>
> –D.H. Lawrence

If you can get someone to help you do this, wonderful. If not, imagining a person is assisting you will be quite effective, although maybe not as much fun.

*Sit comfortably in a straight-backed chair with your feet on the floor. Think of a future you want to be living, as vividly as possible. Imagine it is over there, on the other side of the room.*

*You are going to get out of your chair and move toward it. But let's add a challenge to make it more real. Imagine (or have) someone behind you, leaning their forearms on your shoulders. She or he is not pushing down, but they are leaning their weight on you. Now try to get up.*

If you are like most people, you picked your feet slightly up off the floor and used your energy to go *up*, against the force of the other person's forearms. We are taught to push against; our center of gravity goes in the struggle, to the place where we are stuck. If your real or imagined challenger is bigger than you, your center may even move *into* that person. If not, it may move above the person (overpowering).

*Please stand up and shake that out.*

*This time when you sit down, imagine a tube of toothpaste is lying on the floor. The cap is off and a large foot comes along and steps on the tube. What happens to the toothpaste? Right— it squirts out forward. And if an even bigger foot comes along with even a harder step? Right. The more challenge, the more forward movement. The toothpaste does not have a rational mind. It has not learned to push against.*

*Now feel your passion about that future you have imagined. Make it so important to yourself that a "no matter what" (NMW) will arise in your body. For me, right now, it could be, "NMW, I am going to complete this book with enjoyment and loyalty to myself." Find a future that revs the engine of your desire. Find a purpose that makes you want to be alive.*

*Feel the fire that fuels the sun in your belly. Imagine it spiraling and expanding forward, forward from your belly. Across the room from you is your future. The energy in your belly stretches toward that future, is pulled by it, attracted naturally to it as if forming a magnetic force field. Your feet can draw support up from the earth into your belly the way a tree draws sustenance.*

*Now bring back your challenger (real or imagined). Remembering the toothpaste tube, choose to respond to the challenge by allowing the weight to propel your energy forward, toward your future. The movement originates in your belly and you are pulled forward from there, all the way to the other side of the room. Thus, the challenge has contributed to your forward motion, instead of blocking it.*

"Commitment is the love that binds energy and desire."

–Anon.

Most people don't believe this practice until they do it a few times. They think the challenger is cheating, putting less weight on their shoulders the second time. Then they begin to discover that there is a choice point, between the impulse and the action. Will you choose to use your energy "against" or "toward"? Will your center be in the struggle or moving toward a proactive future, no matter what? It becomes obvious that power exists not in what happens to us, but in how we choose to respond to what happens to us.

The following practice will help you increase your awareness of ways you can enact your commitment. Find the sequence that most fits your way of learning:

*Create a gesture or posture that describes the way you used to be blocked by your enemy.*

*Develop a gesture or posture that symbolizes the lessons you have learned about relating to your enemy and supporting yourself.*

*Watch your hands go from one gesture to the other as if they were dancing a continual story of your own evolution.*

*Continue the process visually: create a doodle or mark that represents the way you used to relate to your enemy on one edge of the paper, and another that represents how you have learned to support yourself in this process. Find a way to connect them.*

*Continue this process verbally: describe to yourself in words, phrases or sounds the things you used to say to yourself in your old way of relating, and then the new statements of self-support you have developed. A very effective way for going from the old to the new is to acknowledge the old by simply saying, "Hello." For example, "Oh, Hello criticism." No long conversation or analysis. Just hello. Some people also find that they can bridge from the old to the new by writing down what the old subvocal statements are and then ripping up the paper.*

These mini rites of passage can be daily reinforcements of your commitment to change. In your morning mirror, you can watch yourself make the dance or gestures or postures. On your note pad, begin the doodles, mumble the words or hum the tune to yourself while driving or riding in the subway. Each time you bring one to mind, you ripen your own evolution.

*"My commitment is to truth not to consistency."*

*–Gandhi*

*"You will find as you look back upon your life, that the moments that stand out, the moments when you have really lived, are the moments when you have done things in the spirit of love."*

*–Henry Drummond*

# 15 Hands Which Can Make Violence Obsolete:
## Connecting With the Community

"Being in touch with the kind of suffering we encountered during the war can heal us of some of the suffering we experience when our lives are not very meaningful or useful. When you confront the kinds of difficulties we faced during the war, you see that you can be a source of compassion and a great help to many suffering people. In that intense suffering, you feel a kind of relief and joy within yourself, because you know that you are an instrument of compassion. Understanding such intense suffering and realizing compassion in the midst of it, you become a joyful person, even if your life is very hard."

–Thich Nhat Hanh

There's no way to complete a journey on the wisdom trail, since it is a spiral of learning, healing, serving, learning. Each straightening by fire cracks opens the shell of numbness and stagnation around our heart, exposing our raw, human fragility. As we dip back into the river of our lives, we discover the muscles of learning that have strengthened on the trip, the truer voice, the clearer eye, the stories that live down close to the bone.

Through this turning point, we have discovered that we are ultimately alone. Through it, we also discover how much we all belong to each other, and how it is possible to do together what we cannot do alone.

The problems we face in our world are fundamentally a spiritual crisis created by a loss of a sense of connection to one another and our values. In his book, *No Boundary*, Ken Wilbur states, "These lines are actually there, but these lines, such as the shoreline between land and water, don't merely represent a *separation* of land and water, as we generally suppose. They equally represent precisely those places where the land and water *touch* each other. That is, lines *join and unite* just as much as they divide and distinguish." Nothing exists except in relation to something else. A shoreline could not be without a body of water; night could not be without day. Everything we do, everything we are, depends on our responses to other people and events and their responses to us.

Most illnesses of body, mind, and spirit are as much disturbances in the connection *between* each of these, and a rupture between "I" and "we" as anything else. More and more research is emerging that indicates social support makes a significant difference in the healing of many diseases, such as heart disease, arthritis, cancer; that it boosts the immune system, reduces pain and depression.

But how do you weave the threads of understanding you've gathered on this journey into a fabric of support? This chapter is about the relationship between the wounded

*"No one can see who does not kindle a light of their own."*

*–Buddha*

*"When we give up the illusion that the world is created of separate, unrelated forces we can then build 'learning organizations' where people continually expand their capacity to create the results they truly desire, where new and expansive patterns of thinking are nurtured, where collective aspiration is set free, and where people are continually learning how to learn together."*

*–Peter Senge*

301

ones and the world—the interconnections. Having explored ways you can sustain the changes you've made on your own, it's time to have a conversation about collaboration and empowerment, so you'll have skills to receive support within your network of family and friends for those changes.

This chapter is also about extending out into the community, giving support to those around you. It is about how a reclaimed life can be a shared strength. It is about telling the truth and breaking the conspiracy of silence, so we can find the courage to be understood as well as the compassion to understand.

## Objects In the Mirror Are Closer Than They Appear

In Latin, *conversation* means a turning together. So let's begin by conversing about your life and what support is there for you already, what's available for you to build on.

You've made a commitment to yourself. What are specific steps you could take to live out that commitment? Be sure to underwhelm yourself and define concrete, specific, attainable steps you can accomplish in the immediate future. What could people do that would help you take those steps? For example, is there someone who could send you a post card each week for a while with words of encouragement? Who is your support community now? It doesn't have to be a group of twenty-five that meets each Thursday in the American Legion Hall. Maybe it's only your cat and your tulip plant. Just allow yourself to notice where you get support from in your life already.

How does the behavior of your support team reinforce your limitations? How could it sustain your growth? What could they do that would support you taking your next steps? How could you expand your community of sup-

"Each of us must be the change agent we want to see in the world."

–Gandhi

"Living in one piece is important for healing–in other words knowing what your deepest values are and living by them–so that there is a coherence between who you are and how you live. "

–Rachel Naomi Remen

port? This may mean adding one or more people, or it may mean gathering the people that already exist on a regular basis to do something that would be food for your spirit.

The following practices will give you the opportunity to learn some very useful skills involved in creating an alliance for change.

# Receiving Support

I'm including two versions for this practice, taught to me by Sensei Kuboyama. The original is to be done with another person. If you can't wrangle someone else into doing this with you, there is a variation for you to do by yourself:

*"Everywhere, hands lie open to catch us when we fall."*

*–Anon.*

*1. Person A is the Supporter. S/he rests on hands and knees like a horse. Person B will practice three ways of getting supported. S/he stands at A's side, resting forearms on his or her back, as if leaning on a table top, committing weight on it. This is the first way, which we call "Finally I've found someone I can trust," or putting your center in your support.*

*Without warning, person A collapses to the floor. B notices what happens. Did you collapse on top of A?*

*2. Both people resume their positions, but this time B gets smart and even though their forearms seem to be leaning, no weight is committed, because s/he is preparing at all times in body and mind for the collapse that will come. This second way is called, "I won't trust anyone ever again" or putting your center in your head.*

*Without warning A collapses to the floor. B notices what happens. The chances are B did not fall, but did you receive any support at all?*

*3. Both people resume their positions. B commits full weight, but this time imagines his/her forearms are absorbent and drink in the support all the way to his or her belly. You are aware*

> "We who lived in concentration camps can remember the men who walked through the huts comforting others, giving away their last piece of bread. They may have been few in number, but they offer sufficient proof that everything can be taken from a man but one thing: the last of the human freedoms–to choose one's attitude in any given set of circum-stances, to choose one's own way."
>
> –Victor Frankl

simultaneously of your own center and the support that is there for you. This third way is called, "I'm trusting myself with your support when it's there, and myself when it's not..," or keeping your center at home.

Without warning A collapses to the floor. Notice how B can keep in contact with both A and self.

## Solo Version

Name one hand A and one B. The basic position is with both elbows on the table, one hand resting on top of the other about eight inches off the table, both palms facing down. Follow directions above with A being supporter underneath, and B learner on top, putting all of its weight on the bottom hand.

In the last step, the palm of B absorbs support down to your center.

There are profound learnings on both sides of this practice. Many of us believe we have to hurt ourselves to help someone else. I was taught not to take in help, not to receive it because it would hurt too much when I lost it. The first ten times I did this exercise, my entire belief system frazzled. I had learned a way to receive support when it was there, and to take it in very deeply, since I knew I *would* be losing it!

How can you use the learnings from the above practice to deepen the way you receive that support?

## Coaching: Teaching Others To Support You

Most of us know little about the kind of support we need and are unsure of what to offer others. Andy devel-oped this practice to help people learn what they need, and how to give it to people they care about. You can do this with an imaginary partner or a tape recorder, but a fleshly friend is much more effective.

*Set up a small obstacle course for yourself—three or four objects will do, spread out over six or more feet. Stand with your back to the objects, eyes closed. Your task is to walk backwards through the obstacle course—blindfolded!*

*Your partner stands by your side to coach you. He or she cannot tell you where to go or even when you are going to crash into an obstacle.(After all, life doesn't often give warnings.) You must teach them how to support you. They can hold your hand (but not lead you). They can tell you specific things, remind you to breathe, check in on you. As you begin to move through the course, you might find yourself stopping to breathe, while your partner reassures you that you can go at your own rhythm. If you bump into something or go out of the boundaries of the course, your partner might follow your instructions to stabilize you and help you find your way back on path again.*

An important part of coaching is helping you feel satisfied. Make sure that your coach cheers or celebrates with you in some way when you make it. Many people forget and just keep going from goal to goal, without ever savoring the delight of accomplishment.

When you're done, document what you learned about the kind of support that helps you in the unknown. People will not be able to read your mind to find out what kind of support you want. *If you don't teach them, they'll give you exactly what they would need in your situation, which might be exactly the wrong thing for you.* So, get some paper or a tape recorder and just begin with the sentence stem, "If you want to give me support, . . ." and write or speak until the pen or your mind runs dry. "If you want to give me support, touch my feet when I'm hurting, and hum Gregorian chants to me. Call me once a week and ask me if I'm keeping my commitment. Don't tell me what to do

> "I'm not called to be successful. I'm called to be faithful."
>
> –Mother Teresa

or try to fix me. Listen to me and just breathe very loudly."

When you are all done, stand in front of a mirror and read or listen to the tape as if you had written it to yourself. Change the pronouns if necessary, to make it work, "Dawna, if you want to give yourself support, rub your feet and hum Gregorian chants in your own ears." Inevitably, what you have written will be true for you, and knowing that makes it possible for you to get support, even if no one else is around or responds to your requests.

Make your tape or writing available to everyone who supports you and ask them to make one for you. I suggest that families post lists that say, "if you want to support Dad . . .," etc. It's made clear to everyone that these are requests, not demands.

As an example, after her separation from a fourteen-year relationship, a friend of mine wrote a letter to all of her friends, sharing the story of what had happened and asking very specifically for such support as frequent phone calls, invitations on Sundays to do things, inclusions in parties, etc. A man wrote a similar letter to his community of friends, telling them what he *didn't* want: "Don't tell me about her. Don't try to fix me up or slip in gossip about who she's seeing."

## Using Imagery To Connect With Others

For those times when you may feel isolated or alienated from the rest of the world, here's a simple and profoundly effective way to create connective tissue between you and the people in your community:

*Bring your mind back to the symbol of the resource your unconscious mind gave to you to help meet the needs of your enemy. You put it in a safe deposit box someplace in your body.*

> *"Self-esteem plays as much a part in the destiny of nations as it does in the internal lives of individuals."*
>
> *–Gloria Steinem*

> *"We will conquer for ourselves the energies of wind, gravity, waves, but one day we will harness for God the energies of love and then for the second time in the history of the world, we will have discovered fire."*
>
> *–Teilhard de Chardin*

*You may want to place your hand over that place to bring it into your awareness.*

*Whenever you are in a group of people with whom you'd like to feel a connection, imagine each of them has the same symbol in the same place in their body. If, for example, your unconscious mind gave you the symbol of a crown and the place you put it was in your heart, then as you scan the other people, imagine each with a crown in the center of his or her chest. Notice the effect.*

## Creating a Community of Commitment

I've heard that if you stroke a violin and there is another one in the room, the second will resonate in the same tone as the first. We can connect to one another in such a way. Here's an example. When Melissa, a woman in one of our groups who was recovering from a history of childhood sexual abuse, shared a song that was part of her commitment of change, there was a resonance among all of us, more profound than she ever expected. As she sang, many people began to close their eyes and rock. Her voice, in its wholeness, was a tuning fork.

*"Everyone has his own specific vocation or mission in life . . . therein he cannot be replaced, nor can his life be repeated. Thus, everyone's task is as unique as is his specific opportunity to implement it."*

*–Victor Frankl*

> *Some way baby, gonna make it right*
> *Oh sweet child*
> *some way baby gonna see you smile*
> *Oh sweet child*
> *'cause it's all over now*
> *it's all over now*
>
> *Little darlin, gonna wash your body clean again*
> *with tears, tears of fire*
> *Ain't nobody gonna hurt you like they did before*
> *I'm here, here by your side*
> *And it's all over now*
> *it's all over now*

*Never again will I leave you in silence afraid*
*I'll speak my truth, I'll defend you*
*I will keep you safe*
*I promise this to you*
*I will stay with you*

*Some day Baby your joy is gonna rise up*
*out of all you've been through*
*some day darlin your heart is gonna sing again*
*I promise this to you*
*cause it's all over now*
*it's all over now*

Because her song was so true to her own experience, it was also universal. As the gift of her voice faded in the silence of the room, I could feel its vibrations in the canyons of my bones.

After receiving feedback, Melissa shared with all of us how afraid she had been to put herself "out there in the world." She re-claimed that responsibility for herself and asked people in the circle to help her live out her promise by brainstorming ways she could share her music with more people.

The conversation went on late into the night. Others spoke of their dreams to tell their stories in music. Andy talked about his dream to be part of a collaborative effort to create an album of music such as Melissa's, where each artist would produce his or her own song of getting through a turning point. He offered his expertise in creating professional tapes. Melissa offered her house as a place to rehearse. The energy was hot enough to fry an egg.

Fourteen people met at Melissa's house for four days. Each had his or her song. Each told the rest of the group how he or she wanted to be supported. Some wanted harmony, some foot rubs and reminders to center. Inspiration and realization, intuition and hard-earned reason wove themselves into a thick fabric. Sixteen hour days of practice with no one tired. The group sang through their meals, sang through washing the dishes. They talked to each other about their fears and dreams. They encouraged, cajoled, and seduced the best out of each other. There was no "criticism." Often, after an hour someone would say to the person singing, "That just doesn't feel quite like it. How can you make it more true?"

The group met two more times in the recording studio within the next four months. I kept thinking about underwater colonies of coral, where each separate unit is strong because it is part of a larger whole. Only two of the members had ever recorded anything before. But together they were strong enough to do what individually they were not, or could not do.

The album was ultimately the howling of a pack of wolves into the darkness, breaking their hearts open. Each song, like Melissa's, was a promise bridging an abyss. Each song was a public declaration of a possible future. Each song was a next step which could not have been taken alone.

*"If I had not read somewhere that a man may not voluntarily part with his life so long as a good deed remains for him to perform, I should long ago have been no more."*

*–Ludwig Beethoven*

## Learn, Heal, Serve

The soul wants to grow larger, wider, deeper. Some people try to fill that need by accumulating alot of things, or by eating themselves into larger bodies. Some parents make themselves larger through their children's accomplishments; some politicians through their constituency. Some people enhance the spread of their own souls by creating a community of support that is entwined at the heart.

A friend of mine, Robert Ostermeyer, told me that if you take heart cells from different frogs and place them touching in one dish of saline solution, they will begin to beat at the same rhythm. I'd like to tell you a story about a man, who, at the end of his life, created a sacred saline solution for an entire community.

When I was sick, I spent alot of time with people who were dying. I think I wanted to know what it was like, to be there and see it for myself from the outside. Perhaps I thought it would give me a head start, like a dress rehearsal. That was how I met Elliot.

At first, I thought he was a Native American or Latino. He had dark skin, long hair, a mustache that made dark parentheses around his mouth. It turned out Elliot was Jewish-American—Miami born and bred. The thing I remember most about him was that he learned from the inside out; he had a beautiful, infinite hunger to understand.

Elliot rode down the coast of South America on a motor scooter when he was in his mid-twenties. He did it because he wanted to meet the people, and travel on his own. He was like that. He thought of himself as a lone wolf.

When he came back, he got sick. At first, none of the doctors could figure out what was going on. They thought he had some exotic Amazonian jungle disease, but it turned out to be testicular cancer. His world came apart with a fierce roar. He was carrying the wolf inside and it was devouring him.

A group of his friends decided to form a support team for Elliot. When he was hospitalized, we cooked all his food, from wheat grass and tofu to carrot juice. Three meals a day for months. For some reason, we grew in number. More and more people became involved. I'm not sure why, except that Elliot had an uncompromising willingness to be present.

As we grew in number, he diminished in size. After six months, he weighed only ninety pounds. I used to tell him stories. Some were really trance inductions to help him

*"Sometime in your life, hope you might see one starved man, the look on his face when the bread finally arrives. Hope that you might have baked it or bought it or even kneaded it yourself. For the look on his face, for your meeting his eyes across a piece of bread, you might be willing to lose a lot, or suffer a lot, or die a little, even."*

*–Daniel Berrigan*

with his pain, but some just seemed to come at random. One night, I told him an old one, whose roots were lost in my unconscious mind. It goes like this:

*Once upon a time, there was a king. He had a fiercely loyal dog whom he loved very much, and a new baby whom he also loved very deeply. On the day of this story, the dog ran into the king's chambers, covered with blood. He pulled on the sleeve of the king's robe until he had to stand up and follow his trusted companion. He was led into the nursery and there he was confronted by an awful sight. The crib was empty but, more than that, it was covered in blood and the baby was nowhere to be found. The king imagined what must have happened and drew his sword. With a sharp intake of breath, he slew his dog.*

*Minutes later, the grief stricken king heard a wail. He looked under the crib where it had originated, and there was his child, covered with the dead body of a wolf. The king realized immediately what had really happened—his beloved companion had protected the baby and killed the wolf. The king, in his vengeful anger, had destroyed his ally.*

Elliot grabbed my hand. Tears were rolling down his neck into the sheets, but no sound came with them, no heaving or sobbing. Just silent tears leaking out of him. Finally, he whispered, "Don't kill the wolf, feed it." I wanted to ask him to explain, but I just couldn't do so. Later, no explanation was possible. Or necessary.

He told his friend, John Moody, that he wanted to go back home to die. The medical staff made a huge fuss, but five or six of his support people carried him out of the hospital and back to the farm.

He asked someone to call his parents in Florida and tell them to fly up. When they arrived, they were very upset that he wasn't in the hospital, but Elliot talked to them and they settled down. People walked with his mother, sat with his father, held each of them. We had been learning in all those months. The caring was seamless.

*"Two sources of strength in our world. One is the force of hatred, of those who are unafraid to kill. The other and greater strength comes from those who are unafraid to die."*

*–Jack Kornfield*

311

On his last night, Elliot seemed to collapse under the pain, like a crushed egg. There were about twelve of us in the farm house. We couldn't do much so we gathered around his bed, the way a cloud rests on the shoulders of a mountain.

At 3:33 a.m., Elliot sat bolt upright. His face was luminous, as if all the light of the world had leaked into him for that moment. I had an almost tactile sense of his grabbing at words and phrases, holding onto them as if protecting them in a high wind. Finally, he released them, and said, clearly, oh so clearly, "We're all beings of light." It was a moment beyond despair or desire.

We responded without thinking, by singing his favorite chant back to him: "Listen, listen, listen to our hearts' song. We will never forget you. We will never forsake you." At 4:44 that same morning, his spirit slipped noiselessly from his body. We held his parents and each other, breathing in the silence, until each of us had settled deep inside the layers of ourselves.

We dressed him in the jacket, pants and hat he had worn on his motor scooter ride, and put his body in the back of his red pick-up truck. We carried him into the lobby of the emergency room, and gathered up all the doctors and nurses who had attended him for those many months. Pulling them in a tight circle around Elliot's body, we sang "Listen, listen, listen to your heart's song, we will never forget you, we will never forsake you." Even the doctors cried.

After they took his body to the morgue, each one of us went up to the oncology floor. Elliot had asked us to sit with the other patients and give them messages from him. I gave Nancy, the forty-two-year-old woman with breast cancer who had been across the hall from him, this one: "Remember to feed the wolf, keep a calm mind, and an open heart."

> " I am of the opinion that my life belongs to the whole community and as long as I live it is my privilege to do for it whatever I can. I want to be thoroughly used up when I die. "
>
> –George Bernard Shaw

## From Vulnerability to Veneration

Some people try to get over suffering; some are imprisoned by it; some do everything they can to get rid of it, including creating more pain; and some work it in their hands until it ignites their compassion and wisdom. In my experience, this last group finds a way to keep both the pure infant of their dreams alive and the untamed wolf of their passions well fed.

Clarissa Pinkola Estes, the author, Jungian analyst, and storyteller, describes wolves as relational by nature, highly intuitive and able to adapt to constant change. Our culture considers them dangerous. Too many have caged their wolf, and walk around as if they carry something dead inside. If left there long enough, it may escape and wreak havoc, destroying anything young and free it can find. But the wolf is not evil. It's not even dangerous, if it is nourished and given its freedom. In fact, it is the cage that is unsafe.

Wolves need to howl through dark nights. They need room to roam. And, they need their pack to come back to, for they know they are safer when part of something more than themselves.

The world needs wilderness, wolves and dreamers. When the last ones are gone, the machines and cages will have taken over and the earth will have lost her heartbeat.

*"If we see the suffering and wounds of our addictive life as a lesson that can be passed along to others, we can transform the wound into a gift. Having lived through a life threatening crisis, we become healers."*

*–Linda Leonard*

## The Power Of Witnessing

Those of us who have experienced major traumas and invasions to the boundaries of our selves, are likely to feel alienated, isolated, and terribly vulnerable. We often need to howl in outrage from the pain and terror. There can be a disruption in our trusting relationship with the world—we have discovered it is not safe or fair. We need to know our

313

wound has meaning.

Our friends and family allow a temporary, brief expression of pain and terror, to which they respond with pity. Then we are supposed to get over it, as if "it" were a bad dream. If we continue to howl, the violations that the rest of our community have stacked neatly in boxes inside the secret closets of their mind will begin to rattle. The community cajoles, placates, teases, does whatever it can to shut us up. "Life has to go on. Other people have gone through much worse. Don't break down in front of people. Let it go."

If we continue, their closet doors begin to crack. In panic, they turn their collective backs so they can go on functioning as if the world were a safe and fair place.

If this isn't familiar to you, think of what happened to the Vietnam veterans. I don't believe that we, as a society, do such things because we are cruel. Who wants a secret closet opening and old scabbed-over wounds falling down on our heads? Especially when we don't have much idea of how to deal with pain when we are in it, next to it, under it, besieged by it.

We who were wounded became exiles in our own bodies, negotiating the razor edge between our truth and what the community will hear. There is a fundamental conspiracy of silence that forbids the public telling of terrible truths. If we break that silence, we are denied membership into the club of the "normal" world. Alternatively, our private, violated self may retreat into numbness and alienation from our public, social self.

It is crucially important whether we see ourselves as someone who doesn't matter or as someone who can effect change. The soul sickness of cynicism says you cannot shape and effect your destiny. Cynicism is the opposite of holiness. We who have discovered that humans can inflict horrendous pain, as well as create tremendous beauty, are not victims. We are veterans and we also

*"Mindfulness must be engaged. Once there is seeing, there must be acting. Otherwise what is the use of seeing?"*

*–Thich Nhat Hanh*

have the potential to be teachers. We can be the messengers who alert the community that the Emperor has no clothes, that Mommy and Daddy are not always Bill Cosby and Vanna White, that war does kill babies and that there is a sickness in our times.

One power that is often ignored is that of witness. Even when there is nothing you can do about suffering, you can witness it. That is what storytelling is about. We cannot continue to not know what is going on. If you have ever been hurt or violated in secret, and have the sense that it was yours alone to bear, you know how hard that is. It is a double oppression. If there is just one person who stands beside you and acknowledges that he or she knows how you are suffering, then you and your story can be brought into the community. This is one of the major gifts we can offer one another.

A woman who studies with us, Peris Gumz, is of Croation descent. When the news stories of the women who were being raped in Croatia were broadcast here, at first I was overwhelmed and just clicked my tongue and turned the television off. But gradually, I began to realize that I knew in a cellular way what those women had experienced. Peris and I spoke about what was in the circle of our influence to do. She wrote a chant called "Sestre Nashe," the words of which were the same in all dialects: "Our sisters, our sisters, we know of your suffering, we carry you in our hearts." A friend, Peggy Tileston, and her sister put the words to music.

The ripple of caring witness began to spread. It was sung and taped by a group of women who have all been sexually violated, and their children. The ripple expanded. We raised the money for Peris to go to the former Yugoslavia in a week. She took a tape of the song, letters and drawings, and a stone with a spiral painted on it that had been passed from hand to hand among hundreds of people who wanted the women to know their suffering

*"In the Chernobyl nuclear accident, the wind told the story that was being suppressed by the people. It gave away the truth. It carried the story of danger to other countries. It was a poet, a prophet, a scientist."*

*–Linda Hogan*

*"Action on behalf of life transforms."*

*–Joanna Macy*

315

mattered. Wherever Peris traveled, she gathered women round and they sat silently in a circle, listening, sobbing, knowing they were not alone in shame, as the song laced us all together at the heart.

It is the truth of our experience that makes our message important. We need to find ways to express what we have learned so that it not only helps us heal, but teaches the community at large. The wolves within us need to know they are heard. The sickness belongs to all of us. The world is spiritually sick because it has forgotten how to receive suffering with compassion. It takes suffering as if shaking hands with rubber gloves. Thus, it cannot learn from it, be influenced by it, respond to it, or ultimately stop it. But if the suffering can be received, the gloves peeled off and the truth absorbed, there can be an intimate connection between individual and world healing.

Expressing pain through the creative process enables our message to be carried to the rest of the community in such a way that they will not drown in it. What was paralyzing individual shame then becomes transformed into collective strength.

A man in one of our groups, Roger (K-V-A), was born with half of his arm missing. He has only two fingers on what most would call a "birth defect." His parents tried to ignore the whole thing, pretending that everything was "normal." For most of his life, he wore a prosthesis, and managed quite well in almost everything. But inside he felt a secret shame that could never be articulated.

I told him how the greatest shamans and medicine people are often those with the greatest wounds, because they believe in the innate ability of healing, and have the deepest compassion. In the course of following the same process you have been using in this book, Roger decided he had to find some way to connect with the group—to become a full member, rather than hanging out on the sidelines, as was his habit.

*"For, while the tale of how we suffer, and how we are delighted, and how we may triumph is never new, it always must be heard. There isn't any other tale to tell, it's the only light we've got in all this darkness."*

*–James Baldwin*

*"There can be no vulnerability without risk; there can be no community without vulnerability; there can be no peace–and ultimately no life–without community."*

*–M. Scott Peck*

He wanted to share what it had felt like his whole life to have his arm labeled a defect, but he could not find the words. Rather, he danced his pain in the stillness of an April afternoon session, while the rest of the group became a circle of violins, resonating on the same tone. His dance concluded with a re-birthing ceremony he created to welcome his arm into a world that wanted him. As Roger went around the circle, every person shared his or her equivalent "birth defect" with him—a stammer, a terminal illness, an alcoholic family, a schizophrenic mother, a body that was too fat, blind eyes. In the universal symbolic language of Roger's dance, we heard the lost song that connected each of us to our lost selves and to each other.

*Genius* and *generous* come from the same root. To give to and of yourself, in the way Roger did, is to discover your true genius. It is then that you feel as if you've finally come home. You know you can be safe inside yourself, even in an unsafe world. You know there is something unique which you can give to the world. You know you can make a difference. You know that as you heal, you can teach. You don't have to run workshops or college courses. Maybe it will happen in a bus station or a hospital room or when you are braiding someone's hair. Your story is a sacred saline solution.

*"Participation in meaningful community is the greatest unacknowledged hunger of our time."*

*–Family Therapy Networker*

## Risking Your Significance

This time in which we live reminds me of the period right before a snake sheds its skin. I am told that for a few days a milky fluid collects between the old and the new skins, which causes its eyes to go blind. The snake then has to hide itself for protection. It begins shedding by opening its mouth very, very wide, stretching around its lips until the skin there starts to peel back. When the shedding is complete, its colors are the brightest they have ever been, and its eyes the clearest.

For years I've shrugged at all the gruesome statistics. My eyes have gone milky to the hollowed faces of babies, stomachs distended, twig-like arms and legs enfolded in a dirty rag, as their mothers scratch a shallow grave for them in Iraq, Appalachia, Anacostia, Haiti, Somalia. The layer of milky fluid under my thick old skin has kept me from feeling the despair of the fourteen year-old on the streets of New York selling her body for one vial of crack. I have hidden away in some stone wall in my mind away from the moans of the twenty-eight-year-old composer, dying alone of AIDS in a rooming house in Philadelphia. I crawl out now, stretch my mouth open wide, wide enough to throw my head back and howl, wide enough to say and write the things I know to be true.

We must engage with life *as* we engage with ourselves. It's not possible for us just to heal ourselves. We are interconnected. We have to undertake personal healing *and* we have to undertake social action simultaneously. We have to find a way for what is finest in each of us to transcend hopelessness, bitterness and cynicism. The time for mere self-improvement is over. It is time to support the unending process of a kind of self-discovery that leads to world improvement. We can neither ignore the world until we get better nor ignore ourselves until the world gets better.

We all contain the pressures of so much. Will it compress and collapse us or stretch us? If it is true, as Pogo says, that "We have met the enemy and it is us," then it must also be true that we have met the ally, the way through, and it is us.

Mystics of every variety of religious belief have spoken of an underlying connection between things, a unity. To heal as an individual is to stop fighting the things inside of you, to learn to trust the force of your own mind, to stop and be still, to turn and face the fear, shame and rage, to

*"The Pentagon admits a nuclear war might wipe out life on the planet but says that's no reason to change nuclear doctrine or stop building atomic weapons."*

*–Associated Press, 4/2/85*

*"Human capacity is equal to human cruelty and it is up to each of us to tip the balance."*

*–Alice Walker*

make room for it in the landscape of your life; to make boundaries so you can feed the wolf until you decode the message it is trying to tell you; and ultimately to recognize that you have a responsibility to teach. To heal as a society is to stop and be still until we can find a way to create a harmony between forces in opposition; to bind back together male/female, rational/creative, dark/light, sacred/scientific, sorrow/joy, either/or, individual/community; and ultimately to realize that those we call victims are really our teachers.

Philosopher Teilhard de Chardin conceived the idea of "infurling," an infinitely slow, almost imperceptible coming together of the world and its beings. I am a possibilist. I reach for the possibility of infurling, on a small scale first. I like small scales these days. Things are getting too big. We see so much suffering, we hear so much, we feel so much and know so much, and yet we understand so little about how we can take action. I need to pull the circumference of the world in, to make it smaller as I expand mine, until it is within my own sphere of influence, where I *can* make a difference. How can I support infurling in my own community? How can I receive the support I need to heal and how can I give the support others need?

*"I will act as if what I do makes a difference."*

–William James

## It's Not What We Have, But What We Give That Brings Joy

We are not without guides. I'd like to pass on a true story I read recently about Betty Williams, a woman from Northern Ireland who was a co-winner of the Nobel Peace Prize in 1977. One night, after witnessing the death of several children, she walked outside and knocked on every door she could find, even though there might have been a gun pointed straight at her as it opened. At each, she

*"The fundamental question we must ask of the world is 'Why is the child crying?'"*

–Alice Walker

319

shouted, "What kind of people have we become that we would allow children to be killed on our streets?" Within four hours, there were sixteen thousand names on petitions for peace.

We are not without guidance. There are many great individuals, known and unknown, who have lived through violence and drew light as brilliant as the moon from it, who have influenced whole populations to raise the tide of compassion for human suffering: Martin Luther King, Elie Weisel, Mother Teresa, Victor Frankl. They have broken the silence and more and more in the world are listening. They have created a new sacrament and washed away shame with their tears. *Somos màs!*

I have asked you to make the choice to turn inward with mercy and allow your life experiences to be your teacher, to go through them, down into the root of them, where the needs and resources exist. I have asked you to rethink many of your assumptions about yourself in order to become the agent of your own liberation, your own evolution. Because of what you have done already, there is less suffering in the world today.

I am calling now for your presence, your real bodily engagement with the world. I am asking you to be both the changed and the changer as a result of what you have discovered, uncovered and recovered. Most of all, I am inviting you to come into a sense of real participation in the world around you. The blood of your life flows minute by minute through the place where the challenges of your history can be transformed with the sacramental power of compassion. I am encouraging you to teach the community the truth that pulses way down deep at that level of bones and blood and seed.

This has been a book about possibilities. How does someone as small as one woman like Betty Williams or one man like Thich Nhat Hanh or one reader like you turn a simple truth into a reality that is passionately alive?

*"It's not the great things you do that you matter, but the small things you do with great heart."*

−Mother Teresa

*"When you are inspired by some great purpose, some extraordinary project all your thoughts break their bonds; your mind transcends limitations; your consciousness expands in every direction; and you find yourself in a great new and wonderful world. Dormant forces, faculties and talents become alive and you discover yourself top be a greater person by far than you ever dreamed yourself to be."*

−Patanjali

## Cross-Pollination

To integrate the growth that has occurred inside of your mind as you have been reading this book, you will need to pass it through the movement of your life. One way to do this is with a wholing:

*I invite you to please place each of your hands palm upward on your knees. In one of those hands, imagine you are holding the learnings you have that have had value to you as you've made your way through this book.*

*In the other, you can imagine the persons, places and situations where you would like those learnings to be immediately available to you, to rise in your consciousness as if they were a sun.*

*After you've fully enjoyed a few breaths, you can allow both those hands to rest on your belly, signaling to your unconscious mind that you would like those learnings to dawn from your center in those situations.*

*You might notice an image of some kind in response, that is a signal to you that there is a future self already living those possibilities dormant in you now as seed.*

## In Your Two Hands

You're invited to look in the palm of your hand. Thich Nhat Hanh would say that if you look deeply enough, you'll never be lonely. Each cell of your hand is made from genetic material passed on to you from your mother and father. Whether you adored or despised them, there they are in the palm of your hand. If you look a little deeper, you'll also see your grandfathers and grandmothers. Deeper still, and there are all your ancestors resting snugly in your DNA. Of course, as your eyes really receive that palm, you cannot help but find your link to every being that has ever lived.

*"To be healers we need to go beyond being victims or even survivors of whatever our own private hell might be. We are being called on instead to become transformers of consciousness."*

*–Joan Borysenko*

321

Please look at your fingertips. Milton Erickson suggested that we carry at the end of our fingertips indications of our remarkable uniqueness. Never before in all the history of humankind has there been another with those markings. You are totally unique. Right there, at the very edge of your reach, is the proof. Allow your mind to receive that and you will come to realize what a work of art you are. Your hands can make violence obsolete. You *can* make a difference.

> *Now we will feel no rain*
> *for each of us will be shelter for the other.*
> *Now we will feel no cold*
> *for each of us will be warmth for the other.*
> *Now there is no more loneliness*
> *for each of us will be companion to the other.*
> *There is only one life before us*
> *and our seasons will be long and good.*
>
> -adapted from an Apache wedding blessing

# Appendix

# PERCEPTUAL PATTERNS EXPLORATION

*Directions: For each question, choose the answer that's most true and make a check mark in the appropriate column on page 330. If more than one option is given, choose both. For example, if the answer to #1 is "a," make a check mark in both the AKV and AVK column. Then, count up how many check marks in each column. The one with the most is probably your pattern.*

*From what you can readily notice:*

## 1. How would you describe how you talk?

| | |
|---|---|
| a. Words pour out, in logical order, all the time, without hesitation; have an excellent vocabulary | AKV, AVK |
| b. May be self-conscious or shy about speaking in groups | VKA, KVA |
| c. Use many metaphors and images ("It's like a cyclone, a blue funnel, a whirling top") | VAK, KAV |
| d. Talk mostly about actions, feelings, what's happening | KAV |
| e. Make hand motions before words, must use hands or movement to find words | VKA, KAV |
| f. Talk in circles, ask endless questions | VKA, KVA |

## 2. How would you describe the way you make eye contact?

| | |
|---|---|
| a. Maintain steady, persistent eye contact | VAK, VKA |
| b. "Eye shy," uncomfortable with eye contact for more than a few seconds, look away frequently | AKV, KAV |

| | |
|---|---|
| c. Keep steady contact, but blink or twitch if sustained | AVK, KVA |
| d. Eyes glaze over if listening too long | VKA, KVA |

### 3. How would you describe your handwriting?

| | |
|---|---|
| a. Neat and legible | VAK, VKA |
| b. Difficult to read | AVK, KVA |
| c. Childlike, sometimes letters may be unformed | AKV, KAV |

### 4. What do you remember most easily?

| | |
|---|---|
| a. What's been said, jokes, lyrics, names of people, titles; memorize by saying something repeatedly | AKV, AVK |
| b. What's been seen or read, people's faces, how something looks; memorize by writing something repeatedly | VAK, VKA |
| c. What's been done or experienced, the feel or smell of something; memorize by doing something repeatedly | KVA, KAV |

### 5. How would you describe your physical needs and skills?

| | |
|---|---|
| a. Constantly in motion, jiggle a lot | KAV |
| b. Can sit still easily for long periods | AVK, VAK |
| c. Can feel awkward or get easily frustrated when first learning physical activity | AVK, VAK |
| d. Learn physical skills easily with little or no verbal instruction | KVA, VKA |
| e. Have high level of energy right beneath the surface | AKV, VKA |

**6.** *How do you respond to touch?*

    a. Tend to be shy about physical contact                         AVK, VAK

    b. Like to touch and be touched by people you don't
       know well                                              KVA, KAV

    c. Touch after initial contact                            AKV, VKA

**7.** *How do you express feelings?*

    a. Very private about feelings                              VAK

    b. Feelings seem right beneath the surface              AKV, VKA

    c. Express reasons for feelings                          AVK

    d. Very difficult to put feelings in words                KVA

**8.** *Under what conditions do you "space out?"*

    a. With too much visual detail, being shown some-
       thing, or questions about what has been seen     AKV, KAV

    b. With too many words, verbal explanations, or
       questions about what has been heard           VKA, KVA

    c. With too many choices of what to do, being
       touched, or questions about what is felt         AVK, VAK

**9.** *What do others perceive as your most annoying behavior?*

    a. Can't sit still or stay put                            AKV, KAV

    b. "Show-off"                                        VAK

    c. Wise-crack, "fresh" verbally                       AKV, AVK

d. Get sullen or withdrawn                                   VKA, KVA

e. Interrupt, talk incessantly                               AKV, AVK

f. Complain, "yeah-buts"                                      VKA

**10. *What do you remember most easily after seeing a movie, a TV program, or reading:***

a. What the people and the scenes looked like               VAK, VKA

b. What was said or how the music sounded                    AKV, AVK

c. What happened or how the characters felt                 KVA, KAV

**11. *What's the first thing you do to remember someone's phone number?***

a. Say it to myself or hear it in my head                    AKV, AVK

b. See the phone or the numbers in my head                   VAK, VKA

c. Feel myself picking up the phone and dialing              KVA, KAV

**12. *What's the thing you remember most easily about someone you just met?***

a. What you did with them or how their energy felt          KVA, KAV

b. How they looked                                           VAK, VKA

c. Their name or what they said                              AKV, AVK

**13. *What's the scariest, hardest for you to take?***

a. Mean, hurtful words                                       VKA, KVA

b. Poking, invasive touch                                    AVK, VAK

c. Nasty looks                                                      AKV, KAV

## 14. *How do you put something together?*

a. I read the directions and then do it. Telling me
   confuses me.                                                     VKA

b. I read the directions, ask questions, then talk to
   myself as I do it.                                               VAK

c. I work with the pieces, then ask questions if I need
   to, never read directions.                                      KAV

d. I work with the pieces, look at the diagram, then ask
   questions.                                                       KVA

e. I have someone tell me, then show me how, then I
   try it.                                                          AVK

f. I have someone tell me how to do it; then I try it. I
   only read directions as a last resort.                          AKV

## 15. *What's most important when you decide which clothes to wear?*

a. How they feel, how comfortable they are, the
   texture                                                          KVA, KAV

b. The colors, how they look on me, how they go
   together                                                         VAK, VKA

c. An idea of what's me, the brand name what the
   clothes say about me, what I tell myself about them,
   what calls to me                                                 AKV, AVK

|  | AKV | AVK | KAV | KVA | VKA | VAK |
|---|---|---|---|---|---|---|
| 1. | | | | | | |
| 2. | | | | | | |
| 3. | | | | | | |
| 4. | | | | | | |
| 5. | | | | | | |
| 6. | | | | | | |
| 7. | | | | | | |
| 8. | | | | | | |
| 9. | | | | | | |
| 10. | | | | | | |
| 11. | | | | | | |
| 12. | | | | | | |
| 13. | | | | | | |
| 14. | | | | | | |
| 15. | | | | | | |

# Bibliography

Achterberg, Jeanne. *Imagery In Healing.* Boston: Shambhala, 1985.

Berman, Morris. *Coming To Our Senses.* N.Y.: Bantam, 1990.

Bly, Robert. *A Little Book On the Human Shadow.* S.F.: Harper San Francisco, 1988.

Boffey, Barnes D. *Reinventing Yourself.* Chapel Hill: New View, 1993.

Borysenko, Joan. *Fire In the Soul.* N.Y.: Warner, 1993.

Brown, Norman O. *Love's Body.* N.Y.: Vintage, 1966.

Bush, Mirabai and Dass, Ram. *Compassion In Action.* N.Y.: Bell Tower, 1992.

Cameron, Julia. *The Artist's Way.* N.Y.: Jeremy Tarcher/Perigee, 1992.

Chopra, Deepak, M.D. *Unconditional Life.* N.Y.: Bantam, 1991.

Coles, Robert. *The Call Of Stories.* Boston: Houghton Mifflin, 1989.

Combs, Gene and Freedman, Jill. *Symbol, Story, and Ceremony.* N.Y.: W.W. Norton, 1990.

Cousins, Norman. *The Healing Heart.* N.Y.: Avon, 1984.

Csiksentmihalys, Mihaly. *Flow.* N.Y.: Harper and Row, 1990.

Dobson, Terry and Miller, Victor. *Aikido In Everyday Life.* Oakland: North Atlantic, 1992.

Dolan, Yvonne. *Resolving Sexual Abuse.* N.Y.: W.W. Norton, 1991.

Dossey, Larry, M.D. *Meaning and Medicine.* N.Y.: Bantam, 1991.

Erickson, Milton. *Healing In Hypnosis.* N.Y.: Irvington, 1983.

_____. *Life Reframing in Hypnosis.* N.Y.: Irvington, 1985.

Estes, Clarissa Pinkola. *Women Who Run With the Wolves.* N.Y.: Ballantine, 1992.

Feinstein, David and Krippner, Stanley. *Personal Mythology.* L.A.: Tarcher, 1988.

Ferucci, Piero. *Inevitable Grace.* L.A.: Jeremy Tarcher, 1990.

Field, Joanna. *A Life Of One's Own.* L.A.: Tarcher, 1981.

Fisch, Richard, Watzlawick, Paul, and Weakland, John. *Change.* N.Y.: Norton, 1974.

Frankl, Victor. *Man's Search For Meaning.* Boston: Beacon, 1959.

Gendler, J. Ruth. *The Book Of Qualities.* N.Y.: Harper Collins, 1987.

Gleick, James. *Chaos.* N.Y.: Viking, 1987.

Goldberg, Natalie. *Long Quiet Highway.* N.Y.: Bantam, 1993.

Haley, Jay. *Conversation With Milton H. Erickson, M.D.* N.Y.: Triangle Press, 1985.

Halifax, Joan. *The Fruitful Darkness.* S.F.: Harper San Francisco, 1993.

Herman, Judith, M.D. *Trauma and Recovery.* N.Y.: Basic, 1992.

Hoffer, Eric. *The Ordeal Of Change.* N.Y.: Harper and Row, 1963.

Houston, Jean. *The Possible Human.* L.A.: Jeremy Tarcher, 1982.

Jung, Carl. *Man and His Symbols.* N.Y.: Doubleday, 1964.

Kabat-Zinn, Jon. *Full Catastrophe Living.* N.Y.: Delacorte Press, 1990.

Keen, Sam. *Faces Of the Enemy.* N.Y.: Harper Collins, 1988.

Kopp, Sheldon. *All God's Children Are Lost, But Only A Few Can Play the Piano.* N.Y.: Prentice Hall, 1991.

Kornfield, Jack. *A Path With Heart.* N.Y.: Bantam, 1993.

Kubler-Ross, Elizabeth. *On Death and Dying.* NY: Macmillan, 1969.

Leonard, Linda. *Witness to the Fire.* Boston: Shambhala, 1989.

Levine, Stephen. *Healing Into Life and Death.* N.Y.: Doubleday, 1987.

London, Peter. *No More Secondhand Art.* Boston: Shambhala, 1989.

Lowe, Ed and Siegel, Stanley. *The Patient Who Cured His Therapist.* N.Y.: Plume, 1992.

Macy, Joanna. *World As Lover, World As Self.* Berkeley: Parallex Press, 1991.

Markova, Dawna. *The Art Of the Possible.* Berkeley: Conari Press, 1991.

_____ *How Your Child Is Smart.* Berkeley: Conari Press, 1992.

Metzner, Deena. *Writing For Your Life.* S.F.: Harper San Francisco, 1992.

Miller, Alice. *Breaking Down the Wall Of Silence.* N.Y.: Dutton, 1991.

Mindell, Arnold. *Dreambody, The Body's Role in Revealing the Self.* N.Y.: Viking-Penguin-Arkana, 1986.

_____ *The Leader As Martial Artist.* N.Y.: Harper Collins, 1992.

Moore, Thomas. *Care Of the Soul.* N.Y.: Walker, 1992.

Muller, Wayne. *Legacy Of the Heart.* N.Y.: Fireside, 1992.

Nachmanovitch, Stephen. *Free Play.* L.A.: Jeremy Tarcher, 1990.

Needleman, Carla. *The Work Of Craft.* N.Y.: Knopf, 1979.

Nhat Hanh, Thich. *Being Peace.* Berkeley: Parallex Press, 1987.

_____. *Touching Peace.* Berkeley: Parallex Press, 1992.

_____. *The Blooming Of A Lotus.* Boston: Beacon Press, 1993.

_____. *Peace Is Every Step.* N.Y.: Bantam, 1991.

Purce, Jill. *The Mystic Spiral.* NY: Thames and Hudson, 1974.

Rossi, Ernest, ed. *The Collected Papers Of Milton H. Erickson.* N.Y.: Irvington, 1980.

Rico, Gabrielle. *Pain and Possibility.* Los Angeles: Jeremy Tarcher, 1991.

Siegel, Bernie. *Love, Medicine and Miracles.* S.F.: Harper San Francisco, 1987.

Siler, Todd. *Breaking the Mind Barrier.* N.Y.: Simon and Schuster, 1990.

Somé, Malidoma Patrice. *Ritual.* Oregon: Swan, 1993.

Steinem, Gloria. *Revolution From Within.* Boston: Little Brown and Co. 1992.

Van der Hart, Otto. *Rituals In Psychotherapy.* N.Y.: Irvington, 1983.

Walker, Alice. *The Temple Of My Familiar.* N.Y.: Harcourt, Brace, Janovich, 1989.

Welwood, John. *Journey Of the Heart.* N.Y.: Harper Collins, 1990.

Wisechild, Louise, ed. *She Who Was Lost Is Remembered.* Seattle: Seal Press, 1991.

Wolinsky, Stephen. *Trances People Live.* Conn.: Bramble, 1991.

Zeig, Jeff, ed. *Ericksonian Approaches To Hypnosis and Psychotherapy.* N.Y.: Bruner/Mazel, 1982.

Zuskav, Gary. *The Seat Of the Soul.* N.Y.: Simon and Shuster, 1989.

# Index

Addiction, 5, 8, 20, 27, 32, 35, 39-41, 55-56, 184, 200, 255, 294

AIDS, 99

Aikido, 31, 60-1, 81, 102, 174, 216, 244

*Art of the Possible, The,* 141, 178

Asset-focus, 239-242

Auditory channel, see Perceptual languages, Personal thinking patterns

Awareness, 29, 65-6, 68-9, 214, 235-6; disconnection from, 36-9; in the present, 85-103; of imagery and imagination, 164-80; Practice, 69

Bateson, Gregory, 22

Boundaries, barriers, and barricades, 28-9, 46, 184, 186-90, 192-3, 281-6, 229, 288-91, 319; Practice, 289-91

Breath, 100-01, 102, 122, 192-3, 253; see also peripheral awareness

Bryner, Andy, 6, 26, 73, 88-90, 92-6, 137, 140, 177, 223-4, 230, 232, 243, 256, 265, 285-6, 305, 308-9

Buddha, 67

Cancer, 20, 35, 37, 46-8, 151, 179-80, 214-5, 244-9, 301; as turning point, 52-6; and receiving self, 92-6; and healing imagery, 132-6

Centering, 73-81, 119, 192-3, 204, 216; Practices, 75-76

Ceremony, 271-7

Chaos, 161, 171

Charts: Learning and problem solving, 42; The Wisdom Trail, 62; Spiral of thinking, 115; Personal thinking patterns, 129; Triggers to states of consciousness, 142; Turning in–states of consciousness, 154; Increasing awareness of quality of imagery, 167; How each pattern recognizes imagery, 173

Childhood; abuse, 27-9; and creativity, 43-5; and fear, 99; trauma, 184

Coaching, 305-6

Collaboration, 11, 301-21

Commitment, 96, 281-298; making and enacting, 293-8; support for 302-6; community of commmitment, 307-9

Community, 6, 213, 301-322; of commitment, 307-9

Compartments, 164, 240; four of resources, 243-8; and metaforms, 255-7

Compassion, 5, 8, 31, 35, 46-9, 63-4, 100, 178, 213-17, 221-36, 291; vs. pity, 214

Conscious mind, 40, 116-7, 268, 282; see also States of consciousness

Conspiracy of silence, 314

Context, 199-204, 208-209, 255

Control, 35, 36, 85, 147-8